‘Vivid, funny, tender and warm – no, hot! Red hot.
A simply stunning setting and a gloriously romantic
plot that will put a smile on your face’
Veronica Henry

‘Lovely characters, a wonderful setting, a beautiful story’
Milly Johnson

‘A breathtaking romance in a stunning location:
the perfect summer escape’
Cathy Bramley

‘Shimmering setting and a heart-swelling,
offbeat romance plot . . . a much-needed,
totally immersive escape from real life’
Louise Candlish

The romantic, evocative escape everyone needs this summer’
Rachael Lucas

‘Evocative, emotional and escapist’
Liz Fenwick

‘A one-way ticket to sunshine and romance . . .
compelling, beautiful and wholeheartedly romantic’
Katie Marsh

‘A gorgeous, warm-hearted love story . . .
the very best of tantalising and escapist fiction’
Holly Miller

‘Evocative and escapist’
Laura Jane Williams

Isabelle Broom was born in Cambridge nine days before the 1980s began and studied Media Arts at university in London before a 12-year stint at *Heat* magazine. When she is not travelling all over the world seeking out settings for her escapist novels, Isabelle can mostly be found in Suffolk, where she shares a home with her two dogs and more books than she could ever hope to read in a lifetime.

To find out more about Izzy and her books, read excerpts, view location galleries and gain access to exclusive giveaways, you can sign up to her monthly newsletter via her website, isabellebroom.com.

Also by Isabelle Broom

The Getaway
Hello, Again
One Winter Morning
One Thousand Stars and You
The Place We Met
Then. Now. Always.
A Year and a Day
My Map of You

Isabelle Broom

The Summer Trip

First published in Great Britain in 2022 by Hodder & Stoughton
An Hachette UK company

1

A CIP catalogue record for this title is available from the British Library

Paperback ISBN 978 1 529 38377 5
eBook ISBN 978 1 529 38375 1

Typeset in Bembo by Manipal Technologies Limited

Printed and bound in Great Britain by Clays Ltd, Elcograf S.p.A.

Hodder & Stoughton policy is to use papers that are natural, renewable and recyclable products and made from wood grown in sustainable forests. The logging and manufacturing processes are expected to conform to the environmental regulations of the country of origin.

Hodder & Stoughton Ltd
Carmelite House
50 Victoria Embankment
London EC4Y 0DZ

www.hodder.co.uk

To Cathy Bramley, I will love you forever, kumquat may.

I

The telephone call, the one that started it all, happened on a Monday.

I wonder if I would have answered it had I known what was to follow. If, instead of a standard ring, it had announced shrilly, 'Ava Fox, your life is about to change in the most extraordinary way'? Unlikely.

As it was, the phone merely elicited the same, low-throated tinkle it always did, and given that, save for the occasional cold caller, the only person who ever rang me on the landline was my mother, I concluded begrudgingly that I should pick up, and did so with a determinedly cheery, 'Hello'.

'Ava, is that you?'

Why do mothers always do this? I swallowed the urge to make a snarky reply and settled for a 'yes' instead.

'I never know if it's you or Rosie these days,' she said, punctuating her statement with a weary little sigh, as if my daughter's voice sounding similar to my own was the most tiresome of inconveniences.

'For Rosie to answer this phone would mean she had put down her mobile for more than three consecutive seconds,' I told her. 'Which, I'm afraid to say, is a near-impossibility at the moment.'

My mother clucked with either affection or disapproval – I never have been able to differentiate – and got straight to her point.

'I spoke to Mattie earlier today.'

'And?' I waited a moment, but she didn't elaborate. 'How is she?'

Mattie being my sister, Matilda. Sweet, dependable, and infuriatingly close to perfect – I tried to avoid thinking about her wonderful life if I could help it.

'Fed up,' was my mother's matter-of-fact reply.

That was unexpected. Kind, patient and predictable Mattie did not do 'fed up'.

'What has she got to be fed up about?' I retorted, wincing inwardly at how bitter I sounded but barrelling on regardless. 'Is the sunshine in Greece too hot for her? The sea too blue?'

My mother cleared her throat.

'Sarcasm is the lowest form of wit, as I am sure you're well aware.'

It took a lot of effort on my part not to rise to this. Instead, I said, 'Every time I've seen Mattie, she's seemed very happy with her lot. She is Mrs Positivity.'

'Mattie is so like your father in that way,' my mother agreed. 'Affable to her core. Unlike us,' she added as an afterthought.

I gripped the receiver a fraction tighter, glancing up the stairs in time to see the long, jogging-bottoms-clad legs of my daughter as she ascended, one hand on the banister and the other clasped around her phone. Taking in my expression, she mouthed the word 'Granny', to which I nodded, and then stifled a smile as she hastily beat a retreat. It is not that Rosie dislikes her maternal grandmother, more that she humours my slightly odd relationship with her. Occasionally, she will say things such as, 'God, I can't imagine having a mum I couldn't talk to about stuff,' and I will feel my chest swell with a blend of pride and self-pity.

'Anyway,' my mother went on, 'I think what Mattie really needs is a break. She works too hard – always has done. So, with that in mind, I suggested that she and Niko stay at your house this summer.'

'Here?'

'No, Ava, in your garden shed. Of course, there.'

'Now who's being sarcastic?' I muttered, to which my mother made a tutting sound.

'We don't have any space,' I continued. 'Rosie will never agree to share a room, and even if she did, I would honestly prefer not to bunk up for weeks on end. We'd all be on top of each other – it would be a disaster. Why can't they stay with you?'

'Oh, your father and I are lending the house to a friend of a friend while we're in Thailand – did I not tell you?'

I am on the verge of repeating the word 'Thailand' incredulously, when it dawns on me what this means.

'You're going to visit Ophelia?'

My youngest sibling departed England a little over a year ago to take up a job offer in Australia, only she never made it past her stopover, deciding instead that a better use of her time would be to become a so-called influencer. Which is classic Ophelia. I had not heard from her since, at least not directly, but I was able to keep tabs on her through the endless Instagram posts, invariably featuring a beach, a bikini, some sort of green juice, and a lot of guff about 'living for the moment'. Ophelia always had made her own rules, stepped outside the boundaries of what was expected and followed whatever path led her to the most fun. 'Good for her,' I would always remark. Untruthfully.

'You know how much I miss her,' said my mother.

'That's no surprise, given that she's your favourite.'

'Well, yes.' My mother did not miss a beat. 'That's because she is the most like me, I suppose – a free spirit.'

The fact that I had pulled the pin out of this particular truth grenade myself did little to lessen the pain it caused.

From somewhere upstairs, I heard taps being turned on. Rosie was running a bath; she had one almost every night, tablet propped up on the loo seat so she could watch one of her beloved history documentaries.

It was not fair of my mother to insist that Mattie and her husband be crammed into our house all summer. It would disrupt my daughter's routine, convince her to spend less time at home and then drive her into the arms of one of the hapless-looking boys who occasionally loitered in our street, waiting to walk her to college.

Of course, that was not the only reason I didn't want them here.

'Before you say no again,' my mother pre-empted, 'let me tell you the other part of my plan.'

I sighed.

'Which is?'

'The genius thing is, you won't have to worry about a lack of space,' she continued. 'Because while Mattie and Niko will be in your house, you and Rosie will be in theirs.'

That shut me up.

'Ava?'

'I'm still here.'

'What do you think? Wouldn't it be nice to see Corfu again? And a holiday in Greece would be such a treat for Rosie. You're forever telling me how hard she's worked, studying for her A levels as well as doing all that volunteering – this could be her reward.'

I closed my eyes as I contemplated.

'Mattie thinks it's a brilliant idea,' she went on. 'They had a pool put in last summer and you can see all the way across Kalami Bay from their patio.'

I did not need to be reminded of how blissful my sister's Greek island life was. Why Mattie would agree to swap that for a poky two-bedroomed terrace in Brighton, where it would doubtless rain with gloomy determination all through the summer, I could not fathom. But I also knew that a refusal to cooperate would make me unpopular, and my mother was bound to get word of her plan to Rosie, who I knew would be thrilled by the prospect of a holiday abroad. The school term would be over soon, so I could not feasibly use my own work as an excuse given that I'd been planning to take a break over the summer anyway. And then there was the small matter that I did miss Corfu.

Every day.

Still.

'And you're absolutely sure Mattie is on board with this swap?' I checked. 'She is genuinely prepared to lend me and Rosie the house?'

My mother coughed.

'Yes. I said so, didn't I?'

Her indignation silenced me once again, and I chewed on my retort, swallowed it with several deep breaths.

'So, I'll tell your sister it's all arranged, shall I?' my mother pressed.

For a tantalising second, I allowed myself to picture Corfu, to envisage the myriad hues of the sea, feel the warmth of the sunshine, hear the ambient hum of insects, taste the salty feta and smell the sharp scent of lemons. It was all there, waiting for me. All I had to do was say yes.

And yet . . .

'You can tell her,' I said firmly, 'that I will think about it.'

2

I told myself that it would depend solely on Rosie. That if she warmed to the idea of spending the summer after her A levels in Corfu rather than at home with her friends, then I would properly consider it. Having left the confines of teaching in a primary classroom to instead become a private tutor several years ago, I was fortunate enough to have a flexible schedule and the ability to work from anywhere with a decent Wi-Fi connection. Although I imagined Rosie would be keen to escape for a few weeks, the time frame my mother had proposed was closer to two months. Surely the prospect of being away that long would not appeal – not when Rosie and the crowd she had grown up with would all be scarpering to various universities come September. This would be their last summer together.

I assumed wrong.

'A whole summer in Greece? Seriously? Er, Mum – *of course* we should go. I can't believe you're even questioning it. They have a pool!'

'You don't think you'd miss Ally and the gang too much?' I ventured. We were in our usual spots in the kitchen, me at the sink, pink Marigolds submerged, her sitting up on the edge of the worktop, bare toes curled around the back of a chair.

'Ally never looks up from snogging Tom long enough to notice me these days,' Rosie observed. 'They're basically married – it's so gross.'

'Quite,' I agreed, getting to work on the breakfast plates. 'But two months is a long time to be away. I would completely understand if you would rather not go, and I'm sure Mattie would, too.'

I sensed rather than saw my daughter roll her eyes.

'Probably,' she allowed, 'but Granny wouldn't. She never takes no for an answer. Remember when she nagged you into wearing that hideous tartan dress for Gramps's seventieth? When you saw how bad you looked in it, you actually cried, and even then, she didn't budge.'

I chuckled at the memory.

'And anyway,' Rosie continued, reaching round me to pluck a banana from the fruit bowl on the windowsill, 'I want to go. You went to Corfu for the summer the year you turned eighteen, so it's only fair that I get to do the same.'

'That's another thing.' I paused mid-scour and turned to face her, experiencing as I always did the tug of affection in my chest at the sight of her – my girl. Her blond curls were frizzed by slumber, her Harry Potter pyjamas worn into holes on both knees. I adored the contrasts of her, the burgeoning young woman who painted her nails, made up her face and asked if she could have a glass of wine with dinner kept at bay by the child who was reluctant to grow up, to fall into the trappings of adulthood. I wanted to protect that little girl. The idea of losing her, of that lingering innocence being snatched away before she was ready to relinquish it, made me feel hot and fierce.

Rosie took a large bite of her banana. 'What other thing?'

'Only monkeys chatter with their mouths full.'

She chewed and swallowed. 'What other thing?'

'Your birthday. Turning eighteen is a big deal and it only happens once. I thought you wanted a party on the pier?'

'A pool party in Greece trumps a pier party in Brighton any day.'

'Even if your boring old mum is on the guestlist?'

'Come on, Mum – thirty-seven isn't all that old – and maybe by the time my birthday rolls around I'll have made friends with some of the locals.' Rosie's expression brightened as she added, 'Or you might even have a holiday romance, like that woman did in that film.'

'You had better not be referring to *Shirley Valentine*.'

'That's the one!'

'Who are you and what have you done with my daughter?'

'I'm serious, Mum.' She poked me gently with her big toe. 'It's about time you found yourself a boyfriend.'

'Oh, is it now?'

'Yeah. I mean, as long as you don't spend the entire holiday sucking face like Ally and Tom, obviously.'

'Sucking face? What a delightful description.'

'Dad won't care – he has Laura now anyway.'

My ex-partner Paul had hit the cliché jackpot by falling in love with the life coach he had turned to after the two of us broke up.

'Why would I want to spend time with anyone other than my beautiful, talented, funny and cheeky' – I flicked a froth of bubbles across her feet – 'daughter?'

Rosie hopped down from the worktop and deposited her banana skin in the compost caddy before wrapping her arms around my shoulders.

'Seriously,' she murmured. 'I know you're probably worried about me freaking out at the prospect of you moving on or whatever, but I really won't. I'm cool about it.'

'I know you are.' The words snagged in my throat. 'Thank you.'

Rosie squeezed me a fraction tighter, but rather than relaxing, I felt myself tense up.

'The time,' I said, and we both glanced towards the clock mounted on the wall. 'You had better get a wriggle on. What is it today?'

'History – Tudors mostly, so lots of head-chopping and bonking of cousins.' She groaned, dragging her feet towards the door.

'You'll walk it,' I said truthfully. Because she would. My daughter's ability to remember dates, events and names was nothing short of astounding, and history was her subject, her passion. Writing about it for three hours was less a chore than a pleasurable way to spend a morning, as far as she was concerned. A few months ago, she had returned from spending the weekend with her father and announced that he and Laura had promised her one hundred and fifty pounds for every top grade she achieved, plus a fifty-pound bonus if she managed to achieve this across all four subjects.

'Easiest six hundred and fifty quid I'll ever make,' she'd told me happily. 'I almost feel sorry for him.'

I stared into the murky dishwater, at the curls of scrambled eggs that had detached from the frying pan and were floating on the surface, lost for a moment in the fog of what might have been, how my life could have looked if I had made different choices. Then, feeling irritated with myself, I pushed the image away.

Why are humans built this way? Why must we taunt ourselves with the impossible?

It was the prospect of returning to Corfu that had triggered all this, of course. There was no way I could think about the place without being reminded of what happened all those years ago, of the regret that had lingered inside me ever since. Perhaps returning to the island would act as an exorcism of sorts; maybe it would show me that what I assumed to be perfection was in fact mundane.

I was still standing by the sink when the doorbell rang, and I smiled as I heard Rosie thundering down the stairs.

'I'm off!' she yelled from the hallway. 'Wish me luck!'

'Luck!' I called back.

'Oh, and Mum.'

'Yes?'

'Corfu. We're definitely going, aren't we?'

And, just like that, we were.

3

I have long been of the opinion that those who proclaim airports to be 'such fun' are likely descendants of people who threw slaves to the lions centuries ago.

There is nothing I find less fun than overpriced taxis, endless queues, suitcases wheeled across toes and the awkwardness of being patted down by humourless security staff. *Do I really look like a criminal?* I always think.

Our flight was also delayed. Because of course it was.

'Four *hours*?' Rosie's expression of abject horror said it all.

'I'll buy you whatever you want to eat,' I chivvied. 'And then we can peruse the designer handbags and gasp in horror at the price tags.'

She went easy on me and chose Pret a Manger as our lunch destination. I sipped a burnt-tasting black coffee while she munched her way through a cheese and pickle baguette.

'Aren't you hungry?'

'I had a big breakfast,' I lied. The truth, that my stomach was bound in far too many knots for me to contemplate any food, would have required too much explanation. I kept waiting for my brain to accept that yes, we were about to embark on a flight that would whisk us from dreary Britain to dazzling Greece; that I would once again bathe in the clear water, wake each day and be greeted by sunshine, and that I would revisit all the places I had spent so many years dreaming about.

It still felt impossible.

'Don't you think it's a bit weird that Auntie Mattie isn't going to be there?' Rosie piped up between mouthfuls. 'I haven't seen her since we spent Christmas at Granny and Gramps's three years ago – you'd think she'd want to at least spend a few days with us before she and Uncle Niko fly over here.'

I responded with a non-committal 'hmm'.

'Didn't you ask her?' Rosie persisted.

'I haven't actually spoken to her directly,' I admitted. 'Granny organised everything.'

'If I had a sister, I would speak to her every single day.'

The lack of a sibling was one of Rosie's go-to subjects whenever she was seized by the urge to have an adolescent moan.

'You're so lucky to have two, and yet the three of you barely talk to each other.'

She stated this fact as if the almost-total estrangement between Matilda, Ophelia and myself had somehow passed me by.

'You don't need to talk to a person every day to know they care about you,' I told her. 'My sisters know full well that I'm here for them. Our lives are simply very different, that's all.'

'Auntie Lia is the coolest,' sighed Rosie. 'A true free spirit rather than all those other fakers on Instagram. I wish my life was even half as exciting as hers is.'

'There's pickle on your chin,' I informed her, passing across a napkin.

'Didn't you ever want to go travelling? See the world?' Rosie was not about to let the subject drop.

'When I was young and foolish maybe,' I said.

'You mean before you had me,' Rosie replied. 'If I hadn't come along, you would have had time to do all sorts of fun things.'

'Perhaps,' I allowed, reaching across the table and tapping her lightly on the nose. 'But none of those things would have been half as much fun as raising you. Aunt Lia might well be doing paddleboard yoga on the beach in Phuket, but I got to watch you take your first steps, say your first word, and blow your first raspberry.'

'That last one obviously being the most important.'

'Obviously.'

We smiled at each other, her blue eyes meeting my grey pair, and for a precious moment my anxiety ceased to thrum. Whatever I feared happening when we reached Corfu – how I would feel to be back and what emotional response the island would elicit – was nothing I couldn't handle if I had my girl by my side. My proudest achievement, the beat of my heart, the air in my lungs. My *everything*.

When I thought about life in those terms, my role as Rosie's mother so clearly defined and unequivocal, I felt strong. I believed I had the capacity to be invincible, that I was in control of my emotions. That was what I told myself.

We passed the time in the departures lounge window-shopping, buying novels to read on the beach and playing endless card games, until finally it was time to board. As soon as we were in the air, an exhausted Rosie dropped off to sleep, her mouth slightly open and her lashes casting faint shadows across her cheeks, while I fidgeted beside her, fingers twisting together in my lap, chewing nervously at my lips, plastic glass of white wine untouched on the fold-down table in front of me.

When the plane began its descent, I stared towards a window painted black by night. I knew the sea was below us, that the now-muted landscape was a vibrant mix of golds, greens and blues – but I saw none of it. Right up until the tyres bounced and screeched across the runway, I continued to cling tight to my denial. But then came the standard announcement about the local time and weather, the seat-belt sign was switched off, and my daughter was rubbing her eyes, re-energised by excitement.

'We made it at last – we're finally here!'

Warm fuggy air greeted us, as I had known it would, wrapping itself around me like an old friend. It was all it took to break me, and I brushed the tears from my eyes before Rosie spotted them.

Passports were shown and stamped, suitcases collected, and soon the two of us were buckled into the back seat of a taxi. The Greek driver chatted away amicably with polite interest – *Was this our first time in Corfu? Where had we come from in England? How long would we be staying? The whole of the summer? Bravo!* – while Rosie peered out through the car window, calling out the things she saw when we passed the occasional streetlight.

'Mopeds! The sea! A cat! Boats!'

Her enthusiasm was contagious, and I could not deny that it felt nice to be in Greece, to be able to see it again, smell it again, hear it again. It had been such a long time since I had last been on the island, yet everything was so familiar. I felt both stirred and soothed.

I knew from photographs, and, OK, maybe a little bit of time spent on Google, that Mattie and Niko's home was a sizeable villa situated halfway up the hillside behind Kalami's main road and the horseshoe-shaped bay below. Spread across three levels, with sea-facing balconies on each floor, it was a very large step up from the cluttered terrace we had left behind in Brighton. Rosie was instantly captivated, and as we pulled up outside she gazed up in reverent silence at the shuttered windows while I paid our fare and bid farewell to our driver.

'Granny said the key will be underneath a pot,' I told my daughter, only to then see, as I switched on the torch function of my mobile phone, that there were a great number of large terracotta pots placed at intervals along the front of the house.

'Try the one closest to the entrance,' I suggested, and Rosie pivoted it to one side.

'Nope – nothing here.'

'We'll have to keep trying,' I said. 'You go right, I'll go left.'

As I kept checking, I heard what sounded like metal scraping against concrete.

'What was that?' Rosie paused mid-squat.

'Nothing,' I replied, although we both knew it had been something. It occurred to me then how exposed we were, two women out in the dark. *My bloody, bloody mother*, I thought. And bloody, bloody Mattie for not secreting her key in a more helpful place. I debated if we should perhaps make our way down to the road, where there would be phone reception or an open bar. But before I had time to articulate any of this, there was another sound, this time loud enough to send Rosie scuttling along the pathway into my arms. We clung to one another as the front door creaked open, both of us emitting a scream of fright as an outraged bellow ripped through the darkness.

A man wearing just a pair of boxer shorts had emerged from inside the house with a menacing shout, a shovel in his hands that he brandished at us. In the seconds that followed, I ran the full gauntlet of fear, anger, and then realisation and mortification. But it was Rosie who recovered her composure first.

'It's OK, it's only Uncle Niko,' she said as he lowered his weapon. 'Hello,' she went on cheerfully. 'You probably don't even recognise me, do you? I'm your niece. Rosie.'

Niko glanced towards me, then back at her, his bewilderment clear. 'Rosie?'

'Yep,' she confirmed. Letting go of me, she stepped towards him and took the shovel out of his hands. 'We're here to stay in your house for the summer, but you already know that, right? Can I go inside? I'm absolutely busting for a wee. That taxi took ages.'

'*Naí*.' It was barely a murmur.

'Cool. Thanks,' she said, assuming correctly that the word '*naí*' was Greek for 'yes'. Slipping past him into the house, she stretched out her hand and clicked on a light switch. Niko's face was thrown into shadow, but I could still see his eyes.

Still feel them.

When he uttered my name, it was as if the intervening years had never passed, as if I was eighteen again, running along the beach in the darkness to be swept into waiting arms, to be kissed, caressed, and gazed at as ardently as if the stars had fallen from the sky and were shining out from within me.

I thought I had left that girl behind in Corfu half a lifetime ago, but I was wrong.

She was still here.

I was still her.

4

I stared.

He stared.

Neither one of us spoke.

The shovel, which Rosie had balanced against the outer wall, fell to the floor with a loud crash, snapping Niko out of whatever horrified trance he had fallen into at the sight of me. He opened his mouth, closed it again.

I heard bare feet hurrying across tiles.

'What is going on down here— Oh. Oh my God – Ava?'

My sister Mattie appeared in the gap behind her husband, her thick dark curls sticking up at all angles. Of the three of us Fox siblings, she is the most like my father, and I registered his pale eyes and neat, oval face as she stepped into the light.

'Hello,' I said weakly.

'This is . . . What are you . . . ? What a lovely surprise.'

Mattie always defaulted to politeness.

Rosie had returned from the bathroom, and greeted her aunt with all the enthusiasm I should by rights have mustered up. Niko remained mute, standing there in his boxer shorts. The same dark hair that covered his head and jawline also spread across his chest, and when I allowed my gaze to inch downwards, I saw large hands and thick muscular thighs. The lithe youth of the past was very much a man now.

Mattie ushered me towards her with an outstretched hand and pulled me into an embrace. Embarrassed by the unexpected physical contact, I went limp.

'You had no idea we were coming, did you?' said Rosie.

'None whatsoever,' Mattie agreed.

Far from being perturbed by this, or even curious, the two of them merely laughed at the absurdity of it all, as if they were in on a joke that Niko and I were not.

'Granny told us we were having this house for the summer and that you were having ours,' my daughter explained. 'Is that not the case?'

Mattie glanced towards her husband.

'Niko, do you know anything about this? Did you and my mother cook up this little scheme between yourselves?'

We were all still crowded in the open doorway, and the temptation to bolt was a strong one. If I had not had Rosie with me, I would have fled.

Niko shook his head. '*Ochi*,' he said firmly, glancing towards me and then reverting from his native tongue into English. 'This is nothing to do with me. I have not spoken to your mother for many months.'

Hearing his voice, that baritone accent with its deliberate emphasis on each syllable, made me feel light-headed.

'This must be her idea of a joke,' I said. 'A prank at my expense – send Ava off to Corfu under a misapprehension; she's gullible enough to fall for it. How amusing it will be when she turns up unannounced.'

'It wouldn't have been amusing if Uncle Niko had bashed us over the head with his shovel,' pointed out Rosie, to which Mattie laughed in delight.

Niko, I noted, did not protest.

'This whole thing is probably my fault,' said Mattie. 'The last time I spoke to Mum, I told her I was sad about the fact that we had lost touch a bit, Ava, and how much I wished you and Rosie would agree to come for a holiday. This must be her way of ensuring we all saw each other. And, you have to hand it to the wily old bird – her plan appears to have worked perfectly.'

Wily was far too generous a word to describe my mother.

'The last thing Rosie and I want to be is a burden,' I said. I was already casting around for my suitcase, wondering how soon I could book us a flight home, plotting our escape from this hideous situation. As far as I was concerned, the holiday had come to an end.

'A burden?' exclaimed Mattie. 'Don't be daft – it's brilliant that you're here. And of course you must stay. We have plenty of room, and Rosie, you're going to love the new pool. I've been dying to have some guests here to show it off to, and now here you both are. It's a better turn of events than I could ever have wished for. Isn't Granny clever?'

I gawped at her.

Clever?

Could she not see that this was agony? That being here, with her and with *him*, was breaking me apart from the inside out?

'We can't stay,' I blurted. 'This is your house – you don't want us traipsing about all over it. We'll get a hotel.'

On a different island, preferably.

'No, you will not.' Mattie wrapped an arm around Rosie's shoulders and led her into the villa. 'If you think I'm going to let you scarper now that I finally have you both in my clutches, you've got another think coming.'

The statement was delivered in jest, but I knew there were hollow spaces behind the words where my sister's very real disgruntlement lurked. In her mind, I had done my best to avoid her ever since she'd announced her engagement. I had missed the wedding, feigning illness, and had diverted every invitation since – often, to my shame, using my daughter as an excuse. Mattie had travelled to the UK on numerous occasions, during which I had made sure to spend a moderate amount of time with her, but she had never brought her husband along with her. If she had, I would have swerved those encounters too. It was difficult enough spending time with her, let alone him.

I looked up then to find Niko staring at me. The two of us were alone, just as we had been so many times before. Only now, the air surrounding us fizzed not with electricity but with trepidation. I saw that he felt it, that he understood how hard this was going to be, and I yearned, suddenly, to offer him – and by extension, myself – some reassurance.

When I opened my mouth to speak, however, Niko shook his head as if dismissing me.

'I didn't plan this,' I whispered. 'I promise.'

I waited for him to reply, to nod, to acknowledge me in any way, but he didn't.

Instead, for the second time in my life, Niko turned and walked away from me.

5

Despite being adamant that I would not allow myself to fall asleep, and genuinely believing that I would never be able to, I had somehow managed to drop off. Perhaps it was the result of the long journey followed by the horrible shock, or that I was conscious of not wanting to disturb Rosie, with whom I had insisted on sharing a bed. Mattie was all for separating the two of us – 'we have plenty of bedrooms, take one each' – but I did not want to let my daughter out of my sight. That was the excuse I gave myself, although I suspect it was more to do with not wanting to be alone.

Both windows were shuttered and screened to keep out mosquitoes, and the room was in total darkness when I awoke. The air-conditioning unit on the wall was still purring away like a contented cat; its night-long murmurings had pacified my frantically racing heart.

Groping for my mobile phone, I blinked in surprise – it was almost ten a.m.

'Rosie,' I said softly to the mound of pale-yellow sheets beside me. 'Are you awake?'

'Huh?' came the mumbled reply.

'It's late,' I whispered. 'I'm going to get up.'

'S'OK,' she agreed. 'Mum?'

'Yes?'

'Tej would be nice.'

'Tej' was our word for tea, had been ever since Rosie was a tiny tot still learning how to speak.

I stood up and stretched. 'What did your last slave die of again – remind me?'

She smiled; her eyes were still closed. 'Exhaustion.'

There was nobody on the middle landing when I emerged, and I blinked furiously at the sudden brightness as I made my way first to the bathroom – which was small, neat, and decorated with blue-and-white tiles – then down the stairs. Mattie and Niko had picked the same deep turquoise paint for the banisters as they had for the villa's external shutters, and had wisely chosen not to carpet over the smooth gold flagstones that covered the lower floor. I liked the way they felt beneath my bare feet – cool and rough.

Immediately below the stairs was an open-plan lounge area, sparsely furnished with matching white sofas, a glass-topped coffee table and a series of earthenware pots in various sizes, each containing artful sprigs of dried flowers. The overall effect was reminiscent of a spread from a glossy interiors magazine – but then again, I thought, rather uncharitably, it was far easier to keep your home pristine when you did not have any children. While Rosie no longer drew on the wallpaper with her crayons or left sticky fingerprints on the upholstery, she had developed a maddening habit of putting her feet up – still clad in their shoes – onto whatever item of furniture happened to be in her vicinity when she sat down.

I wondered how much – if any – input Niko had made on the decor, or if he'd given my sister carte blanche to do as she pleased. Having never spent time with the two of them as a couple, I had no clue about the dynamic of their marriage. Niko had not hung around long enough for me to get any sort of gauge the previous night, instead muttering something inaudible to Mattie before leaving the three of us to it.

I couldn't hear anyone else moving around, so I headed over to the kitchen area, where I located a still-warm pot of coffee and everything I needed to make Rosie's tea. One of the chairs at the scrubbed wooden table had been pushed back at an angle and an empty cereal bowl languished in the sink. I stared at the spoon, wondering whose mouth it had been in.

'Morning!'

The greeting caught me by surprise and the spoon, which I had for some reason picked up, clattered loudly as I dropped it onto the worktop.

'Sorry.' Mattie sounded amused. 'I didn't mean to scare you.'

'You didn't.' I returned her smile with a brief one of my own. 'I was miles away. Still half-asleep, probably.'

'It's the Corfu effect,' she said. 'Don't you remember how well we all slept on the first night of our family holiday here? Mum had a hard job rousing us before lunchtime. I reckon it's something to do with all the stress leaving your body, all that Greek warmth whooshing in and washing the badness away.'

If there was anything I was certain of in that moment, it was that no stress whatsoever had exited my body since I had landed in Corfu. If anything, the opposite was true.

But 'That's probably it,' I said, and dropped a teabag into a mug.

'Here.' Mattie slid in beside me and passed the kettle. 'Is this for you, or . . . ?'

'Her upstairs,' I confirmed. 'Despite many years of gentle persuasion, my daughter still cannot abide coffee. She's a tea girl through and through.'

'Gulp!' Mattie chuckled. 'Don't let Niko find out, or she'll be treated to one of his many rhapsodic lectures about why coffee is God's greatest creation.'

I smiled as she turned away to fetch the milk.

'I'll run this tea up,' she said, talking across me as I started to protest. 'You take us out some coffee to the terrace. It was too dark last night to show you the pool or the view, but both are going to take your breath away.'

Being of a naturally effusive nature, Mattie was prone to exaggeration. However, even I had to allow that on this occasion she had a point. When I ventured outside a few minutes later, the heat that greeted me was powerful enough to stop me in my tracks. I had known it would be hot – we were in Greece, and it was summer – but I had forgotten how intense it could be, how ferocious. My eye was drawn immediately out and across the bay below us, the curve of Kalami Beach just visible, the sea beyond it a deep, steely blue. The villa terrace was paved in moccasin-coloured stone, the pool at its heart a rather odd shape, like a lump of cheese from which someone had taken an unruly bite. I could not pretend that it did not look inviting. I felt a sudden urge to hurry down the steps, fling off my robe and dive straight into the glittering water. A faint hint of chlorine hung in the air, but it was no match for the mineral scent of sun-baked asphalt, shifting dust and vegetation. The garden fell away down the hillside, and from my spot on the covered terrace I could see the twisted trunks of olive trees, the firework blooms of purple agapanthus and the swathes of bougainvillea that were artfully draped across the outer boundary walls.

My feelings towards Corfu had for a long time been complicated, but as I stared out at the view, I found that I was able to separate the tangle of all those past emotions from the immediate reeling of my senses. I had never not loved

Greece; I did not blame the island for the events of that summer so many years ago. Corfu was still every bit as gloriously captivating to me as it always had been. What I was experiencing, gazing out as puddles of sunlight warmed my bare toes, was more than a reaction to the beauty laid out before me; it was a sense of rightness, of coming home after a long and arduous journey.

I could easily have wept, but I didn't. I simply stood and stared.

This was how Mattie found me, and for a beat or two after I heard the door open behind me, I remained perfectly still. It was only when I felt the tentative weight of her chin as it came to rest on my shoulder that I closed my eyes.

Whatever spell the island had momentarily cast over me, I had broken free of it.

6

Mattie will do anything to avoid an awkward silence.

The 'anything' in this case being to talk, endlessly and tirelessly, with the level of enthusiasm usually reserved for children's television presenters. I didn't judge her for it. Besides, I rather enjoyed my passive role as listener. The less opportunity I had to speak, the less likely I would be to say what I was really thinking.

Unfortunately, by allowing my sister to dominate the conversation from the moment we sat down to breakfast on the terrace to when we decamped to loungers around the edge of the pool, it was inevitable that the subject of Niko would eventually come up.

'Sorry he didn't wait in to see you both again this morning,' Mattie said, as she rubbed sun lotion into her stubbly shins. She had just spent the best part of ten minutes wrestling with a large canvas parasol, and I could see beads of sweat on her forehead. The two of us have the same colouring, but while Mattie had done little to alter the messy brown curls we were born with, I had bleached, snipped, and straightened my hair into a chin-length white-blond bob.

'Couldn't matter less,' I said, watching as the corners of her mouth drooped a fraction.

'He doesn't mean to be rude,' Mattie hastened. 'It's just that the taverna takes up so much of his time – he's barely at home now the tourist season's properly got going.'

Her tone suggested that this did not faze her very much, and I must have raised an eyebrow high enough to scale the top of my sunglasses, because she quickly laughed and said, 'Not that I don't see plenty of him – I do. I'm usually down there with him, helping out. But what with the two of you showing up and—'

'You can go if you need to,' I assured her. 'Please, don't let us interrupt your schedule. We're fine on our own, aren't we Rosie?'

From a lounger that had been dragged defiantly out from the shade, my daughter looked up from her phone. She had spent the first part of the day filming segments for a TikTok video around the villa, and now she was busy editing. The same tinkly music track was playing over and over, although blessedly at a low volume.

'Huh?'

'I was just telling Mattie that we'll be fine if she needs to go to work.'

'Yeah, sure. Whatever.'

Mattie pulled a face as she shooed away a hovering fly.

'That's very kind of you both, but no way am I leaving you alone on your first day here. And anyway,' she added, lowering her voice to a conspiratorial whisper, 'Between you and me, I'm owed a few days off.'

'So, that's what you do here then?' I asked. 'Work at the taverna and look after this place? You don't have another job?'

'I always thought I'd do something really bonkers with my life, do you remember?' she said, smiling rather wistfully. 'Like become a yacht captain or a pilot – something that would help me see the world.'

'I remember,' I prompted, waiting for her to continue.

'Silly childish dreams,' she said, and we both turned as Rosie emitted an audible groan.

'What?' I demanded.

'You two,' Rosie complained. 'Acting as if your lives are done and dusted when you're only. . . How old are you?'

'I'll be thirty-four in November,' Mattie told her.

'Hardly retirement age then.'

'Feels like it sometimes,' Mattie said, her attempt at humour earning her a stern look from her niece.

'Look at Ophelia.' Rosie passed across her phone, and Mattie and I leaned over to see our younger sister's most recent Instagram post. It had been taken on a beach at sunset. She was sitting cross-legged on the sand, her hands pressed together in salutation. The first two lines of the caption contained a quote about wilderness not being a luxury, followed by something about feeling thankful for nature. I glossed over the rest, my attention waning almost immediately.

'She isn't letting anything get in the way of her dreams,' Rosie went on earnestly. 'And you could both do the same if you wanted to.'

For the first time since I had arrived, I was able to meet Mattie's eyes, our shared bemusement uniting us for a few fleeting seconds before I turned to Rosie.

'Unfortunately, there is a small thing in life called responsibility,' I pointed out. 'A concept that Ophelia Fox has never been able to grasp.'

Mattie passed the phone back across to Rosie, only to freeze in sudden horror.

'What is it?' I asked.

'I've just remembered what day it is,' Mattie got to her feet and started flapping her arms in front of her like an agitated goose.

'What's so scary about Fridays?'

'Friday night dinner. Niko's mother and his brother – plus his wife and their two boys – come over every Friday for a family meal, and because Niko cooks in the taverna all week long, he leaves this meal up to me.' She looked sheepish. 'Don't feel you have to join us if you don't want to. But it would mean a lot to me if you did. And I'm sure Dorothia will enjoy meeting you both.'

I sat up abruptly. 'Where did I put my phone?' I said, picking it up off the floor and tapping at the screen. 'I should start looking at flights home.'

'Mum!' implored Rosie, chiming in with Mattie's, 'Ava.'

I feigned ignorance. 'What?'

'You promised,' my daughter reminded me. 'This is the first time I've ever even been to Greece – and I told all my friends that I'd be here all summer.'

'Plans change.'

I could tell that Mattie was torn between the urge to agree with Rosie and the desire not to offend me.

'Please stay,' she said, sitting back down and putting a hand briefly over mine. 'You only just got here.'

'You're ganging up on me,' I told them, my hopes of salvation sliding away like the outgoing tide. The truth was, I had no good reason to leave so soon – not as far as the two of them were concerned. Sooner or later, one or the other would demand to know exactly why I was making such a fuss.

'We'll stay for a week,' I said. 'Then after that, we'll have to see.'

'Or two weeks?' Rosie grinned at me before returning her attention to TikTok.

Mattie had got to her feet again, and I watched as she bent to rescue a bug from the pool. She seemed incapable of sitting still.

'Why don't you let me help with dinner tonight?' I heard myself say.

Mattie beamed. 'Oh, that would be lovely. Are you sure?'

'I'm sure – it's the least I can do. What do you have planned?'

'Well, I usually pop down and see what Niko has in fresh. Dorothia likes fish, and it really isn't worth trying to change her mind. The one time I dared to serve moussaka, she looked at me as if I'd put a plate of cowpat down in front of her.'

'Who is Dorothia again?' asked Rosie, who had finally put down her phone.

'Niko's mother,' Mattie said, deflating a fraction. 'She's honestly not all bad. I shouldn't poke fun. She's just very set in her ways; she doesn't mean any harm.'

My stomach churned unpleasantly.

'Ava, why don't you head down to the taverna and pick up the fish while I make a start on all the boring veggies?' Mattie said.

'I don't think that—'

'Oh, go on. It'll give you a chance to explore Kalami a bit, too. You must be itching to get down into the village and have a nosy.'

I started to argue, but it was no good. Mattie was already tapping out a text to her husband, informing him to expect me in twenty minutes.

Since the previous evening's rude reacquaintance, I had decided that avoiding Niko as much as possible was my only real hope of getting through the days we spent here, yet now I had no choice but to face him, to speak to him, and to endure the pain of his obvious hostility towards me.

And the worst thing of all was that I only had myself to blame for ending up in this situation.

7

Nineteen years earlier…

A great number of people had told Ava Fox that turning eighteen changed everything, but she could not say that she felt very different at all. Her hair still frizzed out at the sides in the same stupid way, the spot she had been faithfully covering in toothpaste each night remained stubbornly present, and her mother continued to annoy her just as much as – if not more than – she always had.

No, Ava decided, as she stared glumly down at all the clothes neatly folded in her suitcase, eighteen had been a bit of a letdown so far. Her parents had declared that this summer trip to Corfu would be a 'celebration of your passage into adulthood', but apparently this did not extend to funding the extra credit required to use her mobile phone on the island. There was a 'Happy belated Birthday' text message sitting on there from the object of her utmost desire, Paul Donovan from school, and having waited the requisite week so as not to appear too keen, Ava was now desperate to send him a reply. He had added a kiss at the end, which according to Mattie meant that he wanted to kiss her in real life. She may only be fifteen, but Ava had to begrudgingly admit that her sister already had an impressively good understanding of the opposite sex and seemed to know intrinsically how their strange brains worked.

While Ava may not have been as attuned to boys as Mattie was, she did know that someone of tall, blond and popular Paul

Donovan's calibre would quickly lose interest if he believed his feelings were not reciprocated. Perhaps, Ava mused, she should find a telephone box and call him instead – that was if this tiny Greek resort even had a such a thing. It certainly didn't have any signal.

She was halfway into her bikini when the bedroom door was flung open and Ophelia burst in, her hand going immediately up to cover her eyes when she realised that Ava was topless.

'Oops!' she trilled, as Ava fought to fasten her clasp.

'I'm sure I wasn't as annoying as you when I was eleven,' Ava grumbled as she turned, regretting the slight as she saw the smile on her youngest sister's face fall. 'Now that you're here, you may as well help me decide what to wear,' she said, more kindly this time. Ophelia, who was about as interested in fashion as Ava was in her father's long explanations of how things worked, frowned at the three dresses laid out on the bed.

'The blue one,' she said. 'It feels like Greece is a blue place.'

'I hope you mean the sea and the sky, rather than anything to do with auras,' Ava remarked. Her mother had recently developed a fascination with spiritualism and, having long ago given up on converting either Ava or the rambunctious Mattie to her cause, she had focused her sights on her favourite child instead.

'Daddy says we can rent a pedalo today,' Ophelia said, swerving the question she did not want to answer – a Fox family trait, Ava noted wryly, along with irritability, cowardice, and an extremely low boredom threshold.

'Will you come in it with me?' Ophelia went on. 'Mattie always pedals too fast and makes us go round in a circle.'

Ava had crossed to the mirror, her hands poised to give her spot a good squeeze. 'I'm working on my tan today.'

'Please!'

Ava saw Ophelia's pout reflected in the glass behind her.

'Fine.' She sighed, relenting as she always did whenever her baby sister made that face. She and Mattie both craved time alone and had become experts in the art of self-entertainment, but Ophelia was different. Perhaps it was a symptom of being the youngest that always saw her shouldering her way into groups, badgering her big sisters to spend time with her and not taking no for an answer. Ava admired her determination, even if Ophelia's nagging did drive her up the wall.

'Come on, then,' she chivvied, casting a final longing gaze towards her useless mobile phone. Replying to Paul Donovan would have to wait for another day – and anyway, Ava decided, feeling her mood lift as she followed her sister through their beachside apartment and out onto the stones beyond, she stood far more chance of getting that kiss if she returned to Brighton with a tan. It was so hot here in Kalami, and as she stood at the water's edge waiting while Ophelia scampered off in search of the man who rented the pedalos, Ava could practically feel herself changing colour. The sea was crystal clear, the pebbles below her bare feet pure white, and the sky unblemished by even a single cloud. Ava knew there were many terms she could have used to describe what she was seeing, but the one she chose was heavenly.

In that moment, as her mind and her heart were overflowing with the beauty of that word and all its celestial connotations, Ava turned.

And that was when she saw him.

8

A chorus of crickets applauded as I made my way through the villa garden, where vast spikes of cacti and gnarled olive trees flourished in the dry, cracked earth. Loose stones slipped out from under my sandals and tumbled down the curved slope of the path, while the hot air felt thick enough to slice, nature's own weighted blanket.

Instead of turning left when I reached the main road and following the narrow stretch of tarmac towards the north end of the beach, where I knew Niko's family taverna, Elpida, was situated, I walked in the opposite direction, passing a fishmonger's, a small supermarket and a souvenir shop selling all manner of holiday detritus. There were lurid-coloured beach towels with maps of Corfu printed on them, snorkel masks and matching flippers, buckets, spades, and children's fishing nets, as well as a whole range of suncreams, English newspapers, and magazines, plus a dusty rack of novels.

The last time I had wandered along this same stretch of road was half a lifetime ago, yet it all felt familiar – the lemon trees in paved courtyards, the terracotta roof tiles atop apartment blocks, the bitter sweetness of freshly brewed coffee drifting out from open balcony windows, all accompanied by the soft percussion of the sea.

Kalami was a small resort, and it wasn't long before I found myself at the far end of the village, where the road curved around and met the White House. Once the home of writer Lawrence Durrell, it effortlessly dominated the bay with its gleaming walls, neat windows, and general resplendence. The interior of the main house had long ago been repurposed into a series of rentable rooms, while the lower part of the building and the adjoining terrace played host to an upmarket restaurant.

I knew Rosie would enjoy hearing about the history of the place and wished I had suggested the two of us dine there tonight, instead of allowing myself to be roped into a cosy dinner with the extended Balaouras family. I did not believe for a moment that Niko would be thrilled by the prospect either, especially given the fact that he'd chosen not to tell Mattie anything about our shared history. I had always suspected this, but now I knew beyond doubt. Then again, I acknowledged, it was not simply Niko's story to tell. I too could have volunteered the information at any time.

Leaving the road, I stepped onto the stony beach and bent to remove my flip-flops, hooking them over a finger as I made my careful way to the shoreline. The water that lapped over my feet was cool and clear, so unlike the English Channel in Brighton, which frothed angrily and was chilly enough to turn a person's limbs near-blue if they were foolish enough to submerge themselves.

There were three wooden jetties set at intervals along the beach, and I walked towards the closest, unable not to picture my eighteen-year-old self taking the same route. The apartment we had stayed in that fateful summer was unchanged save for a bit more wear and tear. The blue painted shutters were criss-crossed with cracks and the once-white walls tarnished grey, but if anything it afforded the rustic dwelling more charm. Assaulted then by a pang of sadness so acute that it made my eyes sting, I stumbled away and continued down the beach. The further I wandered, the more populated the cove became. The enterprising owners of the four seafront tavernas had set up loungers outside on which their customers could sprawl during the day for a small price.

Reaching into my bag, I took out my phone and stared at the blank screen, willing a message or call to appear – something to provide me with an excuse to stop, to delay the moment I had been dreading ever since Mattie suggested I come down here. Not for the first time, it struck me how nice it would be to have a best friend, someone objective I could call and share my fears with, who would give me advice or listen while I attempted to make sense of this bizarre situation. But there was no such person.

Growing up, I'd had Mattie, the two of us so close that our bond must have seemed impenetrable to the other children our age who might have wanted to play with us. We allowed the occasional guest into our midst, but never let anyone become much more than a casual acquaintance until we were teenagers, and even then, I was not naturally adept at letting people in, nor inclined to do so.

I could recall being vaguely aware that I should try harder, yet never caring enough to make the effort. Most adults I knew talked a lot about the friends they had made at university, so I resolved to wait until then. I would find my tribe when I moved away from home, I was certain of it. But then came that summer and, shortly afterwards, my unplanned pregnancy. When I'd finally made it to university several years later, I'd only had time to attend lectures and seminars before hurrying home to be with Rosie, her father Paul and me juggling parenthood around a chaotic schedule of work and study until we became the very epitome of ships passing in the night. There had been no space in my life for socialising, and even if there had, I was far too enamoured with my baby girl to crave hours away from her. I did what I had to do to get my degree, and that was that. No extracurricular activities whatsoever.

Making friends requires a particular skillset, the key one being time, and I had always been lacking in that department. Any free time I did have, I guarded fiercely. Perhaps because I grew up in a household where everything was shared – clothes, rooms, conversations, attentions – and so being alone felt not sad but triumphant. One of the things Paul had said to me shortly before we went our separate ways was that I'd always made him feel like a visitor in his own home, as if his presence there was a necessary inconvenience that I was tolerating purely for Rosie's sake.

Not wanting to lie, I had said nothing at all in reply.

I had ended up where I wanted to be, in many ways, and for a long time it had felt like enough. But now, I was on the cusp of change. Rosie would soon be off to university, and I would have to rebuild my life around the space she left behind.

I forced myself to put away my phone and stared towards the dark blue parasols of Niko's taverna, thought of the person who waited beyond them. The clench of a fist curled itself around my heart as I contemplated what I had done. By coming here to Corfu, all the work I had put in over the years to accept what I had lost had been erased. And all it had taken was one single glance.

9

Almost as soon as I stepped up from the stony beach onto the outer terrace of Elpida Taverna, a young and startlingly handsome waiter hurried across to greet me, a sheaf of laminated menus clutched in one hand.

'*Geia sas*,' I said, in reply to his own polite hello, then shook my head as he gestured towards an empty table.

'I'm actually here to see Niko,' I ventured, hoping he would understand and smiling when he nodded in confirmation.

I felt nauseous as I stood and waited, barely managing to take in the stripped wooden tables and wicker-strung chairs, the humming bank of glass-fronted fridges pushed against a wall, the waiting staff zipping around with trays piled high, the shouts echoing from the distant kitchen, and the sated expressions on the faces of diners.

'Ava.'

I jumped, then turned to find Niko standing behind me.

'Sorry,' he said, but I shook my head, dismissing his apology.

'Don't be. I was miles away. Just trying to remember what this place looked like when— Well, before. It's been a long time since— It looks great.'

He thanked me in Greek. '*Efcharistó*.'

'*Parakaló*,' I replied automatically with the standard word for 'please', my ease at slipping back into Greek a mild surprise. It had been Niko who had taught me the basics, with patience and persuasion, and the phrases I had gleaned had never left me. Holding on to them had been a way of holding on to the connection we'd once shared.

My efforts were rewarded by a small half-smile, but Niko did not say anything else. As I had been the previous night, in the uncomfortable silence in the dark outside the villa, I was overcome with a need to reassure him.

'I won't hold you up,' I said quickly. 'I can see you're busy.'

Evidence of that was splattered across the front of his white apron, while perspiration had flattened his hair against his forehead. Niko's eyes, although every bit as deep, dark and beguiling as I remembered, were bloodshot, and there were flecks of grey in the stubble that covered his jaw.

Could he still see the shy, frizzy-haired girl he had promised the world to when he looked at me, or was she lost behind all the layers of intervening life?

'You have come for the fish,' he stated, and only then did I realise he was holding a carrier bag. It dripped as he passed it across to me, and I held it out gingerly, not wanting my bare feet to get wet.

'It is only the ice melting,' Niko said. 'It will help to keep the sea bream fresh.'

'Right,' I said. 'Good. Thanks.'

With a final nod, he turned to leave, and I felt something inside me snag.

'Wait,' I called, loudly enough to attract a few curious glances.

Niko stopped, but he didn't come back towards me. Only by the slightest raise of his eyebrows did I understand that he was asking a question – asking me why.

'I . . .' I faltered, and shook my head. 'Never mind.'

Niko's expression was unreadable.

The waiter who had greeted me when I arrived had returned and was hovering between us, a cloth poised ready to wipe the drips off the floor, yet I could not seem to make my body obey my mind. After several awkward moments had passed, Niko took pity and strode back over to me, his hand finding the small of my back as he ushered me away from his customers. I allowed myself to be steered past the bar area, beneath a pergola straining under the weight of a vast grapevine and into a small office. There was a desk covered in neat stacks of paper, several empty coffee cups, a laptop, and a Elpida Taverna-branded mug full of pens. Niko took the seat behind the desk, while I perched on the very edge of a faded yellow armchair that looked older than both of us combined.

There was too much to say, but in that moment, I could not find the courage to say anything at all. It was unlike me to be timid – usually I spoke first and then had to apologise later – but being around Niko again had made me more aware. And not just of what I said, but how I moved, my expressions, even the way I might smell. It was borderline unnerving.

Instead, I waited to see if Niko would speak first, chewing at my lip and twisting my hands together in my lap. The bag containing the fish brushed against my leg, and I shivered. After several more awkward minutes of silence, I started to get up.

'I should get back to Rosie,' I said, but Niko raised a hand to still me. Again, I thought how tired he looked, how beaten down by this situation, by me.

'Are you all right?' I asked. 'You seem . . . upset.'

His eyes met mine and I tried in vain to read what lay behind them.

Niko sighed once more and attempted a smile, his shrug as half-hearted as the assurance that followed it. I did not believe for one second that he was *entáxei* – in Greek, 'OK'.

'You never told her,' I said, my words sounding dull but the pain behind them acute. Neither of us needed to clarify who or what I meant.

'No.'

'You never thought you should – that she had a right to know? Mattie's your wife.'

'And she is your sister,' he rebutted.

'Yes,' I said. 'Exactly. She is *my* sister. Of all the people you could have married, you chose her.'

Niko closed his eyes briefly, then stared down at his fingers, laced together on the desk. The longer I remained in his presence, the more restless he seemed to become, his foot tapping incessantly against the tiled floor. He wanted me gone; he did not want to have this conversation. But we had to; I needed to.

'Listen,' I said. 'I meant what I said last night. I didn't mean for us to be trapped in this . . . situation together. I should have known better than to trust my mother.'

Despite numerous attempts by both Mattie and me that morning, neither of us had yet been able to get through to our mother. But while my sister was content to laugh the whole thing off as a harmless mix-up, I remained furious at having been tricked. Whether her intentions were decent or not, my mother had landed me in an impossible position, and I wanted her to know that I was not impressed.

Niko had not replied; I ploughed on regardless.

'I don't think either of us wants to rake up the past, do we? Not when Mattie stands to get hurt. I can't – no, I won't – have that. I think the best thing we can do is agree to just draw a line, here and now, and make a pact to be civil to one another until I can come up with a good enough excuse to return home.'

If Niko had looked downcast before, now he appeared wretched. His shoulders had slumped, and he rubbed his hands through his hair and across his face as I spoke.

'This was always going to happen, sooner or later,' I said, careful to keep my tone light. 'We were always going to come face to face again one day. And now that it's happened, it's up to us to handle it properly, to not let anyone get hurt. Agreed?'

Niko would not or could not look at me; he nodded – a single curt gesture that felt like a dismissal – and got slowly to his feet.

'I have to go back to work,' he muttered. There was lead in his limbs when he moved, as if he had suddenly been handed a great weight. He stepped towards the doorway, then paused, speaking without turning to face me.

'I . . . I am sorry, Ava.'

I wanted him to clarify what he was sorry for – whether he regretted the choices he had made in the past or was merely apologising for the fact that I was here at all. I said nothing. Niko wanted me gone, that much was obvious without him spelling it out. But then why, I wondered, as I left the taverna and made my way out into the clean, bright, sunshine, did it feel as if the threads that had connected us for so long, those I'd allowed to grow slack over time, had suddenly been pulled taut again?

10

Dinner turned out to be quite the event.

The only memory I had of Niko's mother Dorothia from when I was younger was of a sour-faced woman sitting behind the till at Elpida in a cloud of cigarette smoke. I had not been introduced to her back then, only to Niko's late father, Leonidas. What I had known was that Dorothia was determined to keep her two sons exactly where she could see them – that much, Niko had told me himself. The year we met was the same one he'd lost his father, and I knew that after that he and his younger brother Socrates had been given joint control of the family business.

The younger Niko had nurtured ambitions of studying abroad, of travelling the world and escaping the confines of the small island he had grown up on, but those dreams were all whipped away the day Leonidas died. The high-spirited jester I knew had disappeared overnight, and a cold, hard stranger had taken his place.

I was unsure if Dorothia remembered or knew much of anything about me, but what became very clear from the moment she arrived at the villa was that she did not like me much.

'*Geia sas*,' I said as Mattie introduced us. I had hoped that choosing the more polite Greek word for 'hello' would ingratiate me towards her somewhat, but all I received in reply was a small sort-of grunt. Far from the black-shawled and white-haired old Greek ladies you might see depicted on a postcard, Dorothia had long, rather brassy bleached-blond hair and was wearing tight stonewashed jeans, white high heels and a thigh-length silver shirt decorated with rhinestones. Her face, while lined, was heavily made up, and as she leaned in to offer her son a proprietorial kiss on either cheek, I was almost knocked sideways by the strength of her musky perfume.

'And this is Rosie,' Mattie continued, her tone belying her obvious fluster.

'Rosie.' The older woman rolled the 'R' with relish, making my daughter titter with nervous laughter. '*You*,' Dorothia declared, 'are beautiful.'

I did not miss the glance she threw my way, nor the careful emphasis she put on the first word. Here was a woman accustomed to saying and doing whatever she pleased, without a care for whose nose she happened to elbow out of joint in the process. Mattie, I could see, was terrified of upsetting her, yet Niko appeared oblivious to any tension.

After taking a moment to mentally crack my knuckles, I followed the small party out onto the patio above the pool, where Mattie had set a beautiful table. Recognising the crockery as the same set Paul and I had been gifted by my parents when we bought our first house, I assumed this must be her and Niko's wedding china. Dorothia folded herself into a chair without comment and extracted a packet of cigarettes and a lighter from her handbag.

'I'll just nip inside and fetch you an—' began Mattie, only to emit a small 'oh' as Dorothia took a deep drag and flicked her ash onto a delicately patterned side plate. Rosie's eyes met mine and widened.

'Help yourself to bread,' Mattie urged. She had baked it herself that afternoon, the delicious aroma of it welcoming me home from my expedition to collect the fish.

'*Ochi*.' Dorothia wrinkled her nose. 'I do not like the way you make it. Too many seeds. You should leave Niko to do it,' she added, wrapping the fingers that weren't propping up the cigarette around her eldest son's wrist. 'He knows how I like it.'

Mattie started to apologise, but her words were cut short by a knock at the front door, and she hastily left the patio.

'Mum,' piped up Rosie, 'am I allowed a glass of wine?'

I barely had time to open my mouth before Dorothia interrupted.

'*Naí, naí*,' she said warmly, already reaching for the bottle of red. 'This is a local Greek wine, made here in Corfu, and it is marvellous.'

I ground my teeth together, irritated but determined not to rise to such obvious bait.

'You can have a small one,' I told Rosie, frowning as Dorothia deliberately filled the glass almost to the brim before topping up her own and Niko's. Nobody offered me any wine, but that suited me just fine. I had already decided to avoid alcohol for the duration of the evening, given its propensity to loosen my tongue.

Mattie returned to the table with Socrates, who was shorter, broader and outwardly jollier than his brother, plus his wife Elena and their two sons, Stelios and Thaddeus, or 'Thady', as it soon became apparent he was more commonly known. While Socrates pulled me against him for a robust hug, Elena was more reserved. Her chaste kisses felt tissue-dry on my cheeks, and her 'hello' – said in English, I noted – was little more than a murmur. The two boys – aged nine and six respectively – were both carbon copies of their bouncy father, and as soon as the new contingent had taken their seats around the table, the strained atmosphere caused by Dorothia's arrival eased somewhat. Bread was broken, bottles were uncorked, and a rousing cheer went up as Mattie staggered outside with a large tray laden with dishes. As well as the sea bream – which my sister had cooked in white wine, fresh herbs, and lemons from her very own trees – there were pink mountains of whipped taramasalata, stuffed vine leaves silken with oil, roast potatoes, platters of tomato and onion salad, a large dish of olives, and parchment parcels of oozy, salty feta.

'These potatoes,' boomed Socrates, spearing three with his fork. 'They are very good.'

'We have Ava to thank for those,' Mattie told him, as seven pairs of eyes swivelled towards me. 'Boiled in their skins and roasted with olive oil – that's right, isn't it?'

'I'm sure it's the local olive oil we have to thank,' I replied, knowing this would please the Greeks at the table. Sure enough, Socrates beamed at me, while Elena, who was sitting beside me, touched a warm hand to mine. Unable to resist, I stole a glance at Dorothia and was rewarded with a withering stare. All she had on her plate were a few slices of tomato and three olives, which she was pushing around with her fork. I registered how downcast Mattie was behind the plastered-on smile, and felt my own mood darken defensively.

'*Ela*, Thady,' Elena admonished, as her youngest son made a grab for the last chunk of bread. 'He does not ever stop eating,' she said to me, adding to the table at large, 'Whatever I prepare, it is never enough. It is always, "More Mama – give me more."'

Dorothia chuckled affectionately, smoke from her cigarette curling out through her nostrils. Struck by an image of a dragon wearing a peroxide wig, I was forced to suppress a smile.

'Socrates and Niki were the same,' she went on. 'It is the best thing for growing boys – let them have whatever they want.'

Elena looked as if she was going to reply, then thought better of it. Socrates merely laughed appreciatively, while Niko continued to chew his fish in silence.

'I think giving in to a child's every whim is a mistake,' I said evenly. 'If I hadn't said no to Rosie's incessant pleas for an ice cream when she was a toddler, she would have lost all her teeth by the age of ten – and I likely would have lost my mind, dealing with the repercussions of all that sugar in her system.'

Dorothia narrowed her eyes. 'Boys are different,' she said. 'You do not have a son?'

'No,' I agreed. 'But the principle remains the same. We, as the adults – the parents – have to set some boundaries, whether that be meal choices, curfews or hours spent on screens.'

Rosie, who was sneaking a look at her phone beneath the table, promptly reddened.

'It is different with daughters,' Dorothia persisted, flicking yet more ash onto Mattie's best crockery. 'Boys must be allowed more freedom when they are young, they must be indulged more by their mamas.'

Her comment was preposterous enough to make me laugh, and even Rosie made a small noise of disagreement. I was surprised that Mattie did not react, but then, she probably didn't dare. If Dorothia's treatment of her tonight was anything to go by, I could only conclude that my sister's resolve must have been trampled underfoot years ago. However, while there were a great many things I could have said in reply, I had to make some allowances. Dorothia had lost her husband, and who wouldn't dote even more ardently on their children following the death of their spouse?

'*Ela*, Mattie – why don't you join us in this debate?' Dorothia craned her head so she could see to the far end of the table.

My sister had frozen with a forkful of salad leaves halfway to her mouth.

'Me? Oh, you know, I don't really have . . . I'm not sure if I should—'

'*Mamá* . . .'

There was a warning undertone in Niko's voice. Beside me, Elena lowered her wine glass, and I saw her dart a look across at her husband. It felt as if a storm cloud was hovering a few feet above us, the thunder of unease rumbling while the lightning prepared to strike.

'*Ochi*,' Dorothia drawled, 'perhaps it is best to say nothing. You are not a mother, and so how can you know what is best?'

Mattie's eyes widened before she lowered them to the table, her cheeks aflame. She said nothing and furiously I turned to Niko, willing him to step in, to tell his ghastly mother not to be so rude. He did not so much as murmur.

I thought about all the times Mattie had supported me when our mother needled, how she had defended Dorothia earlier when we were sitting by the pool, and of all the hours she had spent preparing this meal, laying this table, all the while trying her best to ensure that everyone had an enjoyable evening. She did not deserve to be spoken to like this, and if Niko was not prepared to say so, then I would.

Putting my knife and fork together, I fixed the older woman with a hard stare, hoping she would be able to feel it, that she would turn to face me and regard me with the same disdain she had been all evening. The candles flickered between us, and I heard the faint buzz of a mosquito. In fact, that was what Dorothia reminded me of – not a dragon, but a parasite circling for blood.

I cleared my throat pointedly, but no sooner had the words of my for once carefully constructed rebuttal begun to form on my lips than they were interrupted by a loud knocking at the front door.

'I'll go!' My sister leapt up from her chair so fast that Socrates had to steady both his and Rosie's wine glasses. We all listened in silence to the soft slap of Mattie's bare feet on the tiles, and the shrill exclamation of surprise that followed.

'Come through, come through,' she said a few seconds later, sounding near giddy with excitement. 'Everyone's out here – the whole gang.'

Not my parents, I thought in horror – it couldn't be. They were in Thailand, had only flown out a few days ago. But if not them, then . . .

'Oh my God!' enthused Rosie, who had clambered out of her chair and was peering through the open doorway. 'Mum, you won't believe who's just turned up.'

'Who?' I said, but the question was already redundant because there, standing on the terrace, looking even more wild-haired, wild-eyed and wild-clothed than the last time I had seen her, was my youngest sister Ophelia.

11

'What are you doing here?'

I had asked the question, but the words had burst out of me so rapidly that at first, I wasn't sure if someone else had spoken. Ophelia looked every bit as surprised to find me sitting there as I was to see her.

'I could say the same thing to you,' she said. 'How did y—'

'Mum,' put in Mattie, which was, after all, explanation enough.

'Did she call you, too?' piped up Rosie. 'Granny tricked us into coming here – we thought we were doing a house swap. But I'm really glad that she did because . . .'

Whatever my daughter was going to say withered and died on her lips as a stocky young man came into view behind Ophelia, his form filling the doorway and his smile of greeting far less nervous than mine would have been.

'This is Sam,' said Mattie, catching my eye and giving me a rather meaningful look. 'He's Ophelia's . . . friend.'

'Boyfriend?' I clarified, only for the man, Sam, to shake his head.

'We prefer the term "open relationship",' he explained. "Neither Lia nor I conform to the constraints that society tries to place on us.'

I glanced instinctively at Mattie and saw my own bemusement playing out across her features.

'That's so cool,' sighed Rosie, turning pink as Sam winked at her. I watched as he took her proffered hand and shook it, his gaze lingering a little too long for my liking. Mattie was now busy making more introductions, and Niko had stood to kiss his second sister-in-law on each cheek. Dorothia did not rise from her chair, choosing instead to light yet another cigarette, watching in silence as proceedings unfolded.

The last time I had seen Ophelia had been a little over a year ago, when she had been preparing to leave for the Australia job that never happened. We hadn't arranged to meet, she had simply turned up at my door early one evening, wondering if she could beg the sofa for the night. The two of us had barely spoken in months, so at first the conversation had been stilted. Rosie was out with friends, and I had just opened a bottle of red wine, so I'd offered Ophelia a glass. This seemed to relax her, and by the time she had drained it, she had begun to open up, admitting how scared she was at the prospect of starting a new life overseas.

'I am making the right decision, aren't I?' she'd said, wanting me to provide the reassurance she was incapable of finding within herself.

I'd had no idea, but knowing she needed a definitive answer, I'd opted for the easiest response.

'Of course,' I had told her. 'Think of it as the first day of the rest of your life.'

'I wish you could come with me,' she'd said then, to which I had laughed. Because it was a ludicrous thing to say – an impossibility. Ophelia's face had fallen. She hated being mocked, I should have remembered that. Of the three of us sisters, she was the one least able to cope by herself. I had never been able to understand why.

'You hardly need your boring older sister cramping your free-spirit style,' I'd said. 'You'll soon make friends – don't worry about it.'

'If you say so,' she'd replied, but I could tell that I had done little to console her.

The Ophelia that I remembered from that night was not the woman standing in front of me now. She had lost weight to the point of scrawniness, her once softly rounded cheeks now hollow, the skin pulled taut around deep-set eyes that were haloed by dark smudges of fatigue visible even beneath her dark tan. In the many Instagram pictures she posted, Ophelia appeared to be glowing with health and vitality, but that must all have been filters, because under the tan she seemed tinged with grey. There were twists of coloured thread and beads plaited into her unbrushed hair, and when I glanced down at her sandalled feet I saw the chipped remnants of nail polish, and what looked like a tattoo of a hummingbird on her ankle.

Sam, in contrast, reminded me of a banker on holiday. His heavy flop of brown hair was coiffed just so, his chino shorts ironed to a crease, and his navy-blue polo shirt neatly tucked in. The only hint of a vice was the rolled-up cigarette tucked behind his left ear – and the superior smirk on his face. Whenever I looked in his direction, he returned my gaze with a steadiness that I found unnerving, as if he was sizing me up the way one might look at a new outfit, trying to work out if it would fit. Resolved to ignore him, I focused my attention on Ophelia.

'Did Mum not tell you that she and Dad were flying out to Thailand then?' I asked, to which Ophelia shook her head. Mattie had immediately fetched plates of food for the two of them, but while Sam was tucking in with enthusiasm, Ophelia had barely seemed to register it. I noted, however, that she had accepted a glass of wine someone had poured for her, and was making short work of it.

'No, but I wish she had. She's going to go mad when she realises that I'm here.'

'Serves her right,' I said, ignoring Mattie's small gasp of disapproval. 'Karma.'

Niko pushed back his chair and muttered something about fetching more wine.

'What prompted you to come here anyway?' I continued.

Ophelia made a show of shrugging. 'Oh, you know, it was coming into rainy season over there, and there's only so much swimming and sunbathing you can do before it all becomes a bit samey.'

She must have read the incredulity in my expression because she quickly added, 'Thailand can be a bit full-on, so many backpackers everywhere and parties every night. I guess I – we – needed a change of scene.'

'Well, you're both welcome here for as long as you like,' Mattie said warmly, then jumped as Niko shut the terrace door behind him with a bang.

Sam put his knife and fork together. 'You're so sweet, Mattie,' he said. 'Lia told me you were.'

'What did she say about me?' I asked, and saw his eyes narrow a fraction.

'Different things.'

'Such as?'

'Don't, Sam.' Lia tutted. 'He's winding you up,' she insisted. 'I haven't said anything bad about any of you, have I, Sam?'

'Can I?' he said to Dorothia instead of answering, his hand hovering above her lighter. The older woman nodded out a bored-sounding '*nai*', and I did my best not to sigh with irritation as Sam fussed around flattening out and then lighting his roll-up.

'Nothing bad,' he agreed finally. 'Although everyone has a different definition of what "bad" means, don't they? I mean to a vegetarian, killing an animal for meat is bad, but to us carnivores, it's completely necessary.'

As if on cue, Thaddeus leaned across the table, speared a large chunk of fish and popped it triumphantly into his mouth. Elena laughed, which broke the strange tension, and I felt my shoulders slacken with relief.

Instead of eating her food, Ophelia was chewing her nails, the hand not raised to her lips gripping the fragile stem of her wine glass. Noticing me looking, Sam reached over and patted her absently on the side of the head.

'You seem on edge,' I remarked, when it became apparent that nobody else was going to point it out.

'Usually, we'd be having a spliff at this time of night,' Sam explained. 'Bit of a toke to wind down the day. I don't suppose anyone has a bit of the old wacky baccy going spare, do they?'

Mattie choked on her wine. I glanced at Rosie and saw her eyes widen in awe.

'This is Greece,' Niko said coldly. 'We do not tolerate drugs of any kind.'

Sam smirked. 'If you say so.'

Niko was not impressed. The ferocity of his glare was powerful enough to shatter tarmac.

'This is a very serious matter,' he said. 'You must not ask anyone in Kalami about drugs. It would not be a good idea.'

It was clear that he was telling, not asking, and nobody spoke through the stalemate of silence that followed. Ophelia topped up her wine glass, her slim arm shaking under the weight of the full bottle, and took a grateful sip. And it was then that Dorothia finally chose to speak.

'It is late,' she announced. 'I think that dinner is over.'

12

I would tell myself later that I had tried to like Sam, but any inclination I had to overlook my initial impression of him did not last very long.

I was willing to ignore his ridiculous swagger, his proprietorial behaviour, and even his ill-advised comment about thc 'wacky baccy', but I found it harder to forgive what came next.

It started that first night, when he and Ophelia were given the bedroom next door to the one that I was still sharing with Rosie, and the two of them proceeded to christen it. Repeatedly and extremely loudly. Knowing how even the sight of her best friend kissing a boy turned my daughter's stomach, I felt that I had little choice but to knock on Mattie's door to ask if there was another room free for us to sleep in. As it transpired, my sister was not in there, so I had to endure the added discomfort of explaining the situation to Niko, whom I had woken up, and who clearly thought I was overreacting.

The following morning – our first Saturday on the island – I got up to find Ophelia and Sam swimming naked in the pool, which necessitated me whisking Rosie out for breakfast down at the beach before she noticed what was going on – and of course, she insisted that we go to Elpida. Cue yet another awkward encounter with Niko, who I assumed felt obliged to leave his post in the taverna kitchen to sit with us a while. Presumably tired on account of me having woken him up in the small hours, he ordered a double espresso and sipped it in between answering Rosie's endless questions about the island, the food, and what he thought of a video she'd found on TikTok of a man tossing banana skins onto the heads of passing strangers.

We had eaten and were about to depart when Ophelia breezed up in some sort of kaftan made from a fishing net, worn over a pink thong bikini, and ordered herself and Sam a cocktail. 'Start as we mean to go on, eh?' he said to me, before offering Rosie a sip. When I suggested politely that ten in the morning might be a tad early to start drinking, he told me not be such a 'fuddy-duddy'. The man certainly excelled when it came to using absurd alliteration.

I did not hang around to witness what happened next, but according to Mattie – who received an irate phone call from Niko two hours later – Ophelia had started dancing on his tables and was encouraging his unimpressed customers to follow suit. Mattie had to hurry down there and tempt the pair of them back to the villa, after which they returned to their bedroom for another amorous – and extremely vocal – session of lovemaking.

By this stage of the afternoon, I was ready to return to Corfu airport with Rosie and, if necessary, hitchhike on the runway to get us home. Predictably, however, my daughter was having none of it.

'At least two weeks,' she reminded me. 'You promised.'

I had. And so, we stayed.

Sunday dawned, and, having managed around two hours of agitated sleep, I decided to venture down to the beach early for what I hoped would be a reinvigorating swim. There were no signs of life as I crept silently through the villa clad in a swimsuit and a large towel, my water shoes dangling from one hand. Sneaking out was a skill I had perfected during my first summer in Corfu, although I wondered now if my parents would have cared all that much if they had known what I was up to. Back in those days, my mother repeatedly encouraged all three of us girls to challenge convention, push boundaries, and embrace experiences.

'Go, seek out your dreams!' she would declare, and I'm sure in her head she was the epitome of a cool mum. Having said that, at least part of my more adventurous side had come from my mother, so I probably had her to thank for some of the foolhardiest moments of my life; the times that came before Rosie. I struggled now to recall how it felt to be so free, to have nothing and nobody preventing me from whatever it was I wanted to do.

Perhaps that was why it felt so wonderful to be standing alone on the shoreline, preparing to plunge headfirst into a purely self-indulgent act. All my angst from the past few days seemed to wash away as I waded through the shallows, my breath catching in my chest as the cold water splashed up over my legs, my stomach and, finally, my shoulders. I lifted my arms and dived forwards over a wave, feeling the sea rush over me, tugging my hair with its invisible fingers. There were no sounds save for the whisper of the waves, a melancholic beat keeping time with the rhythm of my own heart as I floated, my face to the sky, thinking of everything and of nothing, grateful simply to be there, in this moment, on this island; the place I had once believed would someday be my home. Had wished and wished that it be so.

I wasn't sure if I had heard his feet on the stones or if a part of me somehow sensed that he was close by, but when I turned my gaze back towards the beach, Niko was there.

I raised a hand.

There was no point pretending he hadn't seen me. We were the only two people on the beach. Like me, Niko had not bothered to dress in more than he planned to swim in, but I noticed that he had also brought a rucksack along. This he dropped on the ground beside my towel before striding into the sea. I had ventured far enough from land to be out of my depth, but was struck by an urge to kick my way back into more shallow water. I suppose I wanted the seabed to be within touching distance in case I needed to make a quick getaway. In the end, Niko and I met each other halfway.

'*Kaliméra*,' he said, in a solemn sort of voice.

I gave myself a moment to take him in, to watch as he pushed his sodden hair off his face and then shook his head like a dog, spraying me with droplets.

'Oi,' I chided gently, and for once, Niko's tired smile of reply felt genuine.

'*Ela*,' he said. 'You are wet already.'

'Did you follow me?' I asked. I had meant to exude nonchalance, but the question came out sounding more as if I was hopeful that he had.

'*Ochi!*' he exclaimed. 'Of course not. I do this every morning. I think you know that.'

I did. The two of us had swum together many times during that summer, after all.

'I couldn't sleep,' I told him, rolling my eyes as I added, 'Ophelia,' by way of explanation.

Niko blinked as the clouds above us parted, the rising sun behind them turning the surface of the water into molten gold.

'Oh, well,' he said, seemingly nonplussed. 'They are young and in love.'

I had to laugh. 'In love? I don't think so. In lust maybe. He'll get bored of her soon anyway. Sam strikes me as someone who approaches life much like a bumblebee – he'll stay long enough to take what he needs, then he'll move on.'

'You sound as if you do not approve,' he said, frowning as I pulled a face. There were two deep lines etched between his eyebrows that did not disappear when he relaxed his expression.

'It's not as simple as that,' I said with a sigh, bracing myself as a small wave buffeted against us. I had fully acclimatised to the temperature of the sea, and it felt almost warm, like one of Rosie's nightly baths that she had lain in long enough for the water to turn tepid. 'I worry about Ophelia,' I admitted. 'I wish she would grow up a bit, stop playing at life and live it instead.'

Niko put his head on one side and examined me.

'What?'

'You are not the same,' he said. 'Once upon a time, all you wanted to do was be free for as long as possible – isn't that what Ophelia is doing? Maybe,' he went on, moving in a circle around me until I was forced to turn, 'you are a little bit jealous.'

'Definitely not,' I said, confident that I was telling him the truth. 'I think the person I wanted to be when I was eighteen might have been, but the me now has no desire to backpack around the world, get drunk at ten in the morning or have sex with men like Sam.'

I shuddered as I said his name, and Niko raised an eyebrow of amusement.

'So,' he prompted, 'you are happy in your life?'

I should have been able to say yes, but his question felt impossible to answer. I never had been able to lie to him and did not want to start now. Instead, I shrugged helplessly.

'Rosie makes me happy.'

'Ah, *naí*,' he said. 'Rosie is beautiful.'

'Inside and out,' I agreed, unable not to smile as I pictured my daughter. 'She is my everything. I can't believe she's going to be eighteen soon.'

Niko then asked when her birthday was, and I guessed he was doing the maths. I had fallen pregnant with her so soon after I had left Corfu that it must have stung him. I know it would have hurt me if it had been the other way round. Niko, however, gave nothing away. He merely nodded.

'We must have a party for her,' he said. 'Perhaps at the house?'

'She would love that,' I enthused, my next sentence swallowed up by the sea as another, more determined wave crashed over us, knocking my feet out from under me. Scrabbling to regain purchase on the sandy seabed, I managed to hook one of my legs around Niko's, leaving him with no choice but to wrap his arms round my waist and steady us both. He lifted me up until my chest was pressed against his, and my lips brushed his ear as I staggered to regain my balance. His body felt strong and warm, the shoulders to which I was clinging broad and knotted with muscle. My skin was pale next to his, barely touched by the sun yet, and I remembered how we used to marvel at our differences. All those hours spent exploring each other, delighting in the pleasure of having found someone we fitted together with so seamlessly. My body had not forgotten how right it felt, and, knowing I was in danger of giving in to its pull, I broke away, removing myself from Niko's grip.

For a moment, neither one of us spoke; the unsaid words too risky, the lingering sensation of each other still dangerously potent. Niko allowed the water to drag him backwards, away from me, and after a while he dropped his gaze and rolled over onto his front. I watched the sea ripple as he cut through it, his movements smooth and focused, and waited for the roar of my heart to slow.

What would happen if I followed him? If I gave in to what I was feeling and simply let myself float out into the blue?

It would be worse than selfish, more than a betrayal – it would be unforgiveable. My life, my real life, was waiting for me back onshore, and it did not matter how much I might yearn for something else. I could not turn the clock back; I had to accept the choices I had made all those years ago.

And so did he.

13

Nineteen years earlier…

As soon as the man – not a boy, thought Ava, not with real stubble across his jaw and those muscles so clearly defined on his torso – was certain that he had her attention, he made his way directly towards her. A smile played at his lips, and when he dipped his chin and raised his dark eyes to hers, Ava felt winded. A warmth began to radiate from somewhere deep below her belly button, and she spluttered out a laugh, loudly and without warning.

'English?' was how he greeted her.

Ava nodded. 'Is it that obvious?'

The man cocked his head, looking her briefly up and down. Ava pulled self-consciously at the hem of her blue dress. She was horribly aware of the heat in her cheeks, and the spot that she had not bothered to conceal with make-up.

'A lucky guess,' he said.

He was Greek, but his English appeared to be word-perfect. This came as a relief to Ava, who had not even learned the words for 'yes' and 'no' yet, let alone anything conversational or – she reddened further at the thought – flirtatious.

'Are you staying here?' he said, gesturing to the apartment behind them.

'Yes.' Ava wondered whether to elaborate. She could not remember ever encountering a man this good-looking before; he was making her nervous. As he raised a hand to push his floppy

dark hair off his face, she caught the scent of him – bitter and lemony – and felt another tug of desire.

'What is your name?' he asked, taking a step towards her. Ava was struck by an absurd urge to reach across and touch him, and knotted her hands together behind her back.

'Ava,' she told him. 'What's yours?'

'Nikolaos,' he replied, his lips parting enticingly as he sounded the 'a'.

She repeated it tentatively, her terrible attempt at a Greek accent making him laugh. 'Maybe call me Niko?' he suggested. 'It is easier.'

'OK,' she agreed, and smiled at him. It was not a smile she could recall having made before, and the broadness of it caused her cheeks to ache happily.

'What are you doing now?' he asked. 'Do you want to come swimming?'

Yes, please, *Ava screamed internally, but instead she shook her head.*

'I can't,' she said, explaining about the planned pedalo trip. She could see Ophelia now, beckoning Ava to join her from further down the beach. 'I should go,' she told him. 'Sorry.'

'Tonight?' he persisted.

Ava laughed again, this time at his audacity.

'I don't even know you,' she pointed out, folding her arms across her chest.

Niko grinned. 'That is why you should meet me.'

'Just like that?'

He fixed his eyes on hers. 'There is a saying in ancient Greek: "While you live, shine." It encourages us to make the most of every moment.'

Ava looked at him, sure that she would detect a hint of mischief behind his words, but Niko's expression was purely serious. She had the sense then that this was a man she could trust, and although she had met him only minutes ago, Ava felt suddenly at ease, as if he had always been there in the wings of her life, waiting for his cue to stride out and join her.

Ophelia had given up waiting beside the rented pedalo and was making her way back across the stones towards them. Ava waved and called out that she would be there in a minute.

'When tonight?' she asked Niko and was gratified when he punched the air in triumph.

'Twelve – perhaps twelve thirty. I will wait for you here,' he said, nodding in the direction of the long wooden jetty.

Then, before Ava had a chance to reply, he took both her hands in his, hesitating only long enough to be sure he had her consent before leaning forwards and kissing her lightly on the cheek.

'What was that for?' she murmured, shivering at the sensation of his breath, hot against her throat.

Niko let go of her hands.

'I was right,' he said. 'You do shine.'

14

It was Mattie who decided that we should all go to the beach.

She had told me that Sunday was one of the busiest days at the taverna, so I'd been half-expecting her to be occupied by work. But despite her offering, Niko had apparently told her to take as many days off as she liked. Socrates, she told me, had been hauled from his usual position in the back office to take over as Elpida host, and was more than capable of covering for her.

'Niko says that all his brother does in there is play Candy Crush anyway,' she confided over breakfast. I had come back from my swim to find her setting out fresh pastries while a pot of coffee brewed, and for the first blissful half an hour or so, the two of us had the terrace to ourselves. I was glad to sit and listen while she chatted away, happy to latch on to anything that would distract me from dwelling over what had just happened down at the beach, the way it had felt to have Niko's arms around me.

It pleased me that he cared enough about Mattie to rearrange work around the unplanned arrival of first me and Rosie and now Ophelia. I could not help but wonder about their relationship, what it looked like behind closed doors. Having made sure never to spend any time with the two of them, I had assumed Niko must share the same playful and passionate bond with Mattie that he once had with me, but

I'd not seen any evidence of that since I arrived. I had not seen him be affectionate towards her once, nor she to him.

'I was thinking of taking everyone over to Agni Bay,' Mattie announced.

She had summoned me and Rosie over to the white sofas, where Sam and Ophelia had been artfully draped across each other most of the morning, her head on his shoulder and his hand on her bare thigh.

'OK,' I said, hesitating as a memory tugged. I had been to Agni Bay before, but not with Mattie.

'Or we could drive to Kerasia? The beach is better there, which means more space for us to spread out.'

'Let's do that then,' agreed Sam, moving to extract himself from the parcel-tape grip of Ophelia. Rosie, I noticed, could not tear her eyes away from the two of them; I rolled my own.

'Do they have Wi-Fi at Kerasia?' she asked, and Mattie smiled.

'At the restaurant they do. We can set ourselves up as close to it as possible.'

This seemed to satisfy my daughter. She stole a glance at her phone before stowing it in her rainbow-striped beach bag. Aside from yesterday's breakfast at Elpida followed by a wander along Kalami Beach, Rosie had yet to see much of the surrounding area, and I could tell she was excited by the prospect of a day out. Once the five of us had scooped up our belongings, filled water bottles, and I had coated Rosie's exposed back and shoulders liberally with suncream, we locked the villa door behind us and headed over to Mattie's jeep. Giving Rosie the front seat, I squashed into the back with the other two.

That morning's clouds had long ago dispersed under the glare of an uncompromising sun, and I stared up at it through the open roof, blinking behind my sunglasses. I had forgotten quite how richly green the island was, with its abundance of tall cypress pines, holm oaks and eucalyptus. Wildflowers seemed to burst out through every cracked wall, and I saw snatches of pink and gold honeysuckle, purply-blue alkanets, and the bright red bulbs of a strawberry tree.

Rosie's long blond hair rippled and whipped around her face as Mattie drove us north along the coast, tooting the horn in greeting to people she knew, or to warn other drivers that she was approaching a blind corner.

'You have to be so careful,' she called back over the rumble of the engine. 'There was a terrible moped crash a few years ago when some tourists forgot which side of the road they were supposed to be driving on.'

Niko had driven a moped when I met him. He took me everywhere on it and not once did it occur to me to ask him for a helmet, let alone worry that we might have an accident. An image of Rosie doing the same thing appeared in my mind, and I felt my stomach somersault with horror.

Becoming aware of a warmth on my thigh, I glanced down to see that Sam had his leg pressed up against mine, manspreading. I moved pointedly away, causing him to turn and face me, an expression of bemused pity calcifying his features. On his other side, Ophelia gazed out at the landscape hurtling past, her eyes half-closed as the wind rushed across her face and lifted her thick, honey-coloured fringe off her forehead. She was lost in a moment, oblivious to my discomfort.

Sam shifted until his body once again connected with mine, and this time there was no room for me to move away from him.

'Sorry,' he said, without a trace of contrition. 'I can't seem to stop slipping. Must be these leather seats.'

The statement was anodyne, his delivery of it pure ice. He was trying to make me feel uncomfortable, that much was obvious – but I did not know why. He barely knew me.

'Shit!' cried Mattie, her foot coming down roughly on the brake as a cat scampered across the road ahead of us. Caught unawares, Sam was thrown forwards, his knees landing in the dusty footwell. I heard him swear under his breath and made no attempt to disguise my smile of satisfaction as he clambered back up.

'Here,' I said, pulling out his seatbelt and offering it to him. 'You had better buckle up. The leather is very slippery, after all.'

'Thanks, *Mum*,' he muttered, slotting it into place around him.

I was about to hit back with a withering comment when Rosie interrupted, saving me from myself.

'Say cheese, you three,' she called, her phone held aloft, and we all tilted our chins towards the camera. I could tell she was delighted to have captured what she perceived to be a happy moment – a rare moment – of her mum and her cool Aunt Lia together, the shape of their smiles so similar and their hair thrown wildly around them. It would have been a perfect picture, could have been a treasured memory, had it not been for the man between us.

We completed the remainder of our journey without further mishap, but it was still a relief to arrive at Kerasia Beach, where I would be able to put some distance between myself and Sam. I knew he was only young and that for him, life was simply one long game, but I did not like the way he goaded me, nor the disparaging way in which had he referred to me as 'Mum'.

I watched him take Ophelia's hand before beckoning for Rosie to join them and wrapping his other arm around her shoulders, leading her away from the jeep.

'Wait – what about the bags?' I started to say, but Mattie merely clucked affectionately.

'It's only a few towels and packed lunch – we can manage.'

'That's not the point,' I grumbled. 'Rosie should know better than to swan off without helping.'

'She's seventeen,' Mattie pointed out. 'Fun takes precedence when you're that age, if I remember rightly?'

I made a small noise of agreement, knowing that if I told her the truth, which was not that I wanted Rosie to carry bags but that I wanted her as far away from Sam as possible, it would make me sound overprotective – not to mention judgemental. Instead, I said, 'You look nice today, by the way. That colour really suits you.'

'Really?' Mattie blushed as she glanced down at her sunshine-yellow dress. 'It's really old – just like me.'

'Careful,' I warned jokily. 'I'm the eldest here, don't forget.'

Mattie smiled. She had a neat, closed-lip smile – unlike mine, which was all teeth and gums. The soft dark curls that framed her face made her look warm and inviting, whereas my rigid, sharp-edged bob screamed 'do not approach' – or so I assumed. Perhaps, however, it had more to do with the person beneath the hair.

We fell into silence again as we made our way from the parking area to the wide stretch of beach. The shingle in Kerasia was finer and more golden than in neighbouring Kalami, while the undergrowth that surrounded it was dense and noisy with crickets. At the far end of the beach, there was a small shop and taverna, a blue-and-white Greek flag flapping above it in the breeze. The others were busy setting themselves up on wooden loungers outside and, as we neared, Rosie raised a hand and began to wave.

'Look, Mum,' she enthused. 'Prime spot or what? And the Wi-Fi is fast!'

I lowered the bag of lunch to the ground, averting my eyes as Sam pulled open the halter strap of Ophelia's bikini top.

'Hey!' she exclaimed, batting him away in mock outrage.

Ignoring them, I passed Rosie a bottle of suncream.

'Go on,' I told her, as she pulled a 'do I have to?' face. 'It will have rubbed off on the drive over. Do it to make your old mum happy.'

'You're not old,' she replied automatically, then laughed as Sam leaned across and whispered something into her ear.

'Do you want a lilo?' Mattie asked Rosie, unfolding a deflated one from a bag.

'If she does, she's more than capable of blowing it up,' I said, taking it from her before she had a chance to get her mouth around the air hole. 'Why don't you just relax, sis?'

I had never referred to Mattie as 'sis' before, and the word sat awkwardly between us for a moment, reminding us of the estrangement we'd allowed to form. The one that *I* had allowed to form . . .

The moment was saved by the arrival of a tall and willowy blond-haired woman, who had clocked Mattie from across the beach and was now striding towards us with obvious delight.

'Hello!' she called, and I saw my sister's face light up. Abandoning the towel that she was in the process of arranging on a lounger, she hurried forwards and enveloped the woman in an enthusiastic embrace.

A flurry of conversation followed, with enough ease to illustrate that this woman, whoever she was, must be a close friend. Perhaps even a best friend. The two of them were no longer hugging, but they had not let go of one another either – Mattie's hands clasped the woman's elbows, anchoring her to the spot.

'Hi,' I said eventually, because I was standing less than two feet away from them and it was becoming awkward.

'Oh God, how rude of me!' exclaimed Mattie, wheeling round. 'Ava, this is my Dutch friend Fenna. Fenna, this is my big sister Ava.'

I was tall, but Fenna was taller – and she was striking too, with wavy golden hair, straight, symmetrical features, and eyes of the palest blue. She was dressed in khaki shorts and a plain black vest, and had a bumbag strapped round her waist.

'Ava,' she repeated, smiling at me with confidence. 'It is very good to meet you.'

Mattie introduced Fenna to the others, of whom Rosie was the only one polite enough to stand up from her lounger. I watched as Sam inspected the new arrival with only the mildest of interest, his murmured 'alright' perfunctory at best.

'I saw the jeep, so I thought I would come and say hello,' Fenna explained.

'What brings you all the way out to Kerasia?' Mattie asked.

'I received a telephone call about some abandoned babies.'

Rosie gawped at her in confusion.

'Babies?'

'Ah, sorry,' Fenna corrected. 'Baby cats – kittens.'

'Oh, I see.' My daughter looked relieved for a second before concern overtook her. 'The poor things!'

'Sadly, it happens quite often here,' Mattie said. 'Fenna does her best to look after them. She's amazing,' she added, turning to smile at her friend. 'Funds it all herself, with the help of a few donations here and there, and drives all over the island picking up strays and making sure they're fed and inoculated.'

'That's so cool of you,' said Ophelia, who had sat up on her lounger and was busy attempting to plait her scraggly hair. Sam, I noticed with irritation, was lying down, his back towards the rest of us as he played a game on his phone. *Rude.*

'Do you need any help locating them?' Mattie asked Fenna. 'You guys will be all right without me for half an hour or so, won't you?'

'Of course we will,' Rosie assured her.

'You're sure you don't mind?' Mattie asked. 'I feel terrible for leaving you all here – I'm supposed to be the host and—'

'Go!' I told her, shooing her away.

'I'll be as quick as I can – and please start lunch. Don't wait for me! I'm not even hungry and—'

'Oh my God, just go, woman!' implored Ophelia. Sam, who had stood up and was stretching like a sprinter before a race, muttered something under his breath as Mattie and Fenna walked away.

'What was that?' I demanded, failing to check my exasperation.

He ignored me, turning instead to Rosie. 'Fancy a swim?'

'Yes, please!'

She could not have got up any faster if a rattlesnake had slithered out from beneath her towel.

'Wait a minute,' I began, but my words were futile. Sam had my daughter's hand in his and was dragging her towards the shoreline, her excited shriek of laughter making my chest contract. I sat down heavily on her abandoned lounger, exhaling my disgruntlement as I did so. Beside me, Ophelia appeared in contrast to be completely relaxed – serene, as ever, in the capricious fog of irresponsibility.

'And then,' she said airily, 'there were two.'

15

I was seven years old when Ophelia was born.

My mother had insisted on a home birth but had not arranged for anyone to look after Mattie and me during her labour, which was long and loud and difficult. In an effort to create a zen environment for her new arrival, she had placed lit joss sticks in the lounge, the hallway and the landing outside the bedroom, and I have never been able to forget the cloying aroma of cinnamon, cloves and sandalwood that accompanied my mother's moans of agony.

Mattie and I had sat side by side on the bottom bunk in our shared room, me doing my best to reassure her while trying not to cry myself. Whenever we heard the soft tread of my father's feet on the stairs, we would immediately lie down flat beneath the covers, our eyes tightly shut in imitation of sleep. Both of us were worried, but neither of us wanted to worry him – not even then. Mattie was not yet four but already pliant, which left me to assume the responsible role, the same one I have been saddled with ever since.

One of the earliest realisations I had about my mother was that she enjoyed making comparisons. She was the type of person to bite into a cake and remark to my father, 'It's nice, but not as nice as the cake we had in Dorset that summer – remember, Angus? In the café with all the broken teapots in the window.' And true to form, from the moment Ophelia was born, my mother had begun to weigh up the merits of her new daughter against her other two, and it was a relentless discourse.

'Lia is so gentle when she feeds,' she would gush to my father, as Mattie and I sat cross-legged on the floor beside the armchair. 'Ava was such a biter – I had to put cabbage leaves inside my bra.' On a separate occasion, I overheard her talking to another mother at the local park, saying how she'd got 'third time lucky' with Ophelia. I had stored that one deep in my subconscious to hurl at her during my antagonising teenage years, and her response had been to simply shrug and say, 'Well, you were a very challenging child, Ava.'

This propensity she had to pit each of us against another inevitably caused rifts between Mattie, Ophelia and me and, even when the three of us were close, we remained in silent competition with each other, the glow of our mother's affection and praise being the warmth we wanted to bask in. Having Rosie had saved me from all that; she was my chance to rewrite the mothering rulebook. There were no disparaging remarks, no other children to divert my attention, no pursuit my daughter could not try if she was keen, and no moment when I was too busy or distracted to tend to her, support her, love her.

While I had failed in my roles of daughter and wife, I did feel as if I'd triumphed at being Rosie's mum. It was the one thing in my life of which I was wholly proud.

I glanced at Ophelia to see if she was keeping an eye on Rosie and Sam like I was, but she was already facing me with a hesitant smile.

'Don't worry about Rosie,' she said, as if I had picked up a stick and scored my thoughts into the dusty ground between us. 'Sam will look after her.'

I bit back the first response that came to me and said instead, 'I'm fairly sure Rosie can look after herself.'

'Oh, I don't doubt it,' Ophelia agreed, stretching out a foot and examining her chipped green nail polish. 'She seems like a very capable girl – a lot like you were at her age.'

There was no barb to Ophelia's tone, but I felt myself stiffen defensively regardless.

'Rosie is smart,' I said carefully, 'but not street smart. She'd have you believe that she's ready to head out and take on the world, when in reality her favourite thing is curling up on the sofa with a hot chocolate to watch *Strictly Come Dancing*.'

'Mum and Dad never let us watch much TV, did they?' mused Ophelia. 'I remember Mum going on and on about how it would manipulate our minds and confuse our true desires. Do you want a sip?' she added, reaching into Mattie's cool-bag and extracting a miniature bottle of vodka.

'No!' I exclaimed, sounding every bit like the judgemental sister I had tried so hard to leave behind. 'I mean, it's a bit early, isn't it?'

Ophelia twisted off the lid and threw me a wicked grin.

'It's always cocktail o'clock somewhere. And who says the consumption of alcohol must be limited to the hours of darkness? Time is just a construct, something society created to control people.'

I sighed at the absurdity of her argument, at how adolescent she sounded.

'If you want to drink, go ahead,' I said. 'It makes no difference to me.'

'*Yammas*,' she toasted, lifting the bottle to her lips, and wincing as she knocked it back.

Watching her made me feel sad, so I looked away towards the water, searching for a familiar outline. Rosie and Sam had not made it far; I could see the two of them sitting in the shallows, their heads turned inwards towards each other, apparently deep in conversation. As I watched, Rosie tipped backwards as if she was laughing, and a coldness crept across me.

My instinct was to go over there, intervene before Sam did or said something to corrupt my daughter. I was halfway to my feet when Ophelia said, 'Please stay.'

I paused.

'I was hoping we could catch up a bit. I've barely spoken to you since I got here.'

'You've seemed otherwise occupied,' I said as I sat down again, and was rewarded with a rather sheepish expression. It was not something I had witnessed Ophelia do very often – look shamefaced – and it was enough to intrigue me.

'Talk to me,' I prompted. 'Tell me about you and Sam. How did the two of you end up together?'

Ophelia took another gulp of vodka before replying.

'We're not together,' she said. 'At least, not in the traditional sense. I have no claim to him, and vice versa.'

'Was that his idea or yours?'

'Both of ours.'

She sounded convincing, but the way she was fiddling with the ties of her bikini bottoms and avoiding my eyes suggested differently.

'Is that what all the young kids are about these days?' I enquired lightly. 'Keeping things casual. Has commitment become uncool?'

Ophelia emitted a scoffing sound.

'I'm not sure if commitment has ever been *cool*,' she said, adding deliberate emphasis to the last word. 'But me and Sam aren't sheep anyway, we make our own rules. We understand that this thing between us, whatever it is, won't last for ever – but that doesn't mean we can't enjoy it while it does. Neither of us likes putting labels on things. Feelings should be free, experiences unhindered by societal expectation.'

'That is all well and good,' I said carefully, 'as long as nobody is getting hurt.'

Ophelia fixed me with her doe eyes, her full bottom lip set. The wind kept lifting strands of her hair and blowing them across her face. It would have irritated me, but she hardly seemed to notice.

'I can tell you don't like Sam,' she stated, not giving me time to respond before adding, 'but he's harmless, honestly.'

I thought about his leg pressed against mine in the jeep, the coldness behind his gaze whenever he looked at me.

'He was really there for me in Thailand,' she went on. 'I was having a tough— Well, I was alone. I needed a friend, and he was there. He listened and gave me advice, stuck up for me.'

'Why did you really leave Thailand when you did?' I asked. The question had been niggling at me ever since Ophelia had trundled out her vague excuse about the weather. She had never been a convincing liar, and I could sense there was more to the story – something she perhaps wasn't ready, or willing, to share.

'I told you, it was raining all the time,' she said.

'But you'd been there almost a year,' I pressed. 'You must have had a life there? Friends? A job?'

Ophelia stifled a yawn. She had finished her miniature vodka and begun absent-mindedly tapping the empty bottle against the back of her hand.

'Nothing and nobody worth staying there for,' she said. 'Only Sam – and he came with me.'

'And what's next?' I continued. 'Will you go back to Thailand when you leave here, or are you considering coming home?'

This time the scoff was real. 'Home? What, you mean to Brighton, back in with Mum and Dad?'

Ophelia had never quite made the step into independent living in England, claiming she didn't have the funds, that she was reluctant to join the rat race and work simply to live. My mother nurtured this sentiment, of course, and Ophelia was permitted to remain in the house we had all grown up in for however long she pleased.

'Is there an alternative option?' I asked, not meaning to goad, but irritating her nonetheless. A supportive, responsible sibling would have said, 'Come and live with me while you figure out what you want to do – I'll look after you.' But I simply waited for her to fill the silence that had wedged itself between us.

'I don't know about you,' she said resolutely, 'but all this serious chat has given me a raging thirst. I'm going to see what alcohol options there are in the shop – what can I get you?'

I slumped, feeling oddly defeated as I lifted my bottle of water. 'Nothing for me, thanks.'

Ophelia began to rummage in her bag, cursing as a packet of rolling tobacco fell out and spilled across the ground. I had kept half an eye on Rosie and Sam throughout our conversation, and now breathed out a sigh of relief as they started making their way back towards us.

An impulse nudged me then, urging me to do something, to say *something*.

'That thing I said, about you not getting hurt?'

Ophelia had got to her feet, her purse clasped in one hand.

'I only said it because I care about you, Lia.'

'That's nice – but there's really no need to worry.'

When I stared up at her, I saw the warped reflection of myself in her mirrored sunglasses, so small and fragile, so unlike my own perception of who I was, and how I appeared to others.

'I mean it,' she said, again with the same sad half-smile. 'Nobody is going to get hurt.'

16

Nineteen years earlier…

There was a fizzing sensation in the pit of Ava's stomach, as if she had dropped two of the indigestion tablets her father favoured so much into it and they had failed to dissolve. She had somehow made it through dinner at Thomas's Place without giving away how nervous she felt, even managing to eat most of the helping of chicken souvlaki that the beach taverna's kindly Greek owner had placed in front of her. For once, she was relieved to be the invisible one, her parents' lack of interest not rankling as it usually did. Ophelia was regaling them with tales of all the fish they had spotted during their long morning out on the pedalo, and Mattie, attentive as ever, was doing a very good impression of someone genuinely interested. Not even she, the person Ava was closest to in the whole world, had noticed a change in her older sister – and Ava was convinced she must have changed. Niko's gentle touch, his whispered words to her, felt as though they had been scorched onto her skin.

Her first instinct after returning from the beach earlier had been to seek out Mattie and tell her all about the encounter, but then she had reconsidered. All of Ava's life, she'd had to share things – her bedroom, her possessions, her friends. She and Mattie had always come as a pair, so alike in appearance that they were often mistaken for each other, and their lives had meshed over time so that sometimes Ava could not work out where she left off and her sister began. But this was different – Niko had been drawn to her and only her. He did not even know that Mattie existed, and that felt important somehow. She wanted Niko to know her properly first, before she gave him the chance to see her alongside her family, in the role that always made her feel diminished. And so, she hadn't told Mattie. She had not told anyone.

When they returned to the beachside apartment after dinner, Ava feigned tiredness and went straight up to her room, stretching herself out on the narrow single bed. The mattress was hard and the pillows flat, but it hardly mattered. Battling the urge to laugh, she tossed from side to side, kicking out the sheets until the bed looked thoroughly slept in, then fetched an armful of spare cushions from the top of the wardrobe and arranged them under the covers. In the unlikely event of her parents coming to check on her during the night, they would hopefully assume the lumpy mound was her.

It was nearing eleven thirty.

Ava's hands trembled as she fastened her gold 'A' necklace and hooked in her favourite emerald drop earrings. They had been an eighteenth birthday gift from her grandparents on her father's side and were the nicest thing she owned. Without knowing where Niko planned to take her, she was not sure what to wear, and eventually settled on simple denim cut-offs and a tight-fitting white vest. Then, having smudged a little kohl around her eyes and smeared gloss on her lips, she snatched up a thin grey cardigan and her trusty black handbag and crept quietly through the house.

Outside, the beach was deserted, but Ava could still see signs of life over at the White House. Making her cautious way along the rickety wooden jetty, she lowered herself into a sitting position, her feet dangling over water daubed silver by moonlight. Her mother had told all three girls that they would love Corfu; she had been there herself many times as a teenager and had never forgotten how beautiful it was, how welcoming the people, and how effortlessly it helped her to unwind. Ava hated admitting that her mother was right about anything, but on this occasion, she had to allow her a victory.

This place was special.

Ava closed her eyes and tried her best to tune out the rapid flutter of her heart by focusing instead on the steadier breath of the sea: in and out, forwards and backwards. And then, another sound. Pebbles slipping, wooden boards creaking, and then a voice.

'Geia sou, *Ava.'*

She turned but did not stand up, smiling her greeting as Niko came into view behind her.

'Can I sit?' he asked.

'Of course.'

Now that he was here, Ava found that her nerves had receded, chased away by that same innate sense of rightness she'd felt when she met him. Like her, he was dressed simply, in jeans and a T-shirt, but she could tell that he'd put some sort of gel into his hair. For a moment they stared at each other, the dancing light in their eyes saying all the things they could not articulate. Ava dropped her gaze to his lips and felt a pulsing sensation from somewhere deep inside her.

'I didn't know if you would come,' she said, and Niko frowned.

'Why?'

Ava could only shrug.

'This was my idea,' he reminded her.

'Did you think that I might not come?' she asked, and Niko grinned.

'No.'

'You're so modest.'

'Sorry,' he teased. 'I do not understand this word: modest.'

'I could always change my mind and go back,' she told him, although they both knew she had no intention of doing so. He was sitting so close to her that Ava could feel the heat of his body, and, when his knuckles grazed her leg, the jolt of pleasure she felt caused her to flinch. She wondered what spectacular combination of chemicals was hurtling between them now, bursting into sparks as they collided in the dark air.

'How are you?' he asked, not casually as a passing acquaintance might, but seriously, as if he really cared about the answer. Ava's mood was buoyant, yet his words brought unexpected tears to her eyes. It took her a few moments to steady herself, and she considered her reply with care.

'I'm better than I was,' she said, to which Niko nodded.

'I am the same.'

It was the perfect moment for him to kiss her, and Ava burned with the hope that he would. Niko was holding her in place with his dark eyes, and she was a willing captive, so convinced now of what was about to happen that she felt the breath stall in her throat.

But Niko did not kiss her. Instead, he offered her his hand.

'Come,' he said. 'I have something to show you.'

17

It was his voice I heard first.

The bedroom that Rosie and I had moved into following the arrival of Ophelia and Sam was situated directly below the one Mattie and Niko slept in, and both were front-facing with a balcony outside that was wide enough to sit on. I had been upstairs an hour or so, having come up with Rosie when her yawning became less about Niko's Greek mythology spiel and more about genuine exhaustion, but had found it impossible to switch off. While I loved having my daughter so close to me at night, it meant that I couldn't keep the light on and read or listen to the audiobooks that had become my sleeping aid over the past few years, in case I disturbed her. The only option was to lie silently in the shadowy dark, my eyes closed and my thoughts hurtling around like mosquitoes at a human banquet, trying to trick my body into slumber.

It never worked.

I had read somewhere, in a magazine perhaps, that the wisest thing to do for insomnia is to change location; accept that you are awake and remove yourself from the bed, where you will only toss, turn, twitch, and drive yourself mad. That was why I went out onto the balcony, to give my mind a new focus. I thought that would be the trails of twinkling light across the water below, the reflection of the moon and the soft breath of the wind. But it was not to be.

I froze in my seat when the door above me opened and I heard Niko grumble something unintelligible under his breath. There followed a scraping sound as he pulled out a chair, and I pursed my lips tightly together, lowering each of my bare feet from where I had propped them against the balcony wall.

Niko let out a weary sigh. I pictured his hands raking through his hair and across the stubble on his jaw, his eyes set on some point in the far distance as he tried, like me, to quieten whatever it was that had him agitated. Because he *was* agitated. I could sense it.

He muttered something else in Greek, a terse phrase that could only be a complaint of some sort, and then I heard another voice: Mattie.

'*Ola kalá*?' she said. *Is everything OK?*

'*Naí.*' His delivery was blunt; cold.

'It doesn't seem that way to me,' she replied tentatively. 'What's up?'

'What is up?' he repeated, stretching each of the words out, as if pondering his reply. '*Ela*, what do you think is up, Mattie?'

The way he pronounced her name made it sound sharper than it was – the 'Matt' quick and the 'ie' hard. My sister, to her credit, did not snap back at him as I would likely have done. She merely sighed and pulled out the other chair.

'I have no idea, Nik. But I'm here if you want to talk about anything. I want to help.'

There was a beat of silence, during which I barely dared to breathe. I knew it was wrong to eavesdrop, but I could not seem to move. What I should have done was call out, make them aware that I was there before they continued what they believed to be a private conversation. But I did not. Instead, I stayed silent in the darkness, listening.

'*Ela*,' she urged him gently, in the same tone I would once have used on Rosie, back when she was a small child in the throes of a temper tantrum. 'Talk to me.'

Niko cleared his throat.

'When the summer is over,' he said. 'I want us to try again.'

'You mean . . . ?'

'*Naí*. I want us to be— To have a family.'

Adrenaline rushed into my blood; I could hear the thud of my heart inside my ears.

Mattie did not say anything for a while, and I wondered if they were staring at each other, if he was beseeching and she was . . . what? Indifferent? Excited? Scared? I had no idea how Mattie felt about the idea of having a child, because I had never asked her, had never wanted to pick at that scab.

'We can try if you want,' she murmured, and even to me she did not sound convincing. 'But I don't want you to get your hopes up. You know it's not, that I'm not— But we can try if you want.'

'Socrates knows somebody in Athens,' Niko said. 'A doctor. He will be able to help us.'

'We don't need a doctor,' Mattie replied, the speed of her response illustrating her insistence. 'We just need time, that's all. You work so hard, and things are always so hectic around here. I'm sure once we can both relax a bit, things will happen naturally.'

'You have said this before,' he pointed out. 'There is always a reason, an excuse.'

'It's not an excuse,' she countered. 'You make it sound as if I don't want a baby.'

'Do you?' he demanded.

'Of course I do – but I want it to be at the right time.'

'Time, time, time,' he muttered, frustration causing bitterness to leak into his tone. 'There is never going to a right time – now is the time.'

I waited for Mattie to stand up for herself, to tell him that it was hardly up to him, that it was her body and her decision just as much as, if not more than, his. That having a baby is not something you simply wish into being, that there were things the two of them needed to resolve about their own relationship before they brought a new person into the midst of it. Because there were issues to address – that much had become starkly apparent. For years, I had foolishly assumed that it must be Niko, not Mattie, who was delaying starting a family. It seemed I had been wrong. Perhaps I had been wrong about a lot of things.

I heard the scrape of a chair as someone stood up, then Mattie's voice again, this time softer, pacifying.

'Come on,' she said. 'Why don't you come to bed?'

The suggestion behind her words was clear, and they landed like blows. The sensation was one of falling, as if I had walked to the edge of the balcony and thrown myself off.

'*Ochi*.'

There was a serrated edge to his refusal that cut through whatever Mattie was going to say next. She faltered mid-sentence, and it was hard not to picture the hurt expression that I knew must be on her face, the bewilderment that comes in the wake of rejection. She had offered him her body, her affection, herself – and he had said no. I had experienced it and understood the pain; yet my sympathy remained with Niko, with the plight that he was suffering, of his yearning to be a parent. Because I knew there was nothing better, nothing that meant more.

When she spoke again, Mattie sounded less as if she was trying to mollify him. 'It's late,' she said. 'I'm going in. If you change your mind, you know where I am.'

For a long time after she left, there was no sound at all save for the indistinct whisper of the waves far below. It was too late for the birds and the crickets, or the buzz of a passing moped, too late for voices to be swept up by the breeze. The night was subdued by heat, the moon obscured by the roof of the balcony above me where Niko sat, so quiet and melancholic that the thought of him stirred me almost to tears. I wanted to reach up through the stone and take his hand, squeeze his fingers into the knot of my own and soothe his consternation with understanding.

The pain of knowing that I could not, that I would never again be able to touch him with the uncomplicated tenderness I once had, was enough to extinguish my urge to do so. The only thing I could do was be there, with him, in the darkness – an invisible companion to his turmoil – and hope that in some small way, it helped.

18

The following morning, Niko did not go to work.

He was there on the terrace when I ventured outside, a cafetière on the table in front of him and pensive expression on his face.

'*Kaliméra*,' I said and, glancing up, he saw me and smiled. A real smile.

'Good morning to you, too.'

Rosie, for once, had got up before me. I could hear her splashing about in the pool, and craned my neck to see who was in the water with her. It was Sam, of course. From the curl of cigarette smoke drifting up from the loungers, I guessed that Ophelia must be down there as well, but there was no sign of Mattie.

'No work today?' I asked, discreetly putting on my sunglasses. I had barely slept and did not want Niko to see the puffiness around my eyes.

'*Ochi*, there are many flights today, so it is quieter. I am waiting for Giorgos to come with the car, then we will go to town by boat.'

'And Mattie is . . .'

'Out,' he said, flicking his hand as he did so. He did not elaborate, and I didn't press him for any further information. As far as he was aware, nobody else but he and Mattie knew that the two of them had argued the previous night.

There was a shriek from the pool area, and I crossed to the edge of the terrace, squinting down through the foliage to see what was going on. All that was visible of my daughter were her kicking legs and bikini-clad bottom, but she was certainly not drowning. Sam must have flicked water at her or something, baiting her as he had tried to bait me. Unlike me, however, Rosie appeared to be a willing participant in the game.

'I'd like to see Corfu Town,' I said, turning back to face Niko. 'Is there any way Rosie and I could come along?'

Niko lowered his cup.

'We wouldn't hold you up or anything – we can make our own way back.'

'Ta, ta, ta, ta,' Niko tutted, shushing me. 'If you want to come, of course the answer is yes. But only if you can be ready in twenty minutes.'

'We can,' I said delightedly, and thanked him before running barefoot down the outer steps towards the pool.

'Rosie – guess where we're going!'

Predictably, Sam was also keen to be included in the trip, but Ophelia – perhaps sensing that her boyfriend was about as welcome within my orbit as a bluebottle would have been at a picnic – convinced him to stay behind.

'Thank you,' I mouthed over Rosie's shoulder as I passed her a towel, and Ophelia smiled weakly. There was definitely something distinctly off about her mood, but I did not have time to coax it out of her. This evening, I told myself. I would take her to one side and get to the bottom of it.

'Have fun then, kiddo,' Sam said to Rosie. He had heaved himself up out of the water and stood dripping beside us, brown hair plastered across his forehead, red shorts slick against his skin. Extending an arm, he brushed a light finger against her cheek. 'We'll have a rematch later, yeah?'

'Yeah.' Rosie did her best to sound nonchalant, but it was obvious that she was thrilled to be the focus of his attention. I wanted to snarl at him like a guard dog, order him in no uncertain terms to stay the hell away from my innocent, impressionable daughter. But I could not allow myself to fall into that trap; to do so would be to let on how much his behaviour was getting to me.

Ushering Rosie away, I rubbed her arms through the towel, the instinct to dry her the same as it had been when I bathed her as a baby. Every night without fail I would sit with my legs curled beneath me on the raggedy mat in Paul's parents' bathroom, one hand poised in case she slipped, listening as she chattered away about what she'd learned that day at nursery and answering her ever more outlandish questions about the world and her place within it.

I indulged her every enquiry, perpetually proud of my inquisitive, interested and articulate child, and vowed that if a question came up that I could not answer, I would do whatever it took to seek out the truth for her. So many times, I had approached my own mother in search of solutions, so many times I had come away unsatisfied.

I had wanted better for my girl.

'There's no time,' I said, when we reached the bedroom and Rosie made a dive for the hairdryer. 'Just tie it up – here, let me.'

I pulled the bobble off my wrist and began twisting her wet curls into a bun. Water dribbled down her back and she pulled away from me, protesting with a drawn-out 'Mu-um'.

'Wear something that covers your shoulders,' I urged a moment later, and laughed as she pulled a face and tossed the playsuit she had selected down onto the bed.

'Mum,' she said. 'I love you, but you're doing my absolute head in. Please go and wait for me downstairs. I promise I'll choose something suitably demure to wear.'

'I just don't want you to get sunburnt—' I started to say, but she interrupted.

'Out.'

'OK, OK – I'm going. But be quick – I promised Nik— your uncle that we wouldn't hold him up and—'

'GO!'

I chuckled to myself as I closed the bedroom door and made my way down to the ground floor. I felt light on my feet and had to quell a sudden and ridiculous urge to skip. Niko was in the kitchen washing up, while a younger Greek man, who I vaguely recognised as one of the waiters from Elpida, hovered nearby, spinning a heavy set of keys around on his finger.

This, I deduced, must be Giorgos.

We greeted one another in Greek, and I allowed myself to take him in properly, to appreciate the soft brown hair brushed forwards, the thick calves below the shorts, the polo shirt straining across a broad chest. His expression was open – kind eyes, aquiline nose, pale-pink lips, and a smattering of dark stubble. He was the archetypal Greek Adonis, that heady blend of exotic and familiar, and when he smiled at me in the same unselfconscious way Niko had when I first met him, I actually blushed.

I fully expected that Rosie would react to Giorgos as a dish of butter might to a blowtorch, but when she trundled down the stairs a short while later, all he received was a brief hello and a good view of her back as she headed towards the terrace.

'Wrong way,' I called, stopping her just as she reached the door.

'I just thought that maybe Lia had changed her mind,' she said. 'And that she and Sam could come with us after all.'

I was saved from having to come up with a decent excuse not to re-invite them by Niko.

'They went swimming,' he told her. 'At the beach.'

'Oh,' she said. 'Oh well.'

Niko and I exchanged a look then, and I saw that he understood, that he was my ally in the ongoing battle to prevent my daughter from forming any sort of bond with the stranger who had been foisted, uninvited, into our lives. He already cared about Rosie enough to become her protector – she was his niece, an extension of his family, and so she must be cherished as such. When it came to me, however, the waters were far murkier.

'*Ela*,' said Niko, nodding in the direction of the front door. 'It is time to go.'

Any lingering disappointment Rosie might have felt was whipped away almost as soon as we set off across the bay, and she laughed out loud with pleasure as the little speedboat bounced up out of the water only to slap back down again, spraying us with a fine mist of salty droplets.

On the wooden bench seat opposite our own, Niko sat with his knees apart and a small rucksack between his feet, seemingly unfussed by the constant lurch and pull of the sea. Giorgos, who had begged his cousin for the use of this unwieldy vessel, stood up at the wheel, wearing a fisherman's cap that he'd unearthed from a box on the deck.

'It is my captain's hat,' he told us, with a certain amount of pride, to which Niko had groaned in mock despair before leaning across and saying in a conspiratorial whisper, 'He is trying to become the boss of me today, I think.'

'I can't imagine anybody being the boss of you,' I replied, although having now met his mother, I knew this was not strictly true.

The crossing from Kalami to Corfu Town – or Kerkyra, to use its Greek name – took around twenty-five minutes, making it a far quicker journey time than that of the taxi Rosie and I had taken the night we arrived. As Giorgos eased off the throttle and the tempo of the boat's engine dropped from a roar to a gentle chugging, the grand outer walls of the town's old Venetian fort came into view high above us.

'Established by the Byzantines during the sixth century,' Niko said, when he saw Rosie's expression of awe. 'When the Venetians came much later, they added more fortifications and improvements, *katalavaineis*?'

'*Katala* . . . what?' Rosie replied.

Niko slapped a hand against his thigh. 'Ah – *naí*, sorry. I forget that you do not speak Greek. *Katalavaineis* means: do you understand? You will hear me say this a lot, whenever I am trying to teach you something – *katalavaineis*?'

Rosie laughed rather nervously. 'Um . . . *Naí*?' she ventured.

'Bravo!'

I had forgotten how common it was to encounter a Greek who was keen to impart knowledge; so many seemed to have an innate compulsion to learn more, to understand better, to ask questions and be interested in the answers. It was part of why so many tourists returned, year after year; they knew a warm welcome awaited them. In my daughter, Niko had found an extremely willing pupil, and he was now talking animatedly to her about the Turkish invasion of 1716.

'Corfu is the only Greek island that was not conquered by these people,' he said, and I could see the pride in his expression. 'There are many things about my home that I will teach you – reasons why it stands head and shoulders above all the rest.'

'Even Santorini?'

Rosie had long been hankering after a holiday to arguably one of the most beautiful locations in Greece – certainly one of the most recognisable.

Niko, however, merely tutted. '*Ela*, OK, so they have some white houses with blue roofs and stuff like this, but Corfu has four thousand olive trees. It is the only island in Greece where the kumquat plant grows, and there are more than fifty beaches.'

Rosie gazed out at the view before turning back to face him. 'Are kumquats those weird orange things?'

Niko smiled; he had barely stopped smiling throughout this exchange. It was clear he was enjoying himself, and he was a natural teacher.

Mattie must have seen this trait in him, must have realised what a wonderful father he would make, and it puzzled me why she appeared so reluctant for the two of them to seek medical assistance if they were struggling to conceive. Was it fear of what would be revealed if they did, or was it that she simply wasn't ready yet? Niko must have had an assurance from her at some stage that starting a family was something she wanted – likely before they got married. I did not believe that he would have gone through with the wedding at all if there were any question mark hanging over the subject of children – it meant too much to him.

'Earth to Mum.'

I blinked and found Rosie standing up in front of me, her hand ready to grasp mine. 'We're here!'

'Right. Yes. Coming,' I muttered distractedly, deliberately not looking at Niko as I clambered out of the boat, even though I could feel his eyes on me. I was flustered because I felt caught out. I had been doing the exact thing I'd promised myself that I would try not to – look for evidence of trouble in my sister's marriage. Whatever the truth, it was almost certainly none of my business. Unless Mattie decided to come to me herself and volunteer the information, I had to act as if I'd never heard anything.

The only problem with that was, I had.

19

Once we had disembarked in the old port, it was only a short walk across a palm-lined park to reach the warren-like lanes that led into town. There was evidence of the island's centuries-long Venetian rule at every turn, from the vast imposing buildings to the elegant bell tower domed in vibrant red. Both Rosie and I were hushed into reverent silence by the grandness of it all, and it felt extraordinary to me that we had only crossed a small channel of water to get here, as opposed to journeying through the folds of time. The past was an insistent interloper among these cobbled lanes, the whisper of it blown on the same breeze that rustled the leaves and scattered petals through the dust.

It was not long before Giorgos took over Niko's role as our unofficial tour guide.

I suspected this had more to do with his desire to impress Rosie than any keen interest he may have had in the history of Corfu Town. At nineteen he was barely older than her, and two years younger than Sam, but there was a nobleness about him that made him seem more mature than his age might suggest. And in stark contrast to the way I felt about Sam, I trusted Giorgos; it did not irk me that he was paying special attention to my daughter. In truth, as the morning had worn on, I'd found myself willing her to flirt back. To my mind, the stronger an attachment she formed with Giorgos, the less in thrall to Sam she would be. They also complemented one another – she so petite, fair and blonde, he so lithe, tanned and dark – and each had the special glow afforded to those with youth and vitality on their side, their faces untarnished by the myriad stresses of adulthood.

I allowed the two of them walk on ahead and fell into step beside Niko.

'You do not need to worry,' he said, inclining his head towards them. 'Giorgos is a good boy.'

'I can tell. Do you think that he . . .?'

Niko smiled wryly.

'Of course. She is very beautiful and,' he added, 'also very intelligent. This is what matters the most.'

'I don't know how I got so lucky,' I said, only for Niko to frown in disbelief.

'*Ela* – she is the same as you were . . . OK, not exactly, but there are many similarities.'

I recalled what Niko had said to me the first time we ever spoke, how he had seen a shine on me, and wondered if he would extend the same compliment to my daughter.

'They remind me of us,' I said, even though I knew it was madness to stray into these waters, uncharted and treacherous as they were.

Niko stared straight ahead, his features unmoving as he contemplated how to respond.

'*Naí*,' he said finally, sadly. '*Naí*.'

We had reached the edge of a small square populated by two cafés, a clothing store and a wide set of steps leading up towards a church – one of thirty-seven in Corfu Town alone, Niko soon informed us. A woman, resplendent in a flowing red dress, had perched herself on the stoop beneath its grand, arched entrance and was instructing her partner to take photographs on his phone.

You're missing it, I wanted to tell them. *You're missing all the beauty.*

When my eyes trailed over towards Niko, I saw that his were narrowed in thought. I wanted more than anything to continue talking to him about the past – about us – but there was no way into that conversation that did not feel incendiary. I stared at his face in profile, at the grey flecks in his stubble and the dark hollow of his throat. He was as familiar to me as a revisited dream – all the elements were there, but the details had altered, almost imperceptibly.

Rosie had abandoned Giorgos, her attention snagged by a rail of dresses outside the shop, and, glad of an excuse to break free from my lingering memories, I joined her.

'Why don't you get one?' I said, pulling a garment off the rail at random and holding it up against her. The soft cotton fabric was intricately patterned with white and purple flowers, each one budded by golden thread. 'It's my treat,' I added when she looked doubtful. 'You can choose one to wear at your party.'

'What party?'

'The one for your eighteenth, obviously,' I said, shaking my head at the dress she had selected, which was quite the wrong shade of pink for her delicate colouring. 'Niko told me that you can have it at the villa.'

'Really? Like, actually? Am I allowed to invite people?'

'By people, do you mean Giorgos?' I asked hopefully.

Rosie looked momentarily confused. 'Er, yeah. I mean, I guess so – it's not my house, so . . .'

'I'm sure he'd like to come,' I barrelled on. 'And he probably has lots of friends your age that he could bring along.'

She did not look convinced by this, nor by the white and purple dress, which was a shame because it really was lovely.

'Honestly, Mum, I'm happy to just have family there. It's been really nice, you know, getting to know Mattie, Niko, Lia and . . . well, everyone, better. I can't actually believe it's taken until I'm almost eighteen, to be honest.'

She was speaking carefully, avoiding my eyes so she wouldn't have to acknowledge how hard her words had struck.

'You make it sound as if you never saw them growing up,' I said, with forced cheer. 'But I always made sure you did. You can't blame me for the fact that Mattie chose to live here rather than in England. I didn't have the money to fly over and spend the summer holidays in Greece every year. I had to keep working.'

Rosie fingered a swirl of red embroidery on the front of a blue blouse and sighed.

'I know,' she said. 'I know how much you sacrificed for me – you don't have to keep reminding me.'

'I'm not, I just—'

'Just forget about it, Mum – OK? Forget I said anything. A party will be great, but I'm not going to wear that granny dress you're holding – not ever.'

'Granny doesn't have the legs for this dress,' I joked, but my attempt to lighten the mood failed dismally. Rosie did not look amused so much as pitying, and before I had a chance to say anything else, she had walked away.

'Sorry,' I muttered to the Greek woman who'd been watching us from the open shop doorway.

She shrugged out a '*parakaló*' and I smiled gratefully, although I felt unsettled. Rosie and I did not often fall out, and the knowledge that I had disappointed her made me feel constricted by sadness as I hurried back across the square to catch up with the others.

Swallows circled in the sky above us, chirping to one another as they dived through the air catching insects. They were impervious to the fierce heat of the sun, but I could feel my skin turning slick beneath my clothes, the strap of my bag slipping off a shoulder that was damp with perspiration. Raising a hand, I began to fan ineffectually at my face, and, without a word, Niko unzipped his backpack and passed me a bottle of water.

'Thank you.' I accepted it and took a few thirsty gulps.

'Where to next?' prompted Rosie.

'First, we must find oil,' Niko said. 'And then,' he added, raising a mischievous brow, 'I will show you where I get my spices.'

'Did you always want to be a chef?' Rosie asked as we continued to walk.

I already knew the answer but was intrigued to hear how Niko would reply.

He considered the question.

'Food was my father's passion,' he told her. 'He had a great many interests – history, languages, economics, politics – and preparing a meal was how he brought all these things together. He would choose very carefully who to have at his table, then he would create a feast that would help them to relax, to open up and talk about their experiences, perhaps have some kind of debate.'

'You mean like literal seats of learning?'

Niko smiled.

'*Naí* – there were always many people in my house when I was a boy, and I would watch and listen. There is a kind of magic that can be made from the sharing of food. I discovered that the dinner table was a better place to learn than a classroom.'

'Did your father teach you to cook?' guessed Rosie, and Niko nodded, his expression becoming more wistful.

'He taught me most of the things that I know today, although I am a better fisherman than him. He could not sit still and watch the water when there were books in the world that still needed to be read – *katalavaineis*?'

'Oh, I understand that only too well,' Rosie enthused. 'It's why I love history so much – there is always something new to learn, and people are discovering new things all the time.'

'I think my father would have liked very much to have you at his table,' Niko told her.

'I wish I'd met him.'

'*Naí*.' Niko touched a hand to her shoulder. 'Unfortunately, he died the year before you were born. But it is OK,' he continued, quick to shrug off whatever sadness he had unwittingly cast over the conversation. 'Death is nothing to us, since when we are, death has not come, and when death has come, we are not.'

'Did your father say that?' Rosie asked, but Niko laughed.

'No – it was a Greek philosopher named Epicurus. Have you ever heard his name before?'

Rosie admitted that she had not.

'Ah!' Niko declared. 'Then I have much to teach you.'

Having wandered a few paces ahead of us, Giorgos reached our destination first and ducked inside, closely followed by Rosie and Niko, who were still chatting away animatedly to one another. Seeing the two of them together had stirred up some conflicting emotions for me, the keenest of which was a nagging sense of guilt over Paul, the man who should, by rights, be here with his daughter now.

As I watched Niko leading Rosie around the small spice shop, encouraging her to dip her fingers into the sacks of dried oregano, cumin seeds, and ground cinnamon, and rub them together to release all the different aromas, I couldn't help but feel guilty at having allowed her father to leave. More than allowed, I had given him little choice. Paul loved his daughter, but the deterioration of our relationship was such that it threatened to corrode his ability to be the happy dad she needed – and that they both deserved. I should have tried harder; no wonder Rosie was disappointed in me.

'The scent of a food is half of its taste,' Niko explained, selecting a single clove and crushing it between his thumb and forefinger.

'This,' he began, tapping the end of Rosie's nose, 'is just as important as this,' he added, bringing a hand up to his own lips. 'When you put down a plate of food for a customer, the first thing they do is to smell it, and if that is not to their liking, they will not enjoy what they are eating.'

'But I like the smell of coffee and hate the taste,' Rosie protested.

Niko froze.

'Uh-oh,' I murmured to Giorgos, who was busy examining bundles of fresh parsley.

'*Ela* – you are playing some sort of joke on me?'

Rosie looked nonplussed.

'No,' she said. 'I hate coffee. It tastes like old car tyres.'

Niko grumbled out a stream of unintelligible Greek. 'Then you have not been drinking the right coffee,' he proclaimed solemnly in English. 'And it is a very good thing that you came to Corfu, because I can solve this problem. I will make you the best coffee that you have ever tasted.'

'Well, that won't be hard.' She laughed. 'Given that I've hated every sip of the stuff I've tried so far.'

Giorgos and I nodded at each other as if to say, 'She makes a good point,' while Niko continued to look thunderstruck.

Turning away, he addressed the proprietor of the shop, speaking in rapid Greek and shaking his head in mock despair. The older man chuckled and raised a half-full paper coffee cup in Rosie's direction. There followed a flurry of chatter and activity as Niko filled his rucksack with twenty or so varieties of herbs, spices and dried chillies, handed the shopkeeper a fistful of Euros, and ushered the rest of us back out into the street.

'He's not really going to force me to drink coffee, is he?' Rosie asked me as Niko fixed her with a glare that quickly dissolved into a grin.

'Please, no!' she cried, her hands pressed together as if in prayer. 'Don't make me!'

Niko started to laugh, the low, throaty sound that I had missed so much. Giorgos joined in, and before I knew it I was laughing too, and then all four of us were staggering around, clutching each other for support. Nothing particularly funny had even been said, but this only made the situation funnier.

Any lingering tension between myself and Rosie vanished, and when I looked at Niko, it was no longer unease I saw reflected in his eyes, but affection. The young man I remembered was still in there, as I'd known he must have been.

As if he could somehow read what was in my mind, Niko reached a hand towards me, only for his phone to start ringing. The shrill sound of it cut a prompt swathe through his laughter, and he took a few steps away before answering.

'*Naí?*'

I watched as his expression switched from mild to concerned, his features pulling together into a frown as he listened to what was being said.

'What's happened?' I asked as he hung up. 'Is everything all right?'

Niko put his phone back into his pocket and looked first at Giorgos and Rosie, before finally turning his eyes to me.

'It is Ophelia,' he said. 'We must go back to Kalami.'

20

The unmistakeable edginess that I had witnessed smouldering within my youngest sister that morning had erupted in proper, ferocious, obscenity-shrieking style.

And it had happened at Elpida.

Unable to reach Mattie on the phone, Socrates had telephoned his younger brother to request – not unreasonably – that someone come to the restaurant and help him remove Ophelia from the premises.

'He says she is drunk,' Niko explained, as I jogged to keep up with him. 'That she is like a wild beast.'

'Oh dear,' I replied, for want of anything more astute to offer. Rosie, who was on Niko's other side, made it clear that she thought Socrates was overreacting.

'Getting drunk is hardly a crime,' she said. 'I'm sure she didn't mean to cause all this drama.'

'If you believe that, then you really don't know her,' I replied, wincing inwardly as I recalled Rosie making that exact point to me earlier in the day. 'What I mean is,' I hastened, groping for anything that would make me seem less of a villain, 'Lia does like attention – we all know that from her Instagram feed.'

'She should not be drinking in the middle of the day,' muttered Niko, and there was nothing either of us could really say in argument to that. He was right: she had sunk cocktails on her first morning here, and cracked open the vodka on the beach at Kerasia. I had noticed it yet had done nothing to intervene, had not even thought to ask her why.

There was none of that morning's lightheartedness on the journey back. Rosie and I skulked at the rear end of the boat, while a stony-faced Niko stood up beside Giorgos, his phone pressed to his ear as he tried again and again to get through to Mattie. As soon as we docked at the jetty on Kalami Beach, he vaulted over the side and ran across the pebbles in the direction of the taverna, leaving Rosie and me to follow in his wake while Giorgos fastened lines.

It was nearing the peak of the lunchtime rush and every table at Elpida was occupied by holidaymakers, save for one indoors, towards the back. Ophelia sat hunched over it, her head down against the blue-and-white checked tablecloth and a beach towel draped across her shoulders. As I neared, I saw that this was to preserve her modesty, because she was not wearing anything save for a bikini. She looked thin, broken, pathetic – and as fed up as I was at having had our day out brought to a premature end, my overriding reaction was one of sympathy.

'Lia?' I said, crouching down until my chin was level with the table. 'Are you OK? What happened?'

Socrates chose that moment to emerge from the kitchen, a large tray of Greek salads, bread baskets and bottles of oil and vinegar wobbling precariously in his hands.

'Ah,' he barked, giving me a curt nod of greeting before turning his attention to Rosie. '*Geia sou koukla*,' he said with a flash of momentary tenderness, before directing a torrent of Greek at Niko. There was no point trying to understand what was being said, so I turned my attention back to Ophelia instead.

'Where are your clothes?' I hissed under my breath, but she merely groaned.

'Maybe Sam went to fetch her some?' suggested Rosie. 'I can go up to the villa and check if you like. Then I can get some myself, if he's not there?'

I hated the idea of her being alone with Sam – especially if he had anything to do with Ophelia being in this state – but I trusted that she would come straight back.

'OK,' I agreed. 'But be quick. Don't hang around up there, even if you do see Sam.'

'I won't,' she promised, already heading to the exit. I watched her go, feeling my mood sour like unrefrigerated milk.

'Lia,' I said, not bothering to lower my voice despite the surrounding diners. 'What the bloody hell happened?'

'What happened is that she threw a bottle of red wine across my restaurant,' Niko said tersely.

'Well, your staff should have known better than to sell it to her,' I pointed out. 'Isn't there a law in Greece against serving alcohol to someone who is clearly inebriated?'

'She did not order it,' he shot back. 'Socrates told me that she helped herself to the wine from the bar, then threw it at him when he tried to challenge her.'

That, I had no defence against, and for a moment or two we glared at each other as my cheeks burned.

Ophelia lifted her head from the tabletop and looked at me through bleary eyes.

'Sam,' she croaked. 'Where's Sam?'

'Gone for a long walk,' I muttered. 'Hopefully off the end of a short pier.'

'Gone where?' As Ophelia tried in vain to focus on me, I caught the medicinal whiff of alcohol on her breath.

'I don't know, Lia. But I'm sure he's fine. Sam strikes me as the kind of man who is very good at looking after himself.'

Niko grunted then, whether in agreement or consternation I could not tell.

'I don't think we're going to get much sense out of her,' I told him as I stood up, my hand rubbing a listless circle between Ophelia's shoulder blades. 'Not until she's either thrown up or had time to sleep it off.'

'*Naí*,' he agreed, regarding me through eyes that were heavy with concern. Socrates bustled past us with another tray, this time laden with scraped-clean plates, and said something to his brother before disappearing into the kitchen.

Niko smiled wryly. 'He is angry that he is having to do some work for once,' he told me. 'Socrates is a fat cat – he prefers to sleep all day on the chair in the office, not run around out here.'

'If you need to go and—' I began, but he shook his head.

'*Ochi*. It is a good thing for him. He has always had the easy life. Things, they just . . . come to him,' he said, gesturing in the air in front of us. 'Everything lands into his lap.'

'That must be very frustrating for you,' I replied, my mind drifting unwarranted to Mattie, and how she had somehow ended up in the starring role of the life that I had wanted.

Niko shrugged expansively. 'This is just the way it is – some people are born with more luck than others.'

'What does Socrates have that you don't?' I asked.

'A family,' he said without pause. 'Children.'

'You and Mattie are still young,' I said quietly. At first, I thought he hadn't heard me over the Greek music pouring out through the speakers, the crash of pots and pans coming from the kitchen, and the swirl of chatter from occupied tables.

'There is still time,' I said insistently, but Niko shook his head.

'Maybe,' he allowed. 'But I do not know . . . I do not know any more.'

Ophelia raised her head again, blinking at us as if trying to focus. 'I feel sick,' she groaned. 'I need Sam. Have to tell him that . . . Have to say that . . .'

I placed a comforting hand on her bare thigh as I crouched down beside her again, but Ophelia recoiled at my touch. It was hot in the back corner of the restaurant; I could feel sweat beading along my hairline, and shifted to dab my head against the draped towel.

Where the hell had Rosie got to?

'Ava? Oh my God – what on Earth has happened?'

Mattie was suddenly next to me – Rosie, Sam, and Fenna a few paces behind.

'Vodka happened,' I said, my tone matter-of-fact. I turned to Sam. 'Where the hell were you?'

'Asleep,' he said defensively. 'We had a bit of a heavy morning, so I went for a lie-down and when I woke up, Lia had disappeared. The first I knew of all this was when Rosie turned up a few minutes ago and told me.'

'I got home at the same time,' Mattie explained. 'So, we all drove down here together.'

She paused to cringe at the expression on a passing Socrates' face.

'This is all my fault,' she added, as I tried to wrangle Ophelia's limp body into the T-shirt and shorts that Rosie had brought with her. 'I should have been there to keep an eye on her.'

'You're not her babysitter,' I said reasonably, as Niko moved around the table to help me. 'It's not your job to watch over her – she's nearly thirty, for God's sake.'

Ophelia let out a low moan.

'Arguing between yourselves is hardly going to help matters,' pointed out Rosie, who, I saw now with a lurch, was holding tightly to Sam's hand. He was doing a very good impersonation of someone duly distressed, but I was sure I saw the corners of his mouth twitch upward as he surveyed the scene. I stared hard at him, willing those hooded dark eyes of his to look my way so that I might read the malicious intent behind them. But Sam was not playing my game; his focus was all on my daughter.

'I'm sorry,' Ophelia wailed, giving in to helpless tears as Niko, Mattie, Fenna, and I hauled her to her feet and carried her out to the waiting jeep. There was a pet-carrier in the footwell, and Niko directed an enquiring look towards Mattie as he clocked it.

'I just thought that we could—' she started, but fell almost immediately into silence. 'But maybe not. Sorry, Fenna,' she added. Her friend leaned over the passenger door and extracted the carrier. I saw a flash of soft, black fur and piercing blue eyes. A kitten. Presumably one of those that Fenna had recently rescued in Kerasia.

Fenna waved and smiled politely as she walked away from the jeep. Mattie called across that she would ring her later, and promised that she would help her to find someone who could take the kitten in. Niko, meanwhile, was fastening a seatbelt around Ophelia and doing his best to stop her head from lolling to the side.

'I'll go with her,' I offered. 'Can you make sure that Rosie . . .?'

I knew that I could trust him to extricate my daughter from Sam's clutches and bring her safely back to me. If Mattie was surprised by Niko's decision to stay behind, she did not give any indication and, after a brief exchange of nods between the two of them, she turned the key in the ignition, put the jeep in gear, and we set off back up to the villa.

21

It was another hour before we could get any sense out of Ophelia.

Following a prolonged spell in the bathroom, during which she thankfully threw up most of the alcohol she had consumed that morning, Mattie helped her into the shower while I attempted to tidy up her and Sam's bedroom.

Neither one had bothered to hang any of their clothes in the beautiful pale-blue wardrobe stencilled with white flowers, nor had they picked up the discarded cotton pads, empty water bottles or torn condom wrappers from the floor. A large bag of crisps was overturned on the rattan rug, which I carefully scooped up and carried out onto the balcony, tossing all the trodden-in crumbs over the side. I found clean sheets in the bottom drawer of a white wooden dresser, and stripped and remade the bed, plumping up the pillows, as well as putting fresh folded towels on the chair beside the window. It took me three trips to rid the room of empty cups, overflowing ashtrays and general filth, and a decent amount of elbow grease to rid the bedside table of drinks rings. And while I took the time to carefully arrange Ophelia's clean clothes on hangers, I took a certain amount of pleasure in kicking most of Sam's into a corner.

As I completed each task, I felt an increasing calm settle over me, and by the time Mattie had ushered a sheepish

Ophelia through and encouraged her into bed, all vestiges of frustration had been replaced by concern.

'Do you feel up to talking?' I asked, pulling the navy curtains across to shut out the blinding sunshine. Ophelia had left the air conditioning on and the room was starkly cool. Mattie bustled out and returned a few minutes later with a glass of water and a sheaf of tablets.

'These will help your head,' she said kindly, and Ophelia sullenly swallowed a couple down.

'How long has this been going on?' I asked, lowering myself down on the bed. Mattie perched on the opposite side, the hump of Ophelia's feet beneath the sheet between us. 'The excessive drinking – how long?'

Ophelia looked as if she might cry, then pulled herself together. 'I don't know,' she sighed. 'A while. Since the—'

'Since what?' I pressed. 'Since you met Sam? He's encouraging you?'

'No, no – Sam is . . . It's not his fault.'

'Well, he's not exactly doing a good job of looking after you, is he?' I challenged. 'He's a bad sort, if you ask me. You can do a lot better than him.'

'Ava,' said Mattie warningly, as Ophelia put her head in her hands.

'I'm just saying – what do we even know about him? From what I've seen, he's pure trouble.'

'It's me,' muttered Ophelia. 'I'm the one who's trouble.'

She looked so fragile, I thought. Like a baby bird that had fallen from its nest – tiny, blind and helpless. It was impossible not to feel protective, to want to shield her from harm.

'You were going to say something,' Mattie prompted gently. 'About why you started drinking so heavily…'

Ophelia shuddered and pulled the covers further up around herself.

'I get flashbacks,' she mumbled. 'The drink helps me to block them out.'

The blood turned to ice in my veins. 'Flashbacks to what, Lia?'

For a moment, she seemed unable to respond. Mattie and I exchanged an uneasy glance.

'In Thailand,' she said eventually. 'I was at a party – a full-moon party – with some of the people I had met on a tour. We were all dancing together and drinking, then I went to use the loo and lost everyone.'

Dread, like scuttling spiders, travelled up the length of my body.

'It was fine. I mean, I was fine,' she went on, sounding more as if she was trying to convince herself than either of us. 'I'd become used to being on my own, and I was even starting to be fine with it, but then . . .' She faltered, assaulted afresh with an image of whatever it was she had tried so hard, and for so long, to banish from her mind.

'It's OK.' Mattie shuffled down the bed and reached for her hand. 'We're here. There's nothing you can't tell us.'

Ophelia stared up at each of us in turn, her eyes huge below her damp fringe. I was reminded of when Paul and I had been driving home from his parents' house late one night and had almost hit a baby deer. Paul had yelled in shock and swerved across the road without thinking, jerking awake a five-year-old Rosie, who was asleep in the back seat. I have never been able to forget the look of terror on that animal's face, how it felt as if my own fear was being reflected back at me.

'It might help to talk about it,' I said. 'Whatever it is, you can't go on allowing it to consume you like this, from the inside out.'

'I know, I know.' Ophelia nodded through her tears. From somewhere downstairs, I heard a door opening, then Rosie's voice, high and clear, asking if anyone would like a sandwich. The simple sweetness of her enquiry made me smile. *My girl.*

Mattie glanced at me.

'Do you think I should go down and help?' she half-whispered, but before I could reply, Ophelia started to speak.

'There was a group of them. Men, I guess, although some of them looked young, like, barely older than teenagers. One minute I was dancing away, the next, they were all around me and... I couldn't escape them. I mean, every direction I tried to go, they blocked me. They were all so much taller than me, so much bigger.' She had brought up her arms and was hugging herself, her gaze not on me or Mattie but focused intently on a space in the middle distance. I guessed that in her mind, she must be back there, trapped, and scared. Alone.

Ophelia had always hated being alone.

'This one guy, he had tattoos all over his arms and a thick, dark beard. Someone had drawn all over his face with that glow-in-the-dark paint, and I just remember him leering down at me, laughing when I tried to push him out of the way. They all started grabbing me, pinching me, trying to pull up my skirt . . .'

I heard Mattie gasp, felt the lava-like heat of my own rage beginning to rise inside me.

'They were taunting me,' Ophelia whispered, 'telling me how they'd drawn straws for who got to have me first, but that I could be sure that they all would before the night was done. They said it was obvious that I wanted it, that what kind of woman came to a party like this on her own if she wasn't a slag looking for a good time?'

I could not sit still then; the fury was too great. Standing up from the bed, I paced over to the window and moved aside the curtain to peer out at the view beyond. I hoped that the beauty of it would offer comfort, that the distant horizon would dilute the pain that I knew this moment was about to deliver and make it more endurable.

'I was shouting at them to leave me alone, but nobody heard me,' Ophelia said. 'And I was drunk, but not so drunk that I didn't know what they were doing was wrong. They kept telling me that I was the one coming on to them, that they were only following through with what I had set in motion. I knew they were lying, but I was so confused, so tired of being pushed around between them. In the end, I guess I just . . .' She sighed, and it was the cracked and weary sigh of the broken-hearted.

'I didn't want to fight. I thought that if I was nice to them, if I played along, then they would let me go.'

'And did they?' asked Mattie, her eternal optimism somehow still intact. I was already shaking my head when Ophelia confirmed our fears.

'They made me go with them back to the beach huts. There were beer bottles all over the floor and I cut my foot on some broken glass.' She winced as she said it, as if she could still feel the hot pain of those shards slicing through her skin.

'The big one, the one with the beard, he pushed me onto one of the beds and put his hand over my mouth. I tried to bite him, but I couldn't. I started gagging, trying to scream, and he just laughed at me. He *laughed*.'

I only realised that I had unleashed a torrent of swear-words when they both looked up at me, Ophelia's face ashen and Mattie's pinched with misery.

'Sorry,' I muttered. 'But bloody hell – I want to hunt them down. I want to hunt them all down and kill them.'

Ophelia nodded. 'I know,' she whispered, her voice hoarse. 'I thought for sure that they were going to rape me.

That they might even kill me after they were done. But that didn't happen,' she added, and it was as if a heavy weight had been lifted off my chest.

'What did they do?' I asked, still terrified to hear the answer, still convinced that whatever she said next would haunt me for the rest of my life.

'Nothing,' she said, and when her eyes met mine, there was a trace of triumph in them. 'They never got the chance. Someone had followed us down from the party and saw what was going on, so they intervened. They fought their way through and got me out of there.'

'Who?' asked Mattie. 'Who saved you?'

But I already knew the answer.

Sam.

22

Nineteen years earlier…

Ava followed Niko through the deserted taverna on her tiptoes, being careful to avoid the many stacked tables and chairs. He had pressed a finger against his lips as they crossed the threshold, signalling that they should be quiet, and now she was fighting a ridiculous urge to giggle – especially as Niko was creeping along in the manner of Jerry the mouse trying to avoid being caught by Tom.

'Where are we going?' she hissed.

'Ela.' He beckoned her forwards. 'This way.'

They passed the bar area, where faint blue light filtered out from a bank of fridges, then ducked underneath the struts of a bare wooden pergola. Producing a key from the pocket of his jeans, Niko opened a door to the right and ushered Ava inside.

They were in a kitchen, that much was obvious from the huge, blackened grill and the stainless steel countertops, but she still had no idea why. Seeing the perplexity on her face, Niko grinned.

'Are you hungry?'

Ava thought back to the large portion of chicken souvlaki that she had been too nervous to finish. How many hours ago had that been? Three? Four?

'A little bit, I guess.'

'This restaurant belongs to my family,' he explained, crossing the room and pulling open a fridge. Ava's eyes widened as she took in the neatly stacked trays, jars and bottles,

'I'm very glad,' she said lightly. 'I shouldn't have liked to be arrested for breaking and entering on my first ever trip to Greece.'

'I have always been in kitchens,' he told her, as he placed three Tupperware boxes down on the counter and bent to extract a plate from a gleaming stack. 'My father, Leonidas, was taught how to cook by his father, and the same with his father before him. It is a Balaouras tradition.'

Ava made a mental note of the surname: Balaouras. She liked the way it sounded when he said it, how he enunciated each syllable with care. It lent the word gravity, helped it to take shape and settle boldly in her mind. She knew that she would never forget it.

'So, that's what you are?' she guessed. 'A chef?'

Niko paused with his hand inside a cutlery drawer. 'I am many things. I am only nineteen, so I do not yet know all the things that I may be capable of doing. That will come with time, through exploration. There is still much for me to learn.'

'I'm going to university in September,' she said, unable not to smile as she always did when she thought of escape. 'In London. And I can't wait.'

'What will you study?'

'English. I want to be a teacher.'

He glanced up, met her eyes. 'Will you teach me?'

Ava laughed. 'I don't think I need to – your English seems pretty good to me.'

He accepted the compliment with a shrug. 'Good, but not perfect.'

'Well, it's a lot better than my Greek.'

Niko peeled the lid off one of the boxes and, lifting a fork, offered it to her.

Stepping forwards, she peered down into the box, only to recoil in horror.

'Are those . . . octopuses's legs?'

Niko speared one of the purple tentacles with his own fork and popped it into his mouth, smiling at her triumphantly as he chewed.

'Now it is your turn.'

'I'm not eating those!' Ava wrapped her arms around her body as if to shield herself.

'You don't like the taste?'

'I don't like the way they look.'

'Ah.' He nodded. 'OK. Then, close your eyes.'

Ava gawped at him.

'Ela,' *he said, sidling along until he was standing right beside her. 'I will feed you.'*

'I don't think I can,' she whimpered, staring again at the slimy-looking suckers.

Niko steadied her with a hand that was cold from delving through the fridge, and she shivered.

'If you don't like it,' he said, 'you can spit it out.'

'Can't I have an olive instead?' she pleaded. 'Or some of that squeaky cheese?'

'Do you trust me?' he asked, the soft tone of his voice drawing Ava's eyes back towards his. They were such a vibrant brown, his lashes so thick and dark.

She sighed, helpless now under his gaze. 'I do.'

This time when he spoke, it was almost a whisper. 'Close your eyes.'

Ava closed her eyes.

'And now, open wide before I pinch your nose . . .'

Somehow, between her muffled bouts of laughter and his gentle persuasion, Ava found herself eating – and actually enjoying – several pieces of the octopus. Thus encouraged, Niko told her to stay where she was and not to look, before returning with more morsels for her to try. She sampled fat, salty olives, fragrantly spiced and stuffed cabbage leaves, fresh juicy king prawns, and gooey courgette rissoles. At no stage did Niko allow her to sneak so much as a peek, but he talked her through each mouthful as he presented them, telling her how he would use them in his own recipes, which local fisherman had been responsible for catching them, and why this food – his father's food – was by far the best on the island.

'Are you ready for dessert?' he asked, and Ava nodded gratefully.

'Yes, please.'

'Parakaló.'

'Parak—?'

She heard him laughing quietly.

'Parakaló *is meaning please in Greek.'*

'My first Greek word!' she exclaimed, practising it over and over until he silenced her with another forkful of food.

'This is bougatsa,*' he told her. Ava tried her best not to moan with pleasure as the lemon custard oozed across her tongue. The pastry surrounding it was sweet and flaky, the vanilla syrup below that delicate and wonderfully moist. Ava felt as if her tastebuds had just awoken properly for the first time in her life.*

'Good?' he asked.

Because she was still chewing, Ava nodded enthusiastically.

'You can open your eyes now.'

Very slowly, she did as he instructed. 'Thank God for that,' she said, meeting his steady gaze. 'For a moment there, I was worried I would find out this had all been a dream.'

Her words had pleased him; she could tell by the bashful dip of his chin as he smiled.

'Do you want to go home – back to the apartment?'

Ava was horrified.

'No! I mean, not yet. Unless you have plans or need to sleep at some point,' she said, glancing up at the clock on the kitchen wall and seeing that it was now almost one thirty.

Niko reached a hand towards her. 'I am glad,' he said. 'Because there is so much more to see.'

Unthinkingly, Ava slid her fingers through his, pulling him towards her. The need she felt to touch him was so much stronger than anything she had experienced before – it scored right through her nerves, her desire now a fierce adversary to the timid voice in her head that never allowed her to be brave. If Niko was surprised, he didn't show it – not by so much as a flicker. There was barely any space between them now; all she had to do was exhale, and their bodies would be pressed together. But Ava felt then as if breathing was impossible – as if to do so would somehow break the spell.

Very slowly, Niko lifted his free hand to her cheek, his brush so slight yet endless. Ava felt it everywhere – the anticipation of him. If he did not kiss her soon, she would scream. Instead, he smiled and said, 'Not here.'

Ava allowed the tension to drain from her body as she laughingly agreed that yes, a kitchen perhaps wasn't the most romantic setting in the world – not when you happen to be on an idyllic Greek island with the sea lapping gently only a few feet away. She wanted to ask him where, but Niko was already backing away.

'Ela,' *he said softly, motioning towards the door. And this time, Ava did not need him to translate.*

She was his, it was no more complicated than that. And from that moment onwards, she would follow wherever he went.

23

Having unburdened herself, Ophelia slept.

She slept so deeply and for so many hours that Mattie became convinced she was unconscious and wondered aloud if she should try to rouse her. Knowing that oblivion was what Ophelia needed most, I felt compelled to sit, sentry-like, at the end of her bed, guarding her while she rested. She was not in danger here, in this villa surrounded by her family, but I needed her to know that, to really believe it. For years, I had dismissed Ophelia's behaviour as impetuous and self-serving, but on this occasion, I had missed the glaringly obvious: that she was flailing and for good reason. And I felt awful about it.

I sat and I stayed, and I waited for her to wake, all the while berating myself for not being a better sister. It was my job to support and protect her, and all I could think was that I had failed. It had been easier, once I moved away from home, to focus instead on my new family – the tiny unit that Paul and I constructed around the baby neither one of us had planned for. I loved Rosie from the second I saw those two pink lines appear, and I allowed that love to fill in all the cracks in my heart, hardening it against everyone and everything that had come before.

I had turned my back on my old life and, in doing so, I had abandoned the two people I should have held on to the tightest. I had caused all this mess.

The room darkened and then lightened again, the dawn of the following day bringing with it the promise of a new beginning. I knew I had things to fix, problems to solve, and patterns of behaviour to break, but it felt enough for now simply to be here, waiting to take my lead from Ophelia once she awoke. Which eventually, of course, she did, stretching her arms out from under the sheet and blinking at me. Her initial confusion soon morphed into something more shameful, as the events of the past twenty-four hours came slowly into focus.

'Don't worry about it,' I said, cutting off what I guessed was the beginning of an apology. 'Honestly,' I added, as she looked at me uncertainly. 'Nobody is angry with you, Lia.'

'Not even Niko?'

I smiled. 'Not even him.'

'God.' Ophelia struggled into a sitting position and rubbed wearily at her eyes. 'I really fucked things up, didn't I?'

'You're being too hard on yourself,' I soothed. 'What you've been through – it's a hell of a thing. Blotting it out makes sense. I would probably have done the exact same thing as you.'

'You would never have ended up in that situation,' she said glumly. 'You're far too smart for that, Ms Fox.'

'You sound like one of my pupils,' I told her. 'And you're wrong – I'm not smart. Most of the time I'm just forging ahead and hoping for the best. Any good decisions I've made have been on account of luck rather than applied wisdom.'

'Do you ever miss it?' Ophelia asked, reaching for the glass of water Mattie had left beside the bed and taking a large, fortifying gulp. 'Being in the classroom.'

'Oh, yes – all the time,' I confessed. 'Private tutoring has its benefits – such as being able to take time off to swan around in Corfu – but on the whole, I thrived more in the school environment than I do on my own. But it works better, now that Paul and I . . . Well, you know. I'm a single parent now, and I like to be there for Rosie as much as possible.'

Ophelia was nodding. 'Will you go back? After Rosie goes off to university?'

'I've thought about it,' I said mildly, not wanting to admit how sick the thought of Rosie leaving made me feel.

'You should do what makes you happy,' she said, but the words were chased out by a sigh. It was as if she knew, just as I did, that happiness was not simply a new job, hobby, or relationship – it was far more complicated than that.

'I should get up,' she said, when I did not reply. 'I have some apologies to make.'

'I'll leave you,' I said, wincing as I stood. I had been sitting in the same position for so many hours that my limbs had turned stiff and unwieldy.

'Ava,' she said as I reached the door. I turned.

'Yes?'

'Thank you – for staying with me, and for listening and, well, for everything. I'm sorry I've been such a maggot in everyone's apple since I arrived.'

It was what our mother used to say to us when we misbehaved as children, to me most commonly of all, and hearing it again made me frown in consternation.

'I'll go and put the kettle on,' I said, forcing myself to smile. Pushing open the door, I stepped out onto the landing – and started in surprise. Sam was there, leaning against the wall, his arms folded and an expression on his face that fell somewhere between sullen and sanguine. I reminded myself that he was only twenty-one – barely older than a teenager really – and that much of his outward bravado could be attributed to nothing more sinister than immaturity. And, as much as I had not warmed to him in the time that we had known one another, he was responsible for saving Ophelia. I had to allow him a measure of credit for that, if little else.

'Is she—?' he began.

'Awake? Yes,' I confirmed.

He nodded, chewing on his bottom lip. I waited.

'She told you then?'

For the briefest second he looked almost wary, his eyes darting from the tiled floor to the banisters, before settling on the wall behind me. It was exactly this shiftiness that made me feel so on edge around him – he was the twitching end of a lit fuse. It was my turn to say thank you, but I was finding it difficult to form the words.

'It was brave, what you did in Thailand,' I told him. 'We're all very grateful to you.'

Sam shrugged. 'Anyone would have.'

'Clearly not. A whole full-moon party's worth of people could have intervened, but you were the only one who stepped in, by Ophelia's account.'

Sam nodded, but he did not meet my eyes.

'Can I . . . ?' he asked, gesturing towards the closed bedroom door.

'Oh, yes, sorry.' I stepped out of his way. 'Your clothes are all in there, of course. Silly me. I should go anyway, find Rosie.'

Sam had his back to me as he replied, so I didn't catch what he said.

'What was that?'

'Rosie,' he repeated, glancing back at me. 'She probably won't be up for a while. It was a bit of a late one last night, in the end. I'm not sure what time we went up to bed, but it was ages after everyone else did.'

His tone was benign, but I felt goaded by the implication behind his words, and it puzzled me. I could not make the two sides of Sam make sense inside my head, was unable to fathom how a young man who would risk his own safety to save a woman he didn't know would also set out to deliberately upset another. But I did know that whatever issue Sam had with me, I did not want my daughter dragged into the middle of it. If his plan was to use her to get to me, then I would have to make sure the two of them did not grow any closer than they already had.

What I wanted to say in reply to him, I suppressed with a tight, closed-lip smile, and then, very deliberately, I turned and walked away from him.

24

The following few days were blessedly free from drama.

While Niko continued to work, Mattie rushed around running errands, preparing meals, and driving Fenna up and down the east coast of the island to pick up stray cats. Ophelia had started to re-emerge from the dark cocoon of her trauma, but she remained listless and depleted, preferring to lounge by the pool rather than venture down into the village. Kalami was a very small resort and as such, news of her outburst at Elpida would have been common knowledge to all its inhabitants within hours after it happened. As she had vowed to give up alcohol, at least for the time being, I guessed that she could not face the gauntlet of local gossip without a drop or two of liquid courage in her system, and so she was avoiding it altogether.

The Fox family always had been more likely to let a wound fester than rip the bandage off; I could not criticise Ophelia for behaving like the proverbial ostrich, because I had long been guilty of the exact same thing.

The only real problem I had with Ophelia's reluctance to engage much with anything or anyone else was that it led directly to Sam spending increasing amounts of time with Rosie, and therefore I was forced to spend increasing amounts of time with him. He had my daughter fooled, the charm he exuded in her presence laid on as thickly as Dorothia's foundation, and I could practically see the stars that lit up in her eyes whenever he paid her attention. Giorgos had come to the villa one afternoon after a shift at Elpida and done his best to extricate Rosie for a swim down at the beach, but she had resisted, leaving him alone on the poolside loungers while she and Sam splashed around in the water playing a game of volleyball. Watching from my seat up on the terrace, a novel face-down on the table beside me and a pot of coffee slowly cooling in the shade, I had experienced a sharp pang of sympathy for him.

In the evenings, Mattie or I would prepare a meal – usually fish or Greek sausage served with buttery rice or potatoes and piles of peppery salad. I could not get enough of the locally grown cherry tomatoes and had taken to strolling around with a paper bag of them in hand. Every bit as sweet as barley sugar and with a succulent firmness that made popping them between my teeth all the more satisfying, they were as delectable a morsel as I had ever eaten, and a far cry from the chalky and rather tasteless ones I was accustomed to eating back home.

As the sense of general contentment within the four walls of the villa had increased, so too had the temperature in Corfu. The unremitting sun became our constant companion, from the fiery dawns until the sultry dusks, when the sky above the bay became a Rorschach blend of pinks, lilacs and golds. The boats that arrived in Kalami Bay every day were anchored in water as clear as glass, the pattern of their reflections undulating with the endless tug of the tide. I almost couldn't believe it was real – that nature could put on such an extravagant show for free. It felt extraordinary to me that we were here at all, bathing in the warm sea, floating on our backs as we marvelled at the island's flora and fauna, being soothed by the gentle wind.

As it had on my first visit, Corfu worked its way below my skin – and further still; its beauty was audacious enough to coerce my bitter heart into reopening once more. I was reminded that it was not only the person I had fallen for all those years ago, but the place, too. And only one of those had gone on to betray me.

I had begun to gradually move past the strangeness of seeing Mattie with Niko, and as the days had passed, I felt more willing than obligated to spend time with my sister again. The two of us were taking incremental steps back towards the other, and had it not been for my secret, hovering like a dark spot in my subconscious, then I might have believed we could be as close now as we had once been before.

By the morning of the fourth day after Ophelia's revelation, even she was itching to leave the villa.

'Why don't us ladies all go out for lunch somewhere later?' I suggested hopefully, earning myself a black look from Rosie. The two of us had just wandered down to join Ophelia by the pool, but Sam was nowhere to be seen and Mattie had left early for an appointment in town.

'We could go to the White House,' I went on, trying my best to tempt my daughter. 'My treat. Or rent a pedalo? Lia, you used to love going out on those.'

Ophelia frowned. 'When I was eleven.'

'Yes, well, it might still be fun.'

'What about Sam?' prompted Rosie. 'Is he included in your plan?'

I sighed. 'He's not here.'

Rosie scoffed. 'He's just gone to get some tobacco – he'll be back any minute.' She turned to Ophelia. 'What do you want to do today?'

Ophelia glanced from one of us to the other, looking uncertain. 'Don't make me decide,' she begged. 'I'm terrible at making decisions – aren't I, Ava?'

It was true, but I maintained a diplomatic silence.

'I've got an idea,' said Rosie decisively, and, snatching up her phone, she stalked off in the direction of the villa.

I blew air into my cheeks and widened my eyes at my sister. 'Someone got out of bed on the strident side today.'

Ophelia sat up on her lounger and crossed her legs, gazing up at me as if she was a child in a primary school assembly and I was her teacher. 'She must get that from Paul,' she said. 'How is he, by the way?'

It was the first time anyone had asked me about my ex-partner since I had arrived in Corfu, Mattie presumably being too cautious to bring up a subject that had the potential to upset me.

'He's fine,' I assured her. 'Great, in fact. Happy.'

She nodded. 'I'm glad. I always thought that he was a decent person. He was nice to me, treated me like a little sister on the few occasions I saw him.'

I was distracted, my attention on the villa steps, eyes searching habitually for my daughter, so only offered a small murmur of reply.

'Do you ever think that you'll start dating again?' she asked, which was enough to make me swing back round and face her.

'Gosh,' I laughingly replied. 'I doubt I will any time soon, but maybe one day.'

'You know,' she mused. 'I used to look at you and Paul and think you had the perfect life. OK, so you weren't able to go out clubbing any more or sling a backpack on and head off around the world, but you had each other, you had a home, and you had Rosie.'

Unexpected tears pricked, and my reply caught in my throat. 'Nothing is perfect.'

'But it was better,' she insisted quietly. 'Better than anything I had.'

'Lia,' I said, sitting down on the edge of the opposite lounger, 'believe me when I tell you that life for me and Paul, in those early days after we had Rosie, was in no way easy. All of it was difficult.'

'Everything changed after you left,' she replied, her fingers pulling at a loose thread on her sarong. 'Mum was constantly angry, Dad retreated into his den and only ever came out at mealtimes, and Mattie started going out all the time. She was never at home. By the time she left to come and work the season here, the two of us barely spoke.'

I hadn't known any of this and felt a cat's-cradle tightening sensation inside my chest.

'And then she never came back,' I finished, and Ophelia nodded. She had brought her knees up towards her chest and was hugging them against her body. Her arms were matchstick thin, her collarbones jutting through the tanned skin.

'I didn't know what to do,' she admitted. 'Whether to try and follow your example, or Mattie's, but I don't have what you to have – that ability to make anything stick. I just give up as soon as things start to get tough.'

Only a week ago, I would have agreed with her, my scorn at her life choices a judgement that I vowed never to pass again.

'You're looking at it the wrong way round,' I said. 'Assuming that all these things you've tried and failed to achieve are black marks against you, when in fact they're all just stepping stones, each one taking you closer to the destination you were supposed to reach all along. The only way to find out where you're meant to be is to keep trying different places and different people, until you feel as if you're . . . home, I guess, for want of a better word.'

Ophelia unfurled her tight ball of limbs and reached for a bottle of water. 'Mattie must have known all those years ago that Corfu was her true home,' she mused, and again, I felt my throat thickening with emotion.

'But what about you?' she asked. 'Where is home for you? Is it Brighton?'

'No.' I laughed bitterly as I shook my head. 'For me, home isn't so much a place as a person.'

Before Ophelia could reply, the terrace door crashed open above us and Rosie emerged, closely followed by Sam and another person I could not quite make out.

'Hello,' I called, waving up at them as I stood.

Giorgos stepped forwards into view and smiled a greeting. Rosie, I concluded, must have summoned him here.

'We're off out,' she explained, as I raised a hand to shield my eyes from the sun. 'Giorgos is taking us out on his cousin's boat.'

I did not care much for the 'us' – it implied that Ophelia and I had somehow become a 'them'.

'And we're not invited?'

Even from a distance, I saw the exaggerated roll of Rosie's eyes. It was so unlike her to exclude me in such a callous way that I failed to disguise my dismay.

'Of course, yes, you can come as well,' Giorgos said quickly, which was enough for me. Turning to Ophelia, I gestured impatiently towards the villa and, with a reluctant sigh, she rose to her feet.

'I suppose,' she said drily, grabbing my arm to steady herself as she wriggled her feet into her flip-flops, 'a boat is better than a pedalo.'

'We're leaving in five minutes,' Rosie announced. 'So you had better hurry up.'

'Aye, aye, Captain!' Ophelia joked. But I could not so much as raise a smile.

25

Situated less than a mile south of Kalami along the same stretch of coastline, the secluded white-pebble beach of Agni Bay was home to three restaurants and several small holiday rentals. Two long jetties stretched out from the shore into the clear water, and from where I was sitting, a folded towel protecting my bottom from the stones, I had an uninterrupted view of the wooden struts going down into the water, each one coated in twists of seaweed, amber rust, and the frayed ends of twine.

The raggedy cotton tote I used as a beach bag was in a heap beside my feet, and I rooted through it for my bottle of sun lotion, squeezing out a trail along each arm, followed by my chest. It had been years since my skin had encountered what I liked to call 'proper sun', and I was taking no chances. I knew that if we stayed in Corfu for the entirety of the summer, then I would eventually turn the same warm bronze that I had when I was eighteen – although then, I had been far less concerned about wrinkles. And although I stayed reasonably fit thanks to long walks along the Brighton seafront, my stomach and hips remained criss-crossed with the stretch marks I had accrued during pregnancy. Far from feeling ashamed of them, however, I found that I was rather proud to look down and see them there, a testament to the miraculous task that my body had achieved.

As I worked yet more cream into my inner thighs, my gaze roamed the water for signs of my girl. She, Sam and Giorgos were snorkelling a little way out beyond the jetty, where the boat was moored, their flippered feet breaking the surface with a lazy pattern of splashes. Ophelia had joined them for a swim when we first arrived, but I could see that she had since clambered back on board and was now sitting hunched beneath the folds of a towel.

I was on the verge of getting up to go and check on her when I heard someone crunching across the stones towards me, and turned.

'Hello, Ava.' It was Fenna.

She usually exuded unflappability, but today she struck me as unsettled. There were several livid scratches across the backs of her hands, and her normally shiny hair appeared lank and unwashed.

'Are you OK?' I asked.

She did not sit down beside me, and I wondered if maybe I should stand.

'Yes,' she said, then, 'no.'

'No?'

'Oof,' she muttered, kicking at a stone before finally lowering herself down, getting white dust all over her shorts in the process.

'That bad?'

'I was hoping to see Mattie – is she here?' she asked, grimacing rather sadly when I shook my head.

'She's in Corfu Town today, an appointment or something – she'll be back this afternoon.'

'Today is not a nice day for me,' Fenna said, although that much was obvious. 'I am worried that somebody is hurting the cats – deliberately hurting them.'

'Oh no – surely not?'

'My friend Stavros found a cat hiding under his car last night,' she went on gloomily. 'One of the oldest stray cats that live in Kalami – I call him Machtige, which means "mighty one". He was in a very bad way, yowling and limping. When I crawled underneath to fetch him out, he was terrified and lashed out at me, which he has never done before. Then this morning, I took him to the vet, and they think he has been kicked. His ribs are broken, and his little pelvis.' She squared her shoulders in an effort not to cry. 'They are going to save him, but it is going to cost a lot of money. And now I am just walking and thinking, wondering how I am ever going to pay them. I don't know what I am going to do.'

'Kicked?' I exclaimed in horror. 'Are they sure? I mean, could he not have been clipped by a car accidentally?'

Fenna twisted a length of blond hair around her finger distractedly.

'I don't know for sure,' she allowed. 'And I don't want to believe it because who would do that? There is no reason to hurt an animal.'

She was clearly very upset, but I didn't feel that I knew her well enough to offer a consoling hug. Instead, I patted her knee a little awkwardly.

'Poor Machtige,' she muttered, utterly forlorn now. 'He is the best cat, the best boy.'

'Maybe there's a way we can help you pay for his treatment,' I said. 'Raise some funds online, perhaps – my daughter is good at that kind of thing. She ran the Brighton Marathon a few years ago and collected over six thousand pounds in sponsorship money. Why don't I ask her?'

Fenna tried for a smile.

Energised by the prospect of doing something practical to help, I got quickly to my feet and called out Rosie's name, scanning the water as I did so.

'What the hell?' I muttered.

Because not only had Rosie, Ophelia, Sam and Giorgos disappeared, but so had any sign of the boat.

26

The pathway that wound through the undergrowth was dusty and uneven, and as I scrambled along it, my bare shins were assaulted by the scratchy fingers of dry plants, though I was too preoccupied to notice.

As soon as I had realised that Rosie was gone, I'd called her, only to begin swearing in earnest when her phone started to ring from inside my bag. Absurdly, I did not have Ophelia's number, nor did I have any way of contacting the two men, which left me with little choice but to return to Kalami and find Niko, whose phone number was another I did not have saved. He would be able to ring Giorgos and demand that he bring my daughter back at once.

'Oh, bloody hell,' I cursed as I tripped for the second time inside a few minutes. It was better luck than judgement that I had pulled on trainers today in place of my usual flip-flops, because navigating the path in those would have been even more treacherous. I had left Fenna behind on the beach at Agni Bay, calling back a promise to be in touch soon over my shoulder as I hurried away. She must have been confused by my sudden panic, and I supposed that to her, the situation did not warrant emergency status. To me, however, it called for sirens, flashing lights, the works – although generally teenagers sloped off behind their parents' backs all the time, until recently my teenager had not. And despite her obvious preoccupation with Sam and the snarky mood that seemed to have settled over her during the past week, it was still out of character for her to simply vanish without a word, and inexplicable of Ophelia to allow her to do so. I was furious with both of them, with all of them, but I was also being driven by a fear that I could not quite explain – an instinct that something was wrong, and that Rosie was in danger.

I continued to storm along, pushing aside low-hanging branches and stepping over the exposed roots of oak trees, until I reached the narrow cove of Gialiskari, which was littered with sun-bleached driftwood and the decaying carcasses of fat cacti fronds. From there, I banked left and followed the trail inland, panting with effort as it took me up past some roughly quartered allotments before tapering out into a driveway bordered by vast olive trees. I recalled one of Niko's comments to Rosie the day we had all gone into town, about how Corfu had four thousand of the gnarly things growing across it, and experienced the tiniest pinch of comfort at the thought of him.

The asphalt of the main road felt meltingly hot through my shoes as I pounded down towards the White House, only pausing for a split second to gaze up beyond its tiled rooftop to where Niko and Mattie's villa nestled high on the distant hillside, a throb of orange and turquoise amidst a tangled nest of forest-greens. How could such a small place contain so many lives, so much emotion, so many secrets?

I continued on past all the small animal statues that adorned the famous Durrells' former home and took the sloping shortcut down to the beach, progressing as fast as I could across the stony surface in my haste to reach Elpida.

It was busy inside and, instead of dithering until one of the waiting staff was free to approach me, I weaved through the occupied tables and pushed open the door into the kitchen. There was the open grill on the far side of the room, just as

I remembered it, but this time it was aflame, and the wall of heat coming off it slammed into me like a fist.

'Ava?' Niko had turned at the sound of the door swinging shut behind me. He was wearing a blue apron dotted with stains, scruffy once-white trainers, and a terribly unflattering hairnet. There were three other staff members in the kitchen with him, all tending to various tasks, but other than a cursory glance when I barged in they didn't pay me much attention. What became apparent to me immediately was that all four of them, Niko included, were clearly run off their feet.

'I won't keep you,' I said quickly. 'I just need Giorgos's phone number – he's gone off somewhere on the boat with Rosie and I can't . . . I mean, I don't—'

'*Ela éxo*,' he said, ushering me out into a small courtyard where stacks of empty fruit boxes were piled underneath a lemon tree. My words seemed to be coming out in completely the wrong order, and it took me a few minutes to explain the situation properly. Niko did not interrupt me; he merely listened, his intrigue becoming exasperation as I explained about being left behind at Agni Bay. Pulling his phone out from the front pocket of his apron, he stabbed his fingers at the screen, then pressed the handset to his ear, pacing around the small space as he waited for Giorgos to answer, then muttering what sounded like disgruntled obscenities when he failed to get through.

'One minute,' he said, scrolling through his contacts. 'I will call his cousin, Matthias – he has another boat at— *Naí, geia sas*.'

I tuned out as Niko's Greek became too rapid to follow, chewing on a fingernail that was already bitten down to the quick. I could not think what I might have done to goad Rosie into staging a disappearing act, but I knew that I had to find her, no matter what. The obvious solution was to simply wait at the villa until the four of them returned, but that felt too passive, too accepting. I was scared and I wanted my daughter to know it – to see for herself that there were consequences to her actions.

Niko ended the call and ran his fingers through his hair, mercifully dislodging the hairnet as he did so.

'Any joy?' I asked, unable to read his expression.

'Matthias has not seen him, but he thinks they may go to Kouloura – it is where the boat is kept and there is a taverna, as well as Houhoulio Beach.'

'I know Kouloura,' I told him. 'I think we drove past it on the way to Kerasia.'

Niko nodded. '*Ela*,' he said, starting to untie his apron. 'I will show you.'

'But you can't leave in the middle of lunch service,' I exclaimed. 'It's so busy.'

Before he had the chance to reply, the door behind him opened to reveal Dorothia, her long bleached hair swept over one shoulder and a cigarette halfway to her mouth.

'*To mikro mou agori*,' she crooned, which I was fairly sure meant 'baby boy'. '*Ti káneis*?'

I watched in silence as Niko explained what had happened, waiting for the inevitable scorn to emerge on the older woman's face. I was surprised, therefore, when instead of dismissing my reaction as hysterical, she offered to step in and take over in the kitchen.

'It is your daughter,' she said. 'Of course, you must go. And Niko must help you.'

'*Efcharistó*,' I mumbled gratefully, but she waved me away.

'Go,' she insisted, accepting a kiss on each cheek from her son, and within a few minutes Niko and I had left the beach behind and were on our way north along the main road. Unlike me, he'd had the foresight to bring along a bottle of water, but I shook my head when he offered it to me. To stop and sip would be to waste more time, when all I wanted to do, all I *needed* to do, was find Rosie.

'Did you two have an argument?' Niko asked as we walked, striding ahead of me up the hill so fast that I had no choice but to jog in order to keep up.

'No,' I said resentfully. 'I would understand it if we had, but everything was fine – or so I thought. One minute they were all in the sea, the next they'd vanished.' Remembering how I had been distracted by the arrival of Fenna, I told him briefly about the injured cat, to which he winced in sympathy.

'I think probably it was hit by a car,' he said, echoing my earlier suggestion. 'Sometimes this happens, and nobody is to blame.'

'As bad as it sounds, I hope you're right,' I replied, panting a little with the effort of scaling the steep coastal road. 'The alternative is too awful to comprehend.'

'Mattie would like us to have a kitten,' he muttered.

'And you don't want to?' I said, recalling the kitten carrier in the jeep that Mattie had passed regretfully back to Fenna.

'*Ochi*.' He looked across at me, his expression challenging, as if he expected me to argue. 'You will probably think that this sounds stupid, but for a long time, I had an idea, a picture in here' – he tapped the side of his head – 'of my child, playing with a kitten. I think that if we get one now, then it will remind me every day that we do not have a child.'

He trailed off, seemingly embarrassed, and for a while neither one of us said anything. We reached the brow of the hill, and the road blessedly began to flatten. On any other day, I would have insisted that we pause to take in the view across Kalami Bay, of the diamond sparkles where sunlight met water, the shimmer of a far-off horizon shrouded in shades of blue. As it was, I barely registered what I was seeing.

'I don't think it's stupid at all,' I said.

Niko screwed up his face. 'Thank you.'

His reversion to English made his words feel more considered, while the hesitation before he uttered them added gravitas. He wanted me to know how grateful he was that I understood, and how much that understanding meant to him. One of the darkest secrets I concealed from the world was how, in the few months after Rosie was born, I had nurtured a wish that she was not Paul's child at all. I'd allowed myself to indulge in a fantasy version of a life where I had not sought comfort in the bed of a boy I did not love upon my return to England and promptly fallen pregnant, but had stayed in Corfu and somehow had my daughter with Niko instead. It occurred to me then that perhaps he had pondered the very same thing, found himself contemplating what his life would have become had he married the first Fox girl he met, as opposed to the second.

But what was the point in wishing things had been different? In the end, all it achieved was useless frustration.

'Are you OK, Ava?' Niko asked.

'Yes, sorry. I'm fine. I was just . . . I'm fine.'

'You look pale.' He peered at me. '*Ela*, we are almost there.'

He motioned ahead to where the road split open like scissors, one blade up and the other slanting down towards a quaint, horseshoe-shaped stone harbour. There were boats of various sizes, shapes and states of disrepair moored around its curved length, and as we hurried down the slope towards the water, I scanned each one in the hope of spotting Giorgos and the others. There was no sign of them.

'*Perimene*,' Niko said, attempted to steady me as we reached the wooden tables of Kouloura's sole taverna, but I didn't want to wait a moment. I knew already that we were either too late, or that Matthias was wrong and his cousin had not decided to come here after all. However, that was not going to deter me from examining every vessel just in case.

Narrowly avoiding tripping over a low anvil disguised by coloured knots of rope, I crunched across the dried-out shells of fallen olives and followed the wall round to where it met the sea. Most of the boats had red and yellow fishing nets heaped in untidy piles on their decks, but a few were pristine. I recognised two that belonged to restaurants in Agni Bay and another, rather oddly named 'Eckythump'. There was no sign of Giorgos's borrowed boat, its captain, or any of the occupants, and by the time I had reached the far end of the harbour, I felt more than ready to scream.

There was a wooden bench below an old-fashioned lamppost, and I crumpled down onto it, pressing my face into my hands. I should not have been so upset; I could see that I was overreacting, but I was powerless to prevent the tears from forming.

Niko crouched down beside me, his hand coming to rest in the small of my back. Fearing that he would encounter a patch of sweat, I moved jerkily away and he stood abruptly, muttering something under his breath as he did so.

'Just . . . just give me a minute,' I said, wiping furiously at my cheeks. 'I'll be OK in a minute.'

When had it got so hot? I felt as if the world was a microwave, cooking from the inside out.

'I'll be fine in a min—' I started to say again, but my voice collapsed as dark spots appeared in front of my eyes.

Removing my hands from my face, I attempted to get to my feet, only to feel my legs turn to mush beneath me. I failed to get my balance and then I was stumbling sideways, falling as if in a swoon, straight into Niko's outstretched arms.

27

'I'm honestly fine. You're making a fuss.'

Niko narrowed his eyes at me, his fingers tapping out an impatient tempo on the table between us.

'What did you eat today?' he asked. 'For breakfast?'

I didn't want to answer him, but his expression told me I must.

'Nothing. There wasn't time,' I added when his response was to splutter at me in Greek.

'And water? What about water?'

'I had some tea,' I mumbled. 'That loose-leaf green tea that Fenna gave Mattie.'

Niko pulled a face that left me under no illusion as to his feelings towards green tea.

'*Ela mori* – it is thirty-three degrees today. You have to drink water – and you have to eat,' he pressed, waving over one of the waiting staff for a second time. He had half-carried me up to the taverna after my near-faint, ignoring my protests and placing an order for coffee. I had to admit it was a relief to rest for a while, and we could not have been in a more beautiful setting. The taverna itself consisted of a long terrace that looked out over the harbour, while the indoor area, which housed the kitchen and several more tables, was on the opposite side of a sloping path that led down to the water. As well as the vases of dried flowers arranged on each stripped wooden table, there were terracotta pots overflowing with the deep purple wings of oxalis, and clusters of the ever-present agapanthus cast alien shadows against white stone walls.

'I still need to find Rosie,' I reminded Niko, to which he nodded once.

'*Naí*, I know.'

'And you need to get back to the restaurant.'

'Hmm.'

The waitress returned with two frappés and a large slice of baklava, and I watched in silence as Niko methodically opened four sachets of sugar and tipped them into my glass.

'Is now a bad time to tell you I don't actually take sugar?' I said, watching as his lips lifted into the hint of a smile.

'Drink,' he instructed, and gave the frappé a brisk stir before pushing it across the table towards me.

'One might argue that I am sweet enough,' I began, and this time he smiled properly.

I sucked the straw, mildly perturbed by the undissolved sugar granules that flooded into my mouth. The flavour of the coffee was barely decipherable behind the sweetness, but I appreciated Niko's concern enough to overlook it. Once he was satisfied that I had drunk enough, he picked up a fork and dug it slowly through the baklava. Honey oozed out through the thin layers of pastry and dribbled across the plate.

'Now open,' he said.

'What? No! Don't be ridiculous, Niko – you're not going to feed me.'

'*Ela*,' he insisted.

'I'm not some sort of invalid,' I retorted, and clamped my lips together.

Niko frowned. 'Do not make me pinch your nose,' he said warningly, and I let out a laugh as I remembered him saying the very same thing to me years before. As I had then, I deduced that resistance was futile, and opened my mouth.

'Bravo,' Niko said, as I chewed and swallowed.

'I really should—' I began, only to be silenced with another forkful.

My eyes met his.

'Mattie,' I said, as if my sister had just appeared. I had no idea what had prompted me to say it, to have brought her into the narrow gap between us – a space that had become charged with so much else that I dared not articulate.

Niko smiled rather sadly and dropped his gaze to the plate. I thought he was going to feed me another morsel, but instead he lifted the fork to his own lips. I thought of his mouth over mine, of a time when we did not need to share an item of cutlery in order to taste one another. Inviting this memory in was an act of betrayal, yet I welcomed it, savoured the recollection as I had the morsels of sweet, sticky pastry.

'I feel better,' I told him. 'You were right about the sugar. I must have needed it.'

Niko inclined his head.

'*Naí*, I am glad.'

I stretched an arm across the table and dipped my little finger into what was left of the honey.

'Any idea where I should try next?' I asked, as Niko unscrewed the lid from a bottle of water and topped up his frappé. 'Might they have gone over to Corfu Town?'

He shook his head. '*Ochi*. I think, perhaps, it is more likely that they went north, towards Kassiópi.' He pointed as he spoke, out into the vast blue of the Ionian Sea. 'There are many small beaches along the way, lots of possibilities to choose from.'

'How do I get there?' I asked. 'Shall I call a taxi? Can I hire a boat?'

'*Perimene*.' Niko raised a placating hand. 'Drink your coffee.'

'Stop telling me what to do, you bossy bloody Greek.'

Niko grinned at me rather wickedly.

'I'm going to pay the bill,' I announced, and turned round on the wooden bench seat in search of a member of staff. It was past lunchtime, but most of the tables were still occupied with couples, family groups and, in the far corner, two elderly Greek men bent over a backgammon board. They all seemed so at ease, as well they should, given the setting and the heat of the day, and I envied them their laissez-faire mood.

'There is no need,' Niko said. 'The owner is an old friend of mine. There is no charge.'

I slumped, grateful but defeated, and the two of us finished our coffees in something approaching companionable silence. I drained my glass more rapidly than Niko, motivated by the need to get up and move, to find Rosie, to empty my bladder, to drink some water. I felt hot with indecision, strangled by the pull of too many unavoidable tasks at once, and pressed my forehead into my hands.

'Ava.'

His voice sounded low and soothing. I did not want to look at him, and made a small noise of enquiry instead.

'There is a path,' he said. 'It follows all the way up the coast. If we walk along together, I am sure we will find them soon.'

I lifted my head. 'We? Don't you have to go back to work?'

Niko made a show of shrugging. '*Naí*,' he said. 'But, you know, there has to be some benefits of being the boss.'

I was torn between wanting him to accompany me and the guilt of allowing him to do so, and the only apparent answer to this moral riddle was to say nothing at all. I could have insisted that he not come with me, but what would have been the point? Niko was a grown man and he would do exactly as he pleased.

If only, I could not help but think when we stood to leave, he had been this stubborn back then; if only he had done what he wanted instead of what was expected of him; if only he had chosen to listen to the same insistent voice that I had yet to silence within myself, telling him to take a chance, to defy his family, to follow the call of his heart.

If only he had chosen me.

28

Pine needles crackled under our feet as we set off around the coast; the heat that surrounded us was loud in its intensity. I focused on the form of Niko ahead of me, murmuring the occasional thanks when he held aside thistles or warned me of a dip in the path. Tall golden grass caressed my thighs, brambles sagged with fruit, while beside us there was always the sea – a coy dancer, revealing itself through gaps in the dense foliage.

To begin with, neither one of us said very much. I was hopeful that we wouldn't have to venture very far before we came across my errant daughter, but after we had crossed from Houhoulio Beach into the undergrowth, then back out to the water's edge, I started to voice my concerns that we may simply be chasing our tails. Niko's predictable response was to reassure and reaffirm. He was sure we would find them eventually, all we had to do was keep going.

As well as the salt carried in by the wind and the tangy undertone of Niko's aftershave, I could detect the scent of apple mint and something else, far earthier but no less pleasant, suspended in the dust kicked up by our shoes. The island was assailing my senses and stirring up responses I had thought lost to the past. Despite my worry about Rosie and the nerve-jangling awareness that came from being in such close proximity to Niko, I could not deny that I felt strangely invigorated by this unplanned expedition.

Emboldened by this sensation and by the fact that a back turned is a far less daunting prospect than a pair of searching eyes, I said, 'Do you ever think about that summer – the one when we met?'

The quickness of his response surprised me, though I was grateful that he answered without breaking stride.

'Of course.'

'So do I,' I said. 'I try not to, but no matter how many years go by, it's always there in my head, like an echo that never fades.'

'It was a long time ago,' he said. 'We were very young.'

I pictured Rosie, on the verge of adulthood yet still untouched by so many facets of life. Had Niko and I been the same? Had the connection we forged that summer been little more than a flimsy entanglement of teenage desire?

'I guess we were,' I agreed, knowing as I spoke that I was being inauthentic. 'I mean, it didn't feel like we were all that young at the time, but I suppose that's what any eighteen-year-old would say.'

'Is Rosie . . .' he began, pausing to allow a lizard to scurry across the pathway in front of us. 'Has she experienced her first love yet?'

'No.'

This, at least, I could be certain about. 'She would tell me if she had,' I clarified. 'She's always had a lot of friends, but nobody has wowed her enough to reach a boyfriend or girlfriend status. She finds the whole idea of that a bit ick, so far as I can tell.'

Niko turned slightly.

'Ick? What is ick?'

I had no idea what the Greek translation might be and thought for a moment.

'I suppose it means unpleasant, but not in a serious way. You probably thought that girls were a bit "ick" when you were a little boy.'

'*Ochi*,' Niko replied slyly. 'I always did whatever I could to get close to the girls.'

'I remember,' I said. 'You definitely weren't shy.'

'I was trouble,' he proclaimed, not without a certain amount of pride. 'I did not understand what it was to be responsible.'

'That's the beauty of youth, though, isn't it? That you don't have to be. When I think about that summer, I remember it as being the very last time I had that was wholly my own. Being selfish might not be very responsible, but it was certainly a lot of fun – at least for the most part.'

He did not answer straight away, and I was left unsure whether he had understood me properly.

'Look,' he said, and stopped so abruptly that I was forced to step around him. Glancing down, I saw that a butterfly had landed on the front of his T-shirt, its pale apricot wings open in salute of the sun.

'Golden wings mean that someone is envious,' he told me in a hushed tone.

'Is that right?'

I had always been told that a yellow butterfly was a symbol of a happy summer, but then again, that saying had come from my mother, who had undoubtedly read it off the back of a joss sticks packet.

'Some people say that the light colour also reminds you not to take life too seriously,' he added. 'So, even if you do feel envious, you should not worry too much about it.'

'That sounds an awful lot like a saying we have in England about the grass not always being greener,' I said, and explained: 'Someone may look as if they are having a better time than you on the outside, but underneath, their life is anything but perfect.'

Niko cupped a hand around the butterfly and ushered it carefully across to a tumbledown wall. There were lilac flowers that resembled small crocuses growing through cracks in the stone, each plant thriving in spite of its predicament. Nature was like that – it found ways to survive the seemingly non-survivable. Corfu, I knew, was home to a great many plants that had evolved to flourish in drought-like conditions – it was a place that bred strength and endurance from the roots up.

'What about you, Ava?'

I looked away from the butterfly and found Niko staring at me.

'What about me what?'

'Is your life perfect?'

I laughed: a short, sharp bark of amusement.

'No – far from it. But I do have Rosie,' I hastened.

The mention of her name spurred the two of us to continue moving along the path. As before, I was content to let Niko to lead the way.

'And you?' I asked. 'Are you happy with your life?'

We had reached a high point of the pathway and the trees on either side of the track were beginning to thin. Up here on the very edge of Corfu's north-east coast, the sun beat down like a composer's baton, subduing the crickets but not the rapid beat of my heart. I was by no means an idle person, but the gradient of the hills we were scaling, combined with the climate, had started to take a toll.

'Do you need to sit for a while?' Niko asked, as I stopped and rested a hand on each of my knees.

'No,' I panted. 'And don't change the subject.'

'You asked me if I am happy?'

I nodded.

'Most of the time,' he said. Then, with a frown, 'Some of the time.'

'Which is it – most or some?'

He sighed. 'Could I be happier? Perhaps, yes. But could I be sadder? *Naí*. It is not so bad, my life. I cannot complain too much about it.'

I should have dropped the subject, but instead I dug further. 'But there is more that you want?'

'Everybody wants more,' he said. 'If a man climbs to the top of a hill, he then sees a mountain in the distance, then from the top of that, he sees the moon.'

'What's so bad about wanting it all?' I pressed gently. 'It's what I always tell Rosie that she should strive for, even if it is too late for me.'

Niko merely laughed. 'It is human nature to want the things we cannot have,' he said. 'But to be happy, you must accept the things you have already. That is the secret.'

He made happiness sound so easy, as if a person could merely trick themselves into absolute contentment so long as they knew the rules. But I had never been able to do it; the gaps in my own life were too large, the things I yearned for too substantial.

I was attempting to put all that into words when Niko stopped in his tracks.

'Down there,' he said, pointing ahead. I could just about see the curve of a beach below us, a yellowed grin against a cobalt sea. And there, in the shallows not far from the shore, was the distinct shape of a boat.

The boat.

29

I yelled out Rosie's name as I ran down the hill towards the beach, not caring how much of a banshee I sounded, and hurried across the shingle towards the only figure I could see. Ophelia was stretched out on a towel and did not sit up as I approached. It was only when I was standing over her, my shadow blocking out the sun, that she opened her eyes.

'Oh,' she said, surprised, and pulled out an earbud. I could just make out the tinny sound of music playing. 'Hi.'

'Where's Rosie?' I demanded.

Ophelia squinted around, seemingly nonplussed. 'Not sure. She was here a moment ago.'

'Where the hell did you all go?' I was barely able to keep the tremble of rage from my voice. Niko had caught up with me, but he did not say anything. He merely stood, hands on hips, looking every bit as frustrated as I felt. 'You left me at Agni,' I continued accusingly. 'One minute you were there, the next thing I knew you'd all vanished.'

'But—' Ophelia's face fell as realisation dawned. 'You said you wanted to stay behind.'

'No, I did not. Why would I do that?'

'Ah, Giorgos,' said Niko, as the younger man emerged from the treeline that framed the cove. He looked unusually downcast, and when he saw us he immediately dropped his chin to his chest.

'Rosie?' I asked him, talking across Niko's stream of Greek.

Giorgos turned towards me; his expression was sullen.

'There.' He gestured vaguely in the direction he'd come from.

'I remember now,' said Ophelia, crossing and then uncrossing her arms. 'Rosie had to answer a call of nature. I told her to just go in the sea, but she was too embarrassed. But don't worry,' she added as I walked quickly away, 'Sam said he'd stand guard.'

There was no sign of my daughter crouched behind any of the bushes or trees close to the beach, and I could not see Sam either. I ventured deeper into the undergrowth, swearing as a thorn tore through my skin. None of this made sense, not the line Ophelia had spouted about me wanting to stay behind, not Rosie's transparent decision to cut me out of her plans, nor her reluctance to show her face now when her name was being called. I was being ignored, and it rankled.

I paused to dab the blood from my ankle, then froze as I heard giggling. Not an adult laugh, a childish giggle that jittered with nerves. Instinct clenched pincer-like in my chest, and I crept towards the sound, no longer calling but listening, neck taut, as I strained to hear more. There was what looked to be some sort of ruined shack set back behind the trees not far ahead of me, its roof long ago stripped bare and gaping holes where windows would have been. I sensed rather than saw movement coming from within and made my way over as quietly as I could, coming to a stop by the screaming mouth of a door.

What I saw next made the blood come to a standstill in my veins.

Rosie, pinned against the far wall, her pretty blond head pressed to the rough stone and her eyes closed as Sam, the muscles across his bare shoulders fixed with intent, moved against her, kissing the hollow of her throat. For a moment I was so shocked that I could not speak, then I saw Sam slide his hand up under my teenage daughter's dress and the lid finally burst off. All the worry and panic and hurt I had been feeling since that morning erupted from me in a torrent of yelling as I marched across and snatched away Sam's probing fingers.

'Mum!' cried Rosie in mortification. 'What the hell?'

I stared at her, not comprehending her anger.

'It's OK,' I soothed. 'You're safe now – come on, come away from here.'

I attempted to usher her towards me, but she refused to move, her arms folded now in defiance. Sam suppressed a laugh, and I spun round to face him.

'I'm not sure what you're finding so amusing,' I said harshly.

'Mum, please!' begged Rosie. 'You're embarrassing me.'

'I'm embarrassing you?'

We all turned at the sound of stomping feet. Niko glanced at each of us in turn, a puzzled expression on his face as he attempted to make sense of the situation.

'Sam was forcing himself on Rosie,' I said, to which my daughter cried out in protest, 'No, he wasn't, Mum. Nobody was forcing anything on anyone. I fully consented.'

'I don't believe you,' I replied. Niko lowered his head and shook it slowly from side to side.

'Rosie is almost eighteen,' Sam began, only to stop talking abruptly when my daughter threw him a 'don't antagonise her' look.

'What about Lia?' I demanded. 'What is she going to think when she finds out you've been sneaking off into the bushes to kiss her boyfriend?'

'I'm not her boyfriend,' Sam said. His deliberate patience grated. 'Nobody is cheating. This is about consenting adults enjoying each other's company.'

'Oh, shut up,' I snarled.

'Mum!' admonished Rosie. Her cheeks were flaming pink beneath her mussed-up hair, and for a moment I pictured her as a toddler, sleep-crushed and bewildered as she stumbled from her bedroom into mine after waking from a bad dream. It was so easy to comfort her then, to wrap her up in my arms and tell her that everything was fine, that there was nothing to fear, and that I would protect her from the monsters of her nightmare.

'You're not an adult yet,' I reminded her, steadfastly ignoring Sam. Niko had moved in behind me, and I felt stronger knowing he was there. 'And, given the stunt you've pulled today, I don't think you deserve to be treated like one.'

I had never scolded my daughter in this manner before, had never had cause to. The shock on her face must have mirrored my own, although I read more than surprise in her expression; I also recognised bitterness. It was clear that she hated me for doing this to her and knowing so made my loathing for Sam run even deeper.

'What's going on?'

Ophelia had wafted over from the beach trailing her earbuds cable, her sunglasses pushed back so that her fringe stuck up in every direction. When Sam, Rosie and I all started talking at once, all trying to get our version of events communicated first, she calmly placed both hands over her ears.

'Whoa,' she said. 'One at a time. Sam?'

'Don't ask him!' I exploded, just as Rosie began to cry.

'Now look what you've done,' said Sam accusingly, but when he tried to place a comforting arm around her shoulders, Niko stepped forwards to block his path.

'*Ela*,' he said, with a shake of his head. '*Ochi*.'

'Did something happen with you two?' Ophelia asked Rosie, who nodded through her tears. I watched my sister for a reaction, but other than the smallest flicker around her mouth, there was nothing. She even smiled.

'We didn't plan it or anything,' Rosie said earnestly. 'It just sort of happened. And it was only a kiss,' she added, directing this comment towards me. 'Hardly the crime of the century.'

I made a 'pfft' sound. 'The last time I checked, just kissing did not involve someone's hand under someone else's dress.'

'Oh, for God's sake,' tutted Rosie. 'I'm seventeen, Mum – not seven. You really think I haven't done stuff with boys before?'

The phrase 'done stuff with boys' sounded so teenage that I couldn't help but scoff. I also didn't believe her. The Rosie I knew was not that interested in boys, and certainly not enough to fool around with them. I guessed that she must be making all this up to impress Sam, and I understood why. I knew how infatuation felt, how when you experienced feelings of longing for the first time, they burned inside you so fiercely and powerfully that you felt changed in an intrinsic way. All that I knew; but it was not enough to extinguish my anger.

It took some effort, but I made sure I had composed myself before I spoke again. 'This man,' I said, motioning to Sam, 'may not seem all that much older than you, but there is a world of difference between seventeen and twenty-one. And even if there wasn't,' I continued before she could argue, 'there is also the not-small matter that until extremely recently, he was involved in an intimate relationship with your aunt.'

Rosie coloured at this, but I could tell it was with insolence rather than shame.

'Doesn't it bother you?' I insisted. 'Because I'll be honest with you, Rosie, it makes me feel more than a bit queasy.'

'Well, of course it would,' said Sam disparagingly. 'You're thirty-seven going on ninety-five. And just because you haven't had so much as a sniff in the past decade, doesn't mean that other people have to follow a life of abstinence.'

Rosie must have filled him in on the dire state of my romantic life, and as much as I did not want to care what he said or thought about me, my cheeks still burned with humiliation at his words. Niko shifted position, his scruffy kitchen trainers causing the dust to rise. I could not bear to look at him, to look at anyone except my daughter. I expected to find remorse there, but all that greeted me was coldness. I had become the villain of this piece in her eyes, when all I had tried to do – all I ever tried to do – was shield her from harm. I did not want to cry, did not want to give Sam the satisfaction of having his callous words land exactly where he had aimed them. But this left me with limited options. The hurt had to manifest somehow – I could have crumpled, but instead, I snapped.

'Come on,' I said, taking Rosie's hand firmly in mine and pulling her out towards the beach. She twisted away from me and complained that I was hurting her, but I did not let go. I kept dragging her forwards all the way across the shingle until we reached Giorgos.

'Can you take Rosie back with you?' I asked him. 'Back to Kalami?'

Rosie yanked her arm from my grasp. 'Stop it, Mum – you're overreacting. It was just a kiss!'

'The rest of us can walk back,' I said to Giorgos, who was understandably confused. 'Please. Just take her away from here.'

'Ava.' It was Niko. The sight of him standing there, so tall and solid and concerned, almost broke me. In the time that we had been arguing in the shack, several other boats had moored up in the small cove, and the water was peppered with swimmers.

'*Ela tóra*,' he said to Rosie. She had no fight with him, and so she obeyed, throwing me a distasteful look over her shoulder before she waded out into the shallows. Niko said something in Greek to Giorgos, who nodded, then set off after Rosie.

'Thank you,' I said when Niko turned to face me. 'I just wanted . . . I needed her to . . . '

He steadied me, his large warm hands coming to rest on my collarbones, but he said nothing, and I appreciated him for that. Unlike the vast majority of people I knew, who would have offered sympathy, reassurance, or distraction, he merely stood there, illustrating through his continued silence that he understood how futile all those well-practised platitudes really were. Niko did not tell me that everything was going to be all right, because he suspected, just as I did, that the very opposite was true.

30

Nineteen years earlier . . .

'You're hiding something.'

Ava lowered her mascara wand and arranged her features into an incredulous expression. 'No, I'm not.'

Mattie folded her arms. She was standing in the doorway of Ava's room, having opened it without knocking; her hair was crumpled by slumber.

'Then why are you putting make-up on at one in the morning?'

Ava tutted. 'I'm practising.'

'I know you've been sneaking out at night,' Mattie went on, only for Ava to shush her.

'Well, I do,' Mattie hissed, coming further into the room. 'And I won't say anything, but only if you tell me where you've been going.'

'Just . . . out,' Ava replied.

'Out where?' Mattie insisted. 'It's hardly Ibiza here, is it? There's nothing open past about ten p.m.'

Ava dabbed some gloss on her lips and stood up from the small dressing table, stepping around her sister to reach the wardrobe. She had already dressed in a tight black Lycra miniskirt, white vest top, and her favourite lace-up espadrilles, but she wanted to take a cardigan in case Niko took her somewhere on the moped. It could get quite chilly on the back, even when she had her arms wrapped tightly around him.

'Who said I was going out in Kalami?' she said. 'Corfu is a big island.'

'Are you going to meet that man we see on the beach every day?' Mattie said. 'You know, the one that always wears those red shorts with the poo stain on the bum.'

'Very funny.'

'He is always staring at you.'

'How do you know?'

'Because I'm always staring at him,' Mattie said slyly. 'Trying to work out if he really has pooed himself.'

Ava laughed. 'You're disgusting,' she said.

'But you love me anyway?'

'Yes. But only because we're related by blood.'

'Surely you love me enough to tell me who your fancy man is?'

'Mattie . . .'

'. . . Or fancy woman?'

'OK, that's it. Time to go back to bed.'

Ava began to shoo her sister from the room, but Mattie slithered out of her grasp and jumped up onto the bed, kicking over the stack of pillows carefully arranged into the shape of a person.

'Mattie! You'll wake the whole bloody place up if you're not careful.'

'I doubt it, not through Dad's snores. He sounds like a bulldozer would if you switched it on and sent it down a metal staircase.'

'Funny. Now go.'

'Not until you tell me,' she trilled, as Ava made a grab for her pink pyjamas and missed. 'What if this person does something bad to you? I'd need a name to tell the police.'

'He's not going to do anything bad to me,' Ava assured her.

'Oh, so it is a "he". I knew it! Is he better-looking than Paul Donovan? At least tell me that.'

Ava pictured Niko, those dark eyes flecked with gold, the large generous mouth and the soft hands that reached so often for hers.

'Much.' Ava was unable to stop herself sighing with pleasure. 'He's just . . . perfect,' she said simply. 'And that's the thing, Mattie – everything is perfect between me and him, and I don't want Mum and Dad finding out and ruining it, like they ruin everything else.'

She assumed Mattie would leap to their parents' defence, as she seemed compelled to do for any underdog, no matter how little sense it made – but she didn't. She merely considered Ava's words in silence for a moment.

'You really like him,' she said. 'Like, really, really like him – don't you?'

Ava thought about lying, but she knew there was no need. She could trust Mattie with the truth; they had always trusted each other with everything.

'I don't just like him,' she said, smiling dorkily at her sister. 'I'm falling in love with him.'

31

It was the lure of a meal at the White House that eventually persuaded Rosie to emerge from her bedroom, which she had locked herself in, and by the time the two of us had strolled the ten or so minutes from there to Kalami's most famous landmark, my daughter had even deigned to speak a few non-hostile words to me. Granted, these had been 'yes' to the query about whether or not she approved of my long, olive-green dress, and 'no' to my gentle suggestion that she might like to bring along a cardigan in case it turned chilly down by the water. But it was a start.

In order to fill the stony near-silence, I told Rosie about my earlier encounter with Fenna in Agni Bay, and what the Dutch woman had told me about the injured cat, Machtige. This, at last, seemed to stir her out of her aggrieved state of self-pity and, as I had predicted, she was immediately full of plans to help raise the necessary funds in order to pay for his treatment.

'Who would do something so horrible?' she said aghast, only to look immediately affronted when I far-too-eagerly responded with, 'That's what I said.' Rosie did not want the two of us to have the same opinion about anything, because I did not share her view when it came to Sam. He encapsulated the term 'moot point', but I knew better than to challenge her on the subject before we had taken our seats.

The White House restaurant was spread across two levels of a sprawling terrace, half of which was ceilinged by wooden struts that dripped green with trailing vines. Wicker lampshades hung down over tables dressed smartly in pressed white cloth, leather beanbags were tossed in artful heaps along the paths in the long garden, and several of the interior walls and pillars carried framed photos of Lawrence Durrell and his extended family. As we crossed to the front desk and waited to be shown to our table, I noticed a bookcase full of Durrell titles for sale, as well as T-shirts, fridge magnets and other assorted knick-knacks.

'Would you prefer to be outside?' the hostess asked. She was unusually tall for a Greek woman and had the same smooth platinum bob as me.

I glanced at Rosie, who shrugged, and smiled at the woman. '*Naí, parakaló*.'

'I don't know why you do that,' Rosie grumbled as we were led through the throng of tables.

'Do what?'

'Pretend that you can speak Greek when you can't.'

'Ouch.'

'They all speak English anyway,' she continued. 'So, what's the point?'

I did not like her tone, and it took some effort on my part not to tell her so. 'It does me good to practise the few phrases I do know,' I said mildly. 'And I'm sure it's appreciated. It's rude to arrive in a foreign country and assume the people living there will understand you simply because you're British, wouldn't you say?'

'Whatever,' she muttered, and thanked the woman in English as we sat down.

'I think it's enormously arrogant,' I said.

'I think you're enormously annoying.'

'Remind me,' I said blithely. 'What's that spell in Harry Potter that stops people speaking?'

'Silencio.'

'That's the one.'

'You think you're funny, Mum, but you're not.'

Instead of dignifying her comment with a response, I picked up the menu. The food on offer certainly wasn't cheap, but it sounded delicious, and after a quick scan I settled on an orzo and shrimp dish, while Rosie opted for the squid with basil pesto. For once, I indulged my craving for wine and ordered a glass of white, then surprised Rosie by agreeing to her request for a cocktail. I wanted to prove that I wasn't the controlling, possessive dragon she had witnessed breathing flames of fury down at the beach, and to remind her that I was still her easy-going mum most of the time.

'Shall I take a photo for you?' I asked, when her admittedly very fancy-looking drink was placed on the table.

Rosie shook her head. 'I'm not really in the photo-posing mood, to be honest.' She had already checked her phone several times since we arrived, but when I made the mistake of asking her if everything was OK, she practically growled.

'I'm waiting for a message,' she told me. 'From Sam.'

I sighed.

'Why did you have to do that to me, Mum?' she implored. 'It was just so . . . ugh. Embarrassing. You're always on at me to behave like a mature adult, then when I do, you tell me off for it.'

'I mean mature in the sense of taking your grubby shoes off the upholstery and not biting your nails at the dinner table.'

'You bite your nails,' she said accusingly.

'Touché,' I allowed. 'But it's not very adult behaviour to try and pinch someone else's boyfriend.'

Rosie flushed. 'How many times?' she implored. 'Sam is not Lia's boyfriend. And Lia doesn't even care that me and Sam like each other. They're not . . . you know . . . any more.'

I took a sip of my wine.

'What about the fib you told Giorgos and Ophelia, about me wanting to stay behind in Agni? What prompted that?'

Rosie fell into silence as a genial waiter arrived with bread, olives, and a selection of complimentary dips. A dinghy was crossing Kalami Bay from one of the distant super-yachts, its passengers a middle-aged couple whose coiffed hair and tailored clothing reeked of wealth. As they docked alongside the restaurant's floating jetty and another smartly dressed waiter leapt forward to fasten the line, I saw that the woman had a small black pug clutched in her arms.

'The thing is,' Rosie said, the careful tone of her voice anchoring my attention firmly to the table, 'when we're at home, living our normal, regular life, I spend quite a lot of time out and about. I'm at college or hanging out with Ally. You and I aren't on top of each other all the time like we have been here.'

I used my wine glass to hide the downward droop of my lips.

'Today, I guess I just needed some time on my own, away from you. And I don't mean that to sound horrible,' she added quickly, 'just that I'm not used to seeing you all day every day. I feel sometimes as if, you know, you're always just . . . there. Watching me.'

'I like watching you,' I said. 'You're my beautiful daughter and I'm proud of you. But that's why today hurt me so much, because today, when I saw you with Sam, I didn't feel proud at all.'

'Ugh,' Rosie grumbled. 'Please don't pretend that you're disappointed in me.'

'I am disappointed that you lied, and that you let a man like him—'

'A man like him?' she repeated incredulously. 'What – the kind of man that comes to the aid of a woman who's drunk and about to be raped; the kind of man who puts himself at risk to save a stranger? *That* kind of man?'

'One good act does not a perfect man make,' I countered. 'People can be all shades, and if you ask me, there's plenty of shadiness where Sam is concerned.'

'You just don't want to like him because I like him.'

'That is ridiculous,' I said, because it was. 'The only thing that I care about is you, and I happen to think you can do better than someone who a: encourages you to lie to your mother, and b: has slept with your aunt. That's before you consider the fact that he'll likely bugger off again in a few weeks' time, and then where will you be? Dropped like a stone and heartbroken.'

'Oh, so it was fine for me to have a fling with Giorgos, but not Sam?'

She had me there, and she took full advantage of my hesitation.

'I'm not like you, Mum – I'm not going to fall madly in love with the first man who pays me a bit of attention and hanker after him for evermore.'

'What are you talking about?' I said, sitting up a little straighter in my chair. The wine that had been doing such a great job of bolstering me tasted suddenly like battery acid.

'You,' she said insistently, 'and your weird obsession with whoever it was you fell in love with on holiday about twenty years ago, or whenever it was. Dad told me all about it.'

'Dad doesn't—'

'Yes, he does. I overheard him talking to Laura about it once, saying how you'd never really loved him because you never got over your first love. Why do you think I've never had a boyfriend? It's because I don't want to end up like you, Mum – trapped in limbo, all because one bloke broke your heart. No way am I ever going to let that happen to me. If I ever fall in love, I'm going to make sure it's with someone who will never hurt me. You make out like I'm some innocent little fool who has been led astray by the Big Bad Wolf Sam, when the truth is, I'm the one who pursued him. I'm not as naïve as you think I am, and I'm definitely old enough to make my own mind up about who I choose to spend time with and the men I choose to kiss.'

I stared at my daughter, unable to fathom what she was saying, that she had learned such a cruel lesson from me, her parent. That instead of setting her an example of a healthy relationship, I had skewed her feelings about perhaps the best and most pure thing a person ever experiences. I had done it all, and now I could not take it back.

Our food arrived as the sun began to set, setting the sky alight with an explosion of pinks, golds and purples. The dark, dead eyes of the shrimps gazed up at me, their tails coiled tight to their fragile bodies, and I experienced a wave of nausea. Glancing across the table, I saw that Rosie, too, seemed to have lost her appetite. She had got as far as picking up her knife and fork, but now each sat suspended above her plate, poised but purposeless.

'I had no idea you felt this way,' I said. 'Or that your father had said anything about . . . well, about our relationship. I want you to know that I did love him,' I added. 'Perhaps not in the all-consuming way that you read about in books, but there was love there. He gave me you, and there is nothing I love more than you, Rosie, nothing in the whole world.'

'I know.' She nodded slowly before raising her eyes to mine. 'But that's the thing, Mum. There needs to be more

– for you. I'm going to uni in September and after that I'll get a job somewhere that definitely isn't bloody Brighton, and you'll need to fill the gap I leave behind with something else – preferably someone else. A man.'

'I don't need anyone,' I blustered, but was saved from having to explain any further by the arrival of the hostess who had shown us to our table. I assumed she was merely there to check that the food was satisfactory and was surprised when she addressed me by name.

'I'm Ava Fox, yes,' I said.

'Your brother, Niko? He just call me,' she said, sounding apologetic. 'He tell me to ask you to check your phone. I think there is a message for you, but he say it is urgent.'

'What is it?' Rosie asked as I scrambled in my bag for my mobile. There was indeed a message, along with three missed calls from Mattie.

'Is it Lia?' Rosie's cheeks hollowed as she contemplated the worst. 'Has she started drinking again? Oh my God, she has, hasn't she?'

'No, not Lia,' I said bleakly. 'It's my parents.'

'Granny and Gramps? Why? What's happened to them?'

'Nothing's happened to them,' I said, reaching once again for my glass of wine.

Rosie was becoming exasperated.

'Then what?'

I held up my phone so she could see Mattie's message, watching the realisation dawn on her face.

'Oh,' she said. And then, 'But I don't understand – they're in Thailand.'

But my parents were not in Thailand. They had just shown up in Corfu.

32

Aside from sending a terse 'Very funny' text message to my mother in the immediate aftermath of Rosie's and my arrival, I had not had any contact with either of my parents since I had been in Corfu. I knew that Mattie had spoken to them briefly after Ophelia had shown up unannounced, but there had been nothing since – or not that I knew of. I had assumed that the gallivant-loving Martha and Angus Fox were having far too much fun on their extended Asian holiday to concern themselves with what might be happening here, among their adult children. But as with so many assumptions I'd made about my parents over the years, I had clearly been mistaken.

While Mattie and Niko seemed to think I would want to hurry back to the villa as soon as possible, in reality it was with extreme reluctance that I allowed Rosie to rush the two of us through the remainder of our dinner.

To say that I was not keen to return to the house and face my parents would have been an understatement of epic proportions. Of course, if I had given proper consideration to the fact that they'd only travelled to Thailand in the first place to spend time with Ophelia, and that she was, of course, no longer there, then the possibility of the two of them showing up in Greece unannounced might have occurred to me sooner. As it was, I felt woefully underprepared to face them – especially amid this strange ongoing row I seemed unable to resolve with Rosie. The things she had said to me had stung, and I needed time to let the weight of them settle. But there was simply no way that I would be given that time – or, indeed, any time – now that her granny and granddad were in residence.

'Shall we get them some chocolates or something?' Rosie suggested as we trawled back along the main road past the mini supermarket. Whenever I was dragooned into visiting my parents back in England, it had become tradition for us to turn up with a gift of some kind, and it was usually of the confectionery variety, but this time I said no.

'This is different,' I told Rosie. 'It's not their house. If anyone should be bringing gifts, it's Granny and Gramps.'

'What do you think they're doing here?' she asked, every bit as mystified as me, only less hostile.

'I don't know,' I said honestly. 'But I can guarantee we won't have to wait very long to find out.'

Niko was the first person we saw when we pushed open the front door of the villa. He was in the kitchen waiting for the kettle to boil, a troop of blue-and-white mugs standing to attention on the work surface in front of him. Our eyes met.

'On the terrace,' was all he said.

As it had been on our very first Friday in Corfu, the long outdoor table had been laid with the best crockery. Dorothia was seated at the far end, beside the empty space her eldest son had presumably just vacated, while Socrates, Elena, Stelios and Thaddeus had shuffled their chairs around until all four of them were squashed together along one side. On the opposite side, Sam lounged back with his foot balanced across his knee and what looked to be a tumbler of whisky in his hand, his body language exuding the same air of nonchalance that had so irritated me ever since he arrived. Ophelia, in contrast, could not have looked more uncomfortable. She cowered in the chair next to his, a roll-up trembling between her fingers, while on her other side my father, who was wearing an ill-advised shirt printed with a procession of elephants, sat in typical blithe contentment, as ever unaware of any tension between the female members of his family.

'Rosie Posey!' crowed my mother as we stepped onto the terrace. I braced myself as she stood to greet us, her short grey hair just so, bracelets jangling beneath the folds of a long-sleeved sack dress, and threw her arms around my daughter.

'You look wonderful,' she gushed. 'Doesn't she, Angus?'

'Wonderful,' agreed my father. 'Hello, Lany,' he added to me. 'Good to see you.'

'Lany?' enquired Sam.

'Oh, that's what I like to call Ava – her full name is Avalanche, you see, and while everyone else in the family shortened that to Ava, I preferred to use my own moniker.'

'Avalanche?' Sam said slyly. 'That is quite some name.'

'Chosen on account of how rapidly she arrived into the world,' my father explained happily. 'A few twinges, a bit of puff-puff, and she was out. Martha and I barely made it to the hospital in time, isn't that right?'

My mother ignored him, instead turning to bestow a chaste kiss on my rigid cheek. 'You look well,' she said. 'But then, Corfu always did suit you. I'm so glad that you fell for my little ruse and finally made it back over here. I simply couldn't stand by and see the gap between you and your sister widen any further. And I was right, wasn't I? Haven't you been having a wonderful time?'

'Sure, Mum,' I said, then, 'Did Thailand not turn out to be as diverting as you'd hoped?'

For the merest second, I saw something dark pass across my mother's eyes, but she recovered quickly.

'Oh, it was a lot of fun, very colourful,' she assured me. 'But once we realised that Lia wasn't there any longer, there didn't seem much point in eking out the trip. No, in the end we decided that it made far more sense to fly here, where we knew you all were. A proper Fox family reunion at last! I have been trying to engineer one for years.'

'That does make more sense,' said Rosie loyally.

Ophelia stood up. 'I'm just going to . . . I'll be back,' she murmured, and disappeared inside.

'Rosie,' said Sam, patting the now-empty bench seat. 'Come and sit next to me.'

I narrowed my eyes.

Mattie, who had not been on the terrace when we came outside, emerged now through the open doorway carrying a tray of coffees, Niko following behind with a cake tin and stack of small plates. Once again, our eyes met.

'Are you ever going to sit down, Ava?' queried my mother, who had returned to her own chair.

She was using a sing-song voice that set my teeth on edge. Despite wanting nothing more than to flee howling into the night, I sat.

The sheer force of my mother's personality coupled with the resulting awkwardness her presence created had rendered even the gregarious Socrates quiet. He was now silently finishing off Ophelia's abandoned plate of dinner, an expression of pure concentration on his face as he forked up the rice. Elena was staring up at Mattie, who was doing her best to pour coffee around Angus's gesticulating arms. My father loved to hold an audience captive with one of his stories, and was now regaling the table with a tale about thieving monkeys.

'The bloody things are worse than a bunch of yobs,' he said between sips of whisky. 'They get themselves drunk on all the bottles of beer tourists leave lying around and then go off on the rob. One morning, I woke up to the most God-awful screaming. I ran outside and found Martha running along the beach in only her bikini bottoms – the bloody monkeys had only gone and pinched her top.'

'Right out from under me,' said my mother. 'There were bosoms flying all over the place!'

I suppressed a shudder.

'Did you and Lia ever encounter the little blighters?' my father asked Sam.

I glanced across as he answered and saw that he had stretched an arm along the bench seat and was playing idly with Rosie's hair.

'Can't say that I did, Angus. But perhaps it explains why the locals always keep a stick handy.'

'No!' cried Rosie. 'People don't hit the monkeys, do they? Poor little things!'

'You're such a sweetheart,' cooed my mother, shaking her head to Mattie's offer of orange cake. 'But don't worry – I certainly didn't hurt any of the monkeys. I would have had to catch them first.'

She and my father laughed uproariously, but other than Mattie and Rosie – both of whom giggled politely – nobody else reacted. Dorothia was lighting one cigarette after another, her slim legs encased in tight denim and her long, bleached hair brushed forward over one shoulder. Not by even the slightest trace did she betray how she felt about the arrival of my parents, who I guessed she must have met before during one of their infrequent visits to Corfu in the years since Niko and Mattie had married. My father attempted to bring her into the conversation several times as he continued to waffle on about Thailand, but Dorothia merely shook her head as if she could not understand what he was saying.

This, I knew, was not true. Dorothia spoke English every bit as fluently as Niko. However, given that it was my parents who had commandeered the table over which she usually reigned, it did not surprise me in the slightest that the Balaouras family matriarch was sitting this one out.

If only I could have done the same.

'Rosie, I hear you had dinner at the White House tonight?' remarked my mother. 'You must have done something very special to be given a treat like that.'

'Not really.' My daughter shot me a look.

'I'd been meaning to take her since we arrived,' I said. 'Hadn't got around to it yet, that's all.'

Sam coughed loudly, and when I turned to glare at him I found that Niko had done the same. My mother, oblivious as ever, stirred her coffee and asked Stelios and Thaddeus what their favourite subjects were in school.

'Thady is very good at maths,' Elena said fondly, smiling as she watched her son devour his third slice of orange cake. 'But he is finding English much harder. I worry that it will hold him back.' She sighed.

My mother made a sympathetic face. 'Why doesn't Ava give him a few lessons?' she suggested brightly. 'She's an English teacher, aren't you?'

'I'm a private tutor now,' I corrected wearily.

'Yes, but that's the same. In fact, it's even better. Do you do languages?'

'What is this – a job interview?'

'Don't be facetious, Ava.'

I glanced across at Elena. She looked hopeful.

'I don't know if—' I began, but my mother had got the proverbial bit between her teeth.

'Don't pretend that you're too busy. You're always telling me how you need more students, how things are tight now since you ditched poor old Paul and—'

'Mum,' I said sharply, as I noticed Rosie's body stiffen. 'Can we not?'

'Well, it's the truth. If I can't speak openly around family, then I don't know.'

It took all my vestiges of self-control not to tear off the tablecloth, fashion it into a parachute, and leap off the terrace wall into the night.

Elena was saying something to her husband, and he nodded.

'We can pay you.' She directed this at me.

I was halfway through telling her that it was fine, that I would be more than happy to help out, when my mother interrupted yet again.

'Let them pay you if they want to, Ava. It can be very insulting to refuse money from people. I used to do a spot of life coaching, here and there,' she explained to Elena who, I was sure, despite nodding along politely, had no idea what a life coach did. She and my mother had this in common.

'I was forever doling out advice to my friends about their marriages, their children and their careers, so I thought why not start sending a few invoices out?'

She laughed and so did my father. He had always doted on my mother, preferring to view her charging-rhino audacity as a 'caring side'. Not for the first time, I wondered who the hell these people were, and how the hell either one could be related to me.

Having satisfied herself on the subject of Thaddeus, my mother turned her attention to his brother. 'And Stelios, what about you?'

Elena glanced at her husband.

'Stelios will take over the business here,' said Socrates, dabbing at the corner of his mouth with a napkin.

Mattie had stood up to start collecting plates, and Niko jumped violently and swore as a heap of cutlery slid off the topmost one and landed with a crash on the tiled floor.

'*Ela tóra*,' he proclaimed, more snappily than the situation strictly warranted.

'Is that what Stelios wants?' asked my mother. 'To run a restaurant?'

It was the wrong thing to say.

'Traditionally,' said Dorothia smoothly, blowing out a smoke ring while she waited for everyone to look in her direction, 'the family business would be inherited by the first child of my oldest son, Niko. However,' she added expansively, giving a still nervously hovering Mattie a pointed look, 'there is no such child yet, so—'

'*Mamá*,' said Niko shortly, causing everyone at the table to stare. Dorothia took a long drag of her cigarette, danger dancing behind her eyes. I willed Niko to continue, wished he would tell the old cow to keep her snout out of his and Mattie's personal affairs.

Mattie was still frozen to the spot and, recognising her turmoil at the same moment, Elena and I both got to our feet and offered to help clear the table.

'Are you OK?' I said quietly as I passed behind her a few seconds later.

She nodded.

'Don't let the old dragon get to you,' I hissed back, raising a disparaging brow in Dorothia's direction, but my sister did not so much as smile.

'Wherever did Lia get to?' asked my mother and Sam, who had moved his hand from Rosie's hair down to her shoulder, let out a bored-sounding sigh.

'She's probably gone out,' he said. 'I'll go and look for her.'

'Shall I come?' Rosie was already on her feet.

'No,' I said, with enough impetus to snag my mother's attention. 'Granny and Gramps have only just got here,' I pointed out, feeling myself shrink under the weight of her glare. 'I'm sure they'd like a chance to spend more time with you.'

'Why don't we all go?' suggested my father. 'I could do with a leg-stretch – and maybe even a nightcap, if that little bar above the supermarket is still open?'

'That's a great idea,' I enthused, as Socrates and Elena chivvied their boys out of their chairs ready to leave. 'Mattie, you should go too – I can finish the clearing up.'

'Oh no, I couldn't possibly lea—'

'Just go,' I insisted. 'Honestly. It's fine.'

'*Ela Mamá*.' Socrates beckoned for Dorothia to come with him. I could sense that the older woman did not want to be rushed, but she had, it transpired, run out of cigarettes, which was more than enough of an incentive to convince her to depart.

I followed the group containing my own family members to the door, promising to join them down at the bar as soon as I was done, then watched as the five of them wound their slow way down the sloping driveway.

It was a balmy night, the air thick with heat and noisy with the insistent buzz of crickets. I gave myself a moment to luxuriate in the relative tranquillity of a deserted house, to gaze down at the serpent-tail flicker of lights across the water and then up at the milky puddle of the moon. The clamour of everything that had happened on this most confounding of days fell silent for a beat or two, my mind wiped clean by the view of pin-bright stars and undulating sea. The island was the arms into which I felt able to fall, the comfort it offered fleeting but firm – revitalising.

It was with some reluctance that I turned to go back inside, and when I did, I found Niko standing there. Waiting.

33

He was at the bottom of the stairs and smiled a greeting as I shut the door.

'Everyone else has gone,' I said.

'*Naí*,' he said. 'I saw them go.'

The front of his hair was damp, as if he had splashed water on his face.

'Are you OK?' I asked.

He drew in a breath, exhaling slowly. 'My mother,' he began, only to shake his head. 'It does not matter.'

'I was just about to start on the washing up,' I told him, moving towards the kitchen. 'I told Mattie to go. I thought she could use a break for once.'

Niko nodded with understanding.

I thought he would go out onto the terrace, but when I turned on the hot tap and squeezed some washing-up liquid into the sink, he slid in and stood beside me.

'You wash,' he instructed. 'I will dry.'

There was a small radio on the worktop, which Niko switched on, and a moment later the two of us were being serenaded by an old Greek man and his bouzouki. I picked up a stack of plates and lowered them gently under the bubbles, before reaching for the knives, forks and spoons that Elena had left in a pile beside them.

Niko was so close that I could feel the heat of him; was he aware that my heart had begun to gallop? No matter how hard I tried to suppress my physical reaction to him, my body continued to defy me. It yearned for him.

'Did your dinner go as planned?' he asked. 'Is everything better now, with Rosie?'

'I wish it was,' I said, passing him a bowl and watching as he ran a tea towel briskly around the rim. 'It turns out that I am a terrible mother.'

'*Ochi*,' he admonished gently.

'No, I am. I have managed to make my own daughter scared of falling in love and by doing so, I have somehow persuaded her that a man like Sam is a good option. She knows that he practically radiates trouble, but she doesn't care – in fact, I'm afraid to say that's the main attraction.'

'Rosie is not a foolish girl,' he said. 'She will learn.'

'She will,' I agreed. 'But I just don't want her to learn anything the hard way. I don't want her to ever feel the way I . . . Feel sad.'

Niko smiled rather grimly as he accepted a dripping side plate.

'This is life,' he said. 'Sadness is a part of it – it is . . .' He muttered a few words in Greek while he searched through his mind for the English translation.

'Inevitable?' I suggested.

'*Naí* – inevitable,' he said, carefully pronouncing every syllable. 'And without the sadness, you can never know what real happiness is. You must have one to feel the worth of the other.'

'Wise old Greek man,' I joked feebly, and Niko laughed softly.

'I think so,' he said. 'My father used to tell us that there is no problem a Greek cannot solve.'

'I wish I could solve this problem I have with Rosie – or rather, the one she has with me. I just want to protect her,' I murmured. 'It's all I have ever wanted, ever since she was born.'

'That is why you are a good mother,' he said emphatically. 'My *mamá*, she is the same, always protecting us. But also, I think, she wants perhaps to control us a little bit as well.'

'A little bit?' I exclaimed, and he gave in to a defeated smile.

'*Naí, naí* – perhaps it is more than a little. When *Bampás* died, I think she tried to become both mother and father. It was not easy for her.'

'Did she ever know?' I asked, my eyes firmly on the dispersing soapsuds. 'About me – about us?'

When Niko didn't answer, I stopped washing the thick glass tumbler I was holding and looked at him.

'No,' he said, glancing away. 'She knew there was someone, that it was an English girl.'

'Was it that?' I said, my voice barely a murmur. 'The fact that I was English?'

'She worried that I would leave her and follow you to England,' he said. 'It was not where you were from, but what it might mean for me, for her, for the business and the family. I believed that perhaps you would come back.'

There was nothing accusatory in his tone, but I still tasted resentment as I contemplated how best to reply. In the end, Niko answered for me.

'You could not come back, you had Rosie.'

'I didn't know that you wanted me to,' I said, needing him to know, wanting him to understand. 'I thought you didn't care about me any more.'

'*Ela*, Ava.' Niko raised his hands in exasperation. 'Of course I cared.'

I gulped as a sob forced its way into my throat. 'We shouldn't be talking about this,' I said shakily. 'You're married to my sister.'

Niko dropped his chin. I had silenced him, but now suddenly, I wanted more.

'Why did you?' I demanded, my hands gripping the edge of the sink. 'How could you marry Mattie, after everything that happened between us?'

Niko's expression gave nothing away. I looked away from him, not wanting to see the disgruntlement that he must surely feel. He had rolled up the sleeves of his white shirt to reveal a sprinkling of freckles on his wrist, the same freckles I had once counted while I lay beside him, our fingers knotted together. I had changed that summer, in those stolen slices of time. Meeting Niko had reframed me, allowed me to view myself as he did, not as a too-tall girl with a foolish name, but as a young woman worthy of time and attention. That I had gone on to lose him had never dimmed my recollection of how it felt to be so very intrinsic to another person, so vital a cog in whatever force it was that kept the world turning.

I plunged both my hands into the water, my fingers groping for purpose, and felt Niko's slide into mine. For the briefest and most exquisite moment it was as if we had been whisked back through time, to a place when all that mattered was the sensation of the other.

'Ava,' he whispered, his hand gripping mine now with a fierceness that stopped my breath short. His skin was soft, the pressure against me hot, but then I felt something else: a coldness, a hard band of gold that signified so much more than the stirring of our past could ever hope to gain. This had to stop; we had to stop.

I pulled away my hand, yanking out the plug as I did so, and stepped away from the sink. Niko said my name again, but the word froze as he turned with me and we saw, with a stab of alarm that caused me to gasp, the shadowy outline of a face at the window.

34

I had run out of the villa, of course I had, but whoever it was that had been standing there was gone. I told myself that it didn't matter all that much – the only thing anyone would have seen was a man and a woman standing side by side at the sink, me washing and him drying. To a stranger, we would have looked like a husband and wife completing a mundane household chore together; but I very much doubted it had been a stranger. The area was not one that a person would simply happen to pass through on an evening stroll, and Kalami was also not exactly teeming with opportunistic robbers. The only thing that made sense was that it had been someone we both knew – a member of our ever-increasing extended family. But then, if that were the case, why had they not simply come in through the front door? And why had they run away when spotted? The issue was not that we had been seen, because there was nothing to see – the thing that made the hairs stand up on the back of my neck was that someone had deemed the two of us worth spying on.

Niko and I did not discuss it. I came back inside, having searched the area around the pool and the gardens, to find all the dishes and cutlery dried and put away but no sign of the man who had done it. I could still feel the burn of his fingers clasped in my own, and it was this that stopped me going upstairs and knocking on his bedroom door. There was still too much tension in the silent, still air, a sense I could not shake that the two of us were teetering on a line we must not allow ourselves to cross.

Wretched and wrung out by guilt, I hesitated on the terrace for a few minutes, battling with my desire to get away from the villa and my dread at the prospect of more time with my parents. I did not want Rosie to feel the way about me that I did about my own mother, and knew I had to do whatever it took to mend things between us. It was this knowledge that proved the most persuasive, and soon I was trudging, legs heavy with foreboding, down into Kalami village. The night had not cooled, and the stars that decorated the dark sweep of sky were smouldering embers of a fire that had crackled on long since the setting of the sun. I dredged up a smile in reply to those of the many holidaymakers I passed sitting out on their balconies, glasses of wine in their hands and bare toes balanced up on iron railings. It was how I had pictured my own evenings here, back when I was still in Brighton, before I had been tricked by my mother. I waited for the standard wave of irritation to pass over me as I thought of her, but none came. I considered whether I could simply have become weary of treading the same path, or if there was a part of me that might even be grateful to her for sending me here, to this place, back into the orbit of people I loved.

I reached the main road that wound through the village and stopped, craning my head to see if I could make out the lights of the villa behind me. There was one upstairs window aglow, and I wondered again about the mysterious figure Niko and I had caught peering in at us. Was that same person standing there, even now, their eyes once more on me?

'Stop it,' I scolded myself out loud, then turned to see that a skinny ginger cat had paused halfway across the road and was staring at me.

'Not you,' I told it, bending to scratch behind its raggedy ears. The cat rubbed its slim body against my shins, its tail twitching with pleasure as I massaged my fingers along its back. I could feel the outline of every rib through its skin.

'His name is Takjes,' said a soft voice, and I glanced up to see Fenna approaching. She was wearing denim cut-offs and a plain grey T-shirt, her blond hair pulled up into a high ponytail. It was the first time I had seen her with make-up on, and it suited her.

'Is that the Dutch word for ginger?' I asked, and she smiled.

'No, it translates as "twigs". I named him this because he is so thin – but don't worry,' she added, 'He is perfectly healthy, just young. He will fill out as he grows up.'

'Like we all do,' I said with a sigh, patting my midriff. The orzo and shrimp dinner I'd had at the White House was still sitting heavily in my stomach – probably on account of the speed at which I had been forced to consume it.

Takjes greeted Fenna in the same way he had me, although perhaps with slightly more enthusiasm. Delving into her bag, she produced a packet of treats and dropped a few onto the ground for him.

'Are you on your way to the bar?' she asked.

'I'm not sure,' I admitted. 'Everyone else came out looking for Ophelia. My parents are here,' I added, unable to stop my features from falling.

'*Ja*.' Fenna nodded. 'Mattie told me – I am going to meet them now.'

We walked the rest of the way along the road together, Fenna waving cheerfully to the man behind the till in the mini supermarket as we clambered up the stairs into Kalami's only bar. Open-fronted and cluttered with stools, wipe-clean pleather sofas and low tables, the interior was adorned with a colourful mix of British and Greek decoration, and there was a large flatscreen television in the far corner, tuned in to a sporting channel. The Fox family had arranged themselves around a table at the very front of the bar, and I was relieved to see Rosie deep in conversation with my father.

My mother had seated herself next to the apparently no-longer-missing Ophelia and opposite Sam, while Mattie crouched on a small stool to the side. It was she who noticed us first and promptly leapt to her feet in delight.

'Thanks for coming,' she said to Fenna, taking her friend's hand and drawing her towards the others. Introductions were made, and my father stood up to kiss the new arrival on both cheeks.

'So many beautiful blondes,' he said happily, beaming around at Fenna, Rosie and me. My mother, who was completely grey now, threw him a look.

Then, 'No Niko?' she said enquiringly to me.

Hating the blush that I could feel creeping across my face, I shook my head. 'I think he went to bed.' Then, turning to Ophelia, 'Are you OK? Where were you?'

Ophelia tilted her chin and gave me a lacklustre half-smile. 'I went for a walk,' she said. 'Just needed some air and—'

'We found her on the beach,' my mother interrupted. 'Standing on the end of a jetty as if she were trying to spot mermaids. Do you remember how much you wanted to believe in them when you were little, Lia?'

'I believed in a lot of things when I was a child,' she said in a small, hard voice.

'Yes, well,' my mother blustered. 'You always were imaginative – I still think you could have become an artist like me. The two of us are so alike.'

'I don't think I'm much like you at all actually.'

The look my mother threw Ophelia then was stern enough to cause even me to quail. Part of me wanted to cheer my youngest sister on, but a larger part did not want a big row to be ignited, not tonight, not when so much else had already happened today to set my nerves on edge.

Nobody had offered to get Fenna or me anything to drink, so I asked her what she wanted before broadening out my request to the table at large. Everyone shook their heads, except Sam.

'I'll have a Johnnie Walker Black if you're buying.'

There was a half-empty pint glass of beer in front of him, and when he saw me looking pointedly at it, he raised it to his lips.

'I'll be done with this by the time you've been served.'

Done with his cheap beer and ready for his very expensive whisky. Naturally.

'Do you want another one of those?' I asked Rosie, whose umbrella-adorned beverage was a lurid, Smurf-blue colour. I did not particularly like the idea of her having what I assumed, given the empty glass in front of her, would be her third cocktail of the night, but I was not going to say as much – not when Sam was certain to scoff, and my mother was likely to make a throwaway comment about how important it is to allow children to break a few rules.

'I'm all right, thanks, Mum.' She smiled up at me. 'I think I'll just move on to water after this.'

'I'll come with you.' Mattie stood up and we made our way to the bar. She had done something different with her hair tonight, I realised, for once allowing her fringe to flop forwards over her eyes instead of pinning it to one side. She had the kind of oval-shaped face that lent itself to all styles, but she had never been experimental when it came to her appearance. Then again, neither had I, not aside from the bleaching. It was Ophelia who had always pushed against the boundaries of convention. I glanced over at her now. She had slipped off her shoes and her bare feet were propped on the edge of the table, knees up, forming a shield around her body.

'Lia's still not right,' I said to Mattie. 'Perhaps we should suggest that she talk to someone – a professional.'

'I tried that,' Mattie said, making me feel guilty that I hadn't. 'She just keeps saying she's fine. I was actually glad when Mum and Dad turned up tonight because I thought perhaps they'd have more luck getting through to her. She's always been closer to them than we have.'

I gave the bartender my drinks order before replying, 'Did they explain why they'd just shown up without any warning? I mean, it's a bit much, even for them. They knew you had a full house over here already.'

Mattie made a 'who knows?' expression.

'You know what they're like. I'm sure half the kids' parties she dragged us to were ones she'd heard talk of in the playground that we hadn't been officially invited to. You and I were always in our little bubble at school, weren't we? I don't think we minded at all that we didn't have that many friends, but Mum was determined that we should be included. Although maybe it was really her that wanted to be included? I don't remember her having all that many friends either.'

It was hard to see my mother through that lens, as someone desperately seeking the approval of others as opposed to gleefully pushing back against their staid expectations. It was precisely this pattern of behaviour that had convinced me to retreat inwards, to become as unobtrusive as possible and remain on the outer boundaries of friendship. I had people that I spent time with, but none of them knew me, not really, just as I did not know them. Apparently, I did not know my own mother either, not that I had ever tried to. Mattie, of course, had made more effort.

'You're right,' I allowed, unable to shake the sense that there was a bigger reason behind my parents' decision to turn up in Corfu unannounced. They had needed their arrival to come as a surprise – but why?

Mattie took Fenna's drink back to the table, while I followed with my own and Sam's. He didn't say thank you when I put it down, merely ran his gaze up the length of my body, assessing me as he always seemed to do. Was he even aware that he did it? Did he know quite how uncomfortable it made me feel?

'I was just saying to Rosie how much she reminds me of you at the same age,' said my mother.

'I'm sure she was thrilled to hear that,' I said wryly, hooking my foot around a stool and dragging it towards the table, then sitting down. The truth was that my daughter more closely resembled her father Paul than she did me – they had the same neat, upturned nose and wide-set teardrop eyes. She had also got her colouring from him and, unlike me, did not need regular sessions with a colourist to maintain her pale-blond hair. All that was mine were her high cheekbones and defined chin, the latter of which she tilted downwards now as she stared across at Sam through her lashes.

'She has that same sense of fun and exuberance about her that you have,' my mother went on. 'Or used to have, I should say.'

The smile that had begun to form shrivelled and died on my lips.

'I imagine you're absolutely irresistible to all the Greek boys,' she said to Rosie, unaware, as usual, that her casual words of criticism had left me reeling.

'Rosie here is irresistible to all boys, no matter which country they might have come from,' said Sam, sipping his whisky as my mother beamed in appreciation.

Ophelia lowered her feet from the edge of the table and stood up.

'I just need a . . . back in a sec,' she muttered.

'I'll come with you,' hastened my mother, but Ophelia looked uncertain.

'You don't have to.'

'Can't have you sneaking off like a thief into the night again now, can we?' My father laughed. Nobody else joined in.

Mattie, who had shuffled along on one of the sofas so that Fenna could squeeze in beside her, leaned across towards me and said in an undertone, 'Do you think we should follow them?'

I shook my head, then promptly changed my mind. 'I'll go,' I said.

The toilets were behind the main bar, and I pushed open the door as quietly as I could. Inside there were two cubicles, both with the doors fastened shut, and I made sure not to stand where my shadow would be cast underneath them.

'Lia?' I heard my mother say.

'Mm-hm?'

'Are you ever going to talk to me? And I mean properly? You can't bury your head in the sand about this. Sooner or later, you're going to have to face it.'

So, I surmised, she knew about what had happened at the full-moon party. Mattie must have messaged her, shared what Ophelia had told us. I waited in silence for my mother to continue talking, to express the sorrow I know she must be feeling for her youngest and favourite child.

But no such sympathy transpired.

'Running away from a problem will never solve it,' she said, in as stern a tone as I had ever heard her use. 'What you did over there, it was not OK, Lia. You hurt people, good people. Your father and I spoke to them, and they told us how betrayed they felt, how much your actions had devastated them.'

I caught sight of my reflection in the mirror above the basin, my grey eyes widened in shock, my mouth slackened with dread.

'Lia, are you listening to me?'

My mother was worse than cross – she was disappointed.

Lia sighed.

'Yes.'

'Well, then – what are you going to do about it? How do you plan to make it up to them?'

'I don't know, Mum.' Lia had started to cry. 'I don't know.'

I heard the footsteps approaching just in time to avoid being struck by the door and, as the woman from behind the bar bustled past me with a cheery smile, I felt I had no choice but to exit before she alerted the other two to my presence. Not that either would continue to talk now, not when they had an audience.

Whatever it was that Ophelia had done in Thailand, it must have been something bad. Something very bad indeed.

35

Nineteen years earlier…

'Where are you taking me?'

Ava knew it was pointless to ask. After two weeks of sneaking out to meet Niko every night, not once had he given away any of his surprises. Begging him to come clean had become, by this stage, a sort of game. She would ask him, and he would shake his head, that generous mouth of his spreading open in a mischievous grin.

'Ochi,' *he would chide. 'It is a secret.'*

So far, he had driven her north along the coast to Kassiopi, and as far south as Ipsos. He had taken her high up into the hills, and low down to hidden coves and inlets. They had watched the moon dance on the water, lain on their backs and counted the stars; he had taken her hand and pressed it to his chest, had brushed the hair off her cheek with a touch so tender that it almost broke her – but he had still not kissed her. Not yet.

Tonight, when she had crept along the jetty in the darkness, trying in vain to catch him unawares, he had leapt up and pulled her right into his arms, the shock of it making her laugh.

'Shhh,' he said, dark eyes flickering over her shoulder. Ava had stilled, taking advantage of the momentary closeness to arch her body against his. She wanted him to know that it was fine to touch her, needed him to understand how ardently she wished he would. There was no space between them at all, and as she

pressed harder still, Ava had felt him stir against her. Collectively, their breath quickened. She did not care that they were only thirty feet from the front door of her apartment, that behind those blue shutters her parents and sisters slept; she would not have minded if the entire world was watching.

Niko was the first to step away.

'Ela,' *he whispered. 'Come with me.'*

For once, he led Ava straight past where he'd parked his moped and set off on foot up and round the corner, past the White House, and along the road beyond. It was a steep climb, and Ava panted in the effort to keep up with him. He waited until they reached the lip of the hill, then paused, a finger on his lips, as they stole off the main route and down along a wide potholed driveway. There were no lampposts to light their way, which became increasingly uneven the further they went, and Ava made sure to step exactly where Niko had in case she stumbled and fell.

'We must be quiet,' he told her, his voice barely audible. 'This land belongs to a private villa. The owner is a friend of my father, and he will shoot me if he catches us.'

'Shoot you?' Ava repeated incredulously.

'A lot of Greeks have rifles,' he explained. 'For hunting.'

'But he wouldn't actually shoot a human being, would he?'

Niko turned in the darkness, and Ava saw a flash of white teeth.

'Perhaps . . . no,' he admitted. 'But he would tell my father – or even worse, my mamá.'

Niko talked often about his mother. The mutual exasperation each felt towards their maternal parent was one of the things that he and Ava had most in common, and over the past few nights, they had discussed their various disgruntlements at length.

Niko's main frustration was tied up with his mother's high expectations of him, and the fact that she wanted to steer his life in a direction of her own choosing, while Ava's want was simpler: she yearned to matter.

'At least your mother cares where you end up,' she had pointed out to him the previous night. 'I could disappear tomorrow, and I don't think my mum would even notice, let alone worry.'

Niko had nodded, not in sympathy but with acceptance. Ava loved that he was pragmatic rather than emotional; he always said what he believed to be true, rather than the words he thought she needed to hear. There were no grey areas, only the stark brightness of truth, and it made opening up to him all the easier. Ava trusted Niko more than anyone she had ever met, and she knew that she was falling for him, hurtling towards love with a recklessness that made her feel free, and alive in a way she never had before.

If only she could be sure that it was the same for him.

Ava exhaled with relief when Niko ushered her through a gate and past a large patch of cacti onto a small beach. This, he assured her, did not belong to the same gun-toting villa owner whose private land they had just successfully crossed, but it was not their final destination either. After scrambling over a pile of stones that lay between the tangle of undergrowth and the sandy shoreline, Ava found herself on a narrow pathway that snaked up through the trees.

'Are you taking us to Agni Bay?' she asked, having done the geographical maths in her head. She had not been to the beach itself but had passed it while out on a boat excursion with her family not long after they arrived.

'Naí,' he said. 'But that is not where we are going.'

'Now you're just talking in riddles,' she told him, but Niko merely laughed.

There were gaps in the treeline, through which Ava saw flashes of silvery sea, but mostly she kept her eyes on him. The night air felt as warm as a caress, what little breeze there was muffled by the branches that surrounded them. Ava could hear the waves, and the sound of their shoes scuffing the earth, but all else was silent, restful.

The path banked downwards and opened out at the rear of Agni's white-stone beach. Niko did not stop, and so neither did she, and soon they had turned their backs on the water and were following a second path up the hillside on the far side of the bay. Glancing up, Ava saw the distant flicker of lights in windows, illuminating those who were, like Niko and herself, willing creatures of the dark. The higher they climbed, the more determined Niko seemed, urging her to hurry even as her legs felt like they might collapse beneath her. She was coated in sweat now, her freshly washed hair damp against her neck. Niko glanced back over his shoulder.

'Ela,*' he said again. 'We are almost there.'*

'That's what you said fifteen minutes ago,' she muttered, but continued to follow him until finally, thankfully, he stopped beside a high wooden fence.

'You are hot,' he said, as Ava fanned her face with her hand. 'Shall we go for a swim?'

'Very funny,' she replied. 'The beach is all the way back down there, in case you hadn't realised.'

Niko's response was to start climbing the fence, and Ava watched, shaking her head in bemusement. He reached the top and swung over a leg.

'Where are yo—?' she began, but before she could finish her question, Niko had jumped down on the opposite side and disappeared from view.

'Ava,' he called a moment later. 'Come on.'

If sneaking through the overgrown garden of a house belonging to his father's friend was risky, then Ava was not sure how breaking and entering into someone else's house was any better. Because that was exactly what they were doing, she thought, as she heaved herself over the fence. No way could she and Niko claim that they had stumbled into the grounds of what she could see now was a palatial villa by accident.

'Whose house is this?' she whispered, having tiptoed over to join him. They were standing in the middle of a smart, manicured garden. Ava could smell the herby scent of rosemary cut through with the sweet tang of honeysuckle.

'It is OK,' Niko said. 'This place is empty at the moment – the owners are in Athens.'

'How do you know?' Ava hissed, reluctant to venture any further until she knew for certain that they weren't about to get caught.

'When you work in a restaurant, you hear things.' He shrugged. 'Stuff.'

'Stuff?'

'Ela, *Ava – do you think I would bring you to a place where there could be trouble?'*

'No, but—'

'But nothing.' He delighted in winding her up. Ava swung out an arm to give him a playful clout. Niko dodged it easily, stepping sideways out of reach and hurrying backwards away from her. Ava set off after him, the two of them breathless with laughter as they ran across a neatly clipped lawn and around the edge of the house. The walls had been painted indigo by the darkness, while the pool they encountered on the far side was inky black.

Niko looked down into the water, then at her.

'We can't,' she stammered. 'I haven't got anything to swim in.'

In answer, Niko pulled his T-shirt off over his head and started unbuttoning his jeans. She thought he would leave his boxer shorts on, but he didn't; instead he turned round at the last moment, and Ava was treated to a quick flash of pale bare bottom before he leapt straight into the water.

'Don't look!' she giggled, her hands shaking as she removed her vest top before kicking off her trainers and wriggling out of her shorts. Clamping an arm across her chest, she lowered herself down until she was sitting on the edge of the pool, then used her free hand to unhook her bra.

Niko had swum a full length in the time she had taken to undress and was now propped up by his elbows at the far end, watching her.

'I said don't look,' she repeated, but Niko did not move. Pinned to her position on the tiles by a heady mixture of nerves and excitement, Ava waited to see what he would do next.

Niko lowered his arms and pushed himself forwards without once taking his eyes off hers. He kept his head above the water until he was only a few metres away, then he dived below the surface, coming up right underneath her and sliding his hands over her feet. Ava was not remotely cold, but there were goosebumps on her arms and across her thighs. Very gently, Niko moved his hands higher until one was behind each of her knees, then drew her legs slowly apart until there was room for him to stand between them.

'Is this OK?' he murmured, and she nodded, biting her bottom lip as she smiled at him.

Her arm was still clamped across her bare chest, and she watched as Niko ran his fingers along it, a light tickle that made her insides fall away into pure sensation. She could see droplets of water on his chest and was overcome by a primal urge to dip her head and kiss them away. As she bent forwards, however, Niko took a step back and she toppled off the edge, drenching them both with an untidy splash.

'Sorry!' she exclaimed, as he coughed and rubbed water out of his eyes.

'Are you trying to drown me?' He laughed.

'No,' she said, telling herself silently that this was it, the time had come; she needed to know once and for all how he really felt

about her. 'But I think you are trying to kill me. Drive me wild with desire only to leave me hanging.'

He frowned at her words, for a moment not understanding.

'You are wild for me?' he said, and Ava felt her cheeks growing very hot.

'A bit,' she said. 'Maybe.'

Niko beamed.

'Don't pretend you don't know,' she scolded, wrapping both her arms around herself and shutting him out. 'Do you even like me?' she demanded.

'Ela, *of course.'*

'I mean really like me, Niko – more than just as a friend?'

'Is that what you want?' he asked. 'For us to be more than friends?'

'What I want is you,' she said in frustration, getting the words out before cowardice got the better of her. 'I want to be allowed to touch you and kiss you and . . . you know what I mean,' she added helplessly.

Niko put one hand on each of her arms and tried to pull them down, away from her chest. Ava resisted at first, squirming away from him until he released his grip, but then she saw something in his expression that made her still.

'What is it?' she whispered. 'What are you thinking?'

'You really believe I do not like you?' he muttered. 'That I do not think about you all the time, burn to be with you, to hold you – of course I do, Ava. I am half a madman because of it. I cannot do anything else because I am trapped in here' – he tapped the side of his head – 'all day, with you.'

'Then why won't you?' she implored.

Ava did not know if he was unable to answer her or if he chose not to, but this time when Niko reached for her, she allowed her arms to drop. He pulled her gently towards him and, as she had when her body was pressed against his on the jetty, she became immediately aware of his desire. She had messed around with boys before, but this felt different; Niko was a man, and he was looking at her as if she was a woman, not a girl.

She wanted to tell him that whatever was holding him back, they could overcome it, that she wanted more than anything to build a future with him, that she would do whatever it took and follow him wherever he asked her to go. But she did not get to say any of that.

Because Niko, at last, was kissing her.

36

I found out Mattie's secret completely by accident.

The morning had been taken up by my first English lesson with Thaddeus, which I'd enjoyed far more than I was expecting. For the majority of the preceding three years I had tutored mostly teenagers, so it was a refreshing change to coach someone far younger. Thady was an ideal student – eager to impress and quick to grasp new things – and I finished our session feeling wonderfully invigorated.

'Absolutely not, you are family,' I insisted, pushing away the notes that Elena tried to give me when she came to collect her youngest son.

'And honestly, I feel as if I'm the one who should be paying you. It's been such a pleasure, and nice to feel as if I'm doing something useful for a change.'

'Next time, then,' she said, and I smiled.

'We'll see.'

Once I had waved the two of them off and washed up the plate that was sticky from the watermelon I'd sliced into bite-sized chunks for Thady, I locked up the villa and was halfway down the driveway when I realised that I didn't have my bag. Cursing under my breath, I retraced my steps and let myself back in. The ragged old tote was where I had left it, in a heap on my side of the bed, and I snatched it up at speed, keen by that point to join the others down at the beach. When I was halfway down the stairs, the phone on the kitchen wall began to ring. I paused for a split second, then went across and snatched up the receiver.

'Yes, hello?'

'*Geia sas*,' said a polite female voice. 'Am I speaking with Mrs Fox?'

'Ms,' I corrected unthinkingly. 'Yes, this is she. Who is this?'

'I am calling from the Aphrodite Clinic,' she said. 'It is concerning . . .' I heard what sounded like the tap of fingers against a computer keyboard, then she said something in Greek that I did not understand, followed by the word 'appointment'.

'I'm sorry, an appointment for what exactly? I'm afraid I don't speak Greek very well.' What I should have done was told the woman to call back another time, but curiosity had got the better of me.

'Ah, sorry.' More tapping followed. 'It is concerning your repeat prescription for the contraceptive pill,' she clarified.

The pill?

'Right,' I said. 'Of course.'

'And next week is being OK? Wednesday at three o'clock?'

'I . . . sure,' I mumbled. 'That's fine. Thank you.'

I hung up, my head spinning as I tried to make sense of what I'd heard. Mattie – and it could only be Mattie – was taking the pill, had presumably been taking it for some time. This, despite the fact that she and Niko were apparently trying to conceive. I had heard her agree with him, detected the longing in his voice as he suggested they seek medical advice. Had they since had a separate conversation and decided that starting a family was not something they wanted after all? I did not believe that for a moment. Which only left one real option.

One of the sunflowers in the patch beside the terrace steps was bent almost double under its own weight, and I snapped off the head as I passed, tearing out the few remaining petals and scattering them in my wake. The unremitting heat of the past few weeks had gouged great cracks in the earth, and even the bulbous lips of the cactus plants had withered in the drought. I paused to unlatch the gate at the bottom of the driveway, watching with listless half-attention as a sated bumblebee crossed lazily through the air in front of me.

What was it that Niko had once told me? That bees were messengers of gods and honey their wisdom.

I tilted my chin in salute of the sun, before making my way along the main road and then down across the white stones onto Kalami Beach beyond. Everyone from the villa had headed there today; Mattie had suggested earlier that morning that we all have a lazy beach day, and nobody had disagreed.

'Where's everyone else?' I asked my mother as I set my bag down on the lounger behind hers.

'Lia's in the taverna kitchen, helping with the washing up, Mattie went to meet Fenna – something to do with cat posters – and Rosie and Sam have taken a paddleboard out. They're really doing rather a good job,' she said.

'Indeed they are,' piped up my father, whose chest was a rather alarming shade of overcooked gammon. 'Only come a cropper twice so far, which isn't bad going at all.'

'How did Lia get talked into that?' I asked, as I peeled off my dress.

'Oh, she was happy enough to volunteer,' said my mother. 'Niko's usual boy didn't show up for his shift, apparently, and from what I've been hearing, Lia owed him a favour or two after that performance she put on recently.'

'It was hardly that,' I argued, immediately defensive. 'Do you even know what happened to her in Thailand?'

'I know far more than you think,' my mother replied silkily.

'Such as?' I asked, my mind going back to what I had overheard a few nights ago in the toilets of the bar.

'Never you mind.'

I thought about badgering her to explain, but there seemed little point. My mother was an expert when it came to playing her children off against one another, goading each of us with her supposed knowledge of secrets that we had shared solely with her. I was not about to step willingly into the ring just so she could knock me down.

Instead, I smeared suncream across my chest and squinted towards the water in search of Rosie and Sam. They had ventured quite a long way from the shoreline, and even from this distance I could tell that they were laughing as they struggled to keep the paddleboard from wobbling. Rosie was kneeling at the front while Sam stood up behind her, both silhouetted by the bold backlight of the sun. It did not matter how many times I sat here on this beach and stared out across the same bay, there was always some new pocket of beauty waiting to be discovered.

My eyes roamed hungrily across the denim-hued sweep of the sea, the shoal of boats on its surface as stoic as chess pieces, barely a ripple interrupting their gentle slumber. Behind the dropped sugar cube of the White House, the hillside reached dark-green arms into a sky as densely blue as a child's drawing, its canvas untouched save for the merest smudge of cloud.

I could not imagine living anywhere that did not have a coastline nearby; although I could appreciate the appeal of rolling hills, the idea of residing in a landlocked country appalled me. I needed a horizon to gaze out towards, was comforted by the promise of escape it offered. Brighton ticked a lot of boxes, although from where I was sitting now, it felt like a drab and dreary runner-up to a far more colourful competitor. Before too long, I would have to bid farewell to this, my most beloved Greek island, and return to my life in England: to self-service tills and litter dropped in puddles, overpriced coffee served in styrofoam cups and tutoring sessions held in stuffy living rooms. Rosie would go to university, and I would stay behind, my evenings punctuated by the ping of a microwave meal, the splash of wine in a solitary glass, the rustle of pages as I attempted to lose myself in a novel only for my mind to wander again to that horizon, to this view, to all that this island had given me. How would I ever leave? It did not seem fathomable.

My father had started to snore. Mattie and I used to joke that he had developed the ability to fall asleep at will as a way of effectively blocking out my mother's nagging, although she was not above shaking him awake if she wanted to ask him a question that simply couldn't wait.

'Angus?' she said now, then tutted affectionately when he did not stir.

'Shall I put the umbrella up for you both?' I asked.

'Don't do it on my account,' she said, reaching for her wide-brimmed straw hat. She had worn the same one on holidays for as long as I could remember, and the edges were frayed as if chewed by a goat.

I stood up and started to wrestle with the beach umbrella, ignoring the sigh of displeasure from my mother as she pointedly rose and dragged her lounger out from the shade.

'Are you hungry?' she said when I was done.

'Not really.'

'I think I'll wander along to Kostas's supermarket and pick us up some of that wonderful spanakopita. Your father does like a little snack after he's had a nap.'

I considered being the bigger person and offering to accompany her despite my edgy mood, but someone needed to keep Rosie in sight. She had not staged any more disappearing acts since the day she'd abandoned me in Agni Bay, but I did not wholly trust Sam not to talk her into another flit. They were sitting facing each other on the paddleboard now, long legs in the water, wet hair plastered back from their faces.

My mother had swathed herself in a voluminous kaftan and bent to retrieve her bag.

'Are you sure I can't bring you anything back?' she checked. 'Some olives? Crisps? I could get us a bottle of rosé?'

I shook my head, dredged up a smile.

'I'll see what they have,' she decided. 'See if I can't tempt you.'

I closed my eyes and took a deep, fortifying breath, only opening them again when I was sure she had walked away. For the next few minutes, I lay back and luxuriated in the sweltering heat, listening to the faint strains of music coming from the taverna behind me and to the gentle rumble of my father's snores. It would be so easy to slip into slumber, but every time my mind drifted that way it was yanked back by clamouring thoughts of the telephone call, and the implications it had about the state of Mattie and Niko's marriage.

As an image of him strode into my conscience, so the man himself came into view on the steps of the taverna. I had not realised until that moment that I had turned my head in his direction, and he saw me before I had a chance to look away.

'Hello,' I said in reply to his '*geia sou*' of greeting a few seconds later. Niko hunkered down until his knees were only a few inches from my left hand, which was flat against the lounger. The temptation to place it on his warm, tanned skin nudged at me insistently, and I curled my fingers into a fist.

'How are you?' he asked, in a tone that told me he genuinely cared about the answer. I gave myself time to consider a reply.

'I was thinking just now about having to go home, and how hard it's going to be,' I said. 'When we first arrived, all I could think about was escaping, but now . . .'

Niko nodded. 'The house will become quiet,' he said. 'It will feel very empty when everybody is gone.'

'Mine, too,' I agreed. 'It'll just be me. Perhaps I should adopt one of the cats Fenna looks after and take it home with me.'

'Sometimes I think Fenna would like to adopt my wife,' he said, and I laughed.

'Most people would do well with a Mattie in their life.'

He tried a smile. '*Naí*.'

'You can sit down, you know,' I told him, as Niko moved his weight from one foot to the other. He had taken off his apron and I could see the pattern of his chest hair beneath his white T-shirt. 'I'm pretty sure my mother paid for all six loungers.'

He levered himself into a sitting position and grumbled at me in Greek, then said in English, 'You do not need to pay. You are family.'

'All the more reason to support your business, in that case.'

Like me, he seemed to be in a quandary over where to place his hands and kept moving them from his lap to the sides of his face, agitating himself with indecision. Was he thinking, as I always did, of how those same hands would once have been invited to caress and explore? How foolish we had both been to assume that those moments would endure.

He looked out now across the water, his gaze drawn as my own always was to Rosie. I loved that about him, that he checked up on her, that he cared for her. That had been the hardest part of breaking up with Paul, losing not just my partner but my teammate in the game of Mum and Dad. Raising a child relied on both parents batting for the same side, united in the goal of ensuring safety, support and happiness. It was a dynamic that collapsed without trust, or with an absence of honesty, and I hoped that Mattie understood this. If she and Niko were ever to stand a chance of starting a family – and after today, that was looking increasingly unlikely – then they would need to wipe their slate clean of secrets.

Glancing up, I felt myself being drawn in by the sight of Niko, and for once allowed myself to savour the familiar shape of him for a moment. His eyes met mine and we held fast to one another, touching in every way but the physical, the intensity causing everything else around us to blur.

Niko blinked slowly and sat up a little straighter. 'Your mother, she is coming.'

It was his cue to leave, but he waited until her shadow fell across us before he stood and then, so subtly that I would wonder later if I had imagined it, reached down and softly, so softly, brushed his fingers across my cheek.

37

Over the week that followed, I did not mention the fact that I had answered Mattie's phone call to anyone – but I did think about it. I thought about it a lot.

There were so many questions I wanted to ask and so much I did not understand, but everything involving my sister and Niko was so tangled up with my own feelings that I found it impossible to be objective. I was confused as to Mattie's motives, accepting of her choices and simultaneously frustrated by them. And I was finding it ever harder to ignore that small murmuring voice that told me there must be cracks in Mattie and Niko's marriage if she was lying to him about something so important, and that if that were true, perhaps there was hope for me. I trusted myself enough to know for certain that I would never do anything as heinous as act on my feelings, but that did little to stop them rising like a tide inside me.

My mood plummeted and I felt jumpy and irritable, snapping at my parents, Sam, Lia, and even Rosie, whom I had so painstakingly been trying to win back over. So, when Mattie suggested that I accompany her into Corfu Town to pick up a few supplies for my daughter's upcoming birthday party, I agreed without hesitation. A change of scene would do me good and getting away from Kalami for the morning would give everyone else a break from my increasingly unpleasant company.

'You girls go and bond,' my mother said, as if the entire excursion had been her idea. 'Rosie will stay here and keep Granny company by the pool, won't you?'

My daughter lowered her phone and looked up with bleary eyes. It was early, and she had yet to brush her hair. I watched as she twisted a piece of it around with her finger until the end began to fray. It was blonder than it had ever been, bleached by a diet of sunshine and salt water.

'Yeah, sure,' she said. 'Whatever.'

'Don't sound too enthusiastic,' my mother joked. 'I promise we'll have fun. You can tell me all your mum's secrets.'

'That won't take very long,' I said drily, getting to my feet. 'And Rosie?'

'Huh?'

'If you want to leave Kalami for any reason, please check with me first. Send me a text or something, telling me where you're going, so I don't worry.'

This was greeted by predictable disdain.

'Please,' I repeated. 'For me.'

'Gosh, she really is a worrywart, isn't she?' chuckled my father. 'Heaven only knows which one of us she gets that trait from.'

I pursed my lips and said nothing.

'Come on,' interrupted Mattie, with typical jollity. 'Let's get out of here before someone commits murder.'

We went in the jeep, Mattie driving while I sat beside her in the passenger seat, my hair whipping around my face as the warm breeze poured in through the open roof. The road chased the undulations of the coastline all the way down from the Gimari region and through the small resorts of Ipsos, Dassia and Limni, before tapering inland towards Corfu Town. For the first half of the journey, we did not say much to each other. It was only when Mattie had to slow down behind some tourists on a hired quad bike that her pale-green eyes flickered in my direction.

'Have you found it weird,' she asked, 'being back in Corfu after so many years?'

'It was at first,' I told her truthfully. 'But I like to think I've settled in now.'

'I'm so glad you and Rosie decided to stay,' she said, slipping the jeep into second gear as we rounded a tight bend. 'I know it's been a bit hairy at times, what with Lia showing up and now Mum and Dad. It probably isn't what you signed up for when you agreed to come here.'

'Definitely not the Mum and Dad part,' I said, and we both laughed. 'But to be honest, I've got used to life throwing me curveballs. Sometimes the things you don't plan for turn out to be the best decisions. I mean, look at Rosie. The last thing I expected was to be a mother at nineteen, but now I wouldn't swap her for the world.'

'You've done an amazing job.' Mattie smiled below her sunglasses. She had pulled her hair up into a messy bun before we left the villa, but most of it had come undone and was tangled in the clasps of her dungarees.

This was my in.

'How about you?' I asked, as casually as I could muster.

Mattie appeared to grip the steering wheel a fraction tighter. 'What about me what?'

'Motherhood. Have you ever thought about it?'

She hesitated.

'Sorry,' I went on. 'It's probably none of my business. I realise we haven't ever discussed it, and that's my fault. I was so caught up in Rosie that I let all my other relationships slide away out of focus. Only, I couldn't help but notice the extremely unsubtle dig that Dorothia made recently, about you and Niko not having started a family.'

Mattie nodded, her features tightening as though remembering the barb had caused her to wince.

'I think both she and Niko assumed there would be a baby by now,' she said.

'And you?'

Mattie seemed to chew her words before replying. 'I guess I thought the same thing.'

I took a deep breath.

'I've got a confession to make,' I told her. 'I answered a call at the villa last week from the Aphrodite Clinic, about a repeat prescription for the pill.'

'Really?' Mattie said lightly. 'Oh, well, that must have been a wrong number.'

'They definitely asked to speak to a Mrs Fox.'

She had gone very pink, and although it was a hot day, I guessed that the temperature had very little to do with it.

'And she just volunteered the information?'

'Kind of.' I cringed. 'She threw me, asking for Fox, and so I didn't exactly tell her that I wasn't you.'

'Well, perhaps you should have.'

I bit my lip, stung by the truth in her statement.

'Sorry,' she said, when a young couple stepped into the road clutching a large inflatable unicorn and she applied the brakes too sharply. 'I didn't mean to snap at you, I just . . .'

'It's fine,' I said. 'You have every right to snap – it's none of my business. You are allowed to be cross with people,' I added, when she started shaking her head.

'You know me,' she mumbled. 'Allergic to confrontation of any kind.'

'You always were the nicer sister,' I replied. 'I felt like all I did growing up was have endless confrontations.'

Mattie said nothing, and for a while I let the silence fill the gap. She seemed to be struggling to compose herself, so

I turned away and stared out across the water instead. The beach in Ipsos was little more than a narrow strip of shingle, and the sea beyond was tantalisingly close. I wanted to stretch out a hand and run my fingers through its glistening surface.

'Please don't say anything to Niko,' she said, shooting me a desperate look. 'About me still being on the pill, I mean. He wouldn't understand.'

'I won't,' I assured her. 'But don't you think it might be a good idea to talk to him about it?'

She shook her violently at that. 'I can't. Not yet, not while everyone is here. He'll be so cross and—'

'He might not be,' I interrupted gently. 'I know he's outwardly a grumpy old man Greek, but he's a good egg underneath it all.'

'I didn't realise the two of you had got to know each other so well.'

I felt myself blush. 'We haven't, not really,' I said. 'But he's your husband – it's his job to understand.'

Mattie nodded, but she did not look remotely convinced. 'You know when you broke up with Paul?' she said.

'Yes,' I said, unsure of where she was going to go with this line of questioning.

'How did you know when you stopped loving him? Sorry – is that too personal? I realise we never discussed it at the time, but Mum told me that it was your decision, so I sort of just assumed it must be that, but maybe I'm wrong. Am I wrong? Oh my God, he didn't break your heart, did he?'

She had talked herself into a tornado of self-doubt and I had to raise my voice to be heard.

'You want the truth?' I asked, and she nodded.

'I'm not actually sure if I ever loved Paul.'

'But—'

'I was with him for fifteen years? Yes, I know. I had to be, for Rosie. And I wasn't unhappy – there was a lot I really liked about Paul, there still is, but ultimately I never felt that passion towards him that I guess you're supposed to feel.'

I paused to collect my thoughts, knowing I had to be careful with what I said next.

'Does that mean,' Mattie glanced at me, '. . . that you have never been in love?'

I had no choice but to lie, and it hurt me to do so. Mattie looked as dismayed as I felt. We had ground to a stop at a set of lights, the air traffic tower of Corfu airport now visible in the near distance. Soon we would reach our destination and this conversation would end, the two of us distracted by party balloons and streamers. I only had one chance to ask her, and I knew that I must, that I had to know. I opened my mouth to speak, but Mattie got there first.

'Sometimes I wonder . . .' she said, so quietly that I had to lean across in my seat. She looked almost afraid to continue, as though she was scared of her own thoughts.

'Wonder what?' I said, my eyes on the lights that were turning from red to amber.

Mattie's hand trembled on the gearstick, her fingers slipping as the driver behind us sounded his horn.

'*Ela re malakas!*' she yelled, only invoking an even more determined blaring.

The jeep stalled, and Mattie dropped her keys as she fumbled to restart the engine. When she bent to retrieve them, her sunglasses slipped off and I caught a glimpse of her eyes, wide and frightened.

'Shit, sorry – oh, bloody hell. Go around me!' she cried, sticking her arm out and ushering past the impatient motorist.

'Do you want me to drive?' I asked, putting a tentative hand on her arm.

Mattie drew in a long breath. 'No,' she said, with forced cheer. 'Don't be daft. I'm fine – just had a funny few minutes then. Must be PMT or something, it always makes me lose my head.'

'You were about to say something,' I reminded her. 'I'm still listening.'

'Was I?' Mattie shrugged as we moved forwards and joined the flow of traffic.

'It sounded important to me,' I continued, but I could tell I had lost her.

'How weird,' she said. 'It's gone right out of my head. Maybe it'll come back to me later.'

'Maybe,' I agreed, unconvinced.

She had opened the door a crack only to slam it shut again, but I knew it made no sense to push her any further. How could I when I was guilty of the very same thing she was? Both of us were marooned on separate islands, each too afraid to admit the truth, fearful of the tsunami of repercussions that would surely follow.

My head told me that I must be mistaken – that Mattie could not have been about to tell me that she no longer loved Niko – and I wanted to believe it. I could have believed it, too, if only my heart had agreed to play along.

38

The final few days before Rosie's birthday party passed by in a blur of activity. Mostly, this blur could be associated with Mattie's limbs, which barely seemed to stop moving in her haste to get everything ready in time. For an event that was only set to include members of the family and the few Kalami residents my daughter had become friends with since we had been on the island, Mattie was certainly going to a lot of trouble.

I watched her from the balcony as I hung up my towel, which was damp from an early-morning swim. She had dragged one of the kitchen chairs outside and was standing on it as she attempted to string an eighteenth-birthday banner between two pillars. I wanted to call down and tell her to wait for me, that I would help her, but I was worried she might topple right off in fright if I did. Mattie, I knew, was happiest when she was occupied with a task, and she was also a classic ostrich. If she kept herself busy, she would not have to confront anything else. I had started to watch Niko and Mattie more closely since our conversation in the jeep, and not once had I seen them touch one another with any kind of tenderness. They never sought each other out in a group or shared private jokes that would have hinted at intimacy. If I hadn't known they were married, I would have guessed they were merely casual friends.

The two people who were demonstrating every tell of growing closeness were Rosie and Sam, and while I had not witnessed the two of them doing anything like they had in the beach shack the day of our argument, I had seen her clasp his hand beneath the dinner table when she thought I wasn't looking. Rosie knew I did not like the two of them spending any time alone together, but she had got around my rule by organising a series of collection boxes for the injured cats in Kalami and taking Sam with her around the island to beg change from generous tourists. Fenna had driven them in her rusty old pickup truck, so I could not protest too vehemently. I just had to wave them off with a rictus grin and hope that nothing untoward happened.

'He saved Lia and now he's helping Fenna save the cats,' Mattie pointed out. 'He can't be all that bad.'

I remained unconvinced. Nobody who had been within a two-mile radius of the villa when he and Ophelia initially arrived could be in any doubt as to his appetite for sex, and it had been several weeks now since the two of them had stopped keeping the rest of us awake all night. He had lost interest in Ophelia as his preoccupation with Rosie had gathered pace, and I did not believe that he would be patient when it came to taking their relationship, such as it was, to the next level. Every time I had tried to raise the subject with her, I had been told bluntly that it was none of my business. The only card I had to play was that I would not allow anything of that nature to happen under the villa roof, and this she had accepted – for the time being, at least.

The banner had been hung successfully and I heard rather than saw Mattie down on the terrace, shouting something through to my mother that sounded cake-related. There was a vast orange and lemon creation being prepared at the Starenio Bakery in Corfu Town, which someone would have to drive over and collect in the morning, and Sam had spent the best part of the previous afternoon preparing a batch of vegan brownies from a recipe he had been taught in Thailand.

'Shoo, kiddo,' I had heard him say, as Rosie attempted to sneak a taste. 'Birthday brownies can only be consumed on birthdays – that's the rule.'

'I'm going to eat at least five!' she promised him, and I had been forced to turn round so neither would witness the rolling of my eyes.

Dragging my mind back to the present, I closed the balcony door and surveyed the open wardrobe, trying to decide what to wear for the party. Rosie had accumulated a decent haul of new garments since we had been in Corfu, but the only thing I'd splashed out on was a mesh top adorned with intricately patterned butterflies. I planned to wear this, along with black cigarette pants and the spiky heels I had tossed into my suitcase at the last minute. I joked to Rosie that I had chosen an almost all black ensemble to mourn the end of her childhood, but there was another, simpler, reason: I wanted to look nice.

Anticipating a day of villa-based party preparations, I opted for a simple shorts and vest combination, and was applying mascara when my phone began to vibrate with a FaceTime call.

'Paul,' I said, pleasantly surprised to see the friendly face of my ex-partner smiling back at me. 'Long time no speak.'

'I know, I know,' he said, leaning forward in his seat. I could see a bookcase behind him and guessed that he must be calling from his office at home. 'Ro-Ro's been messaging loads, keeping me updated on all your goss.'

'I bet she has,' I replied. 'Not on the road today?'

Paul worked as an estate agent, which sounded dull on paper but which he loved – mostly because he excelled at it. There was something very satisfying about locating the perfect home for people, he always said, and prided himself on securing the very best deals he could with the least amount of tedious red tape. When the two of us had agreed to split, Paul had been the one to find Rosie and me our new home in Brighton and make sure our marital assets were divided fairly. He was a decent man – one of the very best I knew.

'Not due in until ten,' he replied. 'It's only just gone eight here.'

'Of course.' I clapped a hand briefly over my face. 'I am rather good at forgetting about the time difference, I'm afraid. You'd think it would have sunk in by now, but then you know me.'

I was not sure exactly what I had meant by that last statement, but Paul chuckled away politely regardless. His blond hair was beginning to thin now that he was in his early forties, but he had the even complexion and bright, shrewd eyes of a man much younger. He was happy and in love – and it suited him.

'How's Laura?' I asked now. 'Everything ticking along nicely with you two?'

'You could say that,' Paul replied, fidgeting with the knot of his tie. It was green and embroidered with tiny red parrots.

'That sounds . . . ominous.'

'God, no – nothing like that. It's actually the reason I'm calling. I mean, I was going to wait until tomorrow, as it's Ro-Ro's birthday, but then I thought, "sod it".'

'Are you getting married?' I asked, and Paul laughed.

'Same old Ava,' he said. 'Getting straight to the point – no time for small talk.'

'There is nothing I enjoy more than small talk,' I lied cheerfully. 'Did I guess right?'

'Go and fetch our daughter, will you?' he said, still laughing. 'Then I can tell you both at the same time.'

I continued to chat to Paul as I traipsed downstairs in search of Rosie, stopping only briefly to allow a flustered Mattie to say a quick hello.

'Do you know where Rosie is?' I asked her, interrupting Paul's spiel about how much potential a place like the villa would have in the holiday rental market.

'I think she said something about snorkelling,' Mattie said distractedly. 'She and Sam borrowed some masks and flippers from Niko's stash.'

'Is that Martha? Hello, Martha!' Paul called, waving with enthusiasm as my mother approached from the direction of the terrace, her wet feet leaving footprints on the stone floor.

'Pauly!' she exclaimed, snatching the phone from my hand. 'Well, don't you just look the absolute picture of health. What a treat to see you. Angus? ANGUS!'

My father sat up very suddenly from one of the white sofas. He was wearing a panama hat and clutching a crumpled copy of *The Sunday Times*.

'Did someone call?'

'It's Paul,' cried my mother, thrusting the phone under his nose. My father took it from her and squinted at the screen.

'Oh yes, so it is. Gosh, you've barely more hair than me these days.'

'Dad!' I exploded, as if I was still thirteen.

'Don't worry.' My father chortled. 'Happens to the best of us.'

'Sorry about that,' I said, when I had managed to wrestle the phone back from them. 'But you should really know better than to engage my parents in conversation.'

'Noted.' Paul grinned as I shouldered open the front door. 'I can't believe the whole family is there in situ. That must be . . . interesting.'

'You're not wrong,' I told him. 'I am barely clinging on to the last threads of my sanity over here.'

'Looks like nice weather,' he remarked, and I turned the phone round so he could see the view across the bay.

'The air feels like soup today,' I said. 'I think everyone is praying it will rain soon, but nobody wants to say so and jinx the party.'

'While I've got you,' Paul said then, the change in his tone making me flip the phone again so I could see his expression. 'What's the deal with this Sam bloke? Every time I talk to Rosie, she drops his name into the mix. Is he working over there?'

'Sam, work? Not unless he can help it. I assume his parents are funding this extended gap year he's on, although to be honest, I haven't thought to ask. Ophelia brought him with her,' I added, and Paul frowned.

'I see.'

'Did Rosie mention—?' I began, and Paul nodded.

'About Lia's incident in Thailand. Yes. Sounds awful. Is she all right?'

'Getting there,' I said. 'She's been helping out at the taverna here over the past week or so, and that seems to be keeping her out of trouble. Hang on a jiffy.'

I had reached the road and weaved through the rows of parked cars. Most of the properties along the beach were private villas, but many had narrow alleys on either side, linking the main thoroughfare to the spread of white pebbles beyond. I had no idea at which end of Kalami Bay my daughter and Sam had chosen to snorkel, and it was luck as opposed to judgement that brought me out only ten or so metres from where the two of them were sitting side by side on Elpida's landing jetty.

'Here's the beach,' I said, holding my phone aloft as I pointed out each of the four tavernas, as well as the White House at the far end. Paul was suitably impressed.

'No wonder you were so cross when Mattie decided to move there,' he said.

'I wasn't cross,' I lied. 'I was just . . .'

'Jealous then. Oh, come on, Ava, there's no shame in admitting it. Anyone would have been. Hell, even I was a little. Brighton is great and everything, but it's no Corfu, is it?'

I walked towards the jetty. Rosie and Sam had not heard me coming, which gave me the opportunity to watch them for a moment. As Niko and I had so many times during our summer, when we had been too wrapped up in ourselves to notice the continuing flow of the world around us, Rosie and Sam leaned into one another now. Her head rested on his shoulder; his hand traced a pattern across her thigh. It should have been a touching scene, but nothing about their interaction felt pure to me. There was an unsavoury edge to Sam that I could not see my way past. Rosie had accused me of taking against him simply because I was protective of her, and I had to allow that there was an element of truth in that. But it ran deeper; my distrust of Sam felt like instinct.

'Is that him?' Paul asked and, realising the phone was still facing forwards, I angled it back towards me.

'That's him,' I confirmed.

'I looked him up,' Paul admitted. 'After about the third or fourth time Rosie mentioned him, I asked for his surname and looked him up on Facebook.'

'And?'

'And nothing – no sign of him.'

'That doesn't necessarily mean anything,' I allowed. 'Rosie is forever telling me that Facebook is solely the domain of the over-forties these days.'

'Laura told me the same – so I tried all the others and still found nothing. Do you know how unusual it is, in this day and age, to have no digital presence at all?'

'Sam Adams must be a very common name,' I pointed out. 'Perhaps he is there but you didn't scroll through far enough.'

Paul narrowed his eyes. 'You're probably right,' he said eventually. 'I'll have another look. Now, pass me over to the almost-birthday girl if you will?'

I smiled and called Rosie's name.

'It's your dad,' I said, holding out the phone. 'He has news.'

She jumped to her feet and scampered along the jetty, a huge smile already lighting up her face as she caught sight of Paul's frantically waving form on the screen. Sam made no move to join her; instead he turned and stared, his hooded eyes blank as they connected with mine.

Despite the heat of the day, the beauty of the setting, and the joyful sight of my girl in all her effervescent glory, I shivered.

39

Rosie guessed what was up almost immediately.

'Laura's pregnant, isn't she? Oh my God – am I finally going to be a big sister?'

Paul beamed.

'You are. The baby's due in February, all being well.' He reached forwards and touched the edge of his wooden desk.

'Oh, Dad! Congratulations. Where is Laura – can I say hi?'

'She's actually on a call to her parents,' he said. 'We thought we'd tell the news to the most important people in our lives at the same time, which obviously includes you.'

'And Mum,' she added.

'Yes.' Paul smiled. 'And Mum.'

'Do you know if it's a boy or a girl yet?'

'Not quite yet,' he said. 'But we are planning to find out, so as soon as I know, I'll make sure you do.'

Rosie had become a flood of questions. Could she help choose names? Were they planning a water birth in one of those pools? Was Laura going to create a birthing playlist? Would they be moving house? Could she be chief babysitter? It was touching to see her so excited at the prospect of a sibling. Mattie had come along so soon after me that I had never known anything different, while all that Ophelia had represented when she arrived was even less parental attention than before, and an even greater amount of responsibility piled on my shoulders. Rosie was old enough to relish the thought of a baby and would be an asset to her father and Laura – of that, I was sure. Paul had always wanted to have more children, so I was happy for him too.

'How funny that you're having another baby just as your first one becomes an adult,' Rosie said now. 'You were almost home free, Dad, and now you're doomed to another eighteen years of nappies, toddler tantrums, first days at school, teenage angst – the works!'

'I know,' he said. 'And I can't wait.'

'I can't either!' she enthused. Then, turning back towards Sam, 'I'm going to be a big sister!'

'So I heard.' Sam got to his feet and shambled towards us. There was a rolled-up cigarette dangling from his lips and his floppy hair was pushed up behind his sunglasses. Catching me looking at him, he unconsciously tightened the muscles across his chest, reminding me of a gorilla limbering up for confrontation. Then, in a move that could only have been designed to goad me, he stepped forwards and wrapped both his arms around Rosie's middle, pulling her backwards against him. I could no longer see Paul on the phone, but listened as he asked about party plans.

'I can't quite believe my little girl is about to turn eighteen,' he said. 'And you'll be off to university before you know it – you must be getting excited about that?'

Rosie's smile drooped.

'What's with the face?'

'I was thinking, maybe, that I might wait a year. Take some time to think about my options. I've been looking into becoming an influencer, you know, earning some money through TikTok or Instagram. Lia said she would help me.'

'Hang on a minute,' I interrupted. 'What happened to becoming a history teacher?'

Sam glanced at me in disdain. 'Not much money in that,' he said, letting go of Rosie in order to take another drag of his roll-up.

I ignored him. 'Rosie?'

She shrugged, uncomfortable now under the combined scrutiny of both me and her father.

'It was just an idea.'

'There's far too much pressure on young people these days to know exactly what they want to do,' said Sam, as if he, at the grand old age of twenty-one, was an authority on the subject. 'If Rosie needs a few more years to make her mind up, you should be prepared to support her.'

He had caught me unawares, and for a moment or two, I was so angry and taken aback that all I could do was splutter incoherently. Paul came to the rescue in the end, which was typical of him.

'This all sounds like a conversation for another day,' he said cheerfully. 'Maybe me, you and Mum can have a call next week – just the three of us?'

Rosie chewed on her lip. 'OK. Yeah, maybe. Whatever.'

'Tell me what else you've been up to,' he prompted. 'Was that a snorkel mask I saw in the background? Do you remember when we went snorkelling in Turkey and I put my hand on that sea urchin?'

'You looked like you were wearing one of those foam fingers,' she said, smiling as she recalled the image of her father's swollen thumb. Paul had expertly redirected their chat both in subject matter and mood, and within a few minutes Rosie was laughing again. Sam, however, was not – and neither was I. He stared at me, and I glared right back, the impasse only breaking when Rosie cried, 'Oh, there's Uncle Niko! Do you want to meet him, Dad?'

She did not wait for Paul to answer, and I guessed she must be keen to remove herself from the tense atmosphere on the jetty. Grateful to have a valid excuse to move away from Sam, I followed my daughter across the beach and up the front steps of Elpida. She and Niko were standing together, both smiling into the phone, although he with perhaps a fraction less enthusiasm.

'*Geia sou.*' He touched my arm, his dark eyes crinkling as he recognised my distress. '*Eísai kalá*?' he murmured. *Are you OK?*

I nodded quickly, unwilling to burden him. Niko had enough to contend with without me heaping on all my concerns about Rosie's career plans. She was now regaling Paul with an amusing anecdote about how Niko had finally convinced her to drink coffee, and how she was now almost as obsessed with it as he was.

'Honestly, Dad, it's, like, mad how much I like it now.'

'You can now call yourself Greek,' Niko told her gravely. 'You are part of the family.'

'Speaking of which,' said Rosie. 'Is Lia here today? Can I go in the kitchen so Dad can say hi?'

'*Naí*, of course.' Niko extended an arm of invitation and Rosie skipped off between the tables.

'She is very happy today,' he remarked, moving further outside until we were shaded below a large beach umbrella. Giorgos, who was manning the sunloungers, did a double-take when he saw his boss standing beside him and removed his feet from the table, shoving the phone at which he'd been staring deep into the pocket of his shorts.

'She's just found out that she's going to be a big sister,' I said. Niko raised an eyebrow. 'Paul and his girlfriend are expecting,' I clarified.

'And this is . . . You are happy?'

'Yes, very much so. A baby is never bad news, is it?'

I realised too late what I had said and stuttered something else instead. Niko rubbed at his eyes as if he was tired, then gave me a half-smile.

'He is your ex. I thought that perhaps . . .'

'Oh no.' I laughed. 'Paul and I, we're friends. There are no regrets or ill feeling – on either side.'

'That is good.'

'We grew apart as a couple, but the friendship endured. He's a decent man, Paul – he never resented me for not . . . Well, let's just say he was understanding.'

'For not . . . ?' Niko echoed, and again I felt the brush of his fingers against my arm.

'Not loving him enough,' I said with a sigh, because what was the point in pretending otherwise? Creating a narrative around the subject of our break-up was exhausting; it made far more sense to simply tell the truth. 'I loved the part of him that was half Rosie, the father part of him. I still do. But when it came to the other stuff, the romantic stuff, there was never anything real there. Not like there had been . . .'

I did not need to finish; Niko knew what I meant.

'First love is like a wildfire,' he said, his voice thick, the words deliberate. 'It devours everything else in its path. You can plant the seed of a new tree in the scorched earth, but you will never again be able to seek shelter beneath its branches.'

'How do you put the fire out?' I asked, and Niko lowered his eyes.

'Unfortunately,' he said, 'I do not know.'

40

Nineteen years earlier . . .

Ava did not mean to pick a fight with her mother.

Like most of the arguments they had, it had flared up from the tiniest spark. Having exhausted all the options in her own wardrobe, Ava had borrowed a dress from Mattie for the evening, and although it was a size smaller than she usually wore, she'd felt good in it. That was, until she came downstairs ready to head out for dinner.

'Is that really what you're wearing?' her mother said. And that was all it took.

Barbed comments were soon being volleyed back and forth between them. Ava unloaded all the things she had long thought about her mother, but never dared say, branding her 'lazy, incompetent, irresponsible, deluded'. Her mother pretended to be affronted, but there was nothing lukewarm about the insults she threw tersely back.

'Your problem, Ava, is that you're uptight. You wouldn't recognise fun if it was stuck fast to the side of your face. It's probably the reason you don't have any friends.'

'That's rich coming from you,' Ava hurled back. 'You've managed to lose all yours from being so utterly self-obsessed.'

Her father had tried to intervene and calm the situation down, but this had only enraged both women further, and eventually, Ava had fled the apartment and set off at a run down the beach.

'Wait!'

Mattie was barefoot and struggling to catch up.

'Leave me alone,' Ava said, as she fought to stop hot tears from escaping. 'I don't want to talk to anyone.'

'Well, that's OK then because I'm not just anyone, I'm your favourite someone.'

'Seriously, Mattie – go away.'

'I'm not going to leave you by yourself in this state,' Mattie replied. She was always so calm and reasonable. Ava did not understand how anyone could be so patient, so accepting, so utterly determined never to pass judgement. Her sister was everything that she, Ava, would never be. The realisation made her slump in defeat.

'Fine,' she said. 'But I'm not going to talk about it.'

They had come far enough along the beach to be within sight of Niko's family restaurant, but as much as Ava wanted to run inside and seek comfort in his strong arms, she knew she mustn't. Niko had yet to tell his family about her, and she did not want to raise any suspicions.

'Shall we sit?' she said to Mattie. There were a few sunloungers that had yet to be tidied away for the night, and they perched together on the one closest to the shoreline.

'Are you all right?'

Ava turned her mascara-streaked face in her sister's direction.

'OK, silly question.' Mattie laughed nervously. 'But are you though?'

'I will be.' Ava smiled with grim determination. 'Just as soon as I've escaped.'

Mattie sighed. 'You're so lucky to be going away to university. I've still got nearly three years to wait.'

'But you and Mum get on,' Ava pointed out.

Mattie shrugged. 'Only because I never argue back. If I told her what I really thought, she'd probably make me move out and live in Dad's shed.'

'I might not go to university any more.'

'What?' Mattie was aghast. 'Why not?'

Ava fixed her with a serious stare. 'You have to promise that you won't say anything – not to Mum and Dad, not to Lia, not to anyone. Do you promise?'

She nodded.

'I'm thinking of coming back here,' Ava told her. 'To Corfu, I mean. Maybe find a job or something.'

'Is this to do with the boy you've met?'

'Partly.' Ava did not want her sister to think her foolish. 'But it's also because I love it here.'

'I do, too.' Mattie sighed and turned her gaze towards the horizon. 'Everything feels easier here, doesn't it?'

'We can both live here. I can build a life for myself on the island, then you can come and join me as soon as you turn eighteen.'

'Really?' Mattie was delighted. 'You'd let me live with you and your mysterious Greek lover?'

Ava giggled. 'Hopefully by then, he won't be mysterious any more.'

'And we won't tell Mum and Dad where we are – only Lia?'

'I guess we can let her visit,' Ava agreed.

'You're actually serious about this,' Mattie said admiringly. 'You're not joking, are you?'

Ava shook her head. 'I'm very serious.'

'In that case,' Mattie enthused, 'so am I! Shall we shake on it, here and now? Make a pact that one day we will both live in Corfu?'

Ava reached across and took her sister's hand. 'Easiest pact I'll ever make,' she said.

They stayed together on the beach until the sun slipped down below the distant hills, excitedly making plans about what their life on a Greek island would look like, and how shocked their parents would be when they vanished abroad without a word. Ava had been toying with her plan for several days – ever since the night Niko had taken her up to the villa in Agni Bay – but sharing it with Mattie had made the whole thing seem real. She could do this; she could do whatever she wanted to do.

Giddy with possibility and excited by the prospect of telling Niko what she intended to do, Ava did not argue when Mattie suggested that they head to Elpida for some food. He would be in the kitchen, she reasoned, so chances were he would not even see her. She would be able to tease him about it later, pretend that the meal she'd ordered was the worst thing she'd ever tasted, only to fling her arms around his neck and take it all instantly back. He would give her that stern look of his, then he would laugh, his big, beautiful head dipping towards hers as he blew raspberries against her neck in retaliation for her naughtiness.

Perhaps tonight, Ava thought, she would tell him. Tell him just how much he meant to her.

She was so distracted by the scene playing out in her mind that at first Ava didn't realise that something was amiss inside Elpida. It was only when Mattie placed a hand on her arm and gestured towards a sobbing waitress that she stopped and stared around. The staff were all either crying or looking dazed, while customers at their tables were glancing around in mounting alarm.

Without giving herself time to consider what she was doing, Ava hurried towards the back of the taverna, to where she knew the office and kitchen were located. She needed to see Niko, had to know that he was OK.

She got as far as the narrow opening that led behind the bar before a young Greek waiter caught up with her.

'Excuse me, you cannot go through here.'

'What's going on?' Ava demanded, fear making her bolder than usual. 'What's happened?'

The waiter looked at her uncertainly. 'Sorry,' he said. 'We are closing now.'

'Please,' Ava begged. 'Is . . . Did something bad happen?'

The young man pulled an agitated hand through his hair. 'The owner,' he said. 'Leonidas Balaouras.'

Niko's father. Ava felt a horrible nausea wash over her.

'What about him?'

The man blinked at her, shaking his head as if he could not believe what he was about to say. Ava knew what was coming, but the words still hit her like a fist.

'He has died.'

41

I stared at my daughter as she slept, drinking in the clean familiar sight of her, this girl I had grown, whose face I knew better than my own. I absorbed every detail, gazed in awe at the perfect angle of her jaw, the fan of her lashes, the kink in her hair that never lay flat and her lips, which were parted in a dreamlike smile. There was an openness to Rosie that was not mirrored in her mother, me with all my sharp angles and deep-set eyes and my aura of mistrust. I had grown up believing that the world was out to spite me, while my daughter knew only kindness.

She stirred, twisting out a hand from under the sheet to rub away the grit of slumber.

'Morning, birthday girl,' I whispered, not lifting my head from the pillow beside hers.

'Happy eighteen-years-ago-labour to you,' she mumbled. It was a running joke – one that she had come up with in her early teens – and I groaned as I always did.

'Gee,' I said. 'Thanks for the reminder. A real low point in the story of our lives together.'

'Funny,' she deadpanned, stretching like a cat.

'Don't worry,' I said, smoothing the hair off her forehead and tucking it behind her ear, grinning as she immediately shook it loose again. 'Things really went up from there.'

'Worth the pain?'

'Every excruciating minute.'

'Remind me how many of those there were again?'

I closed my eyes as I pretended to do the maths.

'Oh, around one thousand and twenty-four, give or take.'

'Blimey,' she murmured sleepily. 'You really took one for the team, Mum.'

'So,' I said. 'Eighteen. How does it feel?'

Rosie wriggled under the covers.

'Sore,' she replied. 'I really shouldn't have worn that thong bikini yesterday. I've definitely burned my bottom.'

'What has two bums and kills people?' I said, and Rosie rolled her eyes.

'Do we really have to start the day with one of your terrible jokes?'

'It's a tradition!'

She grumbled affectionately. 'Fine. Tell me – what has two bums and kills people?'

'An assassin.'

'I think that might be your worst yet.'

'What?' I feigned surprise. 'Worse than the one about the hippo with no bum?'

'No!' she cried. 'Don't say it!'

'Hippobottomless.'

'That's it, I'm getting up.'

I waited until she had scooped up a towel and headed into the bathroom before I reached for my robe. The air conditioning was on, but I could tell from the glow around the shutters that another scorching day awaited. I had resolved to be kind all day and not to snipe – not even at my mother or Sam. This was Rosie's day, and nothing else mattered to me but her happiness.

Paul and I had agreed to our daughter's pleas and divvied up the cost of a small car as her main present, but I had also splurged on a Victorian peridot and pink sapphire ring that

Rosie had fallen in love with when she'd spotted it in the window of an antique jewellers a few months ago. Unbeknownst to her, I had sneaked back and bought it, then had it resized to fit, and now I could hardly wait to surprise her with it at the party. I wanted her to feel every bit as special as she was, and to know how much I loved her. The butting of heads we had been doing during this trip had upset me, and I suspected the same was true for Rosie. I felt as if the links of friendship between us had broken, and I was desperate to restore them.

As if on cue, there was a knock on the bedroom door and my mother's face emerged in the gap. She was pink-cheeked and explained that she had already been for a walk down to the supermarket.

'I thought as it was a special occasion that we should have fresh bread for breakfast.'

'Nice of you,' I said.

'Yes, I thought so. I'm not half as much of an ogre as you think I am, you know.'

'I don't think you're an ogre,' I protested.

She came into the room and dropped a pile of wrapped gifts on the bed.

'Are those for me?' said an excited Rosie. She was wrapped in one striped towel and had cocooned her wet hair in another.

'Do you know anyone else who is turning eighteen today?' teased my mother, smiling as Rosie fell on the presents.

'They're just little things,' she said, as Rosie pulled out a beautiful pashmina followed by a bottle of champagne. 'Gramps has slipped a few notes in the card for you, so be careful not to rip the envelope.'

Rosie's eyes widened as she unsheathed six fifty-euro notes.

'Wow! Thanks, Granny.'

'Just don't go spending it on a tattoo, or your mum will never forgive me.'

'Ha ha,' I said, folding my arms. 'Rosie is not a fan of tattoos, are you?'

'Well . . .' My daughter looked sheepish. 'I did think that maybe I might look at some designs. Sam says he knows this woman in Thailand that does bespoke Sak Yant tattoos for people.'

I had no idea what a Sak Yant tattoo was, but I knew I did not like it.

'This is so nice, Granny,' Rosie said now, as she held up the very same purple-flowered dress that I had wanted to buy her in Corfu Town – the one she had dismissed, ironically, as being too much of a 'granny dress'.

'Thailand is a very long way to go for a tattoo,' I said, aiming for light-hearted nonchalance and ending up with high-pitched trepidation.

'But if I was there anyway . . .' she began, only to fall silent when she saw my expression.

'Oh,' said my mother, perking up, 'are you planning a visit?'

Rosie deliberately avoided my eye. 'I don't know. Maybe. It was just an idea. Sam said he might go back after the summer and, well, I thought I could defer my place at uni. Loads of people do it,' she added to my mother, before I had the chance to disagree. 'And if I did, I wouldn't need that car after all, Mum – we could sell it and I could use the money to go travelling instead.'

I had hoped she'd forgotten about all this.

My mother, finally sensing that an Everest-sized crevasse had opened in the room, glanced at each of us in turn. Given her own predilection to shun convention and encourage all of us to do the same, I had no doubt that she was thrilled by the prospect of her granddaughter joining the backpacker herd, but for once she managed to hold her tongue.

I reminded myself once again that this was Rosie's day and took a very deep breath. 'Let's talk about it later – or tomorrow? There's still a while to go until the A level results come in, so you don't have to decide right this minute, do you?'

Rosie smiled in relief.

'No, I guess not.'

'Here,' I said, picking up a tube of aftersun and handing it to her. 'Smear some of this on your poor burnt bottom and come down to breakfast – Granny got fresh bread.'

I signalled for my mother to follow me, and the two of us made our way towards the stairs.

'Bloody, bloody Sam,' I hissed. 'This is all his doing.' My anger was such that I had to resist a ridiculous urge to stamp my foot.

'Would it be so terrible if Rosie took a year off?' my mother queried.

I stared at her aghast before ushering her further away from the bedroom. 'Yes, it would,' I said in a low voice. 'Until we came here, and she started spending all her time with *him*, it would not have even occurred to her not to go straight to university. She was so excited about it, and now suddenly – what? She's going to give it all up to please a boy?'

'Careful,' said my mother airily. 'You wouldn't want to be accused of hypocrisy.'

My hand tightened on the banister. 'What is that supposed to mean?'

'You and Paul,' she said, as if it was the most obvious thing in the world. 'You'd known him for, oh, all of five minutes before you decided to throw in your lot with him and to hell with everyone else.'

'I was pregnant,' I reminded her coldly. 'That didn't leave me with much choice in the matter.'

'You chose to go,' she said. 'You didn't have to leave home so quickly. Dad and I would have supported you, but instead you went to live with his family. How do you think that made me feel, to be relegated to third place in your life all of a sudden?'

I gawped at her in bewilderment.

'I went because I had to,' I said, my voice hoarse. 'I didn't want my child to be raised the way we were. With you, it was all about so-called freedoms and letting us "become who we truly were", but all that was just a smokescreen to disguise the fact that you had no real time for us. I grew up feeling like an unwelcome guest in my own home, and I couldn't allow my own child to experience that environment. And anyway,' I barrelled on. 'It wasn't about me or you then, it was about Rosie, and what was best for her. Paul's an only child, his parents had more space, more free time to help us than you did.'

I could see that I had hurt her, but the guilt only fuelled my indignation.

'All I have ever done is put my daughter first. I did what I had to, what a parent has to, what you and Dad should have done for us, instead of leaving us to fend for ourselves ninety per cent of the time.'

My mother took an unsteady step away from me. She seemed to have aged in the past few minutes, the short grey hair thinner, the lines around her eyes more pronounced. Regret surged through me, but it was too late. The damage was already done.

'You can blame me if you want to, Ava,' she said. 'But ask yourself this: if your method of parenting has been so wonderful, then why can't your daughter wait to get as far away from you as possible?'

42

Things did not improve much as the day wore on, and I was not the only Fox family member to think so.

Following a frosty breakfast, during which I managed not to wail in frustration when Sam presented Rosie with a cheap-looking ring that she proclaimed to be the 'nicest piece of jewellery I have ever seen', the morning was mostly taken up with errands to collect platters of food from Elpida and crates of wine from the supermarket. Niko and Socrates' cousin was driving down from Kassiopi to run the taverna kitchen that evening, and Giorgos had been granted a rare night off so that he would be able to attend the party as well.

Rosie, meanwhile, had swanned off in her new purple dress for lunch at the White House with my parents and Sam – an outing that I avoided with the excuse of needing to help Mattie. Not that the island's most capable resident required much assistance. At one point during the afternoon, I pondered aloud if she had ever given any serious thought to retraining as a professional plate-spinner, and got only the briefest smile in reply. In fact, she barely had time enough to glance in my direction. It was only when Fenna showed up that Mattie could finally be persuaded to sit down for a few minutes.

'I'll get them,' I said firmly, as Fenna replied affirmatively to Mattie's offer of a drink. 'I think we've all earned a cold beer.'

I found the fridge in the kitchen stacked precariously full and managed to wriggle out three small bottles of Mythos.

'It's so humid today,' Mattie said, pressing the cold neck of the bottle against her hot cheek. The three of us had come outside onto the terrace, where even in the shade it felt as though you were being slow-dried like Greek tomatoes.

I glanced towards Fenna, who looked party-ready in a jade wrap dress and gold pumps, and raised my drink.

'What are we toasting to?' she asked. Her smile was rather forced. Fenna did not strike me as a woman who played pretend – she was far too straightforward for that. Now, before I could enquire as to what was bothering her, she put her bottle down on the wall and let out a sigh.

'I have some news,' she said.

'Oh?' Mattie's polite reply quivered with trepidation.

'Yes. I am leaving,' Fenna continued without preamble. 'Returning home to the Netherlands.'

'What? Why?'

My sister's dismay had, for once, beaten her faultless enthusiasm to the punch.

Fenna looked at each of us in turn; she appeared to be genuinely sorrowful.

'I thought that I could make a difference here, but I am just one person.' She half-shrugged. 'I feel as if I am, you know, treading water. Life is happening without me, or that is how it feels. I want to be at the front, making things happen, not at the end of a very long line.'

'But what about the cats?' Mattie said. 'Who will look after all the strays?'

'Kostas from the supermarket says he will take over. And I was hoping you would agree to help him,' she added, although I noticed that she could no longer meet Mattie's eye.

Sensing my sister's mounting panic, I asked, 'Do you not even want to see out the summer? Stay for the good weather at the very least.'

Fenna picked at the label on her bottle.

'No, I don't think so.'

'Well, I guess if you've made up your mind,' Mattie began, only to lapse into silence as her features contorted with misery. It seemed to me as if there was a battle going on inside her head, between the words she wanted to say and those she thought she should. I was surprised that the former won.

'I think you're making a mistake,' she remarked.

Fenna looked taken aback.

'Really?' she said, and Mattie nodded.

'Yes, I do. As a matter of fact, I think it's a crazy idea. I think you should stay. You love it here – you're always telling me so.'

I felt suddenly as if I shouldn't be there, as if theirs was a private conversation that I had stumbled into unawares. There was an undercurrent of something that was not being said, and I could feel the tension rising, the atmosphere so taut that I could have struck a match against it.

'I'm not sure if there is anything here for me,' Fenna protested. 'I thought that maybe there was, but I was mistaken.'

I wondered if she had been in a relationship with someone local that had ended abruptly; it certainly sounded as if that might be the case. But then again, there was none of the hurt bewilderment that came with heartbreak – at least not on Fenna's side. Mattie, in contrast, looked as if she'd wandered into a school disco and discovered the boy that she had a crush on was slow-dancing with someone else.

'Don't be silly, there's plenty here for you,' she told Fenna, taking a rather aggressive swig of beer. Pieces of her fringe were plastered to her forehead with perspiration, and she pushed them away in irritation as she spoke. I opened my mouth to say something, then thought better of it. Fenna was clearly uncomfortable; her fingers were still picking, her manner shifty as if she had been caught in a lie. With increasing desperation, Mattie continued to list all the things she believed her friend would miss about the island, eventually running herself aground when they moved from valid to ludicrous. Not once did she say what I guessed she was really thinking, what was at the root of her upset, and so eventually I decided to take matters into my own large mouth.

'The point I think my sister is trying to get across,' I said, 'is that she's going to miss you if you go.'

They both gawped at me.

'That's true, isn't it, Mattie?'

'Well, yes, but it's not the only reas—'

'But it is the main reason?'

I didn't understand her reluctance – why was it so hard for Mattie to admit that she would miss her closest friend? Fenna had not said anything for some time. The label of her bottle was all torn away, and she had begun to peel off the residual glue.

The terrace door opened behind us, and Ophelia emerged. 'Oh,' she said. 'There you are. We just got back with the last of the food.'

My treacherous heart had soared at the 'we' because I knew it referred to herself and Niko. Ophelia had begun helping out at Elpida more often, the Instagram account she had once populated with selfies taken over by a predominance of the delicious Greek dishes she was being taught how to create. Working had given her a purpose, and she had once again begun to glow with the vitality I remembered her having as a child.

'What's the matter?' she asked Mattie. 'Has something happened?'

This was another thing that had changed about Ophelia – she had ceased to be so caught up in herself and was beginning to pay attention to those around her again.

'Nothing – it's fine. I'm fine,' blustered Mattie, then promptly burst into tears. Covering her face with her hands, she let out a moan of frustration and hurried away down the steps towards the pool.

'Was it something I said?' Ophelia looked at both of us enquiringly.

'I've just told her I'm going back to the Netherlands,' Fenna said.

Ophelia nodded. 'That's a shame,' she said. 'Did something happen?'

Fenna shrugged. 'It is just time,' she said.

'Why did you come to Corfu in the first place?' Ophelia asked.

It was a question I had not thought to ask her myself and I was intrigued to hear Fenna's answer.

'For the same reason that many people run away,' she said. 'Because my heart had been broken.'

'By someone in the Netherlands?' Ophelia guessed. 'Then why go back?'

Fenna sighed again. 'It used to be that I was afraid to go home, in case I saw my former partner, but that is no longer the case. She cannot hurt me because I don't love her any more.'

'I guess that's a good thing,' Ophelia mused. 'But then, if she was your reason for running away from the Netherlands, who is behind your decision to leave Corfu?'

Fenna looked stricken. 'I cannot . . . Nobody. It is nobody's fault except mine.'

'I'm going to find Mattie,' I said decisively.

'*Ochi*.'

With a start, I wheeled around to find Niko standing behind us in the open doorway. He was wearing jeans, a faded red T-shirt, and an expression that told me he had been there for some time.

'Do not worry,' he said. 'She is my wife. I should be the one who goes after her.'

43

I should have known better than to let Sam carry the birthday cake outside.

There was something that felt entirely predictable about the way it wobbled and then fell with a resounding splat onto the concrete, instantly transformed from a glorious centrepiece into a sad mess of pale sponge and lemon icing.

Rosie gasped, Niko swore, Dorothia blew out a smoke ring, and I reached for the nearest bottle of red wine.

'I'm so sorry everyone.' Sam did not look or sound remotely contrite. 'Fell over my own feet.'

'Oopsy,' trilled my mother, who had been drinking since lunchtime. I watched in silence as my father hurried forwards and bent to examine the damage.

'Probably a few mouthfuls of it still salvageable if anyone's game?'

Niko's eyes met mine.

'Da-ad.' Mattie had dashed inside, and reappeared now with kitchen roll and a dustpan. 'Don't be silly. There's plenty of food – no need for anyone to eat anything off the floor, even expensive cake.'

'Seems like an awful waste.' He pouted.

Ophelia, who had wandered over from the pool area to see what all the fuss was about, pulled a face and hurried back the way she'd come. Giorgos was sitting on a lounger by the far wall and patted the space beside him as she approached.

I glanced across at Rosie to see if she had noticed, but her attention was focused solely on Sam.

'It's fine, honestly,' she was assuring him. 'I prefer brownies anyway.'

Sam fished his rolling tobacco out of his pocket and began the process of constructing a cigarette. He had unearthed a rather crumpled blazer from somewhere and was wearing it over an open white shirt, his heavy brown fringe pushed to one side and oily with product. Rosie sidled in next to him, all legs in a pink rose-patterned jumpsuit with spaghetti straps and a scooped back. She had spent the best part of an hour curling her hair with the help of a YouTube tutorial, before applying more make-up than I had ever seen her wear. I did not think she needed much enhancement but knew better than to say as much. Relations between the two of us still felt precarious, and I was determined not to have so much as a single cross word with her during the party. The issue about the proposed gap year in Thailand would have to wait until the following day.

As well as the assembled Balaouras and Fox families, Rosie had invited a group of Giorgos's Greek friends and Fenna, while Kostas from the supermarket had brought along his wife Maria and their seven-year-old daughter Eirene. The little girl had thrown a tantrum shortly after arriving because she was told categorically not to jump into the pool in her party dress, then the wails had increased when her father was forced to prise one of Sam's brownies out of her hands.

'If she has too much sugar, she will destroy the whole house,' Kostas said, his laughter nervous enough to convince me that his statement carried merit. Eirene, who had squirmed out of her father's grip as he deposited chunks of mashed-up brownie onto an empty plate, made a lunge for a full packet of Lay's crisps and ran cackling with it into the shrubbery.

'She's a . . . character,' I murmured to Mattie. 'You forget what a handful they can be at that age.'

'We were never like that,' she said.

'No,' I agreed. 'We were way worse.'

My mother tottered over on her wedge heels. 'Good news,' she said, addressing Mattie and ignoring me. 'I found another packet of birthday candles in the drawer by the sink, so we can stick a few into a brownie for Rosie to blow out.'

'I'm not sure I want to encourage any wishing from her tonight,' I muttered, taking another large sip of wine. As I'd abstained from alcohol for most of my time in Corfu, it was hitting the spot at a speed that should have concerned me. For once, however, I was more than ready to fully embrace the wooziness. I needed to relax, and the wine was helping me do so. Everyone else had been drinking for hours now – except Ophelia. I had half-expected her to fall back into her old ways when dropped into a social situation such as this, but every time I checked, she appeared to be clutching the same bottle of water. She had barely looked at Sam in the time we had all been out around the pool, but as far as I was aware they were still sharing a room. Rosie assured me it was a purely platonic arrangement nowadays, but it would not have surprised me if Sam was finding a way to not only drop his cake but have it and eat it too. He was one of life's takers, a vulture who would continue to pick until he got what he wanted. It was part of what unnerved me about him, the sense that he was never quite satisfied, and that he would stop at nothing to improve things for himself, no matter the cost to others.

Mattie was helping my mother with the candles, and both were so engrossed in their task that they failed to notice

Thaddeus, who had sneaked away from his mother to help himself to a meat skewer. Niko had prepared a selection of pork and swordfish souvlaki alongside the chicken option, as well as a sticky mound of dolmades, several vast platters of Greek meze and a mountain of warm pitta to dip in his own-recipe tzatziki, taramasalata and melitzanosalata. There had been much fanfare earlier in the evening when Giorgos arrived with an octopus he had caught specially for the occasion, and Niko had taken it from him and transferred it straight to the barbecue. He was far more comfortable in chef mode than he was standing around making small talk, but I noticed that Dorothia had not left his side since she arrived. Seemingly immune to the heat of the evening, she was channelling Cruella de Vil in eye-wateringly tight black jeans, pointed boots and a long white blouse daubed with red splodges. It looked as if someone had had a good go at her with a carving knife.

I had been wary of Dorothia since I witnessed her hostility towards Mattie at that first Friday night dinner – but we had reached an uneasy détente since the day Rosie had gone missing and she'd stepped in to allow Niko to help me. Her attitude towards me remained one of cold disinterest, or so it felt, but that was preferable to the blatant scorn that Mattie had to tolerate. It was quite possible that the coals on the barbecue had been kept smouldering purely by the venomous looks she kept directing towards her eldest son's wife, as poor, roughshod Mattie scurried around topping up glasses, clearing away plates, and generally being the perfect hostess.

I toyed with the idea of asking Dorothia to explain her animosity towards Mattie, but was reluctant to approach her while she remained within Niko's earshot. Instead, I reached for more wine.

'Where's the birthday girl?' called my mother, wafting past me in a cornflower-blue shirt-dress. My father had been bullied into a tie but had long since taken it off and stuffed it into the breast pocket of his shirt – which, I realised as he shuffled over from the step he'd been lounging on, was covered in pictures of goldfish. Socrates clapped his hands as Rosie stepped forwards ready to blow out her candles, and Mattie called across to Giorgos and Ophelia to come and watch.

'Don't forget to make a wish!' my mother said gleefully as Rosie handed her glass of champagne to Sam. Shutting her eyes, she murmured a few unintelligible words before opening them again and blowing delicately at the flames in front of her. As the smoke curled up, I looked across at Niko and saw that he was staring back at me, not in the pained and regretful way I had become so accustomed to, but with a simple happiness that made the years fall away. He was transformed then into his nineteen-year-old self; the mischievous boy who had burrowed his way deep into my affections and stayed there ever since.

'Mum!'

It was Rosie, right beside me with two large squares of gooey chocolate brownie.

'I couldn't possibly,' I said, shaking my head as she pushed the plate towards me. 'I had too much souvlaki. I'm stuffed.'

'You have to,' she insisted. 'It's my birthday cake. If you don't eat some, my wish will never come true.'

If her wish involved Sam in any way whatsoever, then I did not want it to.

'Your proper birthday cake ended up demolished,' I pointed out, and she groaned.

'Go on, Mum – they're delicious. I've had three bits already. It would mean a lot to Sam,' she said, before hurriedly adding, 'and me.'

I sighed.

'Please!'

'Fine,' I said, accepting the plate. 'But if I pop the button on these trousers, then I'll know exactly who to blame.'

I picked up one of the squidgy brownies and held it between my fingers before taking a bite. As I chewed and swallowed, I became aware of Sam giving me a discreet thumbs-up, and for a fleeting second or two, I wondered if he'd dropped the cake just so he could watch me eat what he'd prepared instead. But that made no sense.

Because why on earth would Sam care if I ate his brownies or not?

44

I didn't think I could remember a time when I had been this relaxed.

It felt as if the tight ball of angst that I had carried with me for most of my life had unfurled, and I was lighter, freer. This new me was not agitated or irritable, she was calm – and she could see things: strange, beautiful things, like the colours in music and the wonder of nature. I felt like I had been let into a very special secret, and while I wanted to tell people, I also could not muster the required effort it would take to move. The chair I had lowered myself into was too comfortable, the sensation it offered me too wonderful to risk abandoning. Whenever I looked up at the night sky above me, it seemed to expand. I knew that if I stared hard enough, if I gazed with my heart as well as my eyes, that I would be able to see the planets beyond the stars.

The goldfish on my father's shirt were swimming. I could see the ripple of their fins as he spun around and around in a dance. Watching him made me happy, perhaps happier than I had ever been before, and for a while I got lost in the swirl of him. When I shifted my eyes away, the shimmering blue of the pool came into view, its surface never still, always moving, just like Mattie. She was there, sitting at the water's edge, and I smiled across at her. Fenna was there too, right beside Mattie, holding her hand. They loved each other, I thought serenely. That was nice.

There was my mother, a walking threat in her dress the colour of riptides. As she made her way towards me, I felt a tugging sensation, as if I were tethered to a balloon and someone had snipped the string.

'Hello, Ava,' she sighed happily, in a voice that had been dipped in honey.

'Shhh,' I said, putting a finger over my lips.

'Shhh,' she agreed, following suit.

'You're being silly,' I told her, and she nodded.

'So are you.'

'Sit in the chair,' I said, getting to my feet, and added in a whisper, 'the chair is good.'

My mother considered the wicker-framed seat for a moment, then sat and closed her eyes. I knew she would be safe and, satisfied that I could leave her, I made my careful way towards the villa. I wasn't sure exactly what I needed to do in there, only that I would know when I reached it.

The back door appeared to be locked. I stared at my reflection in the dark glass panel, frowning as the butterflies on my top began to bat their wings. That was unusual.

I turned the handle again, but the door remained closed. There were other doors, I remembered. And windows. I decided to walk round to the front of the house, but I could not get past the agapanthus. They blocked my path with their long spiky fingers. No, it was easier to sit down on the floor and wait.

I pressed my back against the cold stone, the throbbing heart of the villa pulsing through me, and held out my hands for the butterflies. I wished they would fly away, but they wanted to crawl all over me. I could feel the tickle of their tissue-thin antennae as they writhed and squirmed.

'Shhh,' I told them. The scratching noise was becoming difficult to screen out. I tried to pull in the strains of music, see the colour of the notes as they drifted past me, but they were as slippery as bubbles.

I heard what sounded like a person running up the steps and opened my mouth in a rasping call. A shadow stretched into the pool of light beside me.

'*Geia sou*, Ava.'

It was Niko.

He crouched and I put my hand on his arm. He was so warm.

'It's you,' I said, poking at his face. 'Niko Balaouras.'

'It is me,' he agreed, sounding bemused.

'Where have you been?' I asked.

'What do you mean?'

'I lost you,' I said, frowning as the truth of my words saddened me. 'I knew where you were, but I couldn't find you.'

Niko shifted into a sitting position, his knee resting against my thigh. 'I was here,' he said. 'I am always here.'

I nodded. Smiled.

'Too much to drink?' he asked, but I shook my head.

'I wanted to bring my wine, but it was too heavy,' I explained, and Niko cleared his throat. 'Or maybe I am too heavy. I ate two of the brownies. Did you try one?'

Niko shook his head. 'I am sweet enough.'

'Funny.' I poked him again, this time in the chest.

'*Ela*,' he said, looking at me with a puzzled expression on his face that made me giggle. 'Why are you here alone, on the floor, in the dark?'

There was an answer to his question, but I couldn't remember what it was, so instead I just shrugged.

'You seem to be very . . .' He searched for the words, 'unlike yourself.'

'Well, that can only be a good thing,' I said. 'Old Ava was miserable, new Ava is happy.'

'OK . . .' he said uncertainly. 'Why miserable? I think, perhaps, you were upset because of the baby? Your ex-boyfriend?'

I frowned hard as I tried to make sense of what he meant.

'Oh!' I exclaimed. 'You mean Paul? No, no – I'm happy about that. Babies are always good news – I'd have ten more of my own if I could.'

I blew a raspberry to indicate an end to the subject, and Niko's frown deepened.

'Ava, are you sure that everything is OK with you?'

He was so close that I felt his breath, hot against my cheek. I had turned away from him, distracted by all the movement among the trees. I was sure that the cracks in the paving stones were whispering to me. I wanted to laugh; it felt better to be happy.

'What is funny?' he asked when I could no longer restrain myself.

'You are,' I said, pressing my forehead against his for a moment. My neck felt heavier than usual, and it was a struggle not to lie down and put my head in his lap.

'Me?' He was incredulous.

'You, me, all of us – so very silly.'

Niko looked at me as if I had grown a trunk and floppy ears. Perhaps I had, I thought, raising my hands to my face to check.

'Shhh,' I hissed.

'*Ela* – are you telling me to shush?'

'No, not you.' I shook my head. The butterflies had fallen silent again, and I breathed out in slow relief. Niko's hand was right next to mine, so I took it, anchoring myself to him and to the world.

'I feel weird,' I said, realising as I did so quite how true it was. Everything I looked at seemed to bend and contort, and

I began to blink furiously, shaking my head in a bid to snap out of whatever trance I had fallen into.

Niko's hand was still in mine.

'It is OK,' he soothed. 'I think perhaps you have had too much of Socrates' punch.'

'No, it's not that,' I said. 'It's the butterflies, they won't stop scratching me.'

Niko raised a single eyebrow. 'These?' he asked, touching the mesh of my top.

I nodded.

'*Ela*,' he said. 'Come here.'

I let go of his hand and moved round until I was kneeling in front of him. Niko put his hands on my waist.

'Lift,' he said, and I raised my arms as he gently untucked my top, peeling it up and over the black vest I had on underneath. The mesh snagged on one of my earrings and he hushed me as I started to panic, stilling me with his closeness, his fingers making the hairs on the back of my neck stand up as he untangled the material.

I lowered my hands, not bringing them to my sides but resting them gently on his shoulders. Niko looked at me, his gaze steady, and for a moment I forgot what it was to speak, or to fear, or to feel anything other than a deep, burning desire.

I closed my eyes as the space between us narrowed to a breath, felt the soft rub of my nose against his, the grout of his stubble.

This was wrong. We could not do this.

My fingers tightened into fists of frustration, every part of me wanting, every part of me knowing I could not. Niko's hands were still on my waist, and a rich, insistent sensation poured through me, weakening my resolve. I started to speak, to say the word that would stop us, then

I heard another sound – running feet, a voice shouting my name.

I stumbled backwards in my haste to stand, falling against the agapanthus as Ophelia rounded the corner of the villa.

'There you are!' she cried, her strained voice stoking my panic.

'What is it?' I asked, as Niko clambered to his feet. 'What's happened?'

'It's Rosie,' she said, her eyes not quite meeting mine. 'You'd better come quickly.'

45

Rosie was curled up in a ball halfway down the driveway, her face buried in the gap between her knees. Giorgos was crouched beside her, as was Dorothia – which was a feat in jeans as tight as hers. She glanced up at me as I hurried towards them and I expected to see judgement, but there was none. She was as concerned as I was.

'Rosie, baby girl,' I soothed, scooting down until I was sitting in the dust. 'What's the matter?'

She raised her head at the sound of my voice, but it was as if she couldn't see me. Her eyes were black pools, and even in the darkness I could tell that her pupils were fully dilated. As fear took over, I felt the strangeness I had been experiencing start to drain out of me.

'It's so dark,' Rosie whimpered. 'I can't get out.'

'It's OK,' I said, wrapping an arm around her. 'I'm here, and your Uncle Niko and Granny B.'

Dorothia raised an eyebrow.

'You're safe,' I added. 'Nothing can get you.'

'Mum?' Rosie seemed unsure if I was who I claimed to be. She placed a hand on either side of my face and stared at me in what I could only describe as terror. Mascara had run down her cheeks, and she had pulled off one set of false eyelashes.

'There are spiders,' she whispered. 'They're crawling all over me.'

As she spoke, she began brushing at herself in a panic, pulling the beautiful hair she had spent so long perfecting and crying 'Leave me alone' in a high, strangled voice that made goosebumps rise on my arms. I turned to Niko.

'She's taken something, or more likely been given something.'

His expression dawned with understanding at the same time as my own.

'Sam,' I said, fury making me sound brittle. 'He must have spiked the brownies.'

Niko nodded once. 'I will bring him.'

He took Giorgos and a nervously loitering Ophelia with him, but Dorothia was reluctant to leave Rosie.

'I saw her behaving strangely, so I followed her,' she explained. 'She told me that monsters were after her or something, that she needed to get to the water, but I manage to stop her here, and then I shouted for help.'

'Thank God Ophelia heard you,' I said, and she smiled grimly.

'*Naí*.'

Rosie had begun rocking, her eyes wide as she stared around at the untold horrors I could not see. I remembered the agapanthus flowers, how malicious they had seemed and how I had been stopped in my tracks as I attempted to pass them. Then I recalled Rosie telling me she had eaten three of the brownies already, and watching as she devoured a fourth. All the time, Sam had been there – he had cheered her on.

I heard raised voices coming from the pool area and tried in vain to make out what was being said. It was hard to tell who was talking over the music, which blessedly no longer appeared to have colours.

How could I have been so stupid? Why hadn't I realised earlier what was happening?

'Daddy,' Rosie started to cry. 'Daddy. I need my daddy.'

'I'm here,' I said, wrapping both my arms around her. 'Mum's here.'

I was finding it hard not to cry myself, such was my fear and fury. Even Dorothia had lost her usual calm, which only made the situation scarier.

Rosie tried to pull away from me, straining at the protective loop of my arms. 'I need to get in the sea,' she cried. 'Get in the sea and wash the spiders away, wash them away. Please, Mum – they're all over me, they're inside me. I can feel them.'

I hated that I couldn't make it stop, hated myself for having failed to prevent this from happening to her. My mother was right: I was a terrible parent. I had been distracted by this island, by my memories, by my own sister's husband. How had I let any of this happen?

The sound of approaching feet made both Dorothia and me turn, and I saw Niko emerging through the darkness, his hand clamped around Sam's arm. Ophelia followed with Giorgos and – I recoiled in surprise – my mother, wearing just her pants, bra and wide-brimmed straw hat.

'Mum?'

Niko cleared his throat. 'She wanted to get into the pool to swim with the mermaids, so we thought it was better if we bring her.'

'Jesus Christ!' I rubbed a hand across my face in agitation, the other one clinging on to a still-scrabbling Rosie. She had managed to get onto all fours and was attempting to crawl down the driveway, moaning that she must reach the sea.

'Sam,' I said, directing a cold glare at him that was returned with one of nonchalance. 'What was in those brownies?'

Sam stared at Niko, and then down at the hand that was still gripped around his arm. 'Butter,' he said. 'Eggs, flour, sugar, a lot of chocolate.'

'And?'

'You mean the magic ingredient? I'm not sure I can tell you what that is – it's a secret.'

'Stop being such a bloody child!' I stormed, and saw Niko move a fraction, his body poised to intervene if necessary. He looked every bit as angry as I felt – perhaps angrier.

'Just tell us, Sam,' Ophelia said. She was attempting to restrain my mother, who had wandered off and was trying to converse with an olive tree. 'You're not doing yourself any favours here.'

Sam sighed, as if he found the whole lot of us tiresome. 'A few mushrooms, that's all. I had a stash left over from Thailand, so I thought I'd chuck them in. I was doing you a favour,' he added, as Niko shook his head in disgust. 'You all need to lighten up a bit if you ask me. And you certainly seemed to be enjoying yourself last I saw,' he added with a sneer.

I felt the heat flood into my cheeks, but it did little to stem my outrage.

'Rosie will be absolutely fine,' he went on blithely. 'Kiddo here was having a great time until everyone crowded around her and sent her onto a dark trip.'

'You sent her onto a dark trip the minute you got here,' I thundered. 'She was on her way to the sea – did you know that? She might have drowned if Dorothia hadn't been keeping an eye on her.'

Niko smiled briefly at his mother.

'You're overreacting,' Sam said accusingly. 'As usual.'

'Oh, for God's sake Sam,' grumbled Ophelia. 'Stop winding everyone up – you're just making things worse for yourself.'

'I'm not sure things could be any worse for him,' I spat.

'This old lady isn't very friendly,' piped up my mother, leaning towards a puckered, mouth-like gape in the trunk of the olive tree. 'Do you think she only speaks Greek? *Geia sou!* I say, *geia sou.*'

'Who else ate the brownies?' I asked Ophelia. 'Is anyone else . . . you know?'

'Dad,' she said. 'I thought he was just drunk, but then he told me there was a little green man trying to get him to play hide-and-seek.'

'Great,' I deadpanned.

'And Socrates,' she added sheepishly. 'I think he must have had quite a few, because he was adamant that if we all strapped ourselves into the sunloungers, they would fly us up to the alien craft he could see hovering above.'

'It's not funny,' I snapped at Sam, who had started to titter under his breath.

He looked at me coldly. 'You should all be thanking me for broadening your minds,' he said. 'Freeing your inner souls. Isn't that right, Lia?'

Ophelia stared at her feet.

'You knew about this?' I exploded, turning my laser beam of anger towards her. Rosie had stopped trying to crawl away, but she was still scratching at her skin, trying in vain to brush away all the non-existent insects.

'No,' she said, clearly offended by the accusation. 'Of course not. Sam and I tried mushrooms in Thailand. They put them in milkshakes over there and . . . well, I found the experience to be quite enlightening.'

'It's all about mindset,' put in Sam. 'You have to ride the wave.'

I laughed in exasperation. He sounded so utterly ridiculous. 'Not very easy to ride the wave,' I pointed out, putting deliberate emphasis on the repeated phrase, 'when you have no idea you're supposed to be. Giving somebody drugs without their permission is not only dangerous and morally corrupt – it's illegal.'

'No.' Sam sounded slightly less sure of himself now. 'Mushrooms aren't illegal – they grow in the ground, for God's sake.'

'That is not the issue; the issue is that you gave them to all of us without our knowledge or permission. I'm sure the police would have a thing or two to say about that.'

'*Naí*,' Niko agreed darkly. 'They would.'

'You're not going to call the police over a silly prank,' Sam said, the challenge clear in his tone. 'Nobody died – and most of you have had a great time tonight, thanks to me.'

As if on cue, Rosie knelt up on all fours, muttered something unintelligible about baby Yoda, and promptly threw up.

'Yes,' I said acidly, scraping my daughter's hair off her face. 'Such a great time.'

'Shhh,' hissed my mother, and giggled like a child when we all looked at her. 'This old lady is trying to sleep.'

I was not sure whether she was referring to herself or the olive tree she was hugging, and decided it was probably best not to ask.

'Will you help me get her up to the house?' I asked Ophelia, who nodded and hurried forwards. Between the two of us, we got Rosie to her feet. I saw Sam wrinkle his nose with distaste as he took in the dirt and bile stains all over her beautiful rose-patterned jumpsuit, and had to clench my teeth so as not to scream at him. Niko had let go of Sam's arm now and was attempting instead to persuade my mother to leave behind her 'new best friend' and rejoin the party.

'Your husband will be wondering where you are,' he said, to which my mother cackled wildly, then just as quickly began whimpering the word 'Angus' over and over. My eyes met Ophelia's and she grimaced in shame. I knew she felt guilty by association, given that it was she who had brought bloody Sam into our midst, and I didn't have the capacity to be gracious about it. Not yet, not when I was still struggling with the residual effects of the brownies myself. Mercifully, the hallucination part of my experience seemed to have waned, but I was still acutely aware of every colour and sound, and I still felt hollowed out inside – light enough to float away into the dark air. Now that I knew why I felt this way, I could fight back against it somewhat, and I urged Rosie to do the same as we shuffled her up to the villa. I hated the idea of so much poison being inside her and was glad she had been sick. Surely, I thought, that would help a bit?

It was several hours before I saw Niko again.

Having helped Rosie into the bed we shared and stayed with her until she fell into a fitful sleep, I wrapped myself in a long cardigan and went downstairs. The party had ended abruptly, but there were still a handful of guests in the villa. Stelios and Thady were asleep top-to-tail on one of the white sofas, Elena cross-legged on the floor beside them, while Socrates lay underneath the coffee table, his loud snores making the glass top tremble. I found Mattie sitting at the kitchen table staring into space, Fenna methodically washing up behind her. There was no sign of my parents, but Ophelia assured me they were safely tucked up in bed.

'I've been checking every twenty minutes or so, but they seem fine,' she said. 'Dad is even smiling in his sleep.'

'Lucky him,' I muttered. I could not imagine finding much to smile about for a while.

The door onto the terrace opened and Niko emerged, his lips spreading into a tight smile when he saw me.

'Giorgos and my mother are packing everything away,' he said, glancing towards Mattie. She appeared to have lost the ability to speak and continued to stare gloomily at a spot on the far wall.

'Is she . . . ?' I asked Ophelia.

'Afraid so – although I think she's over the worst. It took me ages to find her, and when I did, she was attempting to play her own ribs like a xylophone. I imagine she'll have a few bruises in the morning.'

'And where is . . . ?'

'Sam? In our room. I told him it was probably best if he stayed out of everyone's way for a while.'

'Or for ever,' I muttered. 'I would prefer that.'

Ophelia knitted her fingers together and brought her hands up to her chin.

'You know he has to go, right?'

She sighed.

'Come on, Lia – surely even you must see what he's really like now? I know you feel indebted to him, but there comes a point where you have to accept that one good deed does not a good man make. Sam is trouble, he proved that tonight.'

'I know, but—' she began, only for Niko to cut across her.

'No buts,' he said. 'He is no longer welcome in this house. He must go.'

'I must, must I?'

We all turned at the sound of Sam's voice. I watched as he sauntered into view, still in his unbuttoned white shirt, feet bare below his black trousers. Niko was looking thunderous, and I could sense the heat in the villa beginning to rise.

'It's for the best,' I said, adopting what I hoped was my fairest most parent-like tone. 'Everyone is upset, and you being here is only going to exacerbate things.'

'Big word,' he said wryly, but I noticed that he had not ventured any further down the stairs.

'Sam,' said Ophelia, taking a few steps towards him. 'Maybe it's best if you went back upstairs, wait until the morning when things have calmed down a bit and—'

'No.' Niko was adamant. 'He must go. Tonight.'

'Go where?' Ophelia responded, her voice starting to wobble. 'It's the middle of the night.'

'This is not my problem.'

'You can't just throw him out onto the street,' she argued, only to quail at the look on Niko's face.

'He can stay with me,' said Fenna, wiping her hands on a tea towel. 'I have a spare airbed.'

Mattie made a movement as if she was going to get up, then stilled. I had never known her to be so quiet for such an extended period.

'You are sure?' Niko checked, and Fenna shrugged.

'*Ja*, of course.'

Sam curled his lip, not yet willing to admit defeat, but Ophelia threw him a pleading look.

'I still think you're all overreacting,' he said. 'Rosie will agree with me, too, once she wakes up. You'll be in the dog-house again,' he added to me.

'I think you underestimate my daughter,' I replied. 'She's far smarter than you.'

Sam thought for a moment, then said with careful deliberation, 'Yes. She is far smarter than all of us.'

I did not like the sly expression on his face, as if he had his hand poised over the lever of a trapdoor and was about to send us hurtling down into the dark earth.

'Just go for tonight,' Ophelia urged quietly. 'We can perhaps have a rethink in the mor—'

'No.' Niko stepped towards Sam, his fists clenched, and I found myself between them, a hand on each of their chests. Socrates chose that moment to try to sit up, his head connecting with the underside of the glass coffee table with a loud bang.

'Careful,' murmured Sam, quietly enough that only Niko and I could hear him. 'Lift a finger and I'll have no choice but to tell everyone what I saw around the side of the villa tonight. The two of you. Together.'

I felt the blood drain from my cheeks. Niko narrowed his eyes.

'Tell anybody, and I will call the police,' he said, the low growl of his voice loaded with menace. 'This is my country, my home – I know many people. *Katalavaineis*?'

Sam rolled his eyes, feigning indifference. I could sense from the twitch of his body that he was riled, angry, spoiling for a fight. Niko must have been able to sense it as well because he moved a fraction closer, leaning forwards and muttering in Greek.

Then, taking a step back and speaking in a voice loud enough for everyone in the room to hear, he said, 'If you ever come into this villa again after tonight, it will be over my dead body.'

46

The rain started not long after Sam and Fenna left the villa.

I had followed them out through the door onto the terrace, and stood there for some time after they went, waiting until I could no longer hear their footsteps, until all I was left with was the sigh and swish of the sea. Most of the tables, chairs and decorations from the party had been tidied away, but I could still see the strings of fairy lights that had been twisted through the trees, twinkling like fireflies in the dark.

The events of the past few hours felt unreal, as if I had watched them unfold on a television screen, not lived through them. I heard Sam's words over and over – *I'll have no choice but to tell everyone what I saw* – and turned cold with dread. He may have disappeared for the time being, but I knew he would not stay away for long – not now he had leverage with which to further manipulate the situation. He would persist until he got what he wanted, and therefore I was left with very little choice over what to do next. There could be no more debate or distraction: it was time for Rosie and me to go back to England.

The air had cooled in the time I had been in the open doorway. I was moved but unmoving, and I watched as the rain continued to fall. It had begun light, barely noticeable, but it intensified as a streak of the brightest blue tore through the sky, cracking it open with an angry roar of thunder.

The downpour became a solid wall of water. I imagined the scalloped roof tiles above me turning from terracotta to the deepest red.

Steam started to rise from paving slabs that had baked all day, and I drew in the strange metallic scent of it, wishing I could go back to a time when my daughter had not been tricked into consuming hallucinogenic mushrooms, to a place where I had not strayed across the line of propriety. However, I could not deny that during those moments, when I had been scorched by the heat of Niko's touch, the glance of his breath and the intensity of his gaze, I had felt alive – reawakened in a way I had not been since the summer I met him. The sensation had been fleeting, but it had wounded me, and now I was destined to carry the scar of what might have been for the rest of my life.

I heard someone approaching. Not the timid, mouse-like scuttle of Mattie, but a firm, purposeful tread. Niko, when I turned to face him, looked utterly wretched – so much so that I told him so.

'*Entáxei*. I am OK,' he murmured.

He had pulled on a tatty, dark-blue hooded sweatshirt with 'Elpida' stencilled across the front, and his feet were bare. 'You do not need to worry about me,' he added, before looking at me enquiringly. 'Are you OK?'

I considered lying but could not see the point. 'Not really, no. I can't believe I did mushrooms.'

He surprised me then by chuckling.

'It's not funny!'

'*Ela*,' he said. 'I know. But sometimes, the only possibility is to laugh. And I was very angry before, with Sam, but anger like this, it is not good for me. I do not enjoy being unhappy.'

'That makes two of us,' I said drily.

For a moment or two, neither one of us spoke. The sound of the rain was almost hypnotic, and there was a part of me that wanted more than anything to step out from the shelter of the terrace and walk right into the deluge, let it soak my hair, my clothes and my skin, drink it in.

'Mattie is upset.'

I turned back to Niko, noticed the set of his jaw.

'Why?' I asked tentatively. 'Did you two have another argument?'

'*Ela*, no. We do not argue.'

'I heard you,' I said, before I could stop myself. 'I didn't mean to. I was out on the balcony one night, weeks ago now, and the two of you were on the one above me, arguing about trying for a baby.'

I thought I saw the colour drain from his face.

'I'm sorry,' I said. 'I shouldn't have eavesdropped, but by the time I realised what you were discussing, it was too late to say anything and—'

'No.' He shook his head. 'It does not matter that you heard. It is not a secret that I want to be a father, and I do not mind you knowing.'

'You would be an incredible father,' I told him. 'I'm sorry it hasn't happened for you yet.'

Niko tried to muster a smile. 'Do you remember what you said to me earlier, at the party?' he asked.

I considered, rubbing a hand across my tired eyes as I did so. 'Bits and pieces. Some of it is a blur.'

'When I asked you about Paul, and his baby, you said that you would have ten more.'

I laughed. 'Did I?'

'*Naí*.'

'Well, then, maybe mushrooms are a truth drug,' I replied. 'I would definitely have another child – although I might not be able to stretch to ten. I'm not quite as young as I used to be.'

We jumped in unison as another bolt of lightning lit up the sky, the thunder that followed it a crash that seemed to reverberate in the air.

'It's funny, you know,' I went on. 'Before Rosie came along, I'd never given much thought to the idea of babies. I certainly didn't plan to be a mother so young.'

Niko had folded his arms, but now he raised a hand to his face and began stroking his stubble.

'So,' he said, 'Rosie was . . .'

'An accident? Yes. A very happy one, but definitely not planned.' I took a deep breath, staring fixedly out at the storm rather than him as I continued to talk.

'When I left here, after you and I . . . after that, I was in a mess. All I wanted to do was blot out the pain, and Paul was just . . . there. I knew him from before I even met you, and he still liked me. The night after we flew home from that holiday, I went down to the beach where I live in Brighton, and there was a party. I drank too much, he drank too much, things happened, and we didn't take any precautions. It was all over in a matter of minutes,' I said. I could feel Niko's eyes on me, but I didn't turn to face him. 'Never in a million years did I think I could have got pregnant, but as you know, fate has a sick sense of humour at the best of times. And Rosie is my world,' I added, suddenly defensive. 'I would never be without her, or the events of the night that delivered her to me, even if I do have complicated feelings about where it led me.'

When Niko didn't say anything, I turned to find him nodding.

'I understand,' he said, and then, 'I waited for you.'

'What do you mean?'

Niko paused to glance over his shoulder, back into the bowels of the villa, then lowered his voice.

'For three years,' he said. 'I hoped you would return to the island, that I would see you again, but instead Mattie came alone. She told me that you were living with the man that you had loved for years, and that you were a mother. I was . . . it was a very difficult time.'

'But you said—' I began, only for Niko to shake his head.

'*Ela*, I know what I said.'

'I had a schoolgirl crush on Paul,' I told him, feeling the need to explain, to reassure, to say all the things I needed to before I took Rosie back to England. 'But it was nothing compared to us.'

Niko's expression was impossible to read, and I looked away from him, frustrated now at the both of us. The rain had not stopped, and I stared hard at the droplets cascading down off the terrace roof, the scene blurring in front of my eyes.

'I know why I had sex with Paul that night,' I said quietly. 'But why did you choose Mattie? Of all the women in the world, you married my sister. Why?'

Niko did not reply, and I forced myself to look at him again, watched him narrow his eyes as if he was in pain.

'Mattie and me, at first we were friends,' he said. 'She was like you, but not like you.' He shrugged helplessly.

'My mother did not want me to marry her,' he continued. 'But I was angry with you, and I was angry with her as well. I wanted to prove to her that she was wrong, and Mattie was . . .' He cast around for the right word, eventually settling on 'kind'.

'Things happened between us, and it was very easy to be with her. I wanted to have a family, to defy my mother, to do what you had done and begin my life.' He shook his head slowly. 'I was young and foolish perhaps. I believed I could make her happy, but I have failed. I think now that she deserves better than me.'

He was not talking like a man who had given up on his marriage; he sounded to me as if he wanted more than anything to fight for my sister, to fulfil the promise of his vows to love, to cherish, to protect. I thought of what Mattie had so nearly confessed during our drive into Corfu Town, of my suspicions that her feelings for him had unravelled. I could tell him what I knew, pull at the threads of their relationship until holes appeared, but I was incapable. I cared about both of them far too much, and that, in the end, mattered to me far more than anything else.

The rain continued to fall, droplets running like tears across the shutters as the sea far below us swirled black with intent. It felt as though the seasons were shifting. I could smell the scent of change in the air – an ending of sorts to the summer trip that had altered all of us. Corfu had marked my passage into womanhood years ago, and now it punctuated a new phase – one that I hoped would be based not on regret but on reality. It was time to accept that my love story was just that – a story – and that far from having more chapters to come, it had, in fact, come to an end a very long time ago.

47

Nineteen years earlier . . .

Niko was not waiting on the jetty for Ava that night, nor the one after.

As she had no phone number for him, no address other than the taverna, which had remained closed, and no way of knowing when he might reappear in their usual meeting place, Ava had no choice but to keep showing up and hoping. She was desperately worried about him, haunted by the knowledge that he must be grieving the loss of his father, and frustrated that she was unable to offer him comfort. For as long as she could remember, she'd had responsibility heaped on her shoulders as the eldest sibling, her life punctuated by an endless stream of demands and stipulations. She was obliged to be there in a supporting role and took it on with weary acceptance. But with Niko it was different. Ava wanted to step into that more adult position and be there for him, yearned to support him, craved the opportunity to help in any way she could, and not being permitted to do so was excruciating. It made her already fractious mood slide towards outright hostility, and by the third day even Mattie had begun to maintain a safe distance.

In the end, it was a full week until Ava saw Niko again, and she could tell as soon as he made his way along the jetty towards her that he was not the same person. He wore his sorrow like a heavy cloak, his body hunched beneath the weight of it, and when he raised his eyes to hers they were dulled by pain.

'Niko,' she said, clambering up from where she had been sitting, in such silence and for so long, waiting for him. Her legs had grown stiff and she almost stumbled, but he did not reach out a hand to steady her.

'I'm so sorry,' she began, and then all the words of condolence she had been storing up in the time since she'd last seen him spilled out of her in a barely coherent rush.

Niko listened, seemingly unmoved, waiting until she had finished before he spoke.

'Are you OK?'

'Me? Of course, I am. I mean, I've been worried about you, but no, I'm fine. Don't worry about me.'

'What have you been doing?'

Ava was confused by the question, and why he would ask it. Who cared if she had been sunbathing and swimming and falling out with her mother? All that mattered was Niko.

'Oh,' she said. 'You know, nothing special. Just hanging out, worrying about you.'

He nodded, looking not at her but down towards the black swirls of water. It felt strange to Ava, being this close yet not touching him. She wished he would pull her into his arms, allow her to hold him and soothe him and tell him that everything was going to be OK, even if they both knew the latter was a lie. Because how could anything for Niko ever be the same again? His father was dead.

'I don't know what else to say,' she said helplessly. 'I wish I could wave a wand and make it all go away.'

Niko frowned. 'The funeral is tomorrow,' he said. 'In Corfu Town, but very early. I have to . . . I cannot stay for long. I must return home to be with my family.'

'Of course,' Ava agreed, although the thought of him disappearing again so soon made her want to weep. 'Is there anything I can do? Anything you need?'

Niko's expression changed then, his anguish making him look almost wild.

'I need my father,' he said, his voice so brittle that Ava was sure it would crack. She tried to take his hand, but Niko moved backwards away from her.

'Sorry,' she said, hurt now but trying her best not to show it. 'I didn't mean to . . . I'm sorry.'

'Ela.' *He sighed. 'It is not—You do not need to.'*

'I want to help,' she pleaded, but even as she said the words, Ava saw him flinch. Nothing she did or said was helping, but she could not simply stand there and do nothing, not when he was so obviously tormented.

'I must go,' he said, although he made no move to leave.

'Thank you,' she said. 'For coming here tonight. I was so scared that I would have to leave before I saw you again.'

Niko nodded as he chewed on his thumbnail. His usually gleaming black hair was lank and lifeless, his trainers tatty and trailing laces. Ava did not know this Niko, but she longed for him nonetheless, her body not yet attuned to the sensitivities of her mind. It was shameful, she knew, to feel such potent desire for a person so utterly broken, yet still it led her forwards.

'When do you go to England?' he asked, the question stilling Ava as she stepped towards him.

'The day after tomorrow,' she said. 'But I can come back! I still want to travel with you, go and explore the world like we planned. That's all I want, Niko, to be with you.'

'Ela.' *He beckoned her towards him at last, opening his arms and wrapping them around her before pulling her tightly against him. It felt so miraculous that for a moment or two, Ava allowed herself to believe what she had wanted to reassure him of earlier – that everything really was going to be OK. But then Niko's grip on her loosened, his arms drooping to his sides as he rested his forehead against hers.*

'We cannot do as we planned,' he said, so forlornly that Ava ducked her head out from below his so she could see his eyes.

'Well, obviously not straight away,' she agreed.

'No.' He took a deep, shuddering breath. 'Not ever.'

Ava's face turned very hot.

'What do you mean?'

'Because my father—' Niko could not bring himself to finish the sentence. 'I must take over from him in the taverna. It is my business now, mine and Socrates', but he has to finish with his schooling. My mother, our family . . . I must make sure that the business can survive.'

'Then I'll help you!' she said. 'I'm not a very good cook, but you can teach me. Or I can work as a waitress or something – anything.'

Niko was shaking his head. 'This is not what I want for you.'

'Well, it's what I want for me,' she insisted. 'It's my life, Niko – I get to decide how I live it.'

'But you want to travel,' he said. 'This life' – he motioned around him at the dark beach – 'it is not enough for you.'

'Yes, it is. I love this island. I love everything about it,' she said desperately. It was the first time she had come close to telling him how she felt, but Niko did not seem to have noticed. He was still shaking his head, dismissing her words, shutting her out with arms that were now folded resolutely across his chest.

'I know you feel the same as me,' she said insistently. 'I know you do.'

Niko gazed at her, stricken. 'It does not matter.'

'How can you say that?' she implored. 'Of course, it matters – nothing matters more.'

'This is a child's view,' he said bitterly. 'Many things matter, Ava. We are not the most important thing. I must put my family first.'

'Why can't you do both?' she said, exasperation making her pace the width of the jetty. 'You can stay here for your family and

have me, too. I told you, I'm happy to come back and live here. I don't care about travelling, or university, or anything else.'

'Stop, Ava,' he said. 'Enough. You are making this difficult.'

The implication behind his words was enough to stop her in her tracks. 'What do you mean "this"?'

'You will go home,' he told her, 'And I will stay.'

'And if I don't agree? If I come back anyway?'

Niko lifted his shoulders in a shrug. 'I must put my family first,' he said again. 'My mother . . . she will not accept you. She has lost her husband and I cannot disappoint her now. It has to be this way.'

Ava could not hold back her tears any longer, and when she began to cry it was with great angry sobs. For a moment, Niko looked as if he was wavering, but then he shook his head, turning away from her so that Ava was forced to grab his arm.

'Wait!' she said, wiping furiously at her cheeks. 'You can't go now, not like this.'

Niko pulled gently away, his head bowed and his eyes down.

'This can't be it,' she wept, not caring now how unhinged she sounded, how racked with self-pity she had become.

Niko reached the far end of the jetty, where the rustic wooden slats met the hard pale stones, and she almost fell as she hurried after him.

'If you really cared about me,' she said, 'you would tell your mother about me; you would find a way to be with me no matter what.'

He turned to face her, the hardness of his gaze ripping apart her final shreds of hope.

'No,' he said, with a steely determination so cold that it felt to Ava as if an ice pick had been driven straight through her heart. 'This thing with us – it was just a game, something to pass the time.'

Ava tried to breathe and found she couldn't.

'But I love you,' she whispered, needing to say it, needing him to understand. 'And you love me. We love each other.'

Niko winced then, as if the mere notion disgusted him.

'You are wrong, Ava,' he said, his features gathering together into a tight knot. She tried in vain to reach him, to talk over him, to do whatever she must to eradicate the heinous truth that she knew he was about to tell her, the final devastating blow that only seconds later would bring her keening to her knees. Four awful words that she would never forget.

'I don't love you.'

48

Exactly as I had grimly predicted, Rosie was furious when she discovered that Sam had gone – and matters did not improve when I told her I'd booked us a flight home.

'What? For when?'

I took a fortifying breath. 'Tomorrow evening.'

'But . . . You can't do that. You promised we'd stay.'

'When you were born, I made a promise to myself that I would protect you,' I told her. 'And given what's happened over the past twenty-four hours, that promise has now trumped any other I may have made since.'

The look of outrage she threw me landed like a thump. I felt winded by it, but I did not waver.

'This way you'll get to spend some time with Ally and the gang before you all go off to uni, and you can all celebrate results day together. That'll be nice, won't it?'

'I'm not even sure if I'm going to uni this year any more, remember? I want to go travelling with Sa—'

'No,' I interrupted. 'Don't say his name – not to me, not after he poisoned you, put your life at risk.'

It was impossible not to miss the exaggerated roll of her eyes.

'Oh, pur-lease. You're overreacting. It was just a prank. Sam would never do anything to hurt me; he's my— We're friends,' she continued defiantly.

'A real friend would want what's best for you,' I countered. 'Namely, a university education.'

'There's more to life than just learning stuff out of some old book. Sam says tha—'

'I don't care what he says, Rosie. Not now, and not ever.'

She opened her mouth to retort but I cut across before she had the chance.

'And before you mention Dad, he agrees with me. I spoke to him this morning and he's holding off from transferring you any birthday money.'

'Then I hate him,' she said, throwing back the bedsheet and flouncing across the room. 'And I hate you, too.'

I waited a few moments before I followed her, my eyes meeting Mattie's bloodshot pair on the landing as Rosie hurried past her and went down the stairs, her mobile phone pressed to her ear. Whoever she was calling must not have answered, because a few seconds later, she swore in earnest.

'Rosie,' I snapped, more loudly than I had intended. 'Language.'

A door slammed.

Given that she was still in the vest top and shorts I'd helped her change into the night before, I didn't think there was much chance that she would leave the grounds of the villa – not even to find Sam – but I thought I had better make sure. Stepping over the puddles decorating the pool area a few minutes later, I sat down beside her on one of the loungers.

'Go away,' she muttered, from within a tangle of arms and tousled blond hair.

'I hate it when we fight,' I said. 'I don't want this to be the way we start your eighteenth year in the world.'

She sniffed.

'You should have thought about that before you sent Sam away.'

'I didn't. It was Niko who told him to go, and it is his house,' I pointed out. 'He was really worried about you – we all were. Well, maybe not Granny, but that was because she was trying to commune with a tree.'

Rosie lifted her head.

'What – really?'

I smiled and pressed my shoulder against hers. 'Really.'

'I wish I'd seen that,' she said, lowering her chin until it was resting against her bent knees. 'I don't really remember much, to be honest. It's all a bit of a blur. I didn't do anything, like, really embarrassing, did I?' she added, suddenly going pale.

'You were fine,' I assured her. 'I think you had what they call a "bad trip", but it didn't last very long. I was seeing stars and you were seeing spiders.'

'See,' she said triumphantly. 'Nobody was hurt. Sam would never have meant to cause trouble. Have you forgotten what he did for Lia, how he saved her from those men in Thailand?'

I decided against responding to this, and for a while neither one of us spoke. The morning had begun overcast, but now the sun had started to emerge from behind clouds that were stringy and grey. Everything seemed cleaner, laundered by rain that had fallen for six solid hours overnight. I wished I could wash away Rosie's resentment towards me as easily. The more I considered what Sam had done for Lia, the less sense it made. I found it hard to accept that he would do anything simply out of the kindness of his heart – not unless he was sure of getting something in return. But then again, he had, hadn't he? He had got free accommodation on a Greek island for the summer, and unfettered access to a beautiful and foolishly besotted young woman.

'If this thing . . . this friendship you and Sam share is the real thing,' I said hesitantly, 'then I'm sure he'll stay in touch. He must have a mother somewhere who'd like to see him. Where are his family based? Does he ever say much about them?'

Rosie squinted down into the pool. Nobody had pulled the cover across it the previous night, and the surface of the water was a mess of twigs and leaves. In the far corner of the terrace, a large inflatable ring had become snagged on a potted cactus, and now lay sad and empty on its side.

'His mum remarried years ago, and they barely speak,' she said. 'I'm not sure where his dad is – whenever I ask, he just pulls a face. I don't think they're exactly chummy. I know he inherited some money from another relative, and that's what he's been using to travel, but not much else.'

'Where did he grow up?' I pressed, remembering how Paul had been unable to find any trace of Sam online.

'Like, the Buckinghamshire area I think,' she said, forehead wrinkled in concentration. 'Either that or Surrey – I can't remember what he said.'

I made a mental note.

'What a shame,' I said distractedly. 'About the family estrangement, I mean.'

Rosie nodded. She seemed to be debating whether or not to say something. 'It's the thing that bonded us,' she admitted. 'In the beginning, family was what we talked about most. I told him about you and Dad splitting up, and he could relate, you know? He understands what it is to come from a broken family.'

Again she had stung me, and once again I had to take a moment to compose myself.

'I'm sorry that your dad and I couldn't make things work.'

Rosie slid her hands into her hair and pulled it forwards until it obscured her face. 'It's not just that part of my family that was broken, though, was it? Until this summer, I barely knew my aunties either and I'd never even met Niko in the flesh. And that is weird, Mum,' she added. 'Most people don't wait seventeen years to meet their closest family members.'

'I know,' I agreed. Because she was right, of course. She lifted her head and fixed her eyes on me. I could feel the weight of her stare, of the question she was asking, and hated myself for letting her down with silence.

'It's getting hot,' I said. 'Why don't we do something fun with our last full day? We could borrow the jeep and drive up to Kassiopi for lunch?'

Anything to get her away from Kalami and the ever-present risk of Sam.

'I don't want to leave,' she said. The sourness had returned to her tone, and when I scooted closer in towards her, she moved irritably away.

'Don't bother,' she said, when I started to apologise. 'All you ever do is say sorry, Mum. But if you're so sorry, why don't you change the way you behave? You have been making bad decisions for years. It was your choice not to see Mattie, never to come and visit her and Niko, it was your choice not to even try to love Dad any more. You're the one that always picks fights with Granny, and the only reason I even applied to university in the first place was because you decided I should. But here's the thing, Mum – not all your decisions are good ones. Some of them are dumb and make no logical sense. In fact, most of them are. So, I don't see why you should be the one who gets to make mine for me any more. I'm eighteen now, I can choose who I see, where I go, and what I want to do with my own future. It's not up to you who I am.'

'This isn't you talking,' I said. My cheeks felt hot, and I knotted my fingers together to quell my emotions. The last thing I wanted was another argument, but I also could not beat down the urge to defend myself. 'These are Sam's words,' I said. 'Not yours.'

It was the wrong thing to have said.

Rosie stood up and stared down at me, her face a mask of barely contained fury and – even worse – pity. She pitied me; my own daughter thought I was pathetic.

'What happened to you?' I asked her. 'Why are you being like this?'

'Like what – honest? All I've done is tell you how I feel. I'm still the same person I always was, just a bit braver, that's all.'

'No.' I shook my head. 'This isn't you. You would never say these things, would never be so cruel. You've changed, and do you know what? I don't like this new you very much. It's why I have no choice but to take you home, Rosie, because this place, for whatever reason, has turned you into someone hateful, spiteful, and more than a little bit entitled.'

I had never said anything so harsh to my daughter before, and the shock of my words hit us both with force. Almost immediately, I realised I had gone too far, but she did not let me begin to say how sorry I was.

'All I've done this summer is grow up,' she said. 'And if I have become hateful, well, I had a good teacher all these years. Because who do you actually love, Mum? Not Dad, not your parents or your sisters, nobody you work with – you don't have any friends.'

I wanted to shout over her that she was wrong, that it was precisely my love for most people that caused me to keep them at arm's length, that in the end, I didn't matter at all anyway, because all that really mattered to me was her – my girl, my Rosie.

'You hate yourself most of all,' she whispered, as if she had only now, in this moment, figured it all out.

I shook my head. 'No. No, I . . . I don't.'

'You do,' she said, more firmly now. As my demeanour had crumpled, so hers had swelled. There was a confidence in her manner that I lacked. I should have stood up, made myself taller than her, challenged her – but I felt too broken.

'I haven't changed,' she said, waiting until I met her eyes before she delivered her parting shot.

'But do you ever think that maybe you should have?'

49

I did not go back into the villa.

Rosie had made it very clear that she wanted to be alone, and for the first time since I had held her in my arms at the hospital a little over eighteen years ago, I was glad to oblige. While my daughter had lashed out verbally before, any previous arguments between the two of us had never been anything more serious than the average teenage boundary-testing – a squabble over pocket money or agreed curfew – but this felt different. Never had she been so calculated in her choice of words, or the manner in which she delivered them; Rosie had set out to hurt me, and she had succeeded.

I knew that Mattie would be bound to come outside in search of me soon enough, and it was this that persuaded me to my feet and down the winding driveway towards the village. Conversation was not something I felt able to face, the clamouring of thoughts inside my head too loud, the sense of regret too bitter. Rosie had been right – I did hate myself; had for so long been unable and perhaps unwilling to forgive myself for never telling Mattie the truth, for allowing her to become a stranger to me. She was disappointed in me; I was a disappointment.

I did not want to leave this island either. Rosie was not alone in that. Given the choice and taking all the other people in my life and all the other responsibilities I had out of the equation, I would have happily remained in Corfu for ever.

I started to make an inventory as I walked, taking mental snapshots to create a collage of all the things I would miss about the place. There was the narrow white house with the blue shutters, a weather-beaten table and chairs propped outside on its mosaic-stone patio, a corrugated metal awning turned amber by rust; trailing power lines and air-conditioning units that hummed like sated bees; lilac fingers of jacaranda, mottled paving stones in squares of yellow and red, a small fishing boat belly-up in the undergrowth, jars of shells on windowsills framed by twists of ivy.

Making sure I did not venture too close to Elpida, I crossed from the road down onto the beach, and stood for a moment absorbing not just the view across the water, but the soft salty scent of the air, and the myriad sounds of shifting sea, displaced pebbles, the muted call of birds and thin strains of music. A couple had rented kayaks and were carrying them down towards the shoreline, while a boy of no more than four or five was pulling a rudimentary net through the shallows. Life, in short, continued to unfurl around me, exactly as it would when I was no longer here to watch.

Having fixed on the furthest jetty as my destination, I walked slowly along the curving lip of the bay, stopping at intervals to gaze up at a sky no longer blemished by clouds, then lowering my eyes when I remembered that I would soon be soaring through it. The flight I had booked for tomorrow evening was not going to be an enjoyable one, but it was unavoidable. I had to get Rosie away from Sam, and I also needed to put a safe distance between myself and Niko. We had grown too close, and I knew that the longer I remained, the harder it would be to leave him behind.

A middle-aged couple waded into the water ahead of me, he full of purpose with a snorkelling mask in hand, while she trailed behind, giggling as she stumbled over the jagged rocks. I wondered how many times they had been to Kalami, whether this was their first visit or if they returned each year, as so many did, lured back by the promise of familiarity. I envied them their companionship, the kind of easiness cultivated over decades spent together. Paul and I never did reach that stage, and I knew it was because I had been unreachable. Yet the reason was not laziness or stubbornness, as Rosie had assumed – it was hope. I had never given up hope that I would somehow end up in the life I had once wanted, and even now, with the flight home looming and the complicated mess of emotions that lingered between me and Niko, it was still there. A tiny sliver of the brightest, shining light.

The jetty was occupied by two sunbathing cats, one of which, I noticed, had a patch of shaved fur and what looked to be the remnants of stitches. A casualty of the mystery attacker, I assumed. With Fenna returning to the Netherlands, I had no doubt that Mattie would step into the role of feline protector – but then who would look after Mattie? She needed an ally and I wished it could be me – but how could it? I had lied to her, betrayed her if not in body, then in mind, and not only over the course of this summer but throughout my entire adult life. My bitterness had eroded the bond we once shared as sisters, and I had allowed it to happen. We may have taken a few timid steps back towards each other this summer, but there was still a very long way to go. To build any kind of new foundation, we would first need to be honest, and I did not know how. The secret that Niko and I shared was ingrained, a part of what held me together, a sinew of my very identity. I was scared what would happen if I gave it up.

Dragged from the depths of my misery by the crunch of approaching feet on stones, I turned to find Dorothia making her way towards me, and immediately assumed the worst.

'What is it?' I asked, adrenaline turning my blood to ice. 'What's happened?'

I had forgotten to revert to Greek, or even to say hello, but this did not appear to faze her very much. Nothing fazed Dorothia very much.

'Nothing has happened,' she said. 'I do not think so anyway. I have not been in the villa today.'

'Sorry.' I shook my head to dispel the images of Rosie, somehow back under the influence of magic mushrooms, about to launch herself off the end of one of the jetties. 'I saw you coming, and I just assumed that— Never mind. My mistake.'

Dorothia peered at me with what looked suspiciously like concern.

'Are you feeling well?' she asked. 'You look a bit . . . grey.' She tapped her cheeks as she said it.

'Grey?'

'*Naí.*' She nodded. 'Grey.'

I shrugged apologetically. 'I didn't get much sleep.'

'I saw you walking,' she explained, with a glance over her shoulder. 'And it made me think of a zombie. I don't know if I am saying the right word . . .'

'You are,' I told her. 'A zombie is essentially a reanimated corpse, so that is probably quite accurate.'

Only by the merest twitch did she betray her amusement. She looked softer than usual today, dressed as she was in a loose, flowing skirt instead of her habitual skintight jeans, while the sleeveless shirt she had tucked into it was a pale lotus pink. Even her bleached hair was pulled back into an elegantly scruffy bun, and she had a patterned canvas bumbag strung round her waist. Digging into it, she produced a packet of cigarettes and a large gold lighter.

'No, thanks,' I said, when she offered me one.

Dorothia arched a single brow and inhaled deeply, a small sigh of pleasure escaping her lips as the same time as the smoke.

'Niko is always telling me to quit,' she said. 'Shall we sit down?'

There was a low tumbledown wall behind us that separated the boundaries of an apartment block from the beach, and Dorothia motioned for me to follow her across to it, slipping off her sandals as she sat down. Given that she had barely spoken to me all summer – aside from a few occasions had hardly even looked in my direction – this turn of events was unexpected, to put it mildly. I was so convinced she was going to tell me off about something that I physically braced myself.

Instead, she said, 'How is Rosie?'

At least she had started with an easy question.

'Angry.'

'With Sam?'

'With me.'

Dorothia took a long drag on her cigarette. 'Ah,' she said. 'This is why you are a zombie today.'

Bending, I picked up a smooth white stone and turned it over in my hands.

'She told me she hates me,' I admitted. 'That I am a hateful person.'

'Why?'

I dropped the stone, listened for a moment to the sound of the sea. 'Because I'm taking her home, back to England. And because I want her to go to university. She doesn't trust me – not any more. She believes that I am no longer qualified to make any decisions about her life.'

Smoke curled in the air between us.

'And what do you think?'

'I think she's probably right,' I said, unable to mask how glum this made me. 'It's not as if I have a qualification in parenting – why should I know what's best for her any better than she does? How do I know if anything I have done over the past eighteen years has been the right thing?'

Dorothia made a tutting noise.

'*Ela*,' she said, reminding me painfully of her son. 'This is what it means to be a mother. Sometimes you must make the difficult decisions because your children cannot, even if it makes you unpopular.'

'I know,' I said. 'But it's hard sometimes – Rosie and I were so close before we came to Corfu this summer.'

The cigarette had burned down, and Dorothia ground it out on the wall. Unzipping her bag, she withdrew a small tin and stowed the butt inside it before sliding out a fresh stick of rolled tobacco to begin the process over again. I looked at the lines around her mouth, the puckered skin that spoke of thousands of greedy inhalations, and experienced a pang of concern. I did not want this woman to come to any harm, and it was not simply because I was worried about the effect it would have on Niko. I wanted Dorothia to remain healthy for her own sake.

'I think when you are a parent,' she said, closing the metal lid of her lighter with a pleasing snap, 'then you cannot also be a best friend.'

I did not agree with her, and my consternation must have played out across my features, because she looked at me askance.

'You do not agree?'

'I would argue that you could be both.'

'*Ochi*. I do not think so.'

Her words had riled me and she must have been aware of the fact, but there was nothing about Dorothia's posture or expression that spoke of regret – far from it. She was unwavering in her self-belief, which I found myself respecting for once. Perhaps because it was so very Greek of her, and so very like Niko, too.

'Maybe it's different with boys,' I suggested. 'I often think that the role of mother is more pronounced for a son than it is a daughter.'

Dorothia considered this, and I was sure I saw a shadow of something pass across her face. She appeared unable to meet my eyes, the hand that held her second cigarette quivering a fraction as she brought it up to her lips.

'Sorry,' I said falteringly, watching nervously as she continued to smoke in silence. 'I didn't mean to suggest that you were a bad mother, or a lesser mother than me, or not friends with Niko and Socrates, or anything bad at all, in fact.'

I had begun rambling but was apparently powerless to stop.

'Niko and Socrates worship you,' I hurried on. 'Those two . . . they would do anything for you.'

'You think that I don't know,' she said, posing it not as a question but a statement.

'That you don't know what?'

'About you and my Niki.'

For a few seconds, I was confused.

'Niko,' she clarified. 'I know. The two of you, that summer many years ago. You thought that you were running around like that all over the island and nobody told me? *Ela* – of course I knew.'

The shock of hearing her admit it so casually rendered me immobile. I gaped at her.

'But . . . nobody knew,' I argued faintly. 'Niko said that—'

'Niki was only nineteen,' she said. 'Still a boy, and not a good liar at all – especially not to his mama.'

I was still trying to comprehend her words when Dorothia touched a hand to mine; her skin felt cool and dry.

'I see you,' she said. 'And I see him with you. The love that you felt as teenagers – it is still there between you.'

I laughed, too loudly. 'I don't love Niko, and he doesn't love me either – not in that way. He's married to my sister,' I reminded her.

Dorothia shrugged. 'So?'

'So? So, Niko and I had a fling, but he told me it was over, that he didn't love me, that it couldn't work after what happened with his father, so I went home to England, got together with the boy I had liked for a long time, Paul, and we had Rosie together. Then, a few years later, Mattie came back to the island, she met Niko, and they fell in love. The end,' I finished firmly, standing up so her hand fell away from mine.

'You are angry.'

'Please,' I implored. 'Stop telling me what I am and how I feel.' I almost followed it up with the caveat 'you're not my mother' but realised in time that this would make me sound every bit like the petulant teenager I clearly still was.

Dorothia looked unfazed. 'You have every right to be angry,' she said. 'You were in love with my son, and I was the one who came between you, the one who put a stop to it.'

'No,' I insisted, shaking my head as I paced up and down in front of her. 'Niko said he had changed his mind, that he didn't feel the same way as I did.'

'*Ela*, Ava,' she said in exasperation. 'He said that to protect me. Leonidas had died, and everything was falling apart in my life. I lost my—'

Her words snagged momentarily in her throat, and I wondered in horror if she might be about to cry.

'Losing my Leo was terrible – *naí*, of course,' she said, pausing to light yet another cigarette. I waited while she steadied herself with a long drag, the process calming her far more successfully than any of my platitudes would have done. In the time since we had crossed from the jetty to the wall, both the sunbathing cats had clambered down and were now rubbing their slim little bodies against the hands of the middle-aged couple I had watched going into the sea. The woman must have popped to the supermarket, because as I looked on she produced a tin of tuna from her bag.

'It was a big shock. To all of us. When something like this happens, it changes everything – it turns over a page that can never be turned back.'

She spoke so eloquently that it was hard to believe English was not her first language.

'I was . . . there was a baby,' she continued. 'I lost her two days after Leo died.'

'Oh no.' I crossed to the wall and sat back down beside her. 'Oh, I'm so sorry.'

'Thank you.' She blew out a solemn plume of smoke. 'Niko, he was the one who found me. The only person who has ever known.'

I pictured his stricken face the night he'd told me we were over, how he had been so adamant that his mother must come first, no matter what.

I slumped forwards; my head felt suddenly too heavy, as if the weight of all my mind contained had pooled like water behind my eyes.

'I had lost my husband and my daughter,' she murmured, talking more to herself now than me. 'I could not lose my son. I had to do whatever I could to make him stay.'

Our silly adolescent plan to run away together, explore the world and to hell with the consequences, had felt so vital to us then. But while I was yet to be burdened by the harsher realities of life, Niko had found himself having to grow into a man overnight. Now, finally, I understood. He hadn't had a choice.

When I turned towards Dorothia, I found her staring out at the view, her eyes half-closed as the sunlight flickered across the surface of the water. I thought about her many snide remarks regarding Mattie's lack of a child, and how she had taken such an interest in Rosie.

'Why are you telling me all this?' I asked.

'Because,' she said, flicking ash to the ground, 'I understand that you are right to protect your daughter, but also that she must be allowed to make mistakes. After Leonidas died, I had to become both *mamá* and *petéras*. I still thought of Niko as my baby. I was very strict with him, you understand why?'

'*Naí*,' I murmured. 'It's what we do, us mothers, when we feel our children slipping away from us – we hold on to them tighter.'

'Yes.' She smiled faintly. 'I squeezed Niko so tightly that I am afraid I crushed his spirit. He is not the same man as he once was. He is not happy.' She paused to extinguish her cigarette, once again stowing the butt inside her tin.

'My mother took the opposite approach,' I told her. 'She never cared how far away we strayed.'

'*Ela*,' she said with a small laugh, then muttered a few unintelligible Greek words under her breath. 'You think your mother does not care?'

'I know she doesn't.'

I could, at least, be confident in this.

Dorothia shook her head slowly from side to side, clearly amused by my statement.

'Why did you come to Corfu this summer?' she asked, and I felt my chest tighten as the truth began to dawn on me.

'Because my mother tricked me into it.'

'Yes.'

I started to say more, only to stop abruptly. My mother could have hatched her house-swap plan at any point since Mattie and Niko got married, if her sole purpose had been to reunite her two eldest daughters. But she had waited until this year, the last summer before Rosie moved away, the final time she could be sure that all of us would be together. But why?

'I think that perhaps your mother sees the same thing as me,' Dorothia mused. She had shrugged off her melancholy mood and appeared to have regained her stride. 'Problems, frustrations, unhappiness, secrets . . .' She ticked each one off with the tap of her bare foot against the pebbles. 'And she wonders if maybe all these things can be solved, once and for all.'

'Then why doesn't she say as much?' I asked in exasperation.

'Ha – because she knows you will probably not listen, or perhaps you are not ready to hear it,' said Dorothia. 'Sometimes we cannot tell our children what to do, but we can try our best to show them.'

'I don't understand, though – what is it she's trying to show me? And why now?'

Dorothia regarded me through eyes that were slitted against the still-beating sun. '*Ela*, Ava,' she said. 'You already know the answer to both those questions.'

50

Going out for dinner was Mattie's idea.

The ideal opportunity for the whole extended family to get together before Rosie and I flew home the following day – a chance to 'make an occasion' out of it, she said. I was not surprised when Elena sent her apologies, explaining that the boys were still tired after the party and that Socrates had a prior engagement. Given that the last time they had chosen to spend time with us all, he had ended up spiked with mushrooms, I couldn't say I blamed them much for choosing to stay well away. I also felt guilty to be abandoning Thady's English lessons so soon after they had begun, although I did offer to continue them via video call once I was back in the UK. It wouldn't be the same, but it was something.

We decided on Thomas's Place, a traditional Greek taverna that had been open for almost as long as I had been alive, and which I doubted had changed much over the years. Unlike several of the other establishments along the Kalami seafront, which had been modernised with sleek chrome and ceiling spotlights, Thomas's Place had retained its rustic charm, with wicker-strung chairs, fishing nets hung on walls, plain white tablecloths and a simple menu that made the most of fresh local ingredients. As the eight of us trooped inside, we passed an open freezer and I saw that day's catch laid across piles of ice, their cold staring eyes still as marble.

'Oh, goody!' boomed my father, who was behind me. 'Swordfish. You still like fish, don't you, Pickle?'

From my other side, Ophelia made a small noise of disagreement.

'I'm a vegetarian, Dad. I stopped eating meat when I was fifteen, remember?'

'Yes, of course,' he blustered. 'I was just hoping you'd grown out of all that nonsense.'

'For God's sake,' I heard her mutter, as we followed a smiling waitress towards a long table at the very front of the restaurant. Dorothia immediately moved towards one end, while my father took a seat at the other. Niko and Mattie moved round to the right side with Rosie, while Ophelia and I headed left, followed by our mother. Bread arrived and, after a brief discussion, so did three bottles of mineral water, a large carafe of white wine and a jug of red.

My mother gave her menu a cursory glance. 'Do you think chef will do me an omelette?' she said.

Dorothia pushed back her chair and lit a cigarette.

'There are so many great options, Martha,' said my father. 'Don't tell me you aren't tempted by a nice bit of local Greek sausage.'

Mattie choked on her water. 'Dad!'

'Sorry, couldn't resist.' He chuckled.

'Why don't we get a selection and share?' I suggested, to which most of the group nodded in agreement.

'I really would rather an omelette,' my mother insisted. 'My stomach hasn't been quite right since the brownies.' She rolled her eyes dramatically. 'I can't abide the idea of anything too rich or oily.'

'I'll just have a tomato and cucumber salad,' said Rosie, who had not spoken to me in more than monosyllables since our argument that morning.

'For starter?' I enquired.

'For main.'

I managed not to say what I was thinking – that a salad was rather a paltry choice for someone who I suspected had not eaten all day – only for my mother to wade in.

'You'll waste away,' she chided.

'If Rosie wants just salad, then that's up to her,' I said. I hoped that if I backed her up she would forgive me, or at least acknowledge me. But Rosie merely began tearing strips off her paper napkin.

'Why don't you order for the table, Niko?'

Mattie grimaced as we all turned to face her. 'I just thought it would be easier.'

'Fine by me,' I said, but my father was frowning.

'I rather fancied the *gavros*.'

My mother pulled a face. 'Must you, Angus? You know how I feel about anchovies.'

Niko topped up his glass. It was unusual to see him drinking. On the rare occasions he indulged, it tended to be a few fingers of whisky, but now he was making quick work of the red wine. I shifted in my seat, uncomfortable on the hard wood and wicker, and tried not to stare at him.

A waiter approached and Niko leaned back in his chair, talking to the man in brisk Greek and gesturing along the table with a sweep of his hand.

'Did he remember my *gavros*?' my father said. '*GAVROS!*' he boomed, drowning out my mother's moan of contrition.

'How much longer are you two planning to stay?' I asked, directing the question at both parents.

'Well, that all depends on Lia,' said my mother. 'And what her plans are.'

Ophelia, hearing mention of her name, looked around me towards the far end of the table. 'What was that?'

'We were just telling Ava that we'll be staying for as long as you need us.'

'Need you?' she repeated. 'Why would I need you? I mean, it's nice of you to care and everything, but I'm fine. I have my work at Elpida and—'

'But that can't go on for ever,' my mother pointed out. 'Niko will close up at the end of the season, then what will you do?'

'I don't know.' Ophelia took several sips of her water in quick succession. 'There must be other jobs, maybe in Corfu Town. I'll find something.'

'What about Thailand?'

My mother's tone had changed; there was more steel in it than I had heard in quite some time.

'What *about* Thailand?' Ophelia asked, placing heavy emphasis on the preposition.

'Don't you think it would be a wise idea to go back?'

My eyes met Niko's; he looked as though he was in pain.

'Why would she do that?' asked Mattie, genuinely perplexed. Rosie had stopped shredding her napkin and was listening intently.

'Martha,' said my father warningly. 'We're about to eat.'

Dorothia crossed one tightly denimed leg over the other and reached for her white wine. She had pulled her platinum hair into a single long plait, which was draped over one of her shoulders. A few days ago, I might have unkindly likened it to a python, but I felt differently towards her since our conversation earlier. The two of us had more in common than I ever would have believed plausible, and I respected her for being honest with me about what she had endured, and the mistakes she had made in trying to control her son.

Niko glanced up once again, as if he could sense my thoughts straying to him, and smiled with a kind of weak exasperation. I understood how he felt, and so I smiled back, for once unafraid of what Dorothia would think if she saw me. She knew, after all. She had always known.

'I'm sorry, Angus, but I've been thinking about it, and I've decided that the best way to deal with all this is to be transparent about it. How can we support Lia as a family when most of the family don't even know the truth of what happened?'

'Mum, please.' Ophelia pinned herself back against her chair, eyes darting like an animal in a trap, searching desperately for an escape route.

I found my voice.

'The truth about what, Lia?'

I was so sure that she was about to bolt that I rested my hand on the back of her chair. My mother breathed out in that fed-up way of hers.

'When your father and I arrived in Thailand and tracked down the last place you'd been living, we were greeted by quite the story, weren't we?'

Lia closed her eyes, shutting us all out, shutting the world out. I recalled what I had overheard that night in the toilets at the bar, and how I had vowed to discover what it was all about only to somehow never find the time.

'As it turned out, Lia had been helping herself to other people's belongings. Stealing.' My mother spat the word out as if it was a rotten anchovy.

'And she wasn't stealing from tourists and travellers, those with insurance who could perhaps afford to misplace a camera or a wallet, but the local Thai people. They had trusted her, invited her into their homes, and she had repaid their kindness by robbing them.'

Ophelia had begun to shake her head, repeating the word 'no' over and over, a mournful mantra that made the back of my nose sting with pity.

'Your father and I paid back what was owed, of course,' my mother went on, busying herself with the task of buttering a slice of bread. 'But we both agree that the right thing for Lia to do is return to the scene of her crime and apologise in person.'

Rosie's eyes widened as she stared down the table towards her favourite aunt.

'I didn't,' Ophelia muttered. 'I don't.'

'Did you know about this?' I hissed across to Mattie, who shook her head. She looked every bit as bewildered as I felt, because she knew just as I did that although Ophelia may historically have been flighty, irresponsible and at times even feckless, she had never been a thief. Nothing about this story was landing right; it was as though my mother was an angry toddler, forcing together jigsaw pieces that did not quite fit.

'And I suppose you have proof of these apparent thefts?' I prompted.

My mother stopped buttering.

'Proof? Why would we need any proof? Lia admitted it all to me the night we arrived. Confessed as soon as I challenged her on it. And before you ask,' she continued, raising a hand to silence me, 'we didn't tell you and Mattie because we wanted to give Lia the chance to do so herself. And I thought she would, I really did. I hate to say it, but I'm ashamed of her. And it's a horrible feeling, you know, to be ashamed of your own child.'

Rosie sought out my gaze then, her expression changing from one of concern for Lia to trepidation for herself. It was all I could do not to stand up and rush round the table to her. I settled on a reassuring smile instead.

'I would have thought you'd be used to that feeling by now.'

Mattie's voice had wavered as she spoke, but she did not back down when my mother threw her an icy glare.

'What on earth are you talking about?'

'You and your shame,' Mattie said, more calmly than I would have managed. 'It's followed the three of us around all our lives, but we've never actually picked apart where it stems from, have we? So, you're ashamed of Ophelia for apparently stealing – if that's even true, which I don't think it is, by the way – and you're ashamed of Ava for what? Not being enough like you? I'm guessing you're ashamed of me for being a pushover, or maybe for not providing you with any grandchildren and being the boring one who settled for the first man who paid her the slightest bit of attention. Yes,' she added, as my mother paled in horror, 'I know how you really feel about us, Mum. We're either too much like you, or not different enough to have learned from your mistakes – and I'm not sure what's worse. Ava and me, we brought each other up after Ophelia was born. We had to stop caring what you thought of us to stand any chance of being happy.'

My mother gawped at each of us in turn. 'And is this how you feel as well, Ava?'

I could practically feel Mattie's gaze as she spurred me on, wanting me to say what I felt, needing me to confront my feelings as she had. It was not like her to poke a rod into the proverbial basket of angry rattlesnakes. On any other day, criticism of my mother would have flowed as rapidly from me as the red wine was into Niko's glass, but I felt suddenly weary at the thought of it. There had been so many terse words exchanged during the past few weeks and I was drained by it all. The conversation Dorothia and I had shared at the beach was still at the forefront of my mind, and I was increasingly beginning to wonder if perhaps I had been too hard on my mother. Had I allowed her to become the scapegoat for everything that had gone awry in my own life? I was almost forty – how much longer could I keep it up?

Unable to formulate any of this into coherent speech, I was relieved to see the waiting staff heading towards us with trays of food. Rosie's meagre salad was slid in front of her, while my father – seemingly oblivious to the fact that in the past five minutes his family had fractured apart – let out a 'hooray' as he spotted his portion of *gavros*.

Mattie looked close to tears, while Ophelia had shrunk into herself, chin down and shoulders hunched.

'What a spread!' declared my father, tucking his napkin into the neck of his shirt. 'Ava, poppet, can you pass me the *gigantes*?'

I reached for the dish of warm butter beans that were swimming in a rich tomato and garlicky sauce and put them down beside him. Niko had also ordered two Greek salads, grilled mushrooms, a portion of French fries, bowls of taramasalata and tzatziki, as well as a vast platter of grilled sardines. It all looked delicious, and although it felt as though my anxious stomach had wizened to the size of a walnut, I helped myself to a little of everything and set about deboning my fish.

'No omelette?' asked my mother, her bottom lip drooping with disappointment. I gripped my fork, becoming aware as I did so of a buzzing noise coming from inside my bag. Whoever was calling, they would have to wait.

Several minutes passed while we all ate in silence. My mother wandered up to the bar and I listened as she placed her order.

'I'd like it to have cheese, onion, peppers, mushroom, ham . . .'

Mattie, meanwhile, stared down into her full wine glass, her expression unreadable.

'I didn't do it.'

I was not sure who had spoken and looked first at Rosie. But she was studying Ophelia, her cutlery abandoned on either side of her plate. My mother returned to the table and sat down with a sigh.

'I said, I didn't do it.' Lia's voice was quiet but steady.

'Now, now, Pickle—' my father began, but Mattie cut across him.

'Let her speak. What were you going to say, Lia?'

Ophelia lifted her chin, defiance giving her renewed strength. Instead of turning to face us, her family, she directed her next comment to Niko, who was sitting directly opposite. She trusted him, I realised – perhaps more than any of us. He had known that she needed more than molly-coddling and, in hiring her to help out at his taverna, he had given her purpose.

'I didn't steal from anyone. I would never do that. I-I couldn't do that.'

Niko nodded, encouraging her with his own brand of kindness, his huge compassionate heart.

'Those people in Thailand, they thought it was me. I let them believe it because I had to.'

'What do you mean, had to?' asked Mattie.

Dorothia's cigarette had smouldered away right down to the butt before Ophelia answered.

'For him,' she whispered. 'I had to lie for him.'

'Who?' said Mattie, but I knew instantly who she meant.

Rosie cleared her throat. She had paled beneath her tan, her forehead a junction of frown lines.

'Do you mean Sam?' I asked softly. 'Was he the one stealing?'

Ophelia nodded. It was barely a movement, but it was all the confirmation I required.

'I owed him,' she said, finally finding the courage to look at us. 'I thought it was only once. I had no idea how bad it was until you got here, Mum, I swear I didn't. He told me he'd made a mistake, that it would never happen again, and I believed him.' She winced as she said the last, appalled, I presumed, by her own naïvety.

'I knew they'd call the police on us, so we ran,' she explained. 'I booked us onto the first available flight, and we made our way here, where I knew you'd look after us.'

She braved a smile in Mattie's direction.

'I'm sorry,' she said. 'I didn't want to lie to any of you, but things just spiralled and Sam . . . he kept on reminding me what he'd done for me, how he'd put himself at risk to keep me safe. I thought it was easier to play along. I never expected you two to turn up having been over there to find me,' she added.

My father, in typical Angus Fox style, had finished the *gavros* while Ophelia had been talking, and we all waited expectantly while he mopped up the oil with a slice of bread. However, it was not either of my parents who spoke next – it was Rosie.

'I'm sorry, Lia, but this all feels a bit convenient. Sam isn't here to defend himself, and you know that everyone at this table despises him. Sounds to me as if you're scapegoating him.'

'Wow,' remarked Mattie. 'Really, Rosie?'

'It's OK.' Ophelia flashed Rosie a rather wan smile. 'I know what he's like – he can make you believe anything, he's a master manipulator.'

'I knew it,' I said, heat and hackles rising. 'I bloody well knew he was bad news. Why would you bring a person like that with you to your sister's home, Lia? Why would you sit there and say nothing at all about his true nature as you watched him wheedle his way into my daughter's affections?'

Ophelia's hand trembled as she pushed her fringe off her face. 'I just . . . I don't know. I'm sorry. I never have been any good at dealing with anything – you know that. Rosie has you to protect her, and I knew right from the start that you didn't trust Sam.'

'You're all wrong about him, you know,' piped up Rosie, with such self-assurance that in any other scenario I might have felt proud. 'He's made a few errors in judgement – so what? He's a good person underneath it all, and that's what matters.'

'Omelette?'

The waiter smiled down at us expectantly. My mother raised a weary hand.

'A few errors?' I said, through teeth that were gritted against outright scorn. 'Stealing from poor Thai people, lying about it, letting Lia take the blame for it, loafing around here all summer sponging off Mattie and Niko's hospitality, leading you astray and, oh yeah, spiking everyone's party food with hallucinogenic mushrooms. Did I forget anything?'

Rosie scowled at me. 'Oh, what?' she demanded. 'And you're so perfect? I know what you did, what you've probably been doing the whole time we've been here.'

'Rosie,' I snapped, but I could see that I had lost her to indignation. In her besotted and clearly manipulated mind, we were all the baddies to Sam's poor misunderstood hero.

'They forgot to add ham,' said my mother, but nobody was listening. Every eye at the table was focused on my daughter, on the lit fuse that was her fury towards not only me, but the person who had sent away the man she liked so very much.

'Sam might well be a liar and a thief,' she said. 'But at least he's not trying to steal his own sister's husband.'

51

A stunned silence followed.

Around us, the busy taverna thrummed with bustle and frivolity, as holidaymakers chatted and laughed, glasses were clinked, and orders were scribbled on notepads.

I felt my stomach plummet.

'Very funny,' I said.

'Is it?' Rosie's defiant demeanour was unchanged. 'I don't see how.'

'It's a load of rubbish.'

I did not look at Mattie, but I could feel her staring at me. My mother, for once, appeared to be lost for words.

Rosie picked up her phone and opened her messages, holding it up so I could see. 'Sam told me. He saw you kissing at my party.'

'He's lying. Tell her, Niko,' I said desperately, willing him to back me up, to do as I was doing and make light of it. The longer he remained silent, the guiltier he seemed.

Niko's features were pinched with misery. He gave me only the most fleeting of glances before turning his attention to Rosie. 'It is not true,' he said. 'There was no kiss.'

'See!' I exclaimed. 'Don't you see what's Sam's trying to do? He's stirring up trouble for Niko because he's angry about what happened – and he's always hated me.'

'No, Mum, you've always hated him,' Rosie corrected, sullen but unwavering. 'You decided not to like him and that was that.'

'Oh, not this nonsense again,' I muttered. 'I did not decide to dislike him – I had a gut feeling that he was not a very nice person. A gut feeling that turned out to be pretty much right, as it transpires.'

'So, you're saying there is nothing going on between you and Niko?' she demanded.

'No!' I cried, exasperation causing me to bang my palms down on the table. I saw my father make a grab for his glass of wine.

Rosie was scrolling through her phone again. 'What about this?' she prompted, holding up the handset. There was a blurred photo on the screen that I had to squint at to see properly. It had been taken through a window and showed myself and Niko, shoulder to shoulder at the sink in the villa kitchen, our arms entwined as I knew our fingers had been. So, it had been Sam lurking in the bushes that night. He had used Ophelia's disappearance as an opportunity to skulk around, looking for leverage with which to manipulate me. Well, I was not about to let him get away with it.

'What about it?' I asked, feigning disinterest. 'It's hardly tabloid-worthy scandal is it, a picture of two people doing the washing up?'

Mattie had leaned across to look and I stole a glance at her expression, trying in vain to read what she was thinking. I wanted her to say something, to shout, to laugh, to react in any way. Her continued silence was unnerving.

'What you should be asking yourself is why Sam was sneaking around in the dark peering through windows,' I said, failing to sound anything other than defensive. 'Doesn't that behaviour strike you as odd?'

Rosie was not ready to back down. 'He suspected something was going on and wanted proof before he said anything. That makes perfect sense to me.'

'Why are you doing this?' I asked, almost pleading with her now. 'This isn't the Rosie I know, the girl I brought up to be kind and good.'

Her eyes widened at the accusation. 'You brought me up to be fair,' she argued. 'To speak up for those who cannot speak up for themselves. It's why I love history so much, Mum, because it's all about learning the stories of those who are no longer able to tell them. I learned my integrity from you, I get my strength from you, but not my honesty. Dad has always told me the truth, no matter what. Can you say the same?'

I deflated, unable to say the single word that I knew to be a lie. Because as much as she was wrong about Sam, she was right about me. I was a liar, had been lying not only to her, but to everyone here, for years. I had even lied to myself.

'Ava?'

Mattie had spoken at last, the pale-green eyes below her dark fringe narrowed not with distrust, but with sympathy. Even now, faced with the possibility that Niko and I had betrayed her, her first instinct was compassion. She was the best of all of us, and she deserved to know the truth.

My phone began to buzz away again from inside my bag and, grateful for the respite it would offer me, I hauled it out.

Paul.

Puzzled, I swiped a finger across the screen. 'Hello.'

'Ava, finally – I've been trying to reach you for ages. Did you not get my messages?'

'Sorry, no.'

I stood up from my chair and went outside. The folded white beach umbrellas looked like sedentary ghosts rising through the gloom, and I walked past them, continuing on until the cacophony of sound drifting out from the taverna was replaced by the purr of the sea.

'We're all out having dinner,' I explained. 'I must not have heard my phone. And listen, Paul, there's something I—'

'Later,' he said. 'First, you need to hear me out. You know how I said I'd looked up Sam online, tried to find a trace of him?'

I felt a coldness creep up my spine. 'Yes, I remember. You came up against a dead end.'

'I thought about what you said, about Sam Adams being a common name – and you weren't wrong about that. But then, I thought, perhaps he had shortened it, so I searched for Sam Adamson, and Samuel Adams, and probably a hundred other variations, and eventually I hit upon something, a Sampson A. Tucker, originally from Guildford in Surrey—'

Paul broke off and I heard what I presumed to be Laura's voice, her tone worried, insistent.

'I know,' he said. 'Don't worry, I'm about to tell her.'

'Paul, what's going on? What did you find out? Is this Sampson person Sam or not?'

'Laura has just been comparing photos from Rosie's Instagram with these old newspaper reports we found, and we both agree that it's definitely the same person.'

My brain had snagged on the words 'newspaper reports'.

'What is it?' I asked, my voice hoarse. 'What has he done?'

'Hang on.' Paul began tapping at something. 'I'll just pull it up on screen so I can read it aloud to you. Here we go.'

I had somehow walked all the way along to the far end of the beach, almost as far as Elpida, and now I turned and retraced my steps, seeing but not registering the reflection of the pale moon in the surface of the water. It had been stifling in the taverna, but out here, at least, there was a breeze.

Paul cleared his throat.

'A young Guildford man has appeared in court accused of a rape that took place a year ago. Sampson A. Tucker is accused of committing the offence against a woman at the home of a mutual friend, during a New Year's Eve party. Mr Tucker, nineteen, entered a plea of not guilty, and his family has strenuously denied any wrongdoing.'

I stopped abruptly, nearly losing my footing as the stones slipped away beneath me.

'I won't read you the follow-up article because it's really long, but he was acquitted. The girl alleged that he assaulted her while she slept, only there was evidently reasonable doubt enough to convince the jury he wasn't guilty. But Ava,' he said, 'it's him. He wasn't pictured in the news reports, but he is on other local sites. Apparently, Sampson was quite the talented water polo player in his school days. There are plenty of photos of him holding trophies aloft with his top off, if you want me to send them over?'

'No,' I said. 'No need. I trust you.'

'I knew it,' said Paul. 'I had a hunch that there was something not right about him, and I know an acquittal doesn't exactly scream guilt, but in so many of these cases, it becomes a "he said, she said" situation. And he still changed his name. The more you read about the story online, the murkier it gets.'

'Oh, don't worry,' I said grimly. 'It's not me you're going to have to convince. Rosie is completely under his spell – we were having another row about it when you called, in fact. Can you send me a link to the articles you found, so I can show her?'

'Of course.' Paul paused. 'And Ava?'

I had set off back towards Thomas's Place, my strides as long as I could safely make them across the uneven ground.

'Yes?'

'Be careful. If this bloke has been using a different name, he is not going to be very pleased when all this comes out. Promise me you won't let Rosie out of your sight until you're on that plane tomorrow?'

'Of course,' I told him. 'I promise.'

52

The mood at the table had shifted in the time I had been gone.

The starters had been cleared away and the jugs of wine replenished, but there was no chatter. Every pair of eyes that glanced in my direction did so warily, as if my return was about to become the catalyst for yet more unrest. And while I hated to disappoint them all by living up (or down) to their dire expectations, I needed to share the information I had gleaned about Sam immediately.

I took my seat, hanging my bag on the back of the chair but keeping my phone in my hand. True to his word, Paul had sent through not only links to the articles, but screen-shots of them too. I shot a meaningful look at Rosie and was about to reveal what I had discovered when my mother reached across and put a hand on my arm.

'Mattie was just in the middle of telling us something,' she said.

'Oh.' I reddened as I remembered what had been said not ten minutes before. 'Yes, of course. But it's just that—'

'Ava, your sister has something to ask you.'

This had come from my father, who for once looked grave.

'I just need to talk to Rosie about something first,' I insisted, and saw my daughter's gaze flicker up towards the ceiling – a gesture that illustrated exactly how uninterested she was in anything I might have to say.

'It's important,' I added. 'That was Paul on the phone and—'

'Ava, please let me speak.'

Mattie's tone was far gentler than that of either parent, but I could tell she was determined not to let me win this round. Niko, on her other side, was staring fixedly into his half-empty glass.

I nodded. 'OK, I'm listening.'

Beside me, Ophelia lifted her knees until they were under her chin and wrapped her arms round her legs, pulling them against her body. Everything about her posture radiated discomfort. Dorothia, in contrast, was leaning back in her seat at the head of the table, outwardly relaxed despite the palpable tension. Catching my eye, she gave me the ghost of a smile – a signal of encouragement, I supposed, to finally tell the truth.

'Has anything ever happened?' said Mattie. 'Between you and Niko, I mean?'

I took a breath, closed and then opened my eyes.

'Yes.'

Ophelia let out a small gasp, as did my mother, but I did not turn away from Mattie.

'When?' she asked, her voice barely audible. Niko shook his head and began muttering under his breath.

'The first summer we came here. I . . . He was . . . well, I guess you would call him my summer fling. You knew about it, remember? But I never told you who it was,' I added. 'We kept it a secret.'

Dorothia cleared her throat, loudly enough for Mattie to hear.

'Sorry,' I corrected. 'We thought we'd kept it a secret, but as I discovered earlier today, Dorothia was fully aware.'

Niko's head snapped up and he glared at his mother.

'*Ixeres*?' he said, dumbfounded. 'You knew?'

She shrugged, cigarette in hand. '*Naí.*'

Mattie looked on the verge of tears. I did not dare so much as glance at Rosie. The shame was too great. It burned through me like battery acid.

'I don't understand,' Mattie said, turning from Niko back to me. 'Niko was your secret Greek boyfriend? Why didn't you tell me – either of you?'

What could I say? That the time I spent with Niko over those weeks had felt precarious in its wonderment, that to openly discuss it would have been to risk it all falling apart? And that I was too selfish, that I wanted to keep him all to myself, to savour our moment for as long as it lasted and not be made to share it, as I had been forced to share everything else in my life up to that point?

In the end, it was Niko who spoke.

'It was my fault,' he said, the words so deliberate and his tone so steadfast that it cut a swathe through all the other whisperings around the table.

'I was the one who insisted that it must be a secret; I was the one who was afraid to upset my parents, and it was I who broke everything into pieces. I did not tell you because I was ashamed.'

Mattie's face was ashen as she looked at him and then across to me. 'But I never would have,' she began. 'We never would have . . . if I had known. Ava, why didn't you say anything?'

It was the same question I had been asking myself for half my life.

'Pride,' I told her. 'Niko had rejected me and chosen you instead – my own sister. By the time you two became a couple, I had a daughter to focus on. I thought it would be selfish of me to bring it up. You seemed so happy.'

'Did you know about this, Martha?' asked my father.

My mother tutted. 'Of course I didn't, Angus. Don't you think I might've mentioned it?'

'But I had a right to know,' Mattie continued. 'Why didn't you tell me?' she said again, swivelling round in her chair to face her husband. Niko had folded his arms, his unshaven jaw set.

'Perhaps for the same reason. Ava had told me that she cared about me very deeply, and I hoped that she would come back to Corfu one day. When you told me that she had been with another man for many years, I felt betrayed – *katalavaineis*?'

'No!' Mattie snapped. 'I don't understand. You're saying you got together with me to what? Teach Ava a lesson? Prove to her that you could have the last laugh? What?'

'*Ela*, Mattie – it was not so simple like this. My father had died, and you were my best friend. I did love you.' His voice cracked, and I wondered if it was the word 'love' that had caused his emotions to become unstuck, or the implication of that feeling being in the past tense.

'Let me get this straight,' said Mattie, raising her hands to quieten us. 'You two had a summer fling that in actual fact was not a fling at all, but a proper falling-in-love affair? Then Niko, you broke it off because you were upset about your father's death, but even so, you thought that Ava would come back the following summer, and that you might get another chance with her?'

Niko grimaced.

'And then, instead of Ava, I eventually showed up and you thought, "Oh, may as well settle for second best if I can't have what I really want. Getting off with Ava's sister will definitely be getting back at her for having a baby with someone else." Is that about right?'

I had never seen Mattie so full of self-righteous anger.

Niko had gone back to shaking his head, but when he tried to take Mattie's hand, she tugged it away.

'I think I can guess why he never told you,' I said quietly.

Dorothia exhaled a slow volley of smoke rings. Every single person at the table was staring at me.

'Because he was scared of losing you,' I said. 'He had lost his father, his freedom to explore the world as he had always planned, even to make his own decisions about the future, and he had lost me. Meeting you must have felt like winning the lottery, so of course he wasn't going to risk scaring you away. It might not have been the most honest approach, but I don't think it came from an inherently bad place.'

Niko reached once again for Mattie's hand, and this time she let him take it.

'The two of you have been married for what – thirteen years?' I reminded her. 'Niko and I were together, if you can even call it that, for less than six weeks.'

Mattie looked uncertain. Her anger had started to break down now, confusion funnelling like water through the cracks.

'You still should have told me.'

'I know.'

She was right, and I had no real excuse other than my desire to protect her from hurt. But in saving her from the embarrassment of having fallen into a relationship with a man who had first been with her sister, I had denied her half a lifetime of a proper sibling relationship with me. If anything was unforgiveable, it was this. I knew that if Mattie had been given the choice between Niko and me back then, she would have opted to keep her sister. It would not even have crossed her mind to turn her back on me as I had her.

What a mess I had made of it all, and what a bigger mess I had ended up in, falling out not only with my sisters and my mother, but with my own daughter. Rosie had remained silent throughout this exchange and I longed to know what she was thinking, even though it scared me to imagine.

'I am sorry, *kali mou*,' said Niko, his tone tender as he squeezed Mattie's hand. Ophelia had lowered her knees and was dabbing at her eyes with a napkin. I stared down at the table, at the blank screen of my phone, and felt insistence tug at my insides. I still needed to tell Rosie what Paul had found out about Sam, selfishly wanted to stick it like a plaster across the rift he had been so instrumental in causing. My secret was finally out, and as gut-wrenching as it felt, there was also a sense of being unburdened. Whatever happened next, I would at least no longer have to lie.

There was a full glass of white wine on the table in front of me, and, picking it up, I took a sip, then another. It tasted of nothing, but that did not matter – all I wanted was for the terrible flames of anxiety to be extinguished. Lifting the glass to my lips once again, I saw the screen of Rosie's phone light up, the name 'Sam' appearing before she had time to snatch it out of sight. She hesitated for a moment, deciding whether to pick up, and then, to my relief, silenced the call. I stared for a moment at her hands; she was still wearing the cheap-looking ring Sam had given her. I had stowed the beautiful Victorian one away in my bag, waiting for the right time to surprise her, but now I wondered forlornly if there would ever be one.

'This wasn't exactly what I thought would happen when I suggested a family meal,' Mattie said, attempting a laugh that was more of a strangled sob.

Niko pulled his mouth into a tight line and stared across at me, hopelessness radiating from him. He was still holding

Mattie's hand, but their fingers were not interlaced; he did not grip her fingers as he had mine. I saw love when I looked at the two of them, but not passion or desire. I recognised it as the shared affection that had kept my relationship with Paul buoyant for so many years.

'This, actually, is very typical for Greek families,' said Dorothia. 'We sit, we eat, we argue – bravo.'

A smattering of weak laughter flowed down the table from every one of us except Mattie. The hand that was not clasped in Niko's was in her mouth, and she was chewing her nails.

'*Eísai kala*?' murmured Niko, bringing his head down towards hers.

I took another sip of wine, watching as Mattie's eyes darted around the table, seeking reassurance. When she looked at me, I did my best to smile, although I could not be sure if it had reached her. She seemed flustered, twisting up her long dark hair and holding it away from her neck as if she was having a hot flush.

'I need to tell you something,' she said to Niko, and Dorothia's eyes met mine.

'I . . . I haven't been honest with you either. It's not fair of me to keep it from you any more. Not now that I know the truth about you and Ava.'

'You do not have to say anything now,' he said, too preoccupied with comforting her to worry what she might be about to tell him. I had a pretty good idea of what was to come, and how bitter a pill it would prove for Niko to swallow.

My attention was focused solely on the two of them, so I did not see or hear Kostas from the supermarket approaching until he was only a few feet away.

'Ah,' he said, when he spotted Mattie, then added a '*geia sas*' to the rest of us. 'Fenna told me you were here,' he explained. 'She is coming now.'

'Fenna?' Mattie dropped Niko's hand abruptly. 'Why? What's happened? Is she OK?'

She started rooting through her bag in search of her phone, but Kostas talked over her.

'It is about the cats.'

'Oh.' Mattie slumped with relief. 'What about them? Not another attack?'

Kostas pulled a rather pained expression.

'*Naí*, about an hour ago. But this time,' he said, holding up his own phone, 'I caught him on the camera.'

The spyware that Kostas had set up through his newly installed CCTV camera had come up trumps and, thanks to the wonder of modern technology, he was now able to show us exactly who had been targeting all the strays in Kalami. Pushing back my chair, I hurried round to the opposite side of the table just as he pressed play.

There was very little to see at first, just a portion of deserted street and a cluster of passing tourists.

'*Perimene*,' Kostas said in a hushed voice.

A small cat had wandered into view on the bottom left of the picture, and I recognised it as one of the kittens Fenna had rescued from the beach at Kerasia. It was pure black except for a distinctive white streak than ran along the length of its tail. I held my breath as a figure came into view and crouched half out of shot, one arm outstretched as if trying to coax the little cat forwards. The kitten watched for a moment or two, then scampered forwards, only to be grabbed roughly with two hands. Mattie let out a cry that matched my own as the figure made its way to the wall that separated the supermarket from the arid patch of wasteland beyond, tossed the tiny form of the cat into the air, and kicked it. Having peered over the wall with what I could only presume was some sort of sick satisfaction, the figure turned to leave, and it was then that the face came into view.

A man's face.

Sam's face.

53

Niko roared with such ferocity that Kostas stumbled backwards in alarm.

'It is OK,' the older man hastened to say. 'The kitten is OK – my wife is looking after it.'

Mattie pressed her hand to her mouth. 'Why?' she said desperately. 'Why would he do something like that?'

'Because he's evil,' I replied, wincing as the clip was played again. I did not want Rosie to be subjected to it but knew she must. When I turned towards her seat, however, it was empty.

'Mum,' I said sharply. 'Where did Rosie go?'

My mother blinked, water glass in hand. 'To the bathroom, I presume.'

I looked to my father, who nodded in agreement. 'She was here a moment or two ago,' he said.

Without another word, I opened Paul's message and clicked on the link before passing the phone across to Ophelia. She twisted a strand of hair around on her finger as she read, only to freeze as she realised the significance of the article.

'You think Sampson Tucker is . . . ?'

'I know he is,' I told her grimly. 'Paul found photos online.'

'Oh, hell,' she said. 'This means that— oh God.'

Ophelia had turned grey beneath her tan. 'It doesn't make sense,' she said, more to herself than to me. 'I don't understand what's happening. I feel as if I'm going mad.'

Dorothia had now watched the video and her expression had darkened with disgust.

'Ah.' Kostas said, gesturing towards the taverna entrance. 'Here is Fenna.'

Mattie pushed back her chair and ran towards her friend; the two of them clung tightly to each other. I stole a glance at Niko, but his attention was on Kostas.

'Are you OK?' Mattie was saying. 'I can't believe it. Where's Sam – have you seen him? Should we call the police?'

Fenna extracted herself from Mattie's arms. It was obvious that she had been crying.

'I went back to my apartment to confront the little arsehole,' she said. 'But he had already gone. The collection box we have been using for the cats is empty, and he has taken my phone and the credit cards I keep hidden in my bedroom.'

'Oh no.' Ophelia had got to her feet and now dragged her hands through her hair. 'This is all my fault. I should never have let him come to Corfu with me.'

'It's OK, Lia,' said Mattie, ready, as ever, to be understanding. 'You're not the only one who trusted him – I did too. And so did Rosie.'

My daughter had yet to return from the toilet. Niko seemed to realise it at the same time as I did and, both rising from our seats, the two of us hurried through the restaurant, weaving around tables at speed.

'Rosie!' I shouted, crashing into the ladies' bathroom, and knocked on each of the three cubicle doors in turn. They all swung open to reveal an empty space, a clean toilet, a small basin unit, and no sign of my daughter.

'*Ela*,' Niko urged, when I met him again outside. 'She is probably just sulking on the beach.'

Taking my hand, he pulled me after him round the side of the taverna and down onto the stones beyond, both of us shouting her name into the still night air.

'She's not here,' I said fearfully, gripped now by a panic of the kind I had never experienced – not even when Rosie had wandered off in a shopping centre once as an intrepid toddler. On that occasion, I had only lost sight of her for three minutes, had barely had time to envisage the possible danger she could be in. But now, I knew exactly where she must have headed, and how dangerous the person she had undoubtedly gone to meet really was.

Niko was trying to calm me down, but I struggled away from his comforting arms, tripping in my haste to get back to the table.

'Rosie's gone!' I cried. 'She must be with Sam. He called her just before Kostas arrived, I saw his name flash up on her phone. They must have arranged to meet.'

'Does he know?' Mattie asked Fenna. 'About the video?'

Fenna chewed on her bottom lip before answering. 'I don't know,' she said. 'I cannot see how.'

'If he doesn't know we're all on to him, then he has no reason to do anything stupid,' reasoned Ophelia, but I shook my head.

'Then why take Fenna's credit cards and all the cash? He must be planning to disappear.'

'Chances are he's summoned Rosie for a fond farewell,' said my father. 'She's a sensible girl. I'm convinced she won't go anywhere with him.'

'You don't know how angry she was with me,' I argued. 'How disappointed. She's also determined to believe what Sam tells her, no matter how much mud clings to him.'

Niko had his phone against his ear. 'Voicemail,' he said, his dark eyes hooded with concern.

I tried to call her again myself, and this time it was diverted immediately.

'Shit,' I swore, ignoring my mother's reflexive flinch. 'She must have switched it off.'

'Sam's not answering either,' said Ophelia, her voice close to a whimper.

'Well, they can't have got very far on foot,' my mother pointed out.

'I will go and look for them on the bike,' said Kostas, heading for the exit, only to run back less than a minute later, his face stricken.

'What?' demanded Niko, who was halfway through counting out a stack of euros to pay the bill.

'My motorbike has gone,' Kostas said. 'Somebody must have taken it. I left the keys underneath the seat.'

'It must have been Sam,' I said, swearing again in earnest.

'They could be halfway to Corfu Town by now,' Ophelia exclaimed. 'What if he tries to convince her to fly somewhere?'

'We have to go after her.' I turned to Mattie. 'Can I take the jeep?'

My mother rose to her feet. 'You've both been drinking,' she said. 'I'll drive.'

'But Mum, you don't—'

'No arguments. This is my only granddaughter we're talking about.'

Dorothia had also stood, and, grinding out her cigarette, she touched a hand to her son's shoulder. 'We can go in my car also,' she said. 'We will go north, the rest of you drive south, towards town.'

'Thank you,' I said, grabbing my bag from the back of my chair. Niko met me at the end of the table, and for a moment we stared at each other.

'I am sorry,' he said, his hands warm as they clutched my elbows.

'It doesn't matter.' I moved gently away from him, shaking my head as I fought to keep my frightened tears at bay. 'Nothing matters now except finding Rosie.'

54

Ophelia leapt in the front beside my mother, while Mattie and I scrambled into the back. We had barely got our seatbelts fastened before the jeep was in gear and screeching along the main road, the driver's wing mirror narrowly missing an elderly couple who had just emerged from the hotel opposite Elpida.

'Jesus Christ, Mum!' exploded Mattie. 'Watch where you're going.'

My mother did not so much as blink. 'Keep your eyes peeled, all of you, and call out if you see anything.'

There were streetlights in the hub of Kalami village, but as we rounded the corner at the north end and the road curved upwards through the trees, everything around us turned black. All we could see was the eerie glow of the tarmac beyond the headlights, and the white bulb of the moon as it flickered on and off among the high branches. Tearing past the junction where the road sloped down towards Kouloura, my mother rammed her foot against the accelerator and steered us on up the hillside.

I had tried Rosie's phone twice more since leaving Thomas's Place, but each time it had gone through to voicemail. On the second failed attempt, I left her a message, informing her as calmly as I could muster that Sam had been the one responsible for the attacks on the cats, and that she should send us her whereabouts as soon as she could. 'Please trust me,' I added. Then: 'I love you.'

'Maybe we should have called the police,' I said, my knuckles white on the inside door handle as we took yet another corner at speed.

'And said what?' replied Mattie. 'Rosie's eighteen now and she's been missing less than an hour. There wouldn't be much they could do at this stage.'

'But she's with him,' I argued. 'And we have proof that's he's a criminal.'

In the front seat, Ophelia sobbed, 'This is all my fault. If anything happens to Rosie . . .'

'Nothing is going to happen.' Mattie said firmly. 'Don't think the worst, there's no point.'

'That's easy for you to say,' I retorted. 'It's not your daughter who's been kidnapped by a cat torturer. Just for once, can you not be so determinedly bloody upbeat?'

'Ava,' scolded my mother, braking hard as another car passed by in the opposite direction. We were on the stretch of highway that consisted of a series of blind corners, and she was barely slowing down for any of them. 'There's no need to be rude to your sister. So what if Mattie prefers to remain positive? Lord knows someone in this family needs to, and it's certainly never been you.'

'It's all right, Mum,' said Mattie meekly, but my mother talked over her.

'No, it isn't. Ava has always been a miserable Myrtle and it's time you stopped defending her.'

'Moped!' yelped Ophelia, as a single headlight came into view around the next bend. My mother applied the brakes and we all let out an 'oof' as the seatbelts were pulled taut against our chests. The bike drew closer, revealing a very old Greek man with a dog riding pillion.

'Keep going,' I urged, only to wince as the gearbox crunched and squealed.

'I haven't heard you apologise yet,' called my mother.

Ophelia let out a bitter laugh.

'What exactly is amusing?' my mother stormed, turning on her youngest daughter.

'You three,' Ophelia said, fear and guilt making her near-hysterical. 'Aren't you tired of playing these roles yet? Ava, why do you think you and Mum don't get on? It's because you're so bloody similar. You expect too much of each other because you're the same, and so one of you always ends up disappointing the other. And Mattie,' she added, turning in her seat, 'you have been stuck in the middle of these two for so long that any gumption you might once have had has been trampled underfoot. You do so much for other people that you've completely forgotten how to please yourself.'

Mattie opened her mouth, then closed it again.

'And, if we're being really honest, I don't think you love Niko,' Ophelia said. 'Not any more. So why the hell would you stay married to him? It makes no sense at all.'

'I . . .' began Mattie, but Ophelia had switched her attention to me.

'I used to envy you so much, Ava. You had the devoted boyfriend, the beautiful daughter, the teaching career, the stability of a home – you had a role. But all it's done is given you one excuse after another not to go after what you really want. The reason you and Rosie have clashed this summer is purely because she doesn't need you as much any more. Your main role in life is being her mum, and now that's under threat from outside influences. You're scared to let her go and she knows that, but I don't think she knows how to deal with it, so she's taken the easy option and simply rebelled. I mean, we all did it. I'm probably still doing it.'

My eyes flicked to the road, and I registered a sign for Barbati.

'It's true,' said Mattie, her face ghostly pale in the moonlight. 'I don't love Niko. I'm not sure I ever did, not in the way you must have.' She looked at me. 'I can still remember how upset you were when we got home from that holiday. You were in pieces. When you started going out with Paul, it felt to me as if you were doing so just to prove to yourself that you were wanted by someone. I should have said something then, but you already felt as if you'd slipped away from me.'

I bit back my tears, nodding in lieu of the words I felt too overwrought to say.

'I wish you'd told me about Niko. Things could have been so different – we could have been proper sisters all this time.'

The jeep slowed, trapped behind a hire car that was, unlike us, travelling at the speed limit. My mother leaned on the horn.

'I don't want to be a pushover anymore,' Mattie went on. 'I want to stop caring so much about what everyone thinks of me.'

'Yes!' cried Ophelia. 'At last.'

'What about you then, Lia?' I asked. 'What's your role in our screwed-up family?'

'That's easy.' Ophelia's punctuating laugh was hard-edged. 'I'm the fuck-up, the drifter, the waste of space naïve idiot.'

'Oh, Lia,' my mother said snappily. 'Just because you're free-spirited doesn't mean you're a waste of space.'

'Who says I am free-spirited?' she said in exasperation. 'I never have. It's you who chose that trait for me, Mum, you who laughed off all my poor decisions and patted me on the back whenever I failed to settle into a job, or a relationship, or any semblance of a normal life.'

I saw my mother's shoulders tense. Now that she was unable to take her frustration out on the gas pedal, the tension was manifesting in her temper, which was rising by the second.

'I did no such thing. All I have ever done is encourage you – all of you.'

'It feels like you want me to live the life that you think you were cheated out of,' Ophelia accused. 'Sometimes I wonder if you regret having us, Mum. That if you hadn't, you might have been free from the awful burden of responsibility.'

'Now you're being ridiculous,' she protested. 'I don't regret having you – any of you.'

We were nearing Ipsos. The road had sloped downwards to sea level and the beach was only a few metres away. Light from the many bars and restaurants that lined the main road of the popular resort flooded into the jeep, and I was able to see the angry spread of red across my mother's neck and face.

Ophelia was not finished.

'All I have ever wanted to do is find a quiet corner of the world, somewhere to settle down in, a place where I can work and sleep and maybe even fall in love without worrying if I'm letting you down all the time,' she said. 'You and Dad think you're helping when you do things like following me to Thailand, but you're not – all you're doing is making it easy for me never to grow up.'

A troop of young British holidaymakers in matching pink tutus were dancing across the road ahead of us, kicking their legs up in a conga and singing. My mother slowed the jeep to a crawl as she waited for them to move out of the way.

'You're my last baby,' she said, hands gripping the wheel, her eyes fixed straight ahead. 'When you don't need my help any more, what use am I?'

Ophelia started to sob, and Mattie, too, looked as if she might cry. Turning my head away, I battled for a moment to make sense of everything I had heard, wondering about all the reasons why I pushed my mother away, and how, despite trying my hardest not to, I had apparently become so much like her.

'There,' Mattie suddenly cried. 'In that bar up ahead – that's them, isn't it?'

I leaned as far as I dared over the open side of the jeep and squinted into the distance, saw the distinctive halo of blond hair, the red straps of the dress she had worn for dinner.

'Hurry!' I said. 'Go, go, go!'

My mother sounded the horn as the tail end of the conga skipped out of the way, but the noise caused both Rosie and Sam to glance in our direction. Hurriedly putting down the drinks he had just brought back to their table, Sam grabbed my daughter's arm and pulled her over to a shabby-looking motorbike parked at the kerb.

'Quick!' I yelled, grabbing the back of the driver's seat. 'He's trying to get away.'

My mother did not need to be told. She tore down the road, scattering tourists as she went, and aimed the jeep straight at Sam and Rosie. We were close enough that I was able to meet Rosie's eyes as the motorbike sped away, and I was sure I saw fear behind them.

'Hang on,' called my mother, as she swung the vehicle round in a wide arc. There was not enough room to manoeuvre, and we were forced to reverse before we could give chase. Mounting the pavement in her haste to get going and smashing off the passenger wing mirror on a lamppost, she powered back up the road just as the motorbike taillight disappeared around a bend.

'Don't get too close,' I pleaded. 'I don't want to risk clipping them.'

I knew how exhilarating it felt to be driven along these dark winding roads by a man you loved, the warmth of his body between your thighs and your arms wrapped round his torso. Niko had shown me the island this way and at no point during any of those night-time adventures did I feel unsafe. He had always looked after me, but I could not trust Sam to do the same for Rosie. He was everything that Niko was not: selfish, violent and dangerous. I was more than scared, I was terrified.

'We're gaining on them,' Ophelia called out, and again I was compelled to caution my mother. Straining against my seatbelt, I begged her not to do anything that would put my daughter at risk.

'It's OK.' Mattie put a hand on my shoulder, eased me back beside her. 'We have them in our sights now. There's nowhere he can go.'

Sam was not slowing down for the blind corners, and to make matters worse, he kept glancing back over his shoulder, checking to see close we were.

'Just pull over, you bastard!' I screamed.

Either Sam could not hear me or he was choosing not to listen, because the motorbike did not slow down. As the highway banked steeply upwards, the smaller engine began to struggle, and the bike swerved from one lane into the other. Rosie clung on, her head buried against Sam's back and her hair twisting out behind her.

'Careful,' I cried. 'Mum, ease off a bit.'

Vast pines merged on either side of us, the road now a tunnel far blacker than the night. Rosie's playsuit was illuminated in the headlights – a slash of red like an open wound on dark skin – and as I stared, I saw her tilt her face towards me.

What happened next felt as if it did so in slow motion. A pair of small eyes shining bright in the darkness, the scream of alarm and the awful screeching sound of rubber against tarmac. Sam had heard Rosie's shout and managed to miss the cat that had appeared in the middle of the road, but he had lost control of the motorbike in the process. I watched, horror-struck and helpless, as the two of them slammed through the treeline with a gut-wrenching howl of tearing metal and smashed glass. For a few dreadful seconds there was silence, then a wail of pain rippled out.

I did not wait for my mother to pull over at the side of the road. I unclipped my seatbelt and vaulted straight out of the jeep, shouting desperately for Rosie as I stumbled over roots and loose rocks. I could see the bike about thirty yards below me, its single headlight casting a torch-like beam through the knotted mass of trees. Ophelia overtook me at speed, far more agile on this treacherous terrain than I was, and I called after her to wait for me.

'I see her,' she shouted back. 'To the left of the bike.'

I followed the line of light backwards and tried to make my eyes adjust to the darkness that surrounded it.

'Call an ambulance,' I screamed over my shoulder, almost falling in my haste to reach the crumpled form of my daughter.

Mattie, who was some way behind us, shouted that she was on the phone to them now.

'Tell them to hurry,' I pleaded. The motorbike engine was still spluttering, and I smelt exhaust fumes as I shoved aside low-hanging branches, tripping at the last moment and sliding the final few yards towards Rosie on my side. The pain burned, but I barely felt it, was unable to register anything except the bloodied face of my baby girl, the limpness of her limbs and the shallowness of her breathing.

'Don't!' Ophelia grabbed my arm as I attempted to turn Rosie over onto her back. 'She may have a spinal injury, and you could compromise her airway if you move her.'

She was right, I knew. 'Rosie?' I crooned, not touching her but leaning over until my mouth was close to her ear. 'It's OK, darling. Mum's here.'

It was not OK though – it had never been further from it.

'Is she conscious?' Ophelia sounded wretched, and I glanced up at her, took in the scratches across her bare shins and the onyx shine of her eyes in the dark. She was angry – it was so potent, I was sure that if I touched her, I would be scorched as if by a hot iron. Below me, Rosie murmured something unintelligible.

'Mum?'

'Yes, I'm here. Oh, Rosie, my poor baby girl.'

Mattie was almost with us now, but as she drew nearer, Ophelia started to move away.

'Where are you going?' I asked, even though I knew.

'You two wait here,' she said. 'I'm going after *him*.'

55

'Lia, wait!' I called.

The only answer was the crashing of her feet as she tore through the undergrowth. Ophelia's fury had transformed her into a rampaging bull, and there was no way that a simple word from me would stop her.

Mattie fell to her knees in the dirt.

'Oh my God,' she gasped, as she took in the cruel angle of Rosie's left leg, and the open gash spilling blood into her blond hair.

'The ambulance?' I said.

'En route, but it could be twenty minutes before they reach us.'

'Did you hear that, darling? Help is on the way.'

Rosie attempted to prop herself up on her elbows, only to cry out in pain. 'My leg,' she whimpered.

'Don't look at it,' I soothed. Mattie had taken off her cardigan and rolled it into a pillow shape, which she slid gently under Rosie's head.

'Where's Granny?'

Mattie patted Rosie's hand. 'She's waiting up on the road so she can show the paramedics where we are.'

My daughter's eyes filled with tears.

'Is Sam . . .?'

I glanced at Mattie.

'Try not to worry about him,' she said placatingly. 'Lia will find him.'

'But what if he's injured?' Rosie wailed, again trying to force herself upright. 'You have to find him, Mum – you have to check on him.'

'I'm not going to leave you,' I said calmly. 'If anyone can find him, it's Lia.'

'Please, Mum?' She gripped my hand. 'I have to know that he's OK; I need to see him.'

She still had no idea about any of it, not the incriminating video, the stolen credit cards, or the accusation of assault that had prompted Sam to change his name. And now was not the right time to tell her, not when she was in such a sorry state.

'I can't leave you here,' I said again.

'I won't be by myself,' she insisted, gritting her teeth in an effort not to cry.

'I'll go after them.' Mattie was already halfway to her feet.

'No, it has to be you, Mum!' Rosie's eyes were wet and beseeching. 'Mattie will just pretend that everything's all right even if it isn't.'

'Actually, I'm trying to get better at not doing that,' Mattie told her lightly. But my daughter was in no mood to listen.

'Please, Mum. Or I'll have no choice but to crawl down this hillside myself.'

I looked at Mattie, who lifted her shoulders in a helpless shrug.

'Fine.' I gave in. 'But if I can't find him inside five minutes, then I'm coming straight back.' Turning again to Mattie, I said, 'If anything happens, call me.'

'Of course – and Ava,' she added, as I kissed Rosie on her hot cheek and got reluctantly to my feet. 'Be careful.'

This time as I pushed my way through the trees, it was grim purpose, as opposed to fear, that drove me. I could not stop shaking, the adrenaline that had surged through me in the moments I had watched that bike leave the road now draining out of me in great, shuddering waves. I hated this, hated leaving my daughter lying broken on the ground, but I had promised her that I would do as she asked.

I only had a vague idea of the direction Ophelia had taken, but she had left a conclusive trail of splintered branches and flattened plants in her wake. As the distance between the tall pines started to widen, I heard the sound of raised voices and increased my pace. I told myself that all I would do was get a glimpse of Sam, check that he was in one piece, then return to Rosie, but when I reached the point where the treeline met the water, what I saw made me stop in my tracks.

Sam and Ophelia were below me on a rocky outcrop, circling one another like big cats poised to strike. As I stared, Sam lunged forwards with his arms outstretched as if to shove, causing Ophelia to stagger and almost fall.

'No!' I cried, and they both swung round in surprise. 'Don't you dare touch her,' I snarled. Sam held up his hands in mock surrender, his face a grotesque mask of scorn.

'Why?' Ophelia demanded. 'Why would you hurt a load of poor innocent cats?'

Sam's laugh was as hard as granite. 'Why not?' he said, his cruel deep-set eyes twinkling with menace. 'Because I could, because I'm at the very top of the food chain. Fenna goes on about caring for them all, but she's no better than me. You know she's abandoning them, don't you?'

'She's a far better person than you,' Ophelia spat. 'You're evil.'

I had clambered down the cliff edge as they had been talking, and looked up in time to see my sister quail beneath his raised fist. Sam was rapidly becoming unhinged with fury – a cornered animal with nowhere left to run. The sea behind the two of them glittered, beautiful but wild, the whisper of the waves a coaxing invitation to become lost.

'We know, Sam,' I said. 'About what happened in Guildford, about the accusation of rape. Everyone knows.'

He scoffed.

'So what? That stupid stuck-up cow was lying. I was acquitted.'

'You're lying,' I snapped. 'I know you did it.'

Sam paced, ran his hands through his hair, muttered under his breath, then he turned and came at me, stopping only inches away, his spittle landing on my cheek. I flinched but stood my ground, held up my hand to warn him not to come any closer.

'Rosie is badly injured,' I said. 'Don't you even care?'

He gestured down at his jeans, which I realised then were ripped and stained with blood. There was a gash on the side of his head, just below his ear, and he was holding his right hand at an odd angle.

'She's not the only one who's hurt,' he said, his voice a guttural growl. 'But she's the only one who matters, I suppose?'

'To me, she is,' interrupted Ophelia, who did not seem to care how much her words would goad him. 'You're screwed up, Sam. You need help – professional help.'

'That's rich coming from you,' he exploded, uninjured hand in the air. 'Lia the drinker, the waste of space, the talentless, dim-witted slag.'

'I am not a slag.'

'Oh, come off it,' he said, mouth agape in a crocodile grin. 'You'll open your legs for anyone who pays you a bit of attention. I wouldn't be surprised if you hoity-toity bitches are both shagging Niko behind Mattie's back. Maybe you're into threesomes – enjoy keeping it in the family.'

'You're disgusting.' Ophelia raised her chin defiantly.

'You were more than ready to suck off every one of my mates in Thailand. I was there, Lia, I saw you in that tight dress with your tits barely covered up. And you say you're not a slag? What a joke.'

I heard rustling, as if someone else was pushing their way through the trees, and then from high above the screech of tyres as brakes were applied, a car door slamming shut and raised voices.

'What do you mean, your mates?'

Sam wavered, but only for a split second. A trickle of blood slid down his cheek, black as tar.

'We took it in turns,' he told her snidely. 'Pick off a girl and separate her from her friends, feel her up a bit until she's good and scared, then swoop in and pretend to be her knight in shining armour. It never failed. Girls are so gullible and, like I said, more than ready to take their knickers off to show their appreciation.'

'No.' Ophelia shook her head violently. 'You're lying – tell me you're lying.'

'You'd like that, wouldn't you?' he went on mockingly. 'You're so desperate for affection that you'd believe me if I told you that you were special. Well, you're not, Lia. Rosie, now she's a classy girl, more than worth changing my ways for – but not any more. She's not going to be such hot property with a tarmac tattoo across her face now, is she?'

'Shut up!' I raged, as Sam began to laugh once more. 'Just shut up.'

'Going to make me, are you?' he taunted, bouncing on the balls of his feet like a boxer. I wanted to press my hands over my ears and drown out the harsh rasp of his laughter, close my eyes to the sight of his cruel, leering face.

I became aware of voices – calls that rang out in unison. Distracted by the noise, Sam glanced up towards the treeline and Ophelia, seeing her chance, stepped between us to form a human barrier.

Sam scoffed at her raised hands, refusing to be placated, and then, with a sudden roar of outrage, he hurled himself in her direction. Ophelia's scream of fright seemed to rip the night in two, and she only just managed to twist out of his grasp and stagger away. All that lay between us and the sea was a dropped crown of jagged rocks, and I shouted at her to watch out. Sam raised his fist, but as he did so, his foot appeared to slip out from under him. I saw his eyes widen as he fell, the sneer on his face collapsing as fear took over. He flailed in the empty air, limbs searching for purchase as realisation dawned.

There was a loud crack, and then, nothing.

56

Five days later . . .

I watched the sun setting from the window; the sky was a blush of violet threaded through with golden light. Hand to the glass, I pressed, seeking the warmth that I knew lay on the other side, but could not feel inside the chilled hospital ward. Dorothia had brought me a blanket earlier that smelt faintly of smoke and perfume, and I wrapped it around my shoulders, drawing comfort from the soft folds. The furthest I had ventured from Rosie's bedside was to the small bathroom at the far end of the ward, where I washed each day and cleaned my teeth. Ophelia had provided me with clean clothes, while Mattie had brought in a pile of magazines and crossword puzzle books, but I had not opened a single one. Ever since the crash, I'd felt as if I was suspended in time, and anything other than tending to my daughter seemed frivolous.

During the hours Rosie had spent in the operating room, my mother had stayed with me and, after some robust coaxing from her side, we talked. Really talked. Talked in a way that we had never before been able to. Afterwards, I had felt an odd sense of calm, as if a locked door had finally been opened and daylight was flooding in. There was still a lot more work to be done, but we had at last made a start.

Today, I had finally told Rosie about Sam, and it had taken her over an hour to cry herself to sleep. She would never again be the same girl she had been at the start of this summer; his death had torn away the last vestiges of her childhood, and I knew she had a long road ahead. We both did.

According to the surgeon who had operated on Rosie, she'd had a lucky escape. Given that she had not been wearing a helmet when she and Sam careered off the road, it was a miracle that her head injuries were only superficial, and her concussion only mild. Her leg was another matter – that had broken in four places and was now elevated above the bed, a metal cage contraption holding multiple pins in place. There was also a nasty scrape down one side of her face, which was covered in a thick dressing, and more scratches across her arms and chest. All of these would heal, Dr Laskaris assured the two of us. There would be little to no scarring.

Except on the inside.

Tomorrow, Paul would arrive, and I would have to endure his agony as well as my own, his guilt on top of mine. He blamed himself for tipping me off about Sam when he did, had himself convinced that the chase would not have happened if he had waited. But it was not his fault. The accident was just that – a thing that simply happened, which none of us could ever have foreseen. I told Rosie this as she wept, holding her as best I could without causing her any further discomfort, but she was not ready to hear it and I understood why. Grief is a complicated beast, the stages of it layered like peaks of a mountain, and helping Rosie navigate her way up and across each one was going to take time and patience. She would heal eventually, and the small part of her that remained broken would only serve to make her stronger in the end. Strong like her Greek uncle Niko. Brave and generous like him.

I turned from the window, diverting my eyes from the rich hibiscus sky to the pale-cream bedsheets and the familiar shape of my daughter beneath.

Rosie stirred. 'Mum?'

I hurried to her side. 'I'm here.'

She blinked until I came into focus, then immediately started to cry.

'You're not in pain, are you?' I asked. 'I can call the nurse if you need me to.'

'Not that kind of pain,' she sobbed. 'I forgot for a moment when I woke up. For a few seconds everything was normal again, and then it hit me. Sam.'

She stared past me, blue eyes full of tears that I wiped gently away.

'I'm sorry,' I said. 'If I could wave a wand and make this all go away, I would.'

'I feel like I'm never going to be happy again,' she mumbled. 'Not ever.'

'You will be,' I soothed. 'Life has a way of surprising us – you just have to trust it.'

When she nodded, I wondered if it was because she believed me, or whether she was simply agreeing with me as a way of avoiding further conflict.

I had so far avoided any mention of the disagreement we'd had in the restaurant, unwilling to cause either of us any additional upset, but she did deserve to know the truth about my past – and more than that, I wanted to tell her. Aside from the night of the accident, when Niko had arrived at the hospital looking like a man possessed, I had not seen or spoken to him. I presumed he was preoccupied with the task of trying to save his marriage, and did my best to cram my feelings about that into the deepest, darkest corners of my subconscious. Now that Mattie had finally admitted how confused she was feeling, they would have a clean slate on which to sketch out their future together. Niko learned from his mistakes, and he would not give up on her.

'How is Lia?' Rosie asked in concern.

'Shaken up,' I admitted. 'But coping.'

'She hasn't started drinking again?'

'Not as far as I know.' I smiled. 'She's a Fox, remember? We're a strong-willed bunch.'

'With weak bones,' she joked half-heartedly.

I suppressed a grimace as I glanced at the holes where the metal rods protruded, but it was impossible not to picture the damage below her bruised skin. She had been through such a trial, yet here she was, scraping together some humour. It gave me hope.

'What Lia really wants is a quiet, settled life,' I said. 'I'm sort of hoping that she finds something more permanent in Corfu, because she was beginning to thrive here.'

'That would make Giorgos happy,' mused Rosie.

'Yes,' I agreed. 'I think perhaps it would. I always thought he was an old soul.'

'Careful,' she replied. 'The only people who say that are old themselves.'

I pulled a face. 'Guilty as charged.'

'For the last time, Mum, you are not, in any way whatsoever, even remotely, old.'

I laughed along with her, but almost as soon as she started the tears took over.

I knew what she was thinking, because I was thinking it too: that Sam would never get the chance to grow old. He had been alive one moment and gone the next, and it was horrible. An undeniable tragedy, but one that had, in the end, brought us all closer together. As much as I had hated him, I had to allow that his presence in our lives over the summer had forced us to confront our past, present, and future behaviour. Without Sam, Lia may never have broken free from her pattern of self-destruction, Mattie would have remained voiceless and powerless in a life she found suffocating, and I might not have learned how cloying and claustrophobic my relationship with Rosie had become. All three of us had confronted our feelings towards our parents, too, and although it still felt slightly as if I was on a tightrope whenever I was around my mother, I could for the first time see a way across, towards a new and more honest relationship with her.

Sam had dug up our secrets, goaded us into admitting them, and in doing so had set us free to make better choices. He had set out to break, only to end up fixing.

'Fenna sends her love,' I told Rosie. 'She left for Amsterdam first thing this morning, and says she'll email us once she's settled.'

'How does Mattie feel about her going?' Rosie asked.

'Sad. I think she'll miss her an awful lot.'

'She shouldn't have to.' Rosie attempted to shuffle up against her pillows, only to wince as she jolted her leg.

'Here,' I said, moving in behind her as the nurses had taught me. 'Let me help you.'

Once she was comfortable, I passed her a bottle of water, which she drank gratefully through a straw. She had not broken any teeth in the accident, thankfully, but her cheekbones were heavily bruised, and she hadn't yet been able to chew any solid food.

'I mean it, I'm serious,' she said. 'Mattie should have just gone with her.'

'You mean to Amsterdam?'

'Yes, why not? I mean, she's in love with her, isn't she?'

'Who's in love? Mattie? Or Fenna?'

Rosie frowned.

'Probably both, but definitely Mattie.'

I laughed uncertainly. 'No, she isn't. She's not . . .'

'Er, yeah – of course she is. I realised as much the very first time we met Fenna.'

'I think you're forgetting something fairly important,' I pointed out, but Rosie merely shook her head.

'What, her marriage? Oh, come on, Mum – that is so over. Niko and Mattie are basically brother and sister at this point, which is a good thing, because he's obviously madly in love with you.'

'I think your dose of pain medication might need reducing,' I remarked.

'I'm right. You'll see.'

'Mattie is not going to leave Niko and run off to the Netherlands after Fenna.'

Rosie let out a long breath. 'Want to bet on it?'

'I refuse to encourage gambling,' I replied.

'See,' she exclaimed. 'You do agree with me.'

'But Mattie is . . . Well, that is to say, she's never given any indication that . . .'

'Oh, Mum.' Rosie spread open her hands. 'You should know better than anyone that when it comes to love, there is no right and wrong, no rules, no boundaries – love *is* love. It's a popular global slogan for good reason.'

Persuaded into contemplation, I eyed my daughter with a wry sense of pride. 'How did you become the adult in this relationship all of a sudden?'

She smiled, tiring now. 'I had a good teacher.'

She closed her eyes briefly, and I hurriedly brushed the tears away from my own, reaching up to smooth her hair, stroke the unbandaged side of her face.

'I lost my ring in the accident,' she said, pensive as she examined her bare, scratched hands. 'The one Sa— That I got for my birthday.'

Bending, I hauled up my bag from the floor and rooted through it until my fingers found the small velvet box.

'You didn't,' I told her. 'The nurses gave it to me before your operation, so I put it in here to keep it safe.'

Rosie took the box, fresh tears causing her to blink rapidly, and eased open the lid.

'The other ring is yours as well,' I said, watching her expression merge from one of sorrow to surprise. The peridot and pink sapphire ring looked burnished beside the shiny stainless steel of Sam's.

'It's Victorian,' I explained. 'A sweetheart ring, hallmarked 1875, which makes it . . .'

'One hundred and forty-seven years old,' Rosie said in wonder. 'And it's really mine?'

'It really is.'

I watched as she extracted each of the rings in turn, examining Sam's rather sadly for a moment before replacing it in the box, and then, after some consideration, slipping the one I had bought her on the third finger of her right hand. It was a perfect fit.

'Thank you, Mum,' she said, holding up her hand so the sapphires caught the light from her bedside lamp. 'It's beautiful'

'Like you,' I replied, smiling as she glanced up to read my expression. 'I hope it will remind you of how precious you are to me.'

She nodded slowly, unable or perhaps unwilling to share her thoughts with me in that moment. Once upon a time, I would have attempted to lure them from her, but not any more. I understood that Rosie was not simply my baby; she was her own woman – a vibrant, generous, brave and kind woman. And while she might still need me, and I would always need her, I had to allow her to make her own path, be her own person, and make her own mistakes. That was life encapsulated: one beautiful, beguiling mystery after another.

'Mum?'

Rosie had lain herself back against the pillows, her eyelids heavy with sleep.

'Yes,' I murmured.

'Will you tell me a story, like you used to when I was little?'

'What kind of story?'

'A nice one; a love story. Do you know any?'

I did, I told her. I knew one, and it began the summer before she was born, on a Greek island nestled west of the mainland, the most northernly in the Ionian Sea. A girl her age had met a boy one year older, a young man with charm enough to make it feel like day when it was night. He showed her his home, and in turn she gave him her heart; together they explored what it was to fall freely into love, each one blissful in their unhindered moment, spurred on by the innocence of youth.

When life then conspired against them, showing its hand of loss and of pain, those feelings that had bloomed so easily began to droop and fade, fragile petals of promise crushed beneath the heavy tread of obligation. As the nights drew in and the rain arrived to quench the parched earth, the young lovers said goodbye to their hopes of a future with each other. It could have been the end of the story, if not for the love.

The girl carried it with her like a talisman, a guiding star every bit as bright as those she gazed up at, wondering if he did the same. If he lay on the jetty with his back against the wood, the sound of the water lapping below him while the fate of the world lay scattered above, a tale told in diamonds, of beauty with no bounds.

Rosie had fallen asleep, lulled into slumber by my words, and I slipped my hand from hers.

Outside, the dark air beckoned, the lure of the night more insistent than ever before. I pushed back my chair and let the blanket fall to the ground. The curtains I had drawn around us hung limply on their hooks, and I eased my way through the gap between them, thinking I would go to the bathroom, splash some water on my face, scrub away the track marks of my tears from my cheeks.

Instead, I found two people waiting for me.

57

My sisters were standing together in the open doorway, and I felt the corners of my mouth lift into a smile that almost became a sob.

Like me, Mattie looked crumpled, as if she'd slept in the same cotton dress and raggedy old cardigan for days. Ophelia, too, had dark circles under her eyes, but there was a poise to her that I had not seen before. She was broken, certainly, but not beyond repair.

'How long have you two been lurking there?' I asked, making my way over to join them.

'Long enough for this coffee I brought you to go cold,' said Mattie, sheepishly holding up a takeaway cup. 'We heard you talking and, well, we didn't feel like we could interrupt.'

My eyes found the polished floor, but I raised them again when Mattie's fingers brushed against my arm.

'It's OK,' she said. 'It was a beautiful story.'

'You know that's all it is, right?' I said quickly. 'Just a story. It doesn't mean anything.'

Mattie and Ophelia exchanged an amused look.

'I told you she'd do this,' said Ophelia. 'Bury her big ostrich head in the ground and pretend nothing's happened.'

'I do not have a big ostrich head,' I exclaimed, only for Mattie to laughingly hush me.

'Come on,' she said quietly. 'Let's take these nice stone-cold coffees outside so we don't wake anyone up.'

We made our way along the corridor to the lift, and a few minutes later we were outside, crossing the road to a small open park. There were benches set at intervals around its perimeter pathway, but instead of sitting on one of these, we headed directly for the centre and sat cross-legged together on the grass.

'How are you both?' I asked. 'And don't say "fine",' I added, as Mattie opened her mouth to reply.

'Why don't you go first?' she said to Ophelia. 'Tell her your news.'

'What news?' I asked, taking a sip of my coffee, and immediately regretting it.

'I've got a job,' she said, flicking her fringe out of her eyes. 'At Elpida – a proper one. Niko has promoted me to the position of trainee sous chef.'

'He's seen a gap in the market for protein smoothies and posh avocado,' added Mattie. 'You know the Greeks – entrepreneurialism comes as naturally to them as apologising does to us Brits.'

'Lia, that's great,' I enthused.

'It is,' she agreed. 'Corfu just feels like home, you know? After what happened with Sam, I thought I'd be desperate to leave, but actually, the thought of going back to Brighton – or anywhere else, for that matter – makes me so sad. I like the pace of life here and being around family.' She glanced at each of us in turn. 'At least for now.'

'Well, I'll be here for a few weeks yet,' I said. 'Rosie's leg has some healing to do, and she's decided to take a gap year instead of starting university right away, so there's no desperate rush for us to get home.'

Mattie was grinning at me.

'What?' I asked. 'Why are you doing your gibbon impression?'

'The ostrich and the gibbon,' she said. 'Sounds like the title of a great children's book.'

'She still doesn't get it, does she?' said Ophelia, shaking her head as Mattie continued to chuckle.

'Nope. Still buried in the sand.'

'Oh my God – what is going on?' I demanded. 'Just tell me!'

Mattie scooted forwards on her bottom, a mischievous expression on her face.

'We're laughing at what you just said,' she began, 'about going home, as in back to dreary old England. Because that's not your home, not really. Corfu is.'

I opened my mouth to argue, then shut it again.

'I think you should tell her your news now,' prompted Ophelia.

Mattie steepled her fingers together and rested her chin on top, composing herself for a moment.

'I've decided to go on a summer trip of my own,' she said.

I knew what she would say next: that she and Niko were going to try again; that they were off on a romantic trip for two somewhere a very long way away from their meddling, messed-up families. I was happy for them, but the smile I had forced onto my face would need scaffolding to hold it in place much longer.

I managed a small 'oh?'

'I was going to tell you before – in fact, I was planning to tell everyone at that dinner we had, but Kostas came running in and then . . . well, you know what happened after that.'

Ophelia had started pulling up clumps of grass, and I put an unconscious hand on her shoulder.

'I'm glad I didn't, in hindsight,' Mattie went on. 'Because it wouldn't have been fair on Niko. He deserved to know first that I had fallen in love with someone else.'

My eyes widened in surprise.

'You mean . . . ?'

'Fenna? Yes, of course I mean beautiful, wonderful Fenna. And it feels so bloody good to say it, to shout it,' she cried, tipping her head back and cupping her hands around her mouth.

'I love Fenna Hendriksen!' she yelled. 'I always have, and I always will!'

Seeing her so utterly joyful made my own heart soar, and Ophelia and I cheered as she got to her feet and executed a truly dreadful cartwheel.

'Does Fenna know this yet?' I asked, as Mattie collapsed back down onto the grass.

'Nope!' she said happily. 'But she will soon because I'm going to fly to Amsterdam and tell her.'

'Wow,' I said, for want of anything more suitable. 'And Niko – what was his reaction?'

Mattie lay down on her back and arranged her folded arms into a makeshift pillow.

'He was confused at first, and then he laughed, and then he kissed me and told me to go for it. I thought he would be so angry with me about it, and because I'd been lying to him about being on the pill all this time, but he wasn't. He understands what it's like to harbour feelings for another life and not want to let it sail away out of reach. I knew that if I had a child with Niko, I would never leave him. I was a horrible coward, but I didn't want to simply up and go. I felt as if I couldn't, as if I would be letting too many people down. But God, Ava, if this summer has taught me anything it's that life is far too short to settle for anything less than the absolute most amount of happiness – and truth,' she added, rolling over onto her side and smiling at me.

'I . . . I don't know what to say. I guess, congratulations?'

'That will do for starters,' she replied. 'But, you know, I don't think I would have done any of this if it hadn't been for you. I feel a lot less guilty about divorcing Niko now that I know I'll be leaving him in such safe hands.'

'I don't know what you mean,' I said, only to start laughing helplessly as their cries of 'shut up' obliterated my protests.

'Ava,' said Ophelia gently, 'we heard the story, we have eyes, we know how you feel.'

'But I can't—' I tried again, and this time it was Mattie who interrupted me.

'Look at me,' she said, sitting up and placing a hand on either side of my face. 'This is me, right here, right now, giving you my blessing. No more excuses, Ava.'

I glanced at Ophelia, who nodded encouragingly, then back towards Mattie, whose smile told me all I needed to know.

'We'll stay here with Rosie,' she said as she stood. 'You go.'

'Go?' I said confused. 'Go where?'

Mattie reached down a hand and pulled me to me feet.

'Oh Ava,' she said with a sigh. 'You know exactly where.'

58

I found Niko in the place I had once lost him, on the end of a jetty painted silver by the moon.

He had his back to me as I approached, one hand resting on the worn wooden walkway and the other raised to his mouth. It fell away as he turned and our eyes met, revealing a cautious smile. Indicating that he should stay where he was, I made my slow way towards him.

'*Geia sou*,' I murmured as I lowered myself down.

'*Geia sou*, Ava.'

'I saw Mattie,' I said.

'*Naí*.' He nodded. 'She is . . . We are . . .'

'I know,' I told him. 'You don't have to say. She told me you were happy for her, but are you really?'

'Of course. She is happy, I am happy – it is for the best, all of it.'

I wanted to say sorry for the part I had played, but sensed it was not necessary. Niko looked refreshed, somehow – younger than he had only a few days ago. I realised dully that I must look like a complete wreck by comparison, and glanced down at myself in dismay. It had not even occurred to me to go back to the villa and change; I had simply got into a taxi outside the hospital and come straight to Kalami Beach.

'Rosie,' he asked. 'How is she?'

'Beautiful,' I told him simply. 'And wise – so much wiser than her mother.'

'*Ela.*' He reached across, took my hand in his. 'None of us are smarter than our mothers.'

'How long have you been waiting?' I asked, looking not at him but at our hands, at my fingers so tightly entwined that I could no longer feel them.

'A little while,' he said, his voice lowering as he added, 'For ever.'

He had taken off his wedding ring, and I ran my thumb over the pale band of skin, feeling him soften at my touch.

'I'm sorry,' I said, but all my words elicited from him was a tighter grip.

'There is nothing to be sorry for.'

He edged a fraction closer. My breath felt as though it had become trapped in my throat, and I was overcome by a sensation of weightlessness, as if the jetty below me was sliding away. All the moments Niko and I had shared over this strange, meandering summer had been so fleeting and fragile, our connection a house of cards that would have toppled with the slightest breeze. I could not yet trust that this moment would prove to be any different.

'It's nice to be outside,' I told him. 'I've missed the stars.'

'You cannot see many from the hospital,' he said. 'There are too many artificial lights.'

'I could see some,' I countered. 'And some is better than none.'

'I used to believe that.' He sighed. 'That some happiness is better than none, some laughter is better than none, some hope is better than none, some love . . .'

I went very still.

'And you don't believe that any more?'

Niko had dropped my hand when he moved closer to me, but now he took it again, his fingertips sliding into the soft spaces between my knuckles.

'Now,' he said, 'I believe that if there is a possibility for a person to have more, then they should do everything they can to seek it. It was a lesson my father taught me, but I let myself forget it. He would be ashamed of me for that.'

'No, he wouldn't,' I chided. 'The fact is, it's not always possible to have everything you want. Isn't it more sensible to be happy with what you have, instead of chasing for what you don't?'

'Maybe,' he allowed. 'But not when it comes to love. Love is too important.'

'Love is complicated,' I corrected, looking away towards the patchwork darkness of the sky. I always thought of it as being black, but tonight it seemed tinged with gold. 'What is that saying?' I wondered aloud. 'That love makes fools of us all.'

Niko shook his head slowly.

'I have not ever heard this, but I do know that you are not a fool. I am the fool, for losing you in the first place, for letting you believe that I no longer cared for you. I am sorry for that.' He tugged at me gently, urging me to look at him; his dark eyes were beseeching as he spoke. 'I am sorry if I caused you pain, Ava.'

'I'm sorry too,' I said, the words tumbling out on a current of relief. It felt wonderful to have said it, and to have heard the same from him; the two of us were finally able to forgive those young and foolish iterations of ourselves. All this time, I had thought I was angry with Niko when in truth I had been every bit as furious with myself.

'I know we made mistakes,' I said. 'But I can't regret them – not any of them. The path that took me away from you led me straight to Rosie.'

'I am glad you feel this way.' Niko smiled. 'Because while the girl that snatched hold of my heart many years ago was pretty, and fun, and exciting, the woman she became is beautiful, wise and brave – being a mother has made her shine even brighter than before. You are' – he searched for the word – 'luminous. Complete. And I am in awe of you.'

Tears were coursing down my cheeks, but I made no move to wipe them away, could not bear to sever the connection between us. He had always made me want nothing more than to suspend time, for the two of us to stretch away from the world and be only with each other, a place of warmth and safety, of mutual understanding. I knew this was love because I felt whole when I was with him. At every other time in my life, from the moment he walked away from me on this beach to the night he opened the villa door ready to clout me with his ridiculous shovel, a part of me had been missing. I wanted to tell him all of this – needed him to know how I felt – but my feelings for him were still too unwieldy. Before I could figure out how to share them, I needed to know they were reciprocated in kind.

'Rosie said tonight that she thinks you love me,' I said, and Niko laughed softly.

'She is a clever girl. I don't think there is much that she does not see.'

'I think she's still an optimist,' I said. 'Despite everything that's happened to her this summer and what she's witnessed happen between me and her dad, she somehow still believes in love.'

'And you?'

I smiled, blinking away yet more tears. 'I never gave up on it – not even when I probably should have.'

He looked at me, his expression suddenly serious. 'You talk often about the past,' he said, 'and how things were with us before.'

He looked to me for confirmation, and I nodded.

'You loved that person, but what about this one?' He tapped his chest. 'I was a boy then; I am not the same now.'

'You have changed,' I agreed. 'But not as much as you think. I can still see the old you in there.'

'But it is him that you want, not me.'

I pulled a face.

'You think I want that boy back? The one that encouraged me to break into people's empty houses and have sex on their pool loungers?'

He grinned rather sheepishly.

'*Naí* – perhaps you think that he was more fun? Maybe you believe that the new version is a grumpy old man who spends too much time at work and drinks too much coffee.'

I let out a small laugh. 'Both true.'

'And I worry that you will soon realise I am not the man you think I am.'

'What about me?' I challenged. 'I am every bit as grumpy as you – perhaps even grumpier. I have barely any friends and a life that consists of a series of pointless tasks, all designed to distract me from the empty shell that has become my existence in every regard other than Rosie. I teach students who care more about grades than learning, bicker endlessly with my mother, and yes, I also drink far too much bloody coffee.'

Niko had started to laugh.

'See!' I said triumphantly. 'Not much to love about me either, is there?'

'It does not matter to me,' he said. 'None of it makes a difference. You are more than you think, Ava. The glow in you, the one that I saw on the beach the day I found you, it is still every bit as bright. If there are things in your life that you do not like, you are free to change them.'

'Just like that?'

'*Naí* – exactly like that. Change is a good thing. It must happen for the world to move forwards. It is why we learn, so that we can progress, become better.'

'Change is scary, though,' I whispered, and he nodded.

'It scares me as well, but that's how I know it is the right thing.'

'That what is right?' I murmured.

'This,' he said. 'Us.'

For the briefest second, I allowed myself to be swept away to the past, back to a girl telling her sister that she was falling in love for the very first time. She had known then, just as I knew now, that it was the truth. Niko and I had travelled together, despite being apart, and somehow, we had found our way back to one another. He was right – it was time to let go of what might have been and focus instead on what it could still be, of what we could be.

Niko leaned towards me. I could feel the heat of his body, and was assailed by the scent of him, this man who smelt of cedarwood and lemon mint, whose presence here beside me was unexpected yet obvious, all at the same time, a plot twist that made every other strand fall into place. The hand that was not holding mine was placed against my cheek, and as I raised my eyes to meet his, I saw the hope I felt reflected back.

'I told Rosie our story tonight,' I said, as his hand strayed down to caress my neck, 'but I didn't get to finish it.'

Niko's fingers were in my hair.

'Why not?' he asked.

I smiled, tilting my head to look at him, to see him without the burden of guilt, the pain of yearning, the awful bottomless well of despair. It felt like waking up after decades of sleep, and I saw it then, the reason for all of it, the why and the what and the how – the answer to that most elusive of riddles: what we were here for.

It was for love, of course.

'Because I thought that our story had ended a long time ago,' I whispered, gazing at him in wonder. 'But this doesn't feel like an end.'

'*Ochi*,' he said, his lips inches from my own. 'This is not the end for us, Ava – it is the beginning.'

The moment was ours, as all those that followed would now be, and we sealed it in the way that love deserves.

With a kiss.

Acknowledgements

I want to start by thanking you, the reader, for choosing this book. I always like to think of my readers closing the final page with a smile on their face, and I hope that is the case for you.

To my agent Hannah Ferguson and the brilliant team at Hardman & Swainson for all the support, wisdom, and continuing enthusiasm.

To my editor, Kimberley Atkins – your faultless energy and optimism never fails to astound me. Thank you for your patience and the brilliant work you did on this book. I must also thank Jenny Platt (for publicity), Amy Batley (for editorial), Alice Morley (for marketing), Jacqui Lewis (for copyedit), Becky Glibbery (for this stunning cover) and Catherine, Sarah, Rich, Isobel, and Lucy (for sales). I am very proud to be published by Hodder & Stoughton.

Nobody understands authors like other authors, and I would never get to the end of a novel without my incredible tribe of writer friends. You are my people and I love you. A special mention must go to Cathy Bramley (to whom this novel is dedicated), who not only convinced me to sneak off to Corfu three times (not that I needed much convincing) but who also makes me laugh more than I thought humanly possible. She already knows that she is an inspiration to me, but I wanted to say it again in writing.

To all my non-writer friends, I can only apologise for replying to every offer of social interaction with the word 'edit' for a large chunk of the year. Thank you for still being there when I re-emerged on the other side.

And finally, to my family, whom I adore and who have championed me and my writing ever since I was old enough to hold a pen. That especially goes for you, Mum. I've lost count of the times one of our plot walks has saved the day (and my sanity). Know that I do it all for you, and always will.

Even when you're lost, love can find you . . .

Discover Isabelle Broom's escapist holiday romance
The Getaway, available now!

'Lovely characters, a wonderful setting, a beautiful story'
Milly Johnson

'Vivid, funny, tender and warm'
Veronica Henry

An invitation from the publisher

Join us at www.hodder.co.uk, or follow us on Twitter @hodderbooks to be a part of our community of people who love the very best in books and reading.

Whether you want to discover more about a book or an author, watch trailers and interviews, have the chance to win early limited editions, or simply browse our expert readers' selection of the very best books, we think you'll find what you're looking for.

And if you don't, that's the place to tell us what's missing.

We love what we do, and we'd love you to be a part of it.

www.hodder.co.uk

@hodderbooks

HodderBooks

HodderBooks